Five champions. Four graves.
One chance to claim the throne.

A romantic fantasy fusion of modern Nordic,
Viking, and Medieval Scandinavian culture,
founded in the author's Norwegian heritage.

For centuries, the ruler of Fjorden has been chosen by the Sonne—a battle to the death hosted every twenty-two years. A month before this year's competition, neighboring Swaymark launches an attack on the east coast, shattering the two countries' shaky truce and forcing Fjorden to balance tradition with war.

Princess Sofia must hold her kingdom—and herself—together as each of the five champions prepares to fight for the throne. But the gods have plans of their own. Although the champions can defeat each other, no one can defeat fate.

ALSO BY KRISS DEAN

Dragon Den

FJORDENSAGA
SAGA OF THE CHAMPIONS

KRISS DEAN

YGGDRASIL PRESS

First Edition

Cover art and design by Nico Nicolaysen

Maps and interior design by Kriss Dean

For the younger me,
who would squeal with delight
just knowing this exists.

Author's Note

Some themes in this story may be triggering for some readers. If you feel content warnings are spoilers and you don't need them, please skip the next paragraph and jump right in.

This book touches on emotionally difficult topics, including but not limited to death (including the death of a child/sibling), violence, assault, grief, anxiety, panic attacks, depression, suicide, suicide ideation, and on-page physical intimacy.

Anyone who believes such content may upset them is encouraged to consider their well-being when choosing whether to continue reading.

Always put yourself first.

xo Kriss

Cultural Notes

This fantasy fusion blends elements from modern Nordic, Viking, and medieval Scandinavian cultures.

Modern Nordic culture places a high value on respect and unity among all people, even during competition.

Beliefs are based on Norse mythology, common until around 1000 AD. As Norse sagas are inconsistent, liberties were taken. The Royal Circle of Valhalla is entirely fictional.

In Viking culture, the chief would claim his place by killing anyone who challenged him. Challenges could come at any time for any reason.

Fjorden's government is loosely based on the modern Norwegian constitutional monarchy.

The terrain is heavily based on the land of Norway. Swaymark's topography is a blend of Sweden's and Denmark's.

The castle is based on Akershus Fortress, completed in the 1300s, and pulls building elements from the Burgund Stave Church (built in 1180) and other churches in the region.

VILLAGES AND BUILDINGS are based on traditional Norwegian architecture, much of which can be found in the Norsk Folkemuseum in Oslo, an open-air museum focused on 1500 to the present, and in the Viking village on Birka.

THE SHIPS are based on Viking ships. Average speeds were 5–10 knots, with longships topping 15 knots (17 mph) at perfect conditions.

WEAPONS described are historically accurate to Viking times. The Vikings also had bows and arrows, used for hunting food.

CLOTHING AND ARMOR elements are based on the fashions of medieval Scandinavia.

MARZIPAN is a common Scandinavian sweet first referenced in European cookbooks from the 1500s. Made with sugar and ground almonds, it originated in the Middle East.

HARDINGFELE (Hardanger fiddles) originated in the Hardangerfjord region of southwestern Norway in the 1650s.

HORSES are short and sturdy with fluffy, thick coats, based on Icelandic horses.

FJORDEN BUILT THEIR WEALTH by trading natural resources. The Vikings originally built wealth using slaves, a practice that ended with the spread of Christianity. Most of the slaves were brought in from all over Europe, including other Scandinavian countries and even islands just off the mainland.

WELCOME TO FJORDEN, DEAR READER.

Pronunciation

Events

CHAMPIONSMATCH (shamp-yons-mahtsh), the competition to become the region's champion

CHAMPIONSFEST (shamp-yons-fest), feast/celebration of the champions

SONNE (SOH-neh), competition to become the victor/ruler

VICTORSFEST (vic-toors-fest), feast/celebration of the victor

Holidays

SIGRBLOT (see-gahr-blohtt), the beginning of summer festival

MIDSOMMAR (mid-soh-mahr), Midsummer holiday traditionally celebrated on June 24th

VETRARBLOT (veh-trahr-blohtt), the after-harvest festival

JOLABLOT (YOU-lah-blohtt), festival celebrated after mid-winter

Norwegian Words

FISKESUPPE (fis-keh-soo-peh), fish soup

FJORD (f'yourd), a long, deep and narrow body of water with steep
sides or cliffs

FY FAEN (fee f'ahn), for fuck's sake

HARDINGFELE (hahr-ding-feh-leh), Norwegian fiddle

HEJHEJ (hay-hay), informal/familiar hello

HELVETE (hell-veh-teh), hell/curses

HNEFATAFL (ne-fa-ta-fal), Viking chess

JAHA (ya-hah), yes/I see

KJÆRE (sh-aeh-reh), a dearly loved one

LEDERSTJARNA (leh-der-styahr-neh), the North Star

MAMMA (muh-mah), mother

MARZIPAN (mahr-zih-pahn), almond dessert

MIDDAG (mih-dahg), dinner/supper/second meal of the day

PAPPA (puh-pah), father

RÖGGVARFELDUR (roh'g-vah-fel-deur), soft tufted fleece blanket

SAGA (sah-guh), Norse prose narrative of events

SAFT (sahft), blackcurrant juice

SKALD (skahl'd), poet who composes and recites poems founded
in Norse mythology that honor the kings

SPRINGDANS (sp'ring-dahns), a traditional leaping dance

TRELLEBORG (treh-leh-boarg), a warrior compound

VELKOMMEN (vell-coh-men), welcome

Characters

Royal Family

Filip (FIL-ip), Prince of Fjorden

Sofia (so-FEE-uh), Princess of Fjorden

Ana-Sofia (AH-nuh so-FEE-uh), Queen of Fjorden

Eirik (aye-REEK), King of Fjorden

Champions

Karsten (cahr-sten), Aldersfoss

Skippere (shipp-eh-reh) / Skip (shipp), Sander

Jostein (you-stine), Hamme

Nicolay (NEE-co-lie) / Nico (NEE-coh), Fryse

Dagny (DAHG-nee) / Dag (DAHG), Morge

Parliament

Tomas (toh-mahs), Morge

Karl (cahrl), Fryse

Warriors and Guards

Max (mahcks), Sofia's guard

Geir (guy'r), gate guard

Alexander (ah-lehk-sahn-dur), gate guard

Chief Ragnar (reigh-nahr), Morge's south camp

Servants

Agneta (ahg-NEH-tah), Sofia's maid

Inga (ihn-guh), head cook

Lars (lahrz), stable master

Places

Regions

Aldersfoss (ahl-ders-fohss), the capital
Sander (sahnd-er), shipping region
Hamme (HA-meh), farming region
Morge (mor-geh), Eastern region
Fryse (free-seh), ice region

Countries

Fjorden (fyour-den)
Swaymark (svay-mahrk)
Marrocs (mahr-rohks)
Romiska (roh-miss-kuh)
Stantland (stahnt-lahnd)
Kiniska (shee-nihs-kuh)
Tunland (tuhn-lahnd)

FJORDEN

FJORDEN
SWAYMARK
MARROCS

TUNLAND
KINISKA
STANTLAND
ROMISKA

YGGDRASIL, THE WORLD TREE

THE NINE WORLDS

ASGARD. "Yard of the Aesir," home of the Aesir gods. Home of Valhalla, the hall of the fallen. Home of Urd's Well.

VANAHEIM. "Vanir's home," home of the Vanir gods.

ALFHEIM. "Elf home," land of the light elves.

MIDGARD. "Middle yard," land of the humans.

JOTUNHEIM. "Jotun home," land of the frost giants. Home to Utgard, the Citadel of the Giants. Home to the Spring of Mimir.

NIDAVELLIR. "New moon fields," land of the dwarves.

SVARTALFHEIM. "Black elf home," land of the dark elves.

MUSPELHEIM. Land of eternal fire. Home of the fire giants.

NIFLHEIM. Land of eternal ice. Kingdom of the dead. Home of Hel and Helheim. Home to the Spring of Hvergelmir.

CREATURES

THE FATES. Urd, Verdandi and Skuld.

JORMUNGAND. Serpent surrounding Midgard.

NIDHOGG. Dragon gnawing the tree's roots in Helheim.

VIDOFNIR. Eagle perched on top.

RATATOSK. Squirrel, scurries up and down the trunk carrying insults between Nidhogg and Vidofnir.

Fjorden's Gods

Heavily based on (the very inconsistent) Norse mythology

Asgard

1. **Baldur** (bahl-duhr). Son of Odin and Frigga.

2. **Bragi** (brah-gee). God of poetry and craft.

3. **Eir** (ai-yer). Goddess of healing.

4. **Forseti** (four-seh-ti). Son of Baldur and Nanna. God of law.

5. **Frigga** (frih-gah). Wife of Odin. Beloved goddess of all.

→ **Fulla** (fuhl-lah). Frigga's handmaiden.

→ **Gna** (g'nae). Frigga's messenger.

6. **Heimdall** (hyme-dahl). Guards Bifrost (the rainbow bridge).

7. **Hoenur** (hoe-nure). Brother of Odin.

8. **Hodr** (hoe-durr). Son of Odin.

9. **Idunna** (ee-doo-nuh). Bragi's wife. Goddess of healing. Keeper of the apples of immortality.

10. **Lofn** (loh-fenn). Goddess of comfort.

11. **Loki** (loh-key). Trickster god.

12. NANNA (nah-nah). Wife of Baldur. Forseti's mother.

13. ODIN (OH-thin). God of kings and war. Oversees Valhalla.

14. SIF (siff). Wife of Thor. Goddess of the harvest.

15. THOR (toor). God of thunder. Protector of warriors.

16. TYR (tear). God of oaths. Symbol of bravery.

17. VIDAR (vee-dahr). Half-giant. Odin's son.

VANAHEIM

18. FREJA (fray-uh). Goddess of lovers. Oversees Folkvangr.

19. FREYR (f'rare). God of harbors. Freja's twin.

→ GERD (gehr'd). Giantess. Wife of Freyr.

20. GULLVEIG (guhl-vigg). Seeress.

21. NJORD (noord). God of fishing and seafaring. Ruler of the sea
   and wind. Father of Freja and Freyr.

→ SKADI (skah-dee). Giantess. Njord's wife.

NIFLHEIM

22. HEL (hell). Half-giantess. Loki's daughter. Oversees Helheim.

MARDÖLL (mahr-duhl). Straight, short sword of golden sheen.

RAGNARÖK (rayna-rok). The twilight of the gods.

Part I

Laughing, shall I die.
In glory, shall I live forever.

ALDERSFOSS

"Charge!" Prince Filip roared into the chilly winds. His noble mount remained silent and brave, ready to lead against the hordes.

He pointed his blade at his enemy, determined to send them cowering in fear. He would bring them to their knees. They had attacked his land, taken his father across the sea, and—

"Filip," his sister called from the hallway. Sofia's slippers padded against the wooden floor and into his bedroom. "Breakfast time."

Fiddlesticks.

"Just another minute," Filip begged. He leaned forward atop his wooden sheep, his wooden sword aimed out the window toward the fjords surrounding the castle.

She chuckled. "Okay. Who are we battling today?"

"Swaymark." Vengeance would be his. "I'm going to win. For Pappa."

With a deep frown, Sofia walked slowly toward Filip, her blue dress swishing around her slippers. She tucked a strand of long, ash-blond hair behind her ear before she placed a hand on his shoulder, her green eyes locked on his. "Filip, the best way you can help Pappa is to grow big and strong. You need breakfast to do that. Would you please come down with me?"

Filip sighed, but he sheathed his sword. Vengeance would be his—later.

Sofia kissed his forehead and stepped back, jostling the hnefatafl board on the floor by her feet. "You should put the game away when you're not playing with it."

"Karsten and I didn't get to finish yesterday." Filip patted his sheep before dismounting. "He had to train with the other new warriors. He said we could finish this afternoon though."

She knelt and adjusted the fallen pieces. "Are you red or white?"

"Red."

"Did you see that Karsten's king is vulnerable? Here," she said, pointing to the board. "Trap him, flit the pawn, and you'll be done in three moves."

Yes, he had seen that yesterday, and he'd begged Karsten to stay until they finished, knowing it would be quick. But *saying* it would be quick might have alerted Karsten to his only chance to salvage the game.

Filip smiled and grabbed Sofia's soft hand, and they took off down the corridor, past the paintings of the old, dead kings, and into the Great Hall. The pair crossed through the sea of wooden tables to the largest at the center of the room, where their mother waited for them. She was wearing her favorite green dress; Sofia had embroidered the flowers along the trim.

"My kjære daughter, my fearless son, good morning."

"Good morning, Mamma." Filip sat on the bench beside her, then waved at the painted ceiling. "Good morning, Odin. Thor. Freja."

"Careful, Filip." Sofia sat across from them. "Some of the other gods might feel left out."

"Good morning, everyone," Filip said. The twenty-two gods looked proudly back at him as the painted serpent Jormungand circled the room's edges. Filip glanced at his father's empty chair at the head of the table. "When will Pappa be home?"

His mother's eyes lit up. "Today."

Filip knocked over his empty mug, and Sofia gasped.

His mother laughed, radiating an excitement that had been missing since the warships had set sail. "One of the guards brought a message this morning. They're on the way."

Filip grinned, piling fresh salmon on his plate. "Do you think they won?"

"Of course, kjære. Pappa is a victor. He has Thor's hammer on his side." His mother sipped her birch tea. "And he's just in time for Midsommar."

The festivities would take over the entire capital. Planning and decorating had already intruded on the castle, and the guards were being assigned additional daily shifts, further disrupting Karsten's availability for playtime.

Filip filled the rest of his plate with rolls and cheese. He counted the painted shields hanging from the walls as his mother and Sofia continued the Midsommar planning. It was silly—as long as there was marzipan, the rest didn't matter.

"Mamma," Filip said once they had finished eating. "Can we still go riding today?"

She hesitated. "Well, I suppose. But not for long. We wouldn't want to be out when Pappa gets back."

Filip clapped, bouncing in his seat. "Sofia, will you come, too?"

Sofia smiled. "I—"

"Have you reviewed the notes from Parliament?" their mother asked.

Her shoulders slumped. "Not yet."

"Then no riding. Sofia, a princess must—"

"Serve the kingdom wholeheartedly." Sofia leaned her elbows on the table. "Why doesn't Filip have to attend Parliament?"

He stuck his tongue out at her.

"Because he's six—"

"Almost seven," Filip interjected.

"—and you," their mother continued, "are eleven. You need to prepare to lead. In a couple of years, you might be married. Helping lead your own country."

"Of course, Mamma," Sofia said. "Sorry, Filip."

Filip nodded, ignoring the sting of disappointment. "Can we go now?"

His mother raised her eyebrows. "What do you say?"

"Thank you for the meal. Now can we go?"

His mother chuckled. "Okay, let's go."

Filip raced outside to the stables, his mother trailing behind. The carved wooden dragons along the castle's rooftop watched as he ran down the gravel path.

"Good morning, Lars," Filip called to the stablemaster before running directly to his magnificent horse. "Hejhej, Apple," he murmured, petting her soft, gray nose.

Lars walked up to them, an apple in hand. "Filip, you're taller than Apple now."

Filip straightened, making sure every inch was accounted for. "I just hit four and a half feet. I'm going to be taller than Pappa."

Lars grinned and held out the apple for Apple, who took it eagerly. "Do you want to ride in the paddock?"

"Not today. Mamma is coming."

"Jaha." Lars hurried toward the saddles.

Filip stroked his horse's neck and shoulders while Lars prepared her for the ride. Once Lars finished tacking her, Filip mounted, ready to go, with his wooden sword at his side.

"Warm her up in the paddock," Lars said.

Apple's hooves clopped along on the rocky ground into the fenced enclosure.

The mountains rose around the castle grounds. Just past the ramparts and the beach, cliffs jutted straight up from the sea. Birds circled over the water in the cloudless, pale blue sky.

Warriors trained on the sparring field, their spears clanging against the shields amid their shouts. Karsten was among them. Filip's shoulders slumped as he steered Apple around the paddock. Karsten would have let Filip spar with them, had it been his choice. Unfortunately, the lead guard had told Filip he wasn't allowed to join. But once the king returned, Filip would surely be allowed to practice with the warriors.

When his mother finally emerged from the stables, Filip guided Apple to her side. They rode through the gate, waving to the guards as they passed under the giant stone archway.

The forest's well-worn path waited for them, welcoming them with birdsong. A light breeze rustled the green leaves of the canopy in its wake.

"Do you think Pappa will want to go camping when he gets back?" Filip asked. The trips formally served as training for the Sonne, but he always had fun up in the mountains. After spending their days hunting and scavenging for fresh berries, his father told battle stories half the night—after they'd built a shelter, of course. On each trip, they'd pile a new cairn to point the way home.

"I am sure he will, *after* Midsommar." She sighed. "You two are so alike. And you'll be a champion and a victor, just like him."

He straightened. Ten years until he'd become Aldersfoss's champion, prove himself in the fjords, and win his place as the king. He'd be the youngest victor in Fjorden's history. He'd make his father proud.

Apple snapped a branch under her hoof, startling Filip. His mother laughed. He laughed along, settling back into the saddle. Nothing to worry about.

A shadow caught his eye—a reindeer?

Filip pulled Apple's reins, guided her to stop, and squinted through the trees. His mother stopped her horse beside him. The shadow darted through the trunks, followed by shouts in a foreign language—he didn't recognize the words.

"Get back to the castle," his mother hissed.

Ice flooded his veins. Heart racing, he turned Apple around and spurred her into a full gallop, his mother close behind him.

The shouts grew louder, and the sound of galloping horses filled the air. Filip looked back just as Apple bucked, throwing him to the ground. The wind knocked out of him, he fought back tears as Apple continued toward the castle, leaving him behind.

His mother stopped her horse and dismounted, rushing to his side. "Filip, get up!" She pulled at his arms, and he rose to his feet. "Go, Filip, go!"

She pushed him toward her horse and put her back to him as the shadows surrounded them. Cloaked figures emerged from the darkness of the forest.

His father's words became his center: *A true king is always brave; a true king will always fight for his people.*

He drew his sword and pointed it toward the closest man. The group snickered.

"What are you going to do with that, little prince?" The man flashed his yellowed teeth in a cruel smile and pulled out his sword, the metal gleaming.

Filip held his ground.

"Let us go," the queen ordered, her voice steady but her hands shaking. It was Filip's job to protect her.

Laughing, shall I die. In glory, shall I live forever.

"I don't think I will." The man took a step toward them.

Filip dodged left around his mother and swung his wooden sword into the back of the man's knees, knocking him over. He kicked the man's side, then slammed the hilt into the man's sallow face, sending a bloody spray across the ground. The man grunted and flailed.

Grabbing the man's heavy metal sword with both hands, Filip held it toward the group, standing in front of his mother.

The surrounding horses whinnied and tossed their heads. The riders dismounted, and the cloaked men closed in on them.

Filip aimed the sword at the nearest, blocking swiftly as another sword came down on him. The iron clashed as he fought back, focused on the man in front of him. *Step, strike, step, strike—*

A blade whistled through the air.

His mother cried out.

Suddenly, Filip was entirely alone, freezing cold.

The men, the horses, his mother—gone.

"Mamma?" he called, looking around. "Mamma!"

Skeletal trees surrounded the grove, their leafless branches reaching menacingly toward the gray sky. Filip ran, pumping his legs as hard as he could.

"Mamma!" He had to find her. He had to protect her.

A shadow fell over him, and terror pulsed through his body. He ran faster, desperate to find his mother, desperate to escape. The shadow crossed over again.

He glanced up, catching the white underbelly of a swooping falcon. It let out a shrill yelp, *kak-kak*, hovering over him.

Filip kept running. "Mamma!"

The falcon dove and landed on a fallen tree trunk, shifting shape into a cloaked woman with long, blond hair.

He stopped. He *knew* her.

He'd seen her every single day, greeted her every single morning.

"Filip," she whispered, opening her arms slowly.

He took a tentative step toward her, then another. His hands shook.

"Filip," Freja whispered again, stepping toward him. She wrapped her arms around him. "Do not worry, little one. This is the will of the gods."

TEN YEARS LATER

SOFIA STARED OUT her bedroom window, her gaze drifting along the waves toward the beach surrounded by fjords and darkened by rain clouds. She and Filip had lived for the sunshine, the warmth, the late-summer sunrise. They'd run along the sandy shore all day, playing in the waves until the sun went down at midnight.

His death had broken a piece of her.

She refocused on her notes for that afternoon's Parliament meeting. All five regions were preparing for the Sonne, and their champions would be at the castle next month.

Filip would have represented Aldersfoss—her home, the capital, where the castle was perched among beautiful fjords carved by thousands of years of ice and motion.

Sander to the southwest, where Filip used to admire the ships being built. Hamme, full of farms she and her family had visited to celebrate the harvest. Fryse to the north, ice-cold all year, the terrain full of amber and other valuables that brought wealth to their kingdom. Morge to the east, the closest to Swaymark.

"Karsten, good morning." The king's voice drifted into her room from just outside her open door. "Are you ready for the Sonne?"

"Yes, sir." Her head guard's tone was low and humble. "I've been training with my father every night for months."

Sofia glanced at the fresh pink flowers on her desk.

"Glad to hear it. Aldersfoss will be well represented."

Well represented, yes. But the victor? They would likely come from one of Morge's camps, like her father had almost twenty-two years ago. They'd be vicious and battle-hardened, considering Fjorden's truce with Swaymark had been shaky—at best—since the assassination. Her stomach churned at the thought.

"Sofia," her father said from the doorway. At six-foot-five, he towered over the staff and most of the warriors. Wrinkles had set in around his wide-set eyes, and his hairline had inched up his fair-skinned forehead, but his white beard was still full on his round face. "Ready for the meeting?"

"Of course." It was the same answer she had given before every meeting over the last ten years, since the moment she had stepped into her mother's role. "We'll review updates from Midsommar, the revised trade agreements with Marrocs, and preparations for the Sonne."

"Good, good." He nodded, then smiled sadly at the portrait on the wall. "Mamma would have been proud of you."

Sofia watched his eyes take in her mother's beautiful smile and the long dimples on her rosy-beige skin. Her mother stood a head shorter than the victorious king beside her in their wedding day portrait. The queen's ash-blond hair was braided into a crown and topped with a sparkling silver tiara that matched the clasps on her cream cloak. Her green eyes reflected the joy of the occasion, unlike her father's gray eyes now.

"You look just like her. Filip did too." He sat on the bench near the wall, perching at the edge, never quite settling in and always ready to move quickly.

"I wish Mamma were here to guide you, kjære," he said. "I had no doubt I'd marry her when I won."

The only way she'd keep her role in the kingdom and be with her family in the Royal Circle of Valhalla was through marriage to the new king, and tradition dictated the victor marry immediately after they triumphed. She had to align with the victor—whoever they were, whatever they had done to win.

She tucked her hair behind her ear. "How did you decide?"

"She was raised to lead. I would have been stupid to marry someone else."

Sofia sighed. "That's not actionable advice, Pappa."

"I suppose not." His expression softened. They both knew it wasn't supposed to be this way.

"Filip would have made quite the victor... always full of energy, chasing us with his wooden sword." Laughter danced in his eyes. "I remember the time he hit you with it and sent you crying into my arms."

Sofia folded her arms across her chest with a grin. "You'd have been scolding me instead of comforting me if I had hit my baby brother back."

"You've always chosen your battles carefully..." He chuckled. "I could never keep up with Filip now. Too old. Too much ale."

"You aren't wrong," she murmured.

Though she'd memorized it, Sofia studied the painting of her parents. The twenty-two-year-old pigments, like the maps, like her memories, like her father's energy, were slowly fading—though only the fates knew when their time would end.

"Sofia... The victor of the Sonne, they will have the strength to fight and to win. Show them your worth. That you belong here."

She swallowed, nodding once.

King Eirik rose and moved to the door, stopping briefly at the threshold. He glanced back before continuing. His footsteps padded down the hall, followed by his door closing.

She gathered her notes into her arms and exited her room.

Karsten's ice-blue eyes locked on her. They were deep-set under thick, straight brows; emphasized by his defined nose and high cheekbones molded from his sandy-beige skin; and serious, like his downward turned lips surrounded by his short beard—cropped close, just like his ash-blond hair. His padded shirt and chainmail fit exceptionally well on his six-foot-six frame and fell to the middle of his thighs, showing off his endless muscles earned with endless training. The champion from Morge would be hard to beat, but Karsten was a force to be reckoned with. Maybe...

Sofia realized she was staring, and her cheeks warmed.

Settling into their usual comfortable silence, they wandered down the stairs and turned down a short corridor, passing guards along the way. Karsten opened the door at the end and walked through first, securing the room. When he nodded to her, she stepped into the vacant library.

A massive tapestry of the mighty Yggdrasil greeted them from the far wall. A carved oak table stood in the center of the room, surrounded by twenty-one chairs ready to welcome Parliament. Bookcases dotted the edges of the well-lit space, each shelf holding books collected by the royal families over centuries, every tome handwritten by scholars and traded for in the east. In front of the fireplace sat a well-worn bench, the wood covered in pillows and sheepskin, with wool blankets stored under the seat to help fend off the cold.

Sofia thought back to when she and Filip were tutored here, the only two students in this ocean of knowledge. They would twitter back and forth until their tutor scolded them, shaming them back to their studies.

She set her notes in a neat stack at the head of the table, picked up a pile of books, and put them back on the shelves, clearing the surface before Parliament. Finished, she reached for a second stack, not realizing how heavy it was. All the books fell to the floor. Sighing, she knelt next to the heap.

"Allow me to assist, Princess." Karsten leaned his spear against a bookshelf, then knelt next to her and piled the books up.

Her guards never set down their weapons—at least, not while on shift—but the library was vacant, and his sword and shield were strapped to him. He must have considered it safe enough.

"Thank you, Karsten." She grabbed a couple of books from the pile, then shelved them and started on the stack in his arms.

He caught her gaze. "Tomorrow, you'll have a new guard on rotation. And Max for the early shift."

"Already?" Had she misread the last missive? "Well, you must have so many preparations, and you haven't taken time off in..." She couldn't remember. "Will you visit your family?"

Karsten hesitated. "I might go camping with my brother."

"They'll be ecstatic to welcome their champion home for more than a sparring session. They're proud of you, I'm sure."

"Especially my father."

"As is mine. You impressed him with your dedication." She took the last book out of his hands and placed it on the shelf as he picked up his spear. So today was his last day... "Would you like to take some ale to your family?"

Karsten's cheeks turned pink. "Yes, thank you. They'd enjoy ale from the castle."

They walked to the busy kitchen, where Sofia turned to one of the staff members and asked for assistance. He nodded, gestured to Karsten to follow, and walked toward the cellar.

She found Inga, the new head cook. "How's your first day?"

"Getting settled for the most part." Inga gave a stiff nod.

Sofia glanced toward Karsten, who still hadn't moved. The poor servant stood waiting awkwardly by the stairs.

"Is something wrong? The strongest warrior in the capital isn't afraid of the dark, is he?" Sofia teased. "I suppose I've never actually seen you go down there."

Karsten looked as unsure as a reindeer caught in the torchlights. "I never leave your side, Princess."

"It's extremely unlikely that anyone would launch an attack in the few minutes it would take to grab the ale, and another guard is standing by the door." Sofia's eyebrows rose. "The most I'd do is trip and fall into the pots."

He smirked. "Still a risk."

"Well, you've invested six years into my safety, so I suppose your last day as my guard is the wrong day to test the waters." Sofia chuckled, walking toward the cellar door. "My side is over here." She gestured to the ground next to her.

Karsten followed hesitantly, his eyes wide. The steep cellar stairs were confining and musty. At the base, a single torch lit the space. Her eyes adjusted to the darkness of the unfamiliar basement, taking in the vast stores of food gathered for the coming winter.

The servant gestured to casks of ale lining the back of the room behind dried meats and fish. Karsten picked up a smaller cask with one hand, his spear still firmly in the other. He quickly scanned the room before his gaze landed on Sofia. "Thank you."

"Of course. I hope your family enjoys it."

They ascended the stairs, Karsten in the lead. He hastily placed the cask on the counter and resumed guard.

She crossed the kitchen straight to Inga.

"Would we be able to add a marzipan cake for the champions' first night?" Sofia asked tentatively.

Inga frowned. "I'll see if we can trade at the market for the almonds. They're much easier to find during the winter holidays."

"Thank you. I'd love to share my favorite dessert with them, but I understand if it doesn't pan out."

Back in the library, Sofia sat at the head of the table, her notes in front of her and Karsten nearby. Three guards entered, two remaining by the door.

"Max." Karsten stepped aside with a nod, allowing him to take his place. Guard changeover. Already three o'clock.

Sofia looked at Karsten, who was looking at her. Surely the next month would fly, and he'd be back—but as a champion, fighting for glory, possibly headed straight to Valhalla.

She smiled wanly, not sure what to say. "Don't forget the ale."

"Thank you, Princess Sofia." With that, Karsten left the library.

She searched her notes for the missive about her guard rotation. *Max will start as head guard the day the champions arrive...* But something obviously changed. She tucked it back in the pile.

The representatives trickled in over the next half hour, taking their seats. Sofia greeted them like her mother used to, like she had for ten years. *A princess must serve her kingdom wholeheartedly.*

Two of Morge's representatives entered, followed directly by the king. He sat in the chair next to her, his chainmail jangling and his sword at his side.

"Velkommen, welcome, welcome." Sofia noted only fourteen of the twenty chairs were occupied. "It looks like a few extended their summer holiday. Before we start, any news to share?"

One of Aldersfoss's representatives gestured with a quick wave. "Ingmarie just started her maternity leave, so she'll be out through Jolablot." Everyone clapped with enthusiasm.

Tomas—Morge's eldest representative—signaled to Sofia, his expression pained. Sofia nodded, forcing herself not to fidget. The last time he wore that expression was at her mother's funeral.

He rose from his seat. "Morge's south camp was attacked by Swaymark two days ago. A quarter of the camp was wiped out."

Anxious chatter took over the room. Swaymark had always been cold toward Fjorden, but this was a brutal ice bath.

Sofia glanced down at her notes, now useless. She swallowed and squeezed her eyes shut, her heartbeat thrashing in her ears.

"Quiet, please," she called out, looking around.

The room became silent, all eyes on her.

Clenching the armrests of her chair, she took a deep breath and turned back to Tomas. The priority was always Fjorden's people. "How is the camp?"

"Exhausted." Tomas sighed, sitting back down. He had circles under his eyes; if they had been caught up in yesterday's attack, Morge's representatives would have ridden through the night to arrive on time for Parliament. "Morge needs reinforcements. We need the king with us."

Sofia's stomach roiled with dread. Her father wouldn't survive the war. She had already lost her mother, her brother; she couldn't lose him, too. "King Eirik's twenty-two years are almost at an end. We're hosting the Sonne a month from now."

"Then we must move the Sonne forward." Tomas maintained an even tone, but his fingers began to tap the arms of the chair.

If the Sonne didn't kill Karsten, he'd be up against Swaymark. She blinked away the dizziness, straightening in her chair.

Disgruntled chatter continued, and another representative stood, his head held high. "This is the wrong time to transition to a new ruler. We should postpone the Sonne until next year."

Postponing would mean certain death for her father. Thor would never be on his side. Her father's twenty-two years would end in blood, whether by war or by the gods.

Her hands trembled as she glanced at her father. He looked down; he was leaving the choice to her. Sofia's sweat-covered hands slipped on the wooden armrests of the chair. She took a deep breath. She had to believe the victor of the Sonne would be ready to fight. The gods would be on their side.

"Pappa," she murmured, "we should move it forward."

The king nodded and rose confidently. Chatter ceased as all eyes turned his way. "By the twenty-two gods, I was graced with twenty-two years of their protection to rule, and not a day more. My time is almost over. A twenty-third year would bring down their fury on both me and Fjorden." He looked around the silent table. "We won't defy their will. We won't let fear stop us from running our kingdom. Fjorden needs a new warrior at the helm who will fight hard to protect it, and the Sonne has given Fjorden a great ruler for more generations than we can count."

"Thank you, Pappa," Sofia whispered as he sat down.

She wiped her hands on her silk dress, then straightened and scanned the representatives—some nodding, some frowning. "All in favor?"

Eleven hands raised around the room. They had the majority.

"Huzzah!" the king shouted, and the representatives chanted it back, officially closing the vote.

She had sentenced the victor to an immediate war to spare her father's life, but the victor of the Sonne would have the gods on their side. Karsten had to win, and if he didn't... she had to align with the victor. That was her priority.

Preparations hadn't started. Planning for preparations hadn't started. Sofia pressed her lips together, considering all she needed to coordinate within mere days.

"First and foremost, all are welcome to Championsfest," Sofia said. "Per tradition, we'll feast the night before the Sonne here in the Great Hall." Cheers erupted around the room. No one would turn down an invitation to celebrate in the castle. "We'll welcome the champions with a private feast when they arrive. While they're here, they can enjoy the castle and see all it has to offer. King Eirik will oversee any sparring himself."

"I've got a bit of fight in me yet!" he chimed in.

Some of the representatives chuckled, the mood lightening.

"You old codger! You couldn't fight a rabbit!" Tomas shot back, raising his eyebrows over his tired eyes.

"I'd fight you for saying that, old friend, but you aren't wrong. Bloody fast, those rabbits!"

The room broke out in hysterics, pounding on the tables. It was a fair assessment.

Sofia let the laughter die, then continued. "Four burial mounds will be prepared this week. When the Sonne commences, each champion will be placed twelve miles apart down the fjord. They will have to survive the elements and each other—and the last champion standing is the victor and the new ruler!"

The room erupted in loud cheers. Sofia rose, capturing their attention. "Aldersfoss is presenting Karsten as our champion." Sofia stood taller and clasped her hands together. "He has been one of my guards for six years. Many of you have already seen him here in the castle. He chose to bring a spear to our Championsmatch at Midsommar, and he knocked out eleven of his competitors." The whole group seemed impressed. "Representatives from Sander, are you ready to present your champion?"

"Yes. We are presenting Skippere. He beat everyone during the sail." The representative smiled, and a couple around the table threw down their fists proudly.

"And Hamme?" Sofia looked toward their representatives.

"Cheers for Jostein! He knocked out seven with a sword. I've never seen such passion brought to the battlefield. Extremely well fought—as good as the wars." Cheers rang out again.

"Fryse?" Sofia asked Karl, the eldest representative.

"Our Championsmatch is set for two days from now. We sail back tonight, and Njord willing, we will arrive just in time to see our champion win their match. Hurrah! Hurrah!" Karl's fist pounded the air, and others echoed his chant.

"Morge?" Sofia asked Tomas, clenching her fists to stop them from shaking.

Tomas shook his head. "Not yet, Princess Sofia. Rest assured, we will find our champion quickly, and our champion will be the victor!" The representatives from Morge screamed in excitement while representatives from the other regions hooted and jeered. Someone started stamping the floor, and half the room joined in, followed by a pounding on the table from the rest.

"Hip hip!" shouted Sofia, aiming to take back attention.

"Hurrah," a couple responded.

"Hip hip!"

"Hurrah," about half the room shouted, and some pumped their fists.

"Hip hip!"

"Hurrah!" came from everyone in the room.

"Any other questions before we move on?" Sofia looked around the table, but no one made a motion. Glancing at her notes, she wondered if any of them would be useful at this point. Probably not. She might as well give them to the trolls. "Right, then. Let's continue."

Fryse

Cliffs rose far above the fishing boat nestled in the center of the fjord. Seabirds circled overhead, though the boat was empty of fish. Nico dropped the hook over the edge, gripping the line. His arms ached; he'd spent the prior evening sparring against a straw man with his family's only sword.

"Did you see the dead walrus that washed ashore last week?" a crew member said from the other side of the boat. "He had to be two thousand pounds!"

"Of course we did," the captain said. "Where do you think the new fishing line came from?" Some of the crew laughed. "And we traded the tusks for a new sweater."

"You dummy!" he shouted. "You could have gotten gold for that ivory."

"Gold can't keep you warm, though, can it?"

All nine fishermen laughed, the sound echoing along the cliffs.

"No word yet on winter supplies. Parliament was supposed to meet yesterday."

"They've broken oaths for years. Don't expect anything."

That got snickers from the crew. Nico ignored them, listening instead to the waves lapping at the boat. The sounds of the world always delivered on their promises.

The captain leaned over the edge of the boat, gazing into the water. "Maybe the salmon will bite today."

"I'd like to catch a couple of herring. I'm tired of cod." Nico jiggled the line. "Though I suppose I'd take anything at this point. Hoping for a big meal before the Championsmatch."

A humpback whale surfaced near the bow, its sleek, dark back coming a foot out of the water. Its spray rose ten feet into the sky as it pushed a rush of air from its blowhole. The boat lurched from the whale's waves as the white splash coated the deck with water. Nico slipped and lost his balance, almost dropping his empty line. He grabbed onto the rail to steady himself, hoping the creature's presence meant fish were nearby.

"We deserve more than this," Nico whispered to the wind. He didn't receive a response, drowned out by the whale's deep song.

Fishing continued until late afternoon, a chorus of plops and waves and wind and banter creating a tranquil hum. The pile of fish grew steadily, along with the crew's relief, and the captain thanked Njord when the last basket was filled.

Hopeful seabirds greeted the crew when they returned to the docks. The fishy smell assaulted Nico's nose as he carried the heavy baskets across the deck and lifted them over the boat's edge, handing them to another crew member. Once they had unloaded the catch, Nico disembarked the rocking boat, climbing onto the wooden dock. His legs wobbled. He took a deep breath, his senses consumed again by the scent of fish.

"A basket for everyone. Thanks, all!" the captain shouted.

Nico found a basket with herring, then guarded it against the birds, watching the boats as they sailed into the harbor. Unfamiliar faces wandered the docks, arriving just in time for the match. When his two younger brothers returned, each with a basket full of fish, they began their walk home.

The wind nipped at the barren tundra while they walked toward the small town. A small weasel the size of Nico's foot ran across their path, chasing its breakfast. Its brown coat was beginning the winter molt, revealing pure white fur that blended in with the snow that would drape Fryse in a beautiful white blanket.

Hammering startled Nico from his reverie. A young couple was building their own new turf house. Soon, they'd pack the wooden shell around the fire pit with dirt, then cover the roof in dirt and grass. It would house the two of them, along with the sheep they had been given for their wedding last month. The whole town had attended the celebration, just like they would all be at the Championsmatch tomorrow.

A few minutes later, the brothers stopped in front of their neighbors' home. Nico placed his basket on the ground and knocked on the door. Sheep bleated as footsteps grew louder, and the door cracked open.

"Oh, hello." Nora opened the door the rest of the way, sending smoke billowing out. "Looks like Njord favored you today. Pappa just finished a batch of sea salt last week, so we can take all three baskets and season some of the fish for the winter."

"Just two," Nico said, glancing at his brothers. Their expressions betrayed their surprise. Their mother had asked them to trade it all, but their family deserved fresh fish, too, and Nico needed a filling meal before the Championsmatch. He could send back wool from the capital once he won.

"Anders, Jonas," Nora said, "could you bring the baskets inside, please?" After they stepped in, Nora closed the door to trap the heat. Nico listened to their footsteps and the thuds as his brothers put their baskets down. "I have the yarn for you." Nora's voice was slightly muffled. "It's right over here." Jonas stepped outside and winked at Nico as the sound of footsteps against the wooden floor continued. Maybe the family would help Anders build a house soon...

Anders appeared a moment later with two skeins of yarn in his hands and a blush in his cheeks. "Thank you, Nora." He bit his lip sheepishly as she smiled back.

Nico grinned as he picked up his basket. "Thanks, Nora."

"Have a good evening." Nora gave them a small wave. "And stay warm. Feels like there will be frost tonight."

As she closed the door, Jonas nudged Anders playfully, almost knocking the yarn out of his hands. "She's very pretty, you know." Anders ignored him. "Marriageable too." Jonas poked Anders in the ribs. Anders's face turned a bright red. They all knew exactly why Anders wasn't competing in the Championsmatch.

When the brothers entered their one-room turf house, the smell of freshly cooked soup complemented the usual woody scent mixed with burning timber.

"Hejhej, Pappa. Mamma. We brought some fish with us." Nico walked the basket to his mother.

Her eyebrows drew together with worry, and she crossed her arms. "Why didn't you trade it for more yarn?"

"They had enough fish already." Nico looked at his brothers, imploring their silence.

She chewed the inside of her cheek as she eyed the basket. "Okay. I'll add fish to our soup tonight, and Pappa can dry the rest."

Small arms wrapped tightly around Nico's waist. "You're back!" Elyse squealed. "Does that mean it's time for a song?"

Nico smiled as he looked at the fire pit, the table, anywhere except at the youngest of the five siblings. "I don't know..."

She narrowed her eyes. "Nico, you promised!"

Of course he had. He did every single morning. "Did I? I don't remember..."

"You did. You definitely did. I heard you say it." Elyse set her jaw as she let Nico go and turned to their mother. "Mamma, didn't you hear Nico say he'd play for us when he got home?"

"Hmm... I'm not sure." Laughter danced in her eyes, replacing the worry.

"Pappa!" Elyse wailed. "You heard him too!"

"Of course I'll play for you, little one." Nico kissed the top of her head. "Let me grab the hardingfele."

The fiddle sat against the wall in the corner of the house, the nine strings waiting for him. He ran his hand along its body, tracing the faded ink rosing along the edges and the mother-of-pearl inlays along the tailpiece. His fingers stopped past the pegbox and on the scroll at the top, which was carved into a dragon, smoothed by time and by the hands of his grandfather and great-grandfather.

Nico picked up the hardingfele and the bow and walked over to the table, standing near the fire. "What would you like to hear?"

Her smile lit up the room. "Something to dance to."

"Whatever you want."

Elyse jumped and clapped, leaving smiles on the faces of her family. "Margareta, won't you dance with me?"

"Okay." His sister rose begrudgingly, walked over to Elyse, and stood next to her, waiting for Nico to begin. He met Margareta's eyes, and they hid their amusement behind identical smiles.

Nico placed his hand at the top of the neck, wrist straight, and put the chinrest under his jaw, aligning the fiddle with his arm. He touched the strings delicately, appreciating the light instrument in his hands. The comfort and familiarity washed over him. Pulling up his bow, he held it gently but firmly, then plucked a couple notes. He rested the bow on the strings, then pulled it down with the weight of his arm, filling the house with a haunting melody.

His feet tapped while his mind went blank and his body moved with the music.

Elyse and Margareta danced along to the quick rhythm. They stomped their feet joyfully, jumping and clasping hands as they moved in a circle facing each other. Jonas and Anders got up, and together the four of them made the circle bigger. They released each other's hands, turned outward, and clasped hands again, the circle unbroken. Jonas and Anders both got down on one knee, grasping a sister's hand and holding it above their head. The girls circled their brothers, alternating back and forth, Nico's music swelling in its delicate but energetic beauty. The brothers clapped and stood up as Elyse and Margareta clasped their hands back in a circle to continue the dance.

As Nico played the last note, he looked over at his mother, her grin radiant.

"Again!" Elyse shouted.

"Food time, Elyse." Their mother placed the pot on the table. She lifted the lid, filling the house with the smell of fish.

Elyse sighed. "Aww, okay. Thank you, Nico."

"You're welcome, little one." Nico put down his fiddle and sat next to her at the table.

"Nico, guess what!" Elyse's eyes brightened with excitement.

"What?"

"Mamma and I picked the last of the blackcurrants today!"

"Did you, now?" Nico and his mother shared a smile.

"Yes! We have saft!"

Nico's mouth watered in anticipation of his favorite summer drink. The cheerful mood remained as their family shared the fiskesuppe meal. Once everyone finished eating, they said their thanks and cleaned up the table together.

Elyse pulled at Nico's tunic. "Can I get a story tonight?"

"Songs *and* stories? What am I? Your personal skald?" Nico narrowed his eyes and pouted his lips.

Elyse giggled, but then her shoulders slumped. "Margareta doesn't want to read to me anymore."

"You always spoil the ending!" Margareta shouted from the corner of the room, startling the goat she was milking. It let out a bleat and stomped on the straw-covered floor.

Nico contemplated the benefits of a one-room turf house. Warmth and safety, yes. Privacy and quiet? Not even in his dreams.

"Girls," their father scolded, "you're behaving like trolls."

"You can have whatever you want," Nico said.

His mother's hands rested on her hips. "You're spoiling her."

Nico laughed to himself; life at the castle would spoil her even more.

He moved his sleeping mat next to Elyse's and grabbed their book. She lay down on her mat, eyes wide.

"Which story do you want to hear tonight?" he asked.

She fidgeted, snuggling under her blanket. "How about a new story?"

"We only have one book, Elyse. Not much material for new stories…" His stomach clenched in disappointment. "How about the story of Odin and Freja? We haven't read that one in a while."

"Okay," Elyse said through her yawn.

Nico carefully turned the thick pages to the Saga of Odin. "Odin ruled over the Aesir tribe of gods and Valhalla, the hall of the fallen—a hall of pure gold, created with the spoils of war."

"Can I go to Valhalla?" Elyse asked, cutting Nico off.

"Not unless you die fighting in battle."

Elyse pursed her lips thoughtfully. "So, I have to be a warrior?"

"The kings and queens go to Valhalla as well."

"I want to be a queen, then." She yawned again and snuggled deeper into the wool nest she had created for herself.

If only it were that easy. "It doesn't quite work like that. But you know, if I become the victor, you could come live in the castle with me and the king consort."

"Really?" Elyse's eyes grew round.

"I have to become champion and win the Sonne first, though."

Elyse rolled her eyes. "You're the best. Of course you'll win."

"Thanks, little one." Nico considered all he was risking for the chance to change the government. To help his family. To help all of Fryse. His stomach churned. But no, his time was his time; his life string was already cut by the fates. He was ready to fight for Fjorden. He would make life better for his family, for everyone.

"The story?" She stared at him.

Nico's attention snapped back. "Right. Odin sent his Valkyries to collect Midgard's fallen, deeming them worthy of sharing his glorious home. Odin loved his home but lusted after Freja, the goddess of love and beauty. She ruled over Folkvangr, the home of the lovers and the artists. Odin wanted to show himself to be a grand partner worthy of her love, so he decided to grant Freja half of those who died in battle."

A tiny snore escaped from Elyse. Nico grinned, closing the book.

"Please keep going." His mother placed her knitting down in her lap. "I was enjoying the story."

"Sure." He flipped through the worn pages. "Freja graciously accepted Odin's gesture, but she was not to be so easily won. She did not believe Odin's love was true. She allowed him to come to her bed, but she guarded her heart zealously from him. Instead, she gave it to her people, who loved her in return. Freja collected her fallen herself, and she welcomed them with generosity."

"Thank you, Nico." His mother's voice was thick with emotion, and her eyes had a far-off look. "I'll miss evenings like this."

He looked over at his sleeping sister and his brothers carving wooden bowls in front of the fireplace. He would miss these evenings too. "I haven't become champion yet."

His mother gave him a knowing grin. "You'll see tomorrow. Next month, you'll be on your way to Aldersfoss."

An hour later, the whole family snuggled into their furs. Nico lost himself to the worries of the coming match.

Nico kept his eyes closed against the light of the fire, thoughts racing through his head. His mother puttered around near the hearth, preparing breakfast.

"I hear a mouse in the house," he whispered to her.

"Gods, Nico, take care of it!" she whispered back.

He opened his eyes and saw her smiling at him.

"Of course, Mamma." Nico pulled off the blanket and rose, leaving his sleeping mat on the floor. He hugged her with an easy affection. "There."

His mother chuckled. "Thank you. You're up early, aren't you?"

"Just a lot on my mind." The Championsmatch, mostly.

She nodded. "Are you hungry?"

"I wouldn't want to wake everyone up yet."

"We can eat, just us."

He hesitated, surprised by her response. The last time they had eaten alone, his siblings hadn't been born yet. "Sure, Mamma, that would be great."

Nico grabbed fresh oat rolls from the fire and goat cheese from the stone-lined hole underneath the trapdoor in the floorboards, placing the food on the table. They whispered and laughed as the table slowly filled with the rest of the family. Stories of snowy days and childhood fun shifted to questions aimed at Nico. Was he ready? Was he nervous? Most importantly, would he send back treats from Aldersfoss? Yes to all of it.

Their mother cut all the siblings off, hurrying them along. They finished their meal, layered on their wool, and prepared to face the chilly morning. Nico grabbed his wooden case of bone needles and thread, attaching it to his belt.

His family filed out of the longhouse, a line of porcelain faces and light golden hair that had been passed down through countless generations. Elyse grabbed Nico's hand and held it tightly as they walked to the Championsmatch.

At the competition area, Nico got caught up in the excitement of the match, wading through what seemed like every person from the region. He stood on his toes and looked over their heads until his eyes found the starting point. The competitors had already begun to line up.

A broad man with a heavy northern accent bumped into Nico. "Excuse me."

"Oh, sorry." Nico let him pass, following close behind, allowing the man to part the throng of spectators for him.

At the starting line, Nico sized up the other competitors; he was completely average in comparison. The representatives from Parliament stood on a raised platform. Nico's pulse sped up when the oldest representative, Karl, stepped forward from the group to speak.

"Welcome, all! And a special welcome to those competing to

be Fryse's champion in the Sonne!" A booming cheer rang out from the crowd. "Before we start, we have a quick update from Parliament. There is still a shortage of goods, which we expect to continue. Fjorden was attacked this week—by Swaymark." The crowd jeered, and many shook their fists.

A few of his fellow competitors dropped out of the line, no longer interested in leading. Nico gulped. An attack meant war, but wars were won by strategy, and he knew strategy. He would fight, and he would win. He took a deep breath, steadying his nerves, standing a bit taller.

"Now, on to the reason you're all here!" Karl shouted. "Our Championsmatch will test speed, skill, and strength, all things a great ruler must have. First, you must run four miles across the tundra, circling back to the shore. Then you'll jump into one of four boats, sailing across the lake."

Nico studied the group, counting heads; about twenty other people were doing the same.

Karl chuckled. "Ah, you all see the predicament you will be in, as those who do not arrive at the boats in time are automatically eliminated. There is a sword and shield in each boat. Those who do make it across the lake will need to climb to the top of the waterfall to defend it. The last one standing on top will be named the champion of Fryse!"

A deafening cheer erupted from the crowd. Arms waved, hands clapped, and feet stomped in excitement.

"We set sail for Aldersfoss at first light, taking the champion to the capital ourselves. In one week, the champion will fight to be the victor!" Karl shook his fist in triumph.

Nico started; he'd be leaving his family immediately. He couldn't see them among the sea of hundreds of bodies, but he'd fight for them, for Fjorden. His chest felt tight and his mouth was dry, but he was ready. With a deep breath, he prepared to run across the flat expanse of tundra.

"Competitors, we wish you all the luck of Thor's hammer. You may begin!"

The entire group took off at once, a stampede racing along the barren landscape. The sound of feet against the rocky ground helped Nico maintain a good rhythm for the first half a mile. Some of the faster racers edged forward, and he debated speeding up. A runner near the front tripped another. Nico decided to stay in the middle of the pack. He passed the fallen competitor, trying to keep a distance between himself and the other bodies. By the time they got up, he'd be well past them.

A few more were tripped or pushed, left behind in the morning fog that had draped itself across the tundra. As Nico watched them drop, his confidence rose. After two miles, the fog obscured his view of the other competitors, leaving him unsure of his current standing. His legs burned, but he knew he'd lose if he didn't keep pace.

Nico finished the third mile and sped up. At only half a mile left, he pushed himself to run the fastest he had in his life. The crowd's cheers grew louder as he approached the shoreline. There was only one competitor visible ahead of him.

A jolt of anxiety hit Nico when he saw only one boat left on the shore. With a final burst of speed, he caught up to the runner in front of him. They both touched the last boat at the same time.

"Get off!" The man shoved Nico, then pushed the boat out into the water.

"We can both go," Nico said through his labored breathing. He narrowly avoided tripping over the sword and shield on the deck as he climbed into the boat.

"No, this is mine!" The man had one leg over the edge.

Nico elbowed him in the nose right as he lifted himself, and the man fell back into the water with a splash.

"Sorry. I offered." Nico shrugged and raised the sail quickly, his breathing still heavy. He was far behind the other three boats, but he was confident in his ability to pull through. And maybe there would only be one challenger left at the top of the rock by the time he arrived. He scanned the water, guessing there were about two more miles across the lake.

The wind gusted hard and picked up speed. Nico let the line out and moved to the high side to add ballast, increasing stability against the wind. As he finished his adjustments, one of the boats in front of him listed to the side. The competitor pulled their line hard, and their boat capsized from the pressure on the sail. Nico sailed by them quickly, watching them cling to the sideways hull. One down, two to go.

Two empty boats were perched along the shoreline. Nico sailed up onto the rocky beach, the keel of his boat digging into the sand. He looked toward the top of the waterfall, his final two opponents locked in a swordfight.

He grabbed his sword and shield and scrambled up the rocks. His legs burned from the run, but this was his only chance.

Halfway up, he heard shouts from the two competitors. The clang of the iron pierced his ears. He was almost at the top when he heard a scream. One of the competitors fell past him and hit the lake with a splash.

As he reached the top, a sword whistled through the air. He dropped down the side, hands scraping against the jagged rocks. Launching up over the edge, Nico dodged and threw his shield up. He held it firmly, moving toward the wall and away from the edge of the rocks, his sword at his side.

A sword crashed down on Nico's shield. His rival stepped back to launch her next attack. She was muscular, more practiced. He didn't stand a chance in combat.

Nico threw his sword on the ground and tucked his shield close. He ran straight at his opponent and rammed her with all his might, knocking her off balance. Seizing his opportunity, he pushed her over the edge with all that was left of his strength. She fell off the rock, toward the lake.

He took a step back and looked out over the fjord.

Nico was officially the champion of Fryse.

"Nico, Nico, wake up," Elyse whispered into his ear, tapping his shoulder impatiently.

"Go to sleep." He cracked one eye open to look at her.

"But the lights!"

He rolled over on his mat and pulled his blanket higher, trying to drown out the melody of his family's slow breathing, rolling, fidgeting, and farting.

"Please, please, can we go outside?" Elyse pulled on his arm.

He turned back to her and took in the pleading look on her face. As he gained consciousness, his heart dropped; this could be the last time they watched the northern lights together. "Okay, just for a few minutes," he whispered. She vibrated with excitement. "Shh... It will be our secret."

Nico pulled off the blanket, stood up, and grabbed Elyse's small, warm hand. They slipped out the front door.

"Look!" Elyse pointed up toward the sky. There, against the black of night, lights danced slowly in front of the stars and around the wispy clouds, lighting up the world with bright ocean waves in shades of green and purple. "They're so beautiful."

"Just like you." He tapped her nose.

Sadness took over her expression. "Why do you have to leave?"

His heart cracked as he looked into Elyse's wide eyes. It wasn't fair that the government wasn't caring for them and sharing the wealth. It wasn't fair that anyone had to struggle. For all the amber and oil Fryse sent south... Fryse deserved so much more. "I'm going to make things better for everyone. Especially for you."

Nico picked Elyse up in his arms, holding her close to keep her warm, and together they watched the lights in silence.

MORGE

Her pendant, a miniature iron spear, hung securely from a leather strap around her neck; she had tied it on proudly sixteen years ago, the day she became a warrior.

She took in the emptiness of her small room, wooden walls surrounding a bed and a nightstand, barely lit by the glow of the dying fire. Other warriors would kill for the privacy and prestige it offered.

They could fight over it—as soon as she was named champion. One more day until Morge's Championsmatch. Then she'd be off to the Sonne.

And she would win. She always won. The fighter, the victor, it was who Dag was at her very core. Eternal glory in the Royal Circle of Valhalla would be hers, and the skalds in Midgard would sing her praises for centuries to come.

She put on brown wool pants and a lightweight wool tunic, then knotted her belt and attached her knife. After slipping on her dark leather boots, she circled the laces up her ankles and tied them tightly.

From its spot beneath her pillow, she pulled out her dagger. A dragon was cast into the pommel, its tail wrapped down the grip. The sharp iron blade glinted in the fading light. Slightly longer than her hand and barely the width of her smallest finger, the blade was needle-thin and made to kill.

Dag tucked it into her right boot, then left her room, weaving through the warriors splayed out on the sleeping mats throughout the snore-filled longhouse.

Stepping outside into the misty fog of the cool morning, she kept her eyes peeled for anything out of place. Dew coated the rocks, and the treetops blended in with the foggy gray sky.

The smell of celebration hung over the camp. Embers were dying from the campfires that had burned the night before, and empty glasses littered the benches. Unlike the rest of the warriors, she had gone to bed early, exhausted after four days of cleanup following Swaymark's attack.

Training will be fun today.

Dag kicked off her run toward the edge of the camp, passing by the longhouses and the dining hall. Her mouth watered from the smell of fresh meat being cooked. She'd fill her stomach when she returned. Grateful to the king for always prioritizing Morge, Dag would do the same once she won the throne.

Fresh air beyond the camp's gates finally allowed her to focus on her body's peaceful rhythm. The buildings surrounded by the palisade quickly disappeared behind her, hidden within the fog.

Small rocks skittered across the land, kicked out from under Dag's feet while she jogged across the flat expanse. With an easy speed to start off, she let her body slowly warm up against the late-summer-morning temperatures.

She aimed for the beach and broke into a run at the edge of the sand. Fog blurred the horizon, erasing the line where the sea met the sky. She followed the water line, breathing in the fresh, salty air as small waves lapped against the rocks along the shore.

Dag kept running as the fog continued to lift, her mind empty and free. When her legs started to burn, she turned around and aimed for camp.

Movement over the water caught her eye as she hit the final stretch of the beach. She stopped, squinting into the distance.

Just a seabird, circling its prey.

She had started to turn back toward the camp when she noticed a hint of green sails below the bird.

Her blood ran cold.

Racing the fastest she had in her life, she slammed open the gate at full speed, startling the guards. Her fellow warriors were meandering toward breakfast. She flew past them all to the center of the camp, soared onto the platform, and slammed the clapper into the walls of the warning bell as hard as she could.

The tolls pierced the lazy quiet of the morning. Clanging metal weapons mixed with the warriors' frantic shouts across the camp, drowning out the resonating bell.

She rushed to her sleeping quarters and donned her chainmail. With her sword at her side and her shield strapped across her back, she grabbed her spear. Dag's legs burned and her stomach rumbled, but fear mixed with adrenaline overtook her discomfort. *One, two, three, four—move, move, move.* She hustled out her door toward the gates.

Chief Ragnar appeared beside her within moments. "Dag, where are they?"

"Offshore, a couple of miles out." She repositioned her shield strap across her chest. "We need to get down to the beach and cut them off. No time to get the boats out, but we can build a line they won't be able to pass."

The chief nodded. "Get out there."

Shouting orders, she raced into the throng of fellow warriors hurrying toward the rocky beach. They created a line that extended parallel to the waterfront—a wall of shields, topped with spears that pointed toward the ocean. Dag squeezed into the front of the line, stunned as more ships escaped the disintegrating fog.

A carved serpent proudly graced the bow of the largest ship, coming fast toward the shore in a sea of green sails.

The Kronan.

Swaymark's flagship.

The clapping of hooves sounded behind her. She couldn't see the horse—it barely reached the shoulders of the warriors—but Chief Ragnar was perched on its back, rising above them all.

"Laughing, shall we die!" he shouted.

Dag joined in with the cries of war. *In glory, shall we live forever.*

The first enemy ship sailed onto the beach, the flat bottom of the wooden boat scraping against the sand. Warriors jumped out, spears aimed toward the line. Ships continued to land, the enemy pouring out.

"Charge!" Chief Ragnar roared.

"For victory!" Dag bellowed, gripping her spear. Those beside her joined in. She moved forward, keeping in step with the rest of the shield wall, ready to protect herself and her fellow warriors. They would win, just like they had five days ago.

The enemy thundered toward the center of Fjorden's line. Dag thrust her spear through the chainmail of a man twice her size, then yanked it back. Blood splattering, he fell in surprise, his eyes draining of life.

Small, but mighty.

She stepped over his body, aiming for another and another, killing five more, painting the ground red. After sixteen years of training, the movements were muscle memory.

Clashing metal rang out as bodies fell to the ground around her, suffocating her with the stench of sweat and blood. She pressed on, maintaining her part of the line.

An animalistic roar ripped away her concentration. Four men down, Swaymark's warriors had broken the shield wall, swarming inward. *Helvete.*

Breathing heavily, Dag raised her shield just in time to block an opponent's spear. Her shield cracked, half of it smashing into her arm. Tossing the scraps to the ground, she thrust her spear into her opponent's neck, taking them out swiftly. While their blood poured onto the sand, she wrenched their shield out of their hands. *They won't need this anymore.*

A sword came down on her spear with a whoosh, splintering the shaft. Its bearer raised it again, aiming at her. She whipped the splintered remains at the warrior's head. He ducked gracefully, then moved forward with force, slicing the iron blade toward her. She evaded, then drew her sword from its sheath. Metal met metal, the clang harsh and shrill.

Around her, Fjorden's forces gained ground, reassembling the shield wall. Behind them, warriors lit torches. *Swaymark's ships will burn.*

Dag pushed her opponent back toward the water, their swords clashing, the metal screeching. Warriors around them continued to fall, but Dag refused to give. She would win, or she would be welcomed in glory to Valhalla. *There's no in-between.*

A torch flew past her, launched at the nearest ship.

"Fall back," someone cried from the enemy's fringes.

Swaymark's warriors jumped into the boats and pushed out onto the water.

Dag's sword was an extension of her arm as she aimed for the kill, forcing her opponent into the blood-tinged waves. With sword and shield, he blocked her blows. The cold salt water soaked her boots, weighing her down, slowing her movement. Still, she kept at it, forcing him back.

A boat on the sand beside her caught fire. Swaymark's warriors scrambled on the deck, a few caught in the flames. Burning flesh assaulted her nose. With her opponent distracted, she landed a hit on his arm. His blood dripped into the waves, but he jerked back before she could cut deep.

"Fall back!" someone screamed, louder this time. Their ships launched into the water, the warriors retreating.

Fjorden's forces pushed forward, the shield wall fully reformed.

Her opponent brought his sword down. Dag blocked with her shield, hitting back harder.

Gold glinted on his sword's hilt.

Prince Magnus. He'd led the attack himself.

He ducked out of the way and ran for the last ship, jumping onto it as the warriors pushed the final boat off the beach.

The warriors of Fjorden let out a raucous cheer. They were exhausted, beaten, bloody—but victorious.

Most began the walk back to camp, towing the injured. A few looked for any of Swaymark's survivors, finishing the job. Dag sheathed her sword and watched the ships sail away in defeat. Once the last ship passed the horizon line, she assessed the damage. Dead bodies were scattered about the beach.

The Valkyries will have their work cut out for them.

"Dag?" a weak voice called. One of the newer recruits lay on the ground between two dead bodies, blood spilling from a gash in his thigh. *Helvete.*

She kneeled, tossing aside her shield. "I've got you."

Grabbing her knife from her belt, she sliced off the end of her pants, then ripped the wool fabric into a long strap. She tied it tightly around the recruit's leg, stanching the blood.

Acceptable—barely.

"Leave the weapons. We'll get them later."

She helped the new recruit to his feet. Together, they stumbled back to camp, moving as fast as they could into the first longhouse past the gates. Dag evaluated the bruised and battered warriors. The iron tang of blood overtook her senses. She helped the recruit onto an empty bench, and one of the warriors' partners hurried to his side, taking over his care.

Safe, for the moment.

Arm throbbing and stomach growling, she went to the dining hall. The meat had burned when the kitchen helpers ran to battle, some of them never to return. *They're celebrating in Valhalla now.* She grabbed a plate, filled it, and sat on one of the benches with her fellow warriors.

"Hel of a fight," someone called out. The table let out a cheer, Dag's voice the loudest and proudest of them all.

DAG WASHED OFF THE BLOOD. She dressed in clean clothes, admiring the purple and green bruise on her arm that had grown overnight. After helping collect the weapons on the beach, she had fallen into her bed and slept like a troll, her entire body sore.

She weaved through the warriors on their sleeping mats and exited the longhouse. A good run would loosen her up before the Championsmatch. She couldn't afford to be slow. Come Hel or high water, she'd win—and she would prove to everyone that she was born to rule.

A dozen pyres burned on the beach, the stench of charred bodies overwhelming, the ground stained by blood. Crackling fire mixed with the sound of the waves. After confirming the horizon was clear, she jogged her usual path along the water's edge.

Back at camp, Chief Ragnar stood in the square, conversing with two companions. They were dressed in simple tunics, and only one carried a sword.

The chief waved her over. "Meet Tomas and Lucia, two of Morge's representatives from Parliament. They arrived late last night."

Tomas scrutinized her. "I hear you alerted the camp before the attack yesterday. And personally fought Prince Magnus."

Dag gave a quick nod.

"She's our best." Chief Ragnar glanced her way, a gleam in his eye. "A true fighter, tough on and off the battlefield."

"So we heard." Lucia smiled.

The chief straightened, clasping his hands behind his back. "I know you've been preparing for the Championsmatch, but our representatives are canceling it after yesterday's attack."

Dag stopped breathing, stopped moving, but her head screamed in white-hot rage. Glory was supposed to be hers—to be the one the skalds sang about, to live in the Royal Circle of Valhalla for all time. She counted to four, then counted to four again, her chance to win ripped away.

"Dag?" Chief Ragnar was watching her.

"Hm?"

"I asked if you still want to be Morge's champion?"

"Yes," she responded immediately.

"Great. Eat, pack, and then our representatives will take you to Aldersfoss."

She nodded once, then raised her chin and suppressed a sigh of relief, hiding her surprise.

"I wish you the favor of the fates." Chief Ragnar put his hand on her shoulder. "You're a force to be reckoned with. May Odin's spear be on your side, and long may you reign."

Part II

The string of life is snipped at birth.

One cannot defeat the will of the fates.

FOUR DAYS

With her new head guard Max close behind, Sofia scurried up the stairs to the guest wing.

She needed to show the champions she ran the castle well, and that started with their sleeping arrangements. They'd spend four days in the castle before leaving for the fjords.

A servant was dusting the ornately carved headboard in the first bedroom. Only two logs rested near the fireplace. A pile of colorful patterned blankets sat on the bed, not yet distributed throughout the rest of the wing. They were behind on the preparations, and the champions would be arriving soon.

"Do you have help?" Sofia asked, stepping into the room while Max remained in the hall.

"They're fetching wood," the servant responded, moving faster and blushing deeply. "We had some delays after the"—he started on the nightstand—"late night with the representatives."

"Understood." Of course they'd had a late night; the remaining members of Parliament had drunk themselves into a stupor after four days of tactical preparations for the Sonne, and the servants had dragged them up the stairs to bed.

A white röggvarfeldur blanket sat on top of the pile, the tufts of fleece tied into the warp to mimic the soft feel of sheep. Sofia draped it carefully over the footboard. "Let's leave this one here."

"Max." Karsten's voice was muffled, calling out from down the hall. Sofia straightened quickly and faced the door, disappointed she hadn't made it back to the hall to greet Karsten properly. He was early, like always. She should have expected it.

He appeared in the doorway dressed in a tan linen tunic with the sleeves bunched up, the muscles of his forearms visible. A small bag was slung over his shoulder, though it seemed empty. Thor's hammer hung around his neck; his mark of a warrior had been hidden beneath chainmail for six years. The sword at his side, resting in its carved wooden sheath, was the only remainder of his guard uniform. It was a welcome change. His eyes looked tired, but his lips quirked into a small grin.

The servant tucked the rag into his apron pocket, then gathered the rest of the blankets into his arms and quickly exited.

"Good morning, Karsten." Sofia's stomach fluttered. "I'm sorry your visit with your family was cut short. How are they?"

"Good health and good spirits, thanks to the cask of ale." He placed his empty bag in the closet, claiming the room. Surely he'd grab clothing and armor from the guards' quarters later. "They're coming to Championsfest."

"Wonderful. We haven't seen them since Midsommar. Pappa will be ecstatic."

He nodded, just once, stoic as always.

She smiled. "Well, I'm relieved you've returned."

"Is the new guard not working out?" Karsten glanced at Max, frowning. "Max should have told me."

"No, the new guard has been great. I..." Sofia pushed through her nerves, thinking back on the conversation with her father about showing her strength, her worth. Karsten was no longer her guard—he was Aldersfoss's champion.

But he was still Karsten.

Fidgeting with her ring, she took a breath. "I missed you being here. I enjoy your company."

"Oh." A shy smile crept onto Karsten's face. "I'm glad to be back, Princess."

"Call me Sofia, please."

Karsten's cheeks turned pink. "Of course... Sofia."

She smoothed her dress, then clasped her hands. "I should be downstairs, to greet the other champions."

"I'll walk you down. I told Geir and Alexander I'd spar with them after I dropped off my bag."

He offered his arm, sending butterflies through her stomach, and escorted her to the entrance hall before continuing outside.

The door to the castle was open to let in the fresh summer air, washed clean from the morning rain. Sofia waited anxiously, ready to greet the rest of the champions. Max stood on guard near the wall behind her.

A clopping of hooves was quickly followed by the stablemaster Lars's mumbled greetings. Gravel crunched as the rider jumped down from their horse. Sofia faced forward, determined to make a good impression, as the next champion entered the hall.

"Welcome to the castle. I'm Sofia."

He hitched up his leather backpack. "Thank you. I'm Jostein."

An inch taller than her, he was somewhat stocky, with a long beard and a cowlick in his short, reddish hair. A light coating of freckles dotted his white cheeks and wide nose. He looked like he spent time outdoors, which would be an asset during the Sonne—and would potentially make him a formidable opponent for Karsten.

"How was your trip over from Hamme?"

"Easy. Fast, since it was just me on horseback." Jostein yawned. He had dark circles beneath his eyes, and exhaustion coated his features. "The road was clear, though I passed by more carriages than I expected."

"We asked Hamme's representatives to send back extra food for Championsfest. Sounds like the additional supplies are en route."

Thor's pendant hung around his neck; the simple black iron dangled from a leather cord. The representatives had failed to mention he was a warrior.

"Parliament members were impressed with your sword work during your match," she said. "When did you retire?"

His forehead furrowed. Sofia gestured to the pendant.

"Ah. The hammer was my father's," he said, voice flat, eyes dull. "He died in the war."

Sofia hid her surprise—traditionally, a warrior would be buried with their pendant. But it must have been a comfort for Jostein to have it, to wear it.

Softly, she said, "I still wear my mother's dresses sometimes."

His serene green eyes glazed over while his mind seemed to wander. Staying silent, his lips curved into a sad smile.

She knew that smile well; she often wore it herself.

"I look forward to watching you spar," she said. "Would you like to get settled in your room? You have plenty of time to rest before middag."

He gave another small nod. A servant escorted him to the guest wing while Sofia remained in the hall, studying a painting of her mother. Max stood on guard a few paces away.

The third champion strutted in shortly after with a sword at his side. His dark, golden-brown hair fell in a mop below his narrow ears, but his wide lips were surrounded by an impeccably-trimmed beard. His nose was slightly hooked, his skin a deep tan.

Vibrant embroidery on his light blue tunic matched one of her favorite dresses that had been imported from Marrocs. This was Sander's champion.

"Welcome, Skippere."

"Princess Sofia. Call me Skip." His close-set, forest-green eyes lit up. He stood less than half a foot taller than her. "You've grown since the last time you visited Sander—but I'd recognize your beautiful smile anywhere."

Sofia's heart ached. During their last visit, her family had been welcomed with a parade, and she and Filip had greeted over half the people in the trading port before the sun set. The next day, they had blessed—

"The *Ana-Sofia*," Skip said.

Sofia blinked. "Yes. How..."

He gestured to the painting on the wall, where the *Ana-Sofia* sailed across the canvas, its rust-colored sail full and its oarsmen at the ready. The carved dragon figurehead pointed out to sea. The ship was a tribute to the queen, commissioned during the Great War.

"She's beautiful," Skip said. "My father said she was the most beautiful ship he'd ever built. I never had the opportunity to sail with her."

And he never would. The ship had been buried—a part of her mother's grave. Her mother, who was waiting in the Royal Circle of Valhalla, who she wouldn't see again if she didn't show herself to be a worthy partner for the victor. She needed to focus.

"Her blessing ceremony was the last time we visited Sander. I do miss the port."

Skip shifted his shoulders back. "My father always let everyone take the day off when the royal family came to visit. He owns the largest shipyard."

"The representatives mentioned you dominated the sail."

Skip smirked. "Accurate."

Footsteps approached from the Royal Wing. Her maid Agneta appeared. "Sorry to interrupt, Princess Sofia, but your father is looking for you."

The fates were not on Sofia's side today.

"I'll head right up." She turned back to Skip. "I apologize for cutting our introduction short. Agneta can take you to your room, and I'll see you later."

Sofia sped up the stairs and went straight to her father's door, knocking lightly before pushing it open. "Pappa? Agneta said you needed me?"

"Come in." Her father gestured at her to close the door, but his eyes remained focused on the letter on the tabletop in front of him. "We just received word from Sander that Swaymark plans to wipe out Morge in two weeks. We need to alert Parliament and Chief Ragnar immediately."

Sofia gulped, taking in his serious expression. Two weeks until the victor would face Swaymark's force. But they'd have the gods on their side. She clasped her hands together to keep them still. "And we're sure this isn't a false alarm?"

"We are working to verify—but it seems legitimate. A dead body wearing Swaymark's colors washed up in Sander. They had notes on them with details of the attack. All written in ancient runes, presumably to keep outsiders from intercepting the message."

At least the fates were looking out for Fjorden. They'd need to craft a missive for Parliament to go out immediately.

"Let me grab my notes," she said.

"Have all the champions arrived?"

"Not yet. We're still waiting on Fryse and Morge." And she wasn't in the hall to greet them. Considering Morge's warrior would likely be the most formidable candidate...

"Let's do our best to be quick, then."

Unlikely, with how the day was going.

When Sofia entered her room, Agneta was cleaning the fireplace.

"Pappa needs my assistance," Sofia said. "Two champions have yet to arrive. Please let one of the servants know so they can escort the champions to their rooms."

Agneta set the iron ash bucket and shovel down with a low clang and exited the room.

Sofia crossed directly to her desk. Fresh, pink flowers waited for her. She caressed the blooms cut from Karsten's mother's garden. He would have dropped them off before finding her in the guest wing; that explained his empty bag.

But if the victor wasn't him...

She glanced out the window at the gray sky—darkening over the fjord, promising rain—before retrieving her notes.

Back in her father's room, she set her notes on the table, covering a corner of a map that was spread across the tabletop. "Where exactly was the body found?"

The king pointed toward the southeast corner. "Right here. They were likely traveling from Swaymark's capital to one of the camps in the north. Only one body, no boat, but—" A knock interrupted the king. "Come in."

Tomas entered, closing the door behind him. "King Eirik." Tomas bowed his head quickly. "I've brought Morge's champion, and I have news of another attack."

Sofia closed her eyes and took a deep breath, pressing the tips of her fingers against her temples and gently massaging them. A quarter of the south camp had already been wiped out. What now?

She took another deep breath and opened her eyes. "Welcome, Tomas. Please give us your updates. Unfortunately, we have some for you, too."

Tomas held a stiff posture; his eyes held a fire Sofia hadn't seen in years. "There was another attack on the south camp by Swaymark a few days ago. Prince Magnus led it himself. Our champion alerted the camp, giving us time to prepare and push Swaymark back." Tomas handed a scrap of paper to the king. "Chief Ragnar asked me to deliver the death count."

"How are the rest of the warriors?" The king glanced at the paper before handing it to Sofia.

Tomas tapped his fingers along his side. "Hanging on, but we need reinforcements."

"I'm not surprised, considering these numbers," the king said. "We'll find them."

Tension knotted Sofia's shoulders. "Hamme and Sander just had their summer recruitment last month. We'll have to go to Fryse next, but they don't usually send many, and the northern towns are so spread out. It could take months to find enough to make a difference."

Brow furrowed, the king traced the outline of Fjorden.

Tomas cleared his throat. "You said you had news?"

The king slammed his fist down angrily on the map, covering Swaymark. "In two weeks, Swaymark plans to wipe out Morge." His tone was sharp, his nostrils flared. "They'll come by sea, from the north and the south—pushing Morge's troops inward before eliminating them. Get the message immediately back to Chief Ragnar. Have him send word to the other camps. We'll send guards from Aldersfoss to Morge the day after Championsfest."

And the victor soon after.

Sweat dampened the paper in Sofia's hands. She set it on the table.

There was no room for fear; her responsibility was to serve the kingdom wholeheartedly, and she had to rise above it. "I'll call an emergency Parliament for the morning of Championsfest. Many of the representatives stayed in Aldersfoss or are already planning to return early."

"We'll send out guards with the alert tonight." The king's eyes remained fixed on the map. "Tomas, we will see you in four days. Take some of our guards with you."

With a sharp nod, Tomas said, "Laughing, shall we die."

The king's cheeks flushed. He was slow to respond. "In glory, shall we live forever."

Tomas exited, and his steps against the wooden floors faded quickly.

Sofia gathered her notes from the table, wondering if they'd ever be useful. Not today, it seemed. "Hamme's representatives will be here tomorrow for a quick review of the winter plans. I'll give them the update during our meeting."

Her father continued to stare at the map. "Less distance for our guards to travel."

"Pappa…" she said. He looked up at her, finally meeting her eyes. "First middag with the champions tonight."

He nodded, then turned back to the map, his jaw clenched.

Sofia sighed as she closed the door gently behind her.

THE SHIP LURCHED, scraping against the beach, and Nico grasped the rail to keep his balance. A dozen other ships lined the shore. The crew buzzed about, preparing the tarp to cover the deck for the evening. They had sailed straight through two storms to make it back to Aldersfoss on time.

"Out with you, Nico." Karl's tone was flat.

Nico disembarked, grateful to be back on solid ground. The

castle loomed from behind eight-foot-high stone walls, covered entirely in wooden shingles. Carved dragons roared toward the sky from the peaks of the roof, declaring war on anyone who tried to attack. Nico followed along the wall to the main gate. A Baldur-sized door covered in carvings opened onto a gravel path. Tall guard towers flanked either side, their stone bases and wooden tops mimicking the towers of the castle.

A guard stepped into Nico's path. His eyes peeked out from his peaked metal helmet, the ocular and nasal guard hiding the upper half of his face. Chainmail glinted from beneath a brown wool cloak. It went down to the middle of his thighs and covered a heavy leather padding meant to keep him safe from attacks. His sword hung from his leather belt, its wooden sheath covered with carved knotwork. He carried a spear at his side, and a painted shield was strapped across his back. Nico would need all that in the fjords.

"What's your business here?" The guard tightened his hold on his spear.

"I'm Nico, one of the champions." He had a sudden desire to flee. But he was a champion—he deserved to be there.

"Where are your representatives?"

"They are still on the beach." Nico kept his voice even. "We just landed a few minutes ago."

His eyes narrowed. "No weapons?"

Nico held back a sigh. "I left them with my family in Fryse. I knew there would be plenty here."

The guard looked him over once more and nodded, turning back toward the castle. "The fifth champion has arrived!" He stepped aside and gestured for Nico to enter, offering no apology.

Nico passed through the gate, awestruck by the full height of the castle perched on the hill. The base was made of rocks, and a wide, stone-hewn step stretched out before the open front door. Carvings covered the entire door, although he couldn't make out the details from his distance. All the windows were high off the ground, trimmed with carved wood. Patches of fresh shingles on the roof and walls showed the care the servants took to maintain the exterior.

This could be his new home. His family's new home.

He started along the curving gravel path. A loud neigh caught his attention. He followed it to the stable. Four horses roamed within a rectangular paddock surrounded by a wooden fence. As Nico approached, one of the horses trotted over to him.

"Hi there." Nico laughed as the horse nuzzled him, begging for food. He picked some grass and held it out to the horse, who ate it from his hand before wandering toward its companions. "If only it were that easy to find food in Fryse."

"Fryse, huh?"

"Oh!" Nico turned around, catching himself. "Hello. Yes, I'm Nico. I just arrived."

The unexpected stranger was tall and blond, his build similar to Nico's. "You're the fifth champion, then?"

Nico nodded. A large dog ran toward them from the stable, letting out a sharp bark.

"Welcome to the castle. I'm Lars."

"Thanks." Nico reached down to pet the dog, who had stopped at his feet.

"Do you ride?"

Horses were meant for traveling; since his family didn't travel far from home, a horse would just be another mouth to feed. "No, but I'd like to learn."

"I'm the stablemaster," Lars said. "Come on down any morning. I'm happy to teach you."

"That would be great." Nico smiled, readjusting his bag.

Lars returned to the stable, the dog tailing him.

Past the horses, a vast, open field stretched all the way to the rocky exterior walls. A group of men sparred with spears, their movements fluid and graceful. Fortunately, they were on Fjorden's side. Nico couldn't match their skill. He wasn't sure he'd survive against them.

After a few minutes, they wandered over to the trelleborg—four identical longhouses built along the edges of a square, with an open space in the middle containing a massive fire pit.

Nico crossed the field toward the camp. As he wandered closer, he smelled meat roasting over a fire.

"Hello," growled a voice behind him.

Startled, Nico turned around. "Oh, hello."

The woman had a pendant of Odin's spear around her neck; she was a warrior. "Are you lost?"

"No, I just arrived."

"Well, welcome. The servants' quarters are over there." She pointed to a set of six matching longhouses lined up next to each other. Servants came and went, all wearing various shades of brown and tan.

"Thanks." Nico smiled bitterly. He sighed as she shuffled past and entered the food hall.

Sheep and goats grazed in the fields, and cows circled a fenced-off enclosure just beyond. His family would have fresh milk daily, with no complaints from Margareta.

He eagerly followed the path up to the castle and into the bustling kitchen. Stone floors stretched wall-to-wall, the room three times the size of his family's longhouse. Vast counters were covered in wooden plates, platters, and bowls. What a feast it would be—all the food could feed his family for a year. Cast-iron pots hung over open flames in giant fireplaces. Shelves lined the back wall from floor to ceiling, filled with all manner of plates and glasses meant to serve a kingdom. His kingdom.

"Why are you just standing there?" a short, heavyset woman scolded. "And you aren't dressed, young man. Didn't you get your new clothes?"

"Sorry, I just arrived." Nico gulped, rubbing the back of his neck.

She tore him down with her stare. "Well, get back out to the quarters and get changed. The champions are arriving today, and we need to be ready. Time is running out."

Nico fought back the urge to flee for the second time within the hour. "Sorry, I think there's a misunderstanding. I'm a champion."

"You are?" The woman's brows drew closer together.

"Yes. I just arrived from Fryse."

Her eyes widened. "Oh, I'm sorry. I'm Inga. I run the kitchens. What are you doing here?"

Nico suppressed a sigh, straightening. "I'm going to fight in the Sonne."

"Yes, but what are you doing *in my kitchen*?" Inga quipped, her tone as sharp as the knife in her hand.

He started. "Oh, well…"

"Never mind, go through that door to the Great Hall. Middag should be served soon." Inga waved him on and turned back to her cooking.

Nico shrank back. "Thanks. Sorry, Inga."

He stepped past the threshold into the hall, stunned by the vast cathedral ceilings covered in paintings of the gods. Odin watched from his golden throne. Njord sailed along—like Nico's brothers, who'd be out fishing today. While he missed them, he didn't miss the fishy smell. The sea serpent Jormungand was painted along the entire edge of the room, its body separating the gods from Midgard.

Massive iron chandeliers hung over the tables and benches, with fresh candles waiting to be lit. Shields hung along the walls, each painted with bright colors only found during the summer back in Fryse.

At the end of the head table, a giant wooden throne beckoned him. Dragons were carved along the edges, and the intricate design continued on the table. He traced his fingers along the pattern.

The table had been set for seven—exactly the size of his family. But this time, it was set for five champions, one princess, and one king.

In the entrance hall, Nico scanned the colorful paintings, mostly of ships prepared for battle, set in gilded frames. Two massive stairways framed the hall, and a giant iron chandelier hung from the center of the ceiling. A guard was posted just outside the open front door.

A small corridor led off the hall. Nico followed it, pushing open a carved oak door and entering a giant library. The shelves were covered in more books than he'd dreamed could exist. Elyse would be ecstatic to find out she could have a new bedtime story every night for the rest of her life. He ran his hand along some of the spines, wondering which one she'd want to read first.

Twenty-one chairs surrounded the giant oak table in the center of the room—nineteen Parliament members, one princess, and one king. He would surely spend a lot of time here as Fjorden prepared for war.

Rusty old weapons hung along the walls. Nico wondered who used to wield them. No one would honor a coward sent to Hel, so they must have been used by someone who had died in glory.

At the end of the room, a giant tapestry of the mighty Yggdrasil and the nine worlds stretched from the floor to the ceiling. It was framed by two giant windows that let in plenty of daylight. Midgard was safely nestled in the center of the tree.

Looking at Yggdrasil, preparing to compete in the Sonne, ready to fight for Fjorden… Nico had never felt so extraordinary and so minuscule at the same time.

It was unnerving. A headache started to form.

He scanned spots of chipping paint on the ceiling, confused. Everything seemed so well-kept. Looking closer, he realized the constellations of the night sky were painted across the dark blue ceiling. The lederstjarna, the brightest star of the north, and the only star needed to find the way home in the dark, graced the center of the vaulted ceiling.

Footsteps entered the library. "What are you doing in here?"

Nico turned toward the gruff voice, taking in another guard. "I'm Nico. I'm one of the champions."

The guard frowned as he narrowed his eyes. "Yes, I know. I've been looking for you. I was waiting by the front door. Please allow me to escort you upstairs."

"Sorry, thanks." Nico followed the guard out the door.

Dag rested her hands on the windowsill, taking in the castle grounds. Four warriors guarded the gate, a short distance from the open door. She breathed easy, confident they were safe behind the tall stone ramparts, exhausted after traveling through the night.

Guards swarmed between the four longhouses like bees in a hive. The trelleborg was built like those back at the south camp in Morge, but the longhouses were smaller. They could only hold a few hundred to protect the castle. Other trelleborgs outside the grounds served the Aldersfoss region.

On the sparring field, warriors attacked each other with spears, undaunted by the threat of rain from the darkening sky.

Two armed guards crossed the field. When they arrived at the gate, all six worked together to close the door. Then four walked back across the field toward the trelleborg. *Guard changeover.*

Dag's stomach rumbled. *Three o'clock.* If the castle stuck to the standard three daily shifts, the next shift would be eleven tonight, followed by seven in the morning when they'd reopen the gates. Most things seemed to run the way they did in Morge. It made sense, since Morge was where King Eirik grew up. *Easy enough to stick to.*

Tomas had given her a sack of clothes, which was now waiting on the bed. She opened it, surprised to find a deep purple silk tunic resting on top. Tan or brown were her usual colors, both easy to wash clean of dirt and blood. Stripping off her tunic, she threw it and her pants to the floor of the closet before shrugging into the soft silk and belting her waist. After dumping the bag onto the shelves, she tossed it to the floor, then rifled through the linen and leather. She pulled on dark leather pants—a bit tight, but she could still move well.

From her hanging cloak, she removed her turtle brooches. They'd become hers the day her mother was killed. Dag had pulled them off her mother's lifeless body and washed them of blood, wearing them almost every day since. The iron was a cool comfort but a heavy weight in her hands. She attached the brooches to the silk, their chains hanging halfway down her chest.

Once she had tied her boots along the sides, she picked up her dagger from the windowsill and tucked it where it belonged: nestled safely in the top of her right boot.

Footsteps approached the door, followed by a knock.

She tensed. "Yes?"

The servant from earlier cracked open the door. "Middag will be held in the Great Hall. We can go down when you're ready."

Dag eyed her sword in the corner of the closet and contemplated whether or not to bring it. *No, let them think I'm weak.* If anyone tried to go after her, she could be just as lethal with her dagger—or even her own two hands when it came down to it.

She followed the servant down the silent hallway, keeping a watchful eye on the doors all the way to the Great Hall. Servants scurried along the edges, and guards watched at the doors. The other champions were gathered around the table in the center.

The tallest of the four had his back to her. She took in his muscular form; he spent hours each day training and had the opportunity to eat enough to fuel his body while he did it. *Karsten, Sofia's guard-turned-champion.* Tomas had warned her that he was a fighter. Seeing him immediately confirmed he would be her toughest competition.

A stocky man sat beside him, possibly slow. Sander or Hamme, the only two places left where he could get enough food to match his body's build. Red hair, brown tunic—could be either region.

The man across from Karsten was lean. Muscular arms. Sailing or... embroidery along his collar, oceanic pattern. Wealthy family. Definitely sailing and trading. Deep tan skin—probably had direct ties and family history with Marrocs. *Sander. Not a threat.*

This meant the stocky redhead was from Hamme. Possibly a threat, especially if he trained as a recruit in Morge.

And the final champion: Fryse. His almost-white hair was too clean for the amber mines. Likely a fisherman, probably slow. *Not a threat.*

That made five champions. Five of the best from their regions. She contemplated getting to know them, then remembered they'd be dead a week from now as she ruled the kingdom.

Dag walked to the table and moved to sit next to Karsten. She was put out when he gestured to the empty seat next to Sander's champion. It was the farthest from the king's chair. But rather than argue, she circled the table and sat, feigning nonchalance.

Sander's champion offered her a pitcher of ale and a grin. "Hi, I'm Skip."

"Dag. Morge." She hoped he'd take the hint. If not, oh well. *He'll be dead soon anyway.*

Karsten looked at her. She stared back brazenly, noting Thor's hammer dangling at his neck. *Silver, not iron.* Wealthy household. He grew up well-fed and well taken care of.

The stocky redhead shifted. "I'm Jostein, from Hamme. Close to the border."

"Have you spent much time in Morge?" Dag kept her tone light.

"No, but we sent food regularly, of course. My family owned a farm."

Perfect. Probably not a threat, although he wore an iron Thor's hammer.

"Oh, to get regular food from Hamme..." Fryse's champion, of course.

"Well, Nico, you're in the castle now." Skip elbowed Nico's side jokingly.

"Where are you from?" Jostein asked Skip.

"I grew up in Sander." He picked up his glass. His hands were calloused—definitely a sailor.

"Did you grow up in Aldersfoss?" Skip asked Karsten.

Karsten nodded silently, offering no further response.

"Has anyone met the princess yet?" Nico asked.

Skip grinned. "Yeah, just before she was called up by her father."

"I met her as well." Jostein seemed tired, unenthusiastic.

"Dag, I assume you didn't meet her yet?" Skip asked, turning back to her. "I think you arrived after me."

"Correct." *Skip pays attention.*

"I hope she comes down soon," Nico said. "I'm hungry."

"What was your match?" Dag asked, ignoring Nico and turning to Jostein. *And did you train in Morge?*

"Hamme held a swordfight," Jostein said.

"Shield-breaking?" Nico asked.

Jostein nodded. "If three of your shields were broken, you were out."

"Obviously you won," Skip said.

"Knocked out seven."

Skip's eyebrows lifted slightly. "So that's twenty-one shields?"

Jostein took a swig of ale. "I actually broke thirty-two."

Dag kept her face schooled. *Definitely a threat.* But she was fast, and speed would be her ally.

"So what was your match, Skip?" Jostein asked.

"Sailing. There was some fighting on the decks during the launch, but I outsailed them all." Skip straightened, puffing his chest. "I was born on the water."

"Our competition involved sailing, too," Nico said. "We also had to run and fight."

Huh. Have I underestimated him?

"That's more intense than ours," Skip said.

Nico nodded as the rest of the champions turned his way. "I was the fastest runner, the fastest sailor, and the... well, the most creative fighter."

"What do you mean?" Skip asked.

Dag leaned in with curiosity.

"During the third leg of the challenge, we had to defend the top of the waterfall with only a sword and shield. Last one standing won."

Skip's eyebrows rose. "What's creative about that?"

"I pushed my final competitor off by running straight for them with my shield. They fell off over the waterfall and into the lake. Enjoyed their swim." Nico chuckled.

One competitor? Dag laughed to herself. *Not a threat.*

"What about you, Karsten?" Dag asked.

"Of course you wonder about *him*," Skip muttered.

Dag bit back her laugh.

Karsten eyed her warily. "It's Aldersfoss tradition to host the Championsmatch during Midsommar. The princess and the king celebrated with the people, and the match was part of the events of the day."

"What was the challenge?" Skip asked.

"Fight to submission."

Skip whistled low. Below the table, Dag clenched her fists. It was cowardice to yield, and no warrior would bow out for anything less than certain death. She squashed her feelings down.

"What was yours, Dag?" Skip asked.

Showing no emotion, she said, "I didn't have one."

"You... didn't have one?" Skip repeated, his eyes narrowing.

"Right. The representatives just sent me."

Dag could see it in their expressions. They were underestimating her. She smiled sweetly and took a swig from her glass. *Let them think what they will.*

Motion by the doorway quickened Dag's pulse.

The princess strode toward their table. Confidence radiated off her, although she lacked grace, stumbling slightly over... *her own feet?* Her steps echoed through the hall, drawing the attention of the rest of the group, who rose in respect.

"Welcome to my home, champions of Fjorden."

SOFIA OBSERVED ALL FIVE CHAMPIONS around the head table, determined to make eye contact and show them she would be a strong and confident partner. "Your greatness is inspiring, and your place here at the castle is well deserved. I hope it will soon feel like home for each of you."

Karsten nodded when their eyes met, gesturing to the space on the bench beside him. Warmth filled Sofia; he had guarded her usual spot and chosen to sit next to it.

"Does your mother have any flowers left to cull, or did you take the rest?" Sofia whispered as they all sat down.

"She's always happy to share," Karsten whispered back. His lip quirked.

Jostein still looked tired, his thick brows furrowed. She'd ask later if he was comfortable—though she doubted she could ease whatever troubled him.

The next face was unfamiliar, but her stoic expression and watchful eyes rivaled Karsten's. Sofia caught her gaze, saying, "My apologies that we didn't have a chance to meet earlier. What's your name?"

"Dag, Your Highness." Her shaggy, strawberry-blond bob was tossed carelessly behind her pointed ears.

Sofia blinked slowly, taking in the powerful muscles that lined Dag's entire body underneath her honey-tan skin. Odin's spear graced her neck. Her strong collarbone was framed by iron turtle brooches connected by chains that hung past her flat chest. This was the body of an athlete, sleeker than a knife blade and far more deadly, forged by the Eastern front.

"Welcome, Dag. Call me Sofia. I'm pleased to meet you. Where are you from?"

Dag straightened. "Morge."

"My father is from Morge. He's been looking forward to your arrival."

Though she remained quiet, Dag seemed pleased. She would definitely be a challenge for Karsten. A scar crept along her neck, from her ear all the way to her collarbone. Sofia wondered who had left the permanent marks on her skin.

"Skip," Sofia said, "apologies we were cut short earlier."

"No worries." Skip toasted her with his glass.

"Nico," Sofia said, turning to the final champion, "I heard you had the guards looking all over for you."

Nico grimaced, running his hand through his short hair—thick and straight, the same shade as his stubble. His gray tunic matched the hooded, winter-gray eyes beneath his thick, rounded brows. "It wasn't intentional."

"I don't mind. It took the focus off me." Sofia waved to one of the servants along the edge of the room. "The king will be down soon. Then the meal can begin."

Karsten straightened next to her, his movement followed shortly by the sound of her father's footsteps. She and the champions rose, facing the door.

"Sit down, sit down," the king bellowed cheerfully as he entered the hall. "One of you will be taking my place in a couple of weeks. If anything, I should be standing. Oh wait, I am!"

A couple of the champions laughed politely as they all sat.

Sofia smiled affectionately at her father.

"Welcome, all." The king settled in his chair. "I sat at this exact table twenty-two years ago, facing the Sonne." He paused, looking at each of the champions. "The five of you are the best of your region. One of you will be the victor. If you're lucky, you might even prove yourself worthy of Sofia's hand. Hurrah!"

"Hurrah!" the champions echoed back. A few of them glanced at Sofia, whose cheeks heated.

"Enjoy some friendly sparring over the next couple of days," he continued unwittingly. "Why wait for Valhalla? Have some fun and get used to the weapons in the armory. They're some of the best in Fjorden."

Karsten grinned. Jostein brightened a bit as well. Maybe the pair would be a good match.

"Speaking of the best." The king gestured toward Sofia, and she straightened her dress, fighting the urge to squirm. "In between meetings and running the castle, including the preparations for this feast and the events surrounding the Sonne, Sofia arranged a sail for all of you—tomorrow afternoon."

"We'll sail in the fjord where you'll be competing," Sofia said. "I haven't been out on the water in a few years, so I'm quite excited."

Skip and Nico looked especially pleased.

"Then Championsfest, and it's off to the fjords for all of you." The king lifted his ale in a toast before taking a swig. "The Sonne begins the moment you're dropped off. For now, let us eat." He gestured to the servants to bring the food over. They laid out a feast of roasted reindeer and vegetables, and Sofia relaxed as the champions eyed the platters of food hungrily. "Dig in."

They all filled their plates, passing the giant wooden serving platters along, harking back to middags when Filip and Mamma were still at the table. A force of longing hit Sofia, leaving her lightheaded. She took a deep breath.

"Which one of you is from Morge?" The king looked around the table.

Sofia gestured to each in turn, saying, "Dag is from Morge. Skip is from Sander, Nico is from Fryse, and Jostein is from Hamme." Her stomach twisted. "And, of course, Karsten." She hoped Karsten didn't notice he'd been skipped when she circled the table.

"Tell me, Dag, how is it out there?" the king asked, unconcerned with the rest of the group. No surprise, with Tomas's report.

"Busy. We successfully defended against two attacks this week."

Nothing they hadn't heard.

"Swaymark has been bolder lately with the Sonne coming up." The king looked around the table, his brow furrowed. "Even though I'll be here as a mentor, the victor will need to be prepared. Ready to fight back."

Dag nodded. "The best skills are learned on the battlefield."

"That they are." His eyes glassed over, his expression familiar; his mind was back on the wars.

Karsten shifted next to her. "Most of my fighting has been here in Aldersfoss. The worst was when we were ransacked by Tunland at Midsommar."

Sofia's eyes widened; she had only known peace in the capital since she took over Parliament. "When was this?"

The king's eyes darkened. "You were nine, and Filip was only three. The queen and the royal guards protected you both." He relaxed his shoulders and took a swig of ale. "The quick actions of the warriors stopped the castle from burning to the ground. They saved countless lives."

"That's right," Sofia said, meeting Karsten's eyes. "I remember the feast after, in the Great Hall. We were thankful to welcome so many, although the cooks were exhausted by the end of it all."

The champions continued to share battle stories. Sofia enjoyed the camaraderie; it was far livelier than she was used to. She stayed quiet for the most part, listening and appreciating the energy they brought with them.

Once the food had been eaten, the servants brought out plated slices of marzipan cake. Sofia's mouth watered. She picked up her spoon and eyed her slice greedily as she waited for everyone else to be served. She took a bite the moment the last plate hit the table directly in front of Dag, savoring the sweetness.

"Mm, the cooks found almonds." Sofia beamed.

"Here, enjoy. I'm full." Karsten pushed his plate toward her.

"You're turning down marzipan cake?" Filip would have been appalled.

Karsten gave her a sly smile. "No one warned me of dessert when they brought out the meal."

She hesitated. He pushed it a bit further toward her.

"Well, I always have room for marzipan." She finished the last bite of her cake and pulled his plate on top of hers. Karsten smiled as she took another bite.

After the plates had been cleared, the king rose. "Have some fun tonight. I look forward to seeing all of you first thing tomorrow on the sparring field."

The champions chorused a goodnight as he exited the hall.

"More ale?" Skip asked.

Sofia nodded and gestured to the servant on the side of the room.

"Maybe some water, Skip?" Jostein asked.

"Only if it's from Urd's well," Skip said dramatically.

Dag laughed. "That can be accommodated as soon as the Sonne starts."

Skip breezily waved his hand at her.

Jostein sighed and shook his head.

Karsten stiffened beside Sofia. His eyes were locked on Nico, who was rummaging underneath the table. Nico coughed under the scrutiny, and suddenly all eyes were on him. His porcelain skin turned a deep crimson as he opened his bag.

"I brought along my hardingfele." Nico pulled it out of the bag ceremoniously.

Karsten relaxed, and Sofia smiled at Nico. He propped the fiddle under his chin, plucked a few strings, and played happily as the group listened and drank.

A couple of songs later, Sofia yawned. "Nico, your playing is exquisite, and I'd love to keep listening. Unfortunately, my eyes don't want to stay open."

"You only need ears to listen," he joked.

Sofia chuckled. "You aren't wrong."

"I'll bring along my fiddle tomorrow night."

"Wonderful." Sofia stood.

Karsten immediately stood as well.

Sofia blushed. "Oh, you can stay if you like."

Ever stoic, he said, "I need sleep before my morning run."

Dag perked up unexpectedly. "Where's your route?"

"Through Aldersfoss." Karsten's eyebrows lifted slightly. It seemed he hadn't expected Dag to perk up, either.

"Mind if I join you?" Dag watched him, eyes far brighter than they'd been all evening.

Karsten swallowed, then nodded. "Sure."

"Thanks." Dag turned back to the table.

"All, please enjoy," Sofia said. "Stay down as long as you'd like. Just don't be late for sparring tomorrow morning, or you won't hear the end of it from Pappa."

Karsten and Sofia exited the hall together, her newest guard following behind.

Sofia clasped her hands in front of her. "I'm glad you're back. It was strange without you here."

"I'm glad to be back."

He smiled, warming Sofia from the inside out. She wanted to say more, but she wasn't sure what. Sofia yawned again, her cheeks heating.

Karsten chuckled. "Sleep well, Sofia."

"See you in the morning."

She meandered back to her bedroom. Her guard trailed behind her, stopping just outside the door. She stepped into her closet but was interrupted by her father's knock.

"Pappa, I thought you went to bed." Sofia stepped back into the room.

"Not yet."

"Do you need help with anything? Was there more to cover?"

He frowned. "I wanted to ask... might one of the champions already be a favorite?"

Sofia's cheeks heated. "Yes. Was it obvious?"

Her father nodded. "It was, kjære. Consider how the other champions might feel about it." The consequences were implied by his expression.

Sofia remained silent, her hands clammy, taking in her father's words with trepidation.

"I think you get it?"

She nodded. "Thank you, Pappa."

"Sofia… just remember, the gods have already decided the fate of each of our champions, and their life strings are already cut. We can't change that."

"Of course, Pappa." She sighed, resigned. *A princess serves her kingdom wholeheartedly.*

He sat on the bench, eyeing the papers on her desk. "Have you shared your favor?"

"Not yet. I haven't finished yet, with all…" With everything.

Her father gazed wistfully at the portrait of her mother. His love was visible in his eyes. "Your mother gave me her favor. Did I tell you that?"

"No, you didn't. What was it?"

"My hammer pendant. Thor's hammer." He pulled a neck chain out from underneath his tunic and held the silver hammer in his hand. "She said it would protect me, and I suppose she wasn't wrong. The fates decided it wasn't my time yet." His thoughts seemed to drift off.

Sofia admired the amulet embellished with filigree rope that twisted around the upside-down hammer. At the top, the filigree rope formed a head with large staring eyes. Always watching, just like the gods.

"It's beautiful, Pappa."

"She broke the rules about making the favor herself, you know." He chuckled. "It came from the Royal Treasury."

Sofia smiled. "Of course she did. She couldn't sew or paint, and the cooks had banned her from the kitchen before I was born, so I suppose her options were limited. Her handwriting was atrocious, too."

Her father let out a deep belly laugh. "It's true. She could have written something, but I wouldn't have been able to read it." Sofia laughed as her father seemed lost in thought, a smile on his face. "Still, she was ferocious. A real dragon. A force to be reckoned with. And if she set out to do something, it would be done."

"Like breaking traditions," Sofia joked.

"I've worn this hammer every day since, you know. I think your victor will cherish your favor too."

Sofia took comfort in the thought. "Yes, I think so."

Her father rested his hand on her shoulder. "None of us know what the gods have decided, but I hope they smile upon you... Whatever happens, I love you and I'm proud of you."

"Thank you, Pappa. I love you too."

He exited the room, his steps fading down the hall.

Sofia pulled her stitching hoop and carved ivory sewing case from the drawer of her nightstand, determined to finish her favor. Settling on her bench, she threaded a bronze needle, then started stitching pink wildflowers—just a simple four-stitch pattern her grandmother had taught her. Quite a contrast to Thor's hammer, which she had stitched in a corner in the same rich, earthy brown of the chain-stitch edges. Her stitches were small and practiced, the small pops of the thread through the linen music to her ears.

Agneta entered with firewood, filling the fireplace for the night. "The handkerchief looks beautiful. Your grandmother loved teaching you how to stitch."

"I always loved spending time with her." Sofia cut the pink thread and switched to green. "Mamma never had the patience, though."

"She would be so proud of you—a beautiful and smart woman who shows just how dedicated she is to Fjorden every single day."

Sofia looked at the painting of her mother. "Thank you, Agneta. I think you're right."

"Of course, I'm right." Agneta shook her head, but her grin hinted amusement. "Don't stay up too late."

With all the thoughts swirling in her head, there was no chance she'd be asleep any time soon.

RAIN PATTERED ON THE ROOF, layering a heartbeat beneath his hardingfele's music. Nico's thoughts drifted along with the melody.

Skip danced alongside the table, another ale in his hand. Jostein and Dag were relaxed, a positive change after their more serious middag. It had been slightly awkward, but new environments, new people, temporary arrangements, and imminent death would do that—especially when piled together.

The king had remained oddly silent. His stories had to be... well, he was the king. Everyone had been curious about Sofia, but who wouldn't be curious about the princess? Karsten had watched her like a falcon for most of middag. Jostein and Skip had watched her as well, though not to the same extent. But Dag. Dag had sized everyone up, watching everyone in turns, and it seemed she had found everyone lacking. The situation in Morge sounded worse than Fryse's representatives had let on, though...

Nico sliced through the last note of the song and placed the fiddle on the table before picking up his glass of ale. Skip relaxed on the bench.

"How long have you been playing?" Jostein asked.

Nico thought back to his grandfather's lessons. "Seventeen years, on and off."

"You play well." Skip toasted him. "We have plenty of musicians in Sander, and you could definitely hold your own against them."

"Thanks." Nico fidgeted a bit, but no one seemed to notice. He took another swig of ale as the rain continued to thrum against the roof.

"Dag, share some of your battle stories," Skip said gaily.

"What sort of story do you want?" Dag's bright eyes betrayed her amusement.

"Which battle led to the death of the sorry soul that gave you that scar?" Skip gestured to her neck. "There is no way that they survived."

Dag's nostrils flared, and her eyes became as cold as ice. "No. They didn't."

No one said a word as the rain thrummed along. Nico picked his fiddle back up and began to play a serene melody, breaking the silence without words.

Jostein shifted uncomfortably. "Skip, why don't you tell us tales from your travels?"

"Tales from the *best* sea captain, you mean." Skip took another swig of ale; the alcohol definitely increased his enthusiasm. "Well, I'm sure no one wants to talk about Swaymark, especially after last week's attack. Trading is difficult at the moment, considering half of them want to kill us and the other half want to enslave us. Our goods are so similar that we don't need to trade anyway, so cheers! Forget them!"

Dag's expression softened as she raised her glass.

"You remind me of my brothers." Jostein raised his glass, his lips quirked in amusement. "So you haven't been to Swaymark in a while, then?"

Skip shook his head. "I miss it, though. The stone-lined streets full of life, the energy of the people, a sheer lightness of being, topped with towering buildings lining the waterfront. All the streets lead directly to the castle in the center of the capital, and we were always greeted with the best parties."

"Really?" Dag looked as surprised as Nico felt, considering Swaymark had attacked twice within the last week. Nico missed his next note, but no one seemed to notice as he played on. Not that Skip was likely to notice much...

"The king and his new bride pulled out all the stops the last time we were there. That was a few years ago now, though."

"Why would he do that for merchants?" Dag asked.

"Not just merchants, Dag. The best merchants, with the biggest ships in the sea. Coveted by *all*." Skip smiled devilishly.

"So where else have you gone?" Dag asked.

"Oh, I've been everywhere." Skip waved his arms. "Marrocs, Tunland, Stantland, but home will always be Fjorden."

"That's not everywhere."

"Fine," Skip huffed. "Everywhere worth going."

Nico laughed to himself, dragging the bow across the strings.

"What is Stantland like?" Jostein took another deep gulp of his drink before waving to the servants to bring more ale.

"Only the most glorious country you have ever seen." Skip's expression betrayed his awe. "Half the buildings are topped with giant domes, and every street in the capital is lined with merchants. Silks in bright colors, spices you've never even heard of, wines so delicious the taste can't be described, silver and gold and coins and jewelry, and all of the vendors love trading with foreigners. We always come home loaded up, but it's the longest sail and the furthest away."

Skip rose, resuming his dance. He jumped twice to the beat of the last few notes.

Jostein's eyes brightened, though Dag continued to sulk. Nico started up another fast-paced song.

"Your shirt is probably from Marrocs, Dag," Skip said.

"How do you know?"

"Silk from Stantland is softer, and the colors are usually brighter. Silk from Kinaska is the highest quality, but it's even farther away unless we sail past Tunland. That route opens us up to a risk of freezing or hitting the icebergs, though. Not usually worth it."

Dag's eyes glazed over, her face otherwise blank.

"We usually send smaller ships to Marrocs," Skip said, finishing a turn. "They're a lot closer, and we only trade for their silks and fruits. Honey too."

Nico played the final note of his song, then started a new one. "Is Tunland like Fryse?"

"The freezing cold is the same, of course, in the north. Their leatherwork is far superior to Fjorden's. Usually, we send smaller ships to Tunland, and leather goods are all they come back with. Tunland already has fur and oils, but they go crazy for our amber. Our wool, too, but we don't trade much of that away."

"Have you ever been to Romiska?" Jostein asked.

"Of course!" Skip jumped up, knocking into the table and spilling his ale as he gestured wildly with his hands. "The best silver and gold, the biggest of the buildings, the grandest of the castles." Skip started to dance again.

"Why didn't you lead with that, then?" Dag quipped.

"I've only been once. Usually my older brothers go."

"Ah, are you the youngest?" Jostein asked.

Skip nodded. "Of five."

Just like Elise; no wonder they had the same energy. Nico ended the tune with a flourish and set down his fiddle while one of the servants brought over more ale.

"I was the youngest of three." Jostein smiled softly.

Skip took another swig of his ale, laughing. "It's the worst, isn't it? The eldest inherits *everything*. Nothing for the rest of us."

Jostein's smile became forced. He nodded and rose from the table. "Well, I'm heading up to bed." Skip's smile dropped, his forehead pinched. "I'll see you all in the morning. When should we be at the sparring field?"

"Probably after seven, since that's when the first shift starts," Dag said. "I think I'll head up too."

Nico and Skip chorused a goodnight. Jostein and Dag exited the Great Hall. Bed was probably a good idea, though he wasn't tired.

Skip gestured to the servants for another glass of ale, so he wasn't going anywhere. Not that Nico minded.

"Another song?" Nico asked.

"Definitely."

Nico swept the bow across the fiddle.

Skip's attention shifted to the painted ceiling.

"Do you know 'The Song of Yggdrasil'?" he asked after Nico ended the tune with a flourish.

Nico began to play, surprised when Skip started singing:

An ash I know stands,
Yggdrasil, its name.
Splashed with pure water,
are its high branches.
From those come the raindrops,
that in the fjords fall.
Green stays the ash tree,
from the pure water of Urd.

As Nico finished the last note, Skip smiled. "Thanks for playing tonight. This was fun."

It *was* fun.

He drank the last of his ale and stood. "See you in the morning."

Nico nodded a goodnight as Skip meandered off, then played the second verse to the vacant hall, singing low:

Out come three maidens,
from Urd's endless well,
found under Yggdrasil.
Urd always comes first,
then Verdandi and Skuld.
They measure the fate,
of all children born.

Nico tucked his fiddle back into his bag, grateful for the small piece of home he'd briefly found.

THREE DAYS

Darkness surrounded Dag. The fire had burned out in her hearth during the night. A chill ran through her, despite the wool nightshirt.

Back at camp, warm bodies had filled the longhouse of the trelleborg, and whoever was awake would throw logs on the fire throughout the night. Heat had always permeated through her closed door, keeping the room warm all night. Now here she was... *Exactly where I'm supposed to be.*

She threw back the covers and placed her feet squarely on the floor. The wood felt fresh, hardly worn, noticeably different from the well-traveled floors of the camp. She ventured to the window and scanned the vacant, moonlit field. Most of the warriors were probably still asleep. *Nothing new there.*

Two guards paced along the tops of the ramparts near the gate, spears in their hands and shields on their backs. Their metal weapons gleamed in the moonlight.

When will Karsten wake? Considering he was a guard who ran every morning... he must have been used to starting at seven with the first shift, so he'd probably be awake soon if he wasn't already.

Dag stripped off the nightshirt; shrugged into her tan wool tunic and pants, the light material comfortable against her skin; and tied up her leather boots, appreciating the familiarity of her routine. From underneath her pillow, she pulled out her dagger, tucking it into her right boot. *Where it belongs.*

She opened the door and stepped into the hallway, scanning thoroughly for any sign of motion. Her footsteps light, she crossed to Karsten's door, listening for any sound of movement. *Silence.* She went down the stairs to the entry hall and stepped outside.

The gravel crunched beneath her boots as she walked toward the castle gate. Hints of moonlight caught on the clouds of smoke rising from the trelleborg's kitchen. A bush rustled. She stopped, scrutinizing it closely. *No, it's nothing.* The rest of the world was silent. She continued on.

"Good morning," Dag called to the guards by the gates.

"Good morning," they responded in unison.

"Could you open the gate, please?"

One of the guards shook their head. "It opens at seven."

"I was hoping to go out running before—"

"Seven." The guard's expression left little room for discussion. "You're welcome to run on the castle grounds."

"Sure, thanks."

Two more hours. Karsten must have been on a later shift if he ran outside the walls every day. She didn't feel like waiting around for him to wake up.

Dag ambled toward the sparring field, unenthusiastic about running in circles—even if they were large. She stopped at the edge of the horse run and watched the castle, backlit by hints of fiery orange creeping upward in the sky.

The door opened, and a bulky form appeared. *Karsten is an early riser after all...*

She met him on the gravel path. He wore his sword at his side. She wondered if she should have worn hers to leave the grounds. Probably, although her speed had gotten her out of plenty of close calls. And she had her dagger.

"Morning." Karsten's voice was full of energy. "I saw you from the window. Ready to go?"

Dag nodded. "The guards said the gates open at seven."

"Yes, they do." Karsten aimed for the gate.

Following behind, Dag could just make out the carved dragons in the wood now that the sky was brightening. "Do you have a back way out?"

"No." They stopped, and Karsten looked up toward the guards. "Good morning, Geir, Alexander."

"Hejhej, Karsten. Morning run?"

Karsten nodded. "Please help crack the gate."

"Unfortunately, we can't let you out this morning."

His brow furrowed. "Really?"

"No champions are allowed off the grounds. The king sent word last night."

"Ah... thanks." Karsten gestured Dag toward the ramparts.

Looks like we are *running along the wall...*

"Which guard is which?" Dag asked as they walked to warm up their muscles.

"Alexander is the taller one," Karsten said.

She glanced back quickly. She couldn't tell who was taller. The two men were on top of a fifteen-foot wall at opposite sides of the gate, shrinking in the distance.

Not helpful.

Dag took her time, getting a feel for the uneven, unfamiliar terrain, venturing out from the wall toward a flat expanse.

"Careful. Those are the dungeons." Karsten continued along the wall. "There are doors dug down into the earth. Harder to see at this angle."

Dag moved back toward him. If she broke her leg from a fall, she'd be easy pickings in the Sonne. "Is anyone in there?"

"Not today, but they were full during the wars."

She eyed the land. "Somewhat unprotected, isn't it? Out here in the field?"

"The guards on the tower keep watch over the dungeons as well. If someone broke in to free the prisoners, it's better to keep them away from the castle anyway. But they're treated well, fed food from the guards' kitchens... Some have been given work as servants after their sentence."

Eyes wide, Dag gazed at the servants' quarters. "Really?"

"Just the ones serving for petty crimes. Some are trained to do work throughout the city. Some have been killed too. Depends."

Who died would be her decision once she claimed the throne. They would be sent straight to Helheim, the greatest dishonor. Fortunately, the old king would be able to mentor her on politics once the Sonne was over.

"Ready to run?" Karsten asked.

They were well past the sparring field now along the ramparts. *The wall is boring.* She missed the shoreline. "Sure."

The pair took off, keeping a steady pace. Karsten ran faster, but Dag hustled to keep up with his longer strides. The wall was a giant curve, no turning—or thinking—required. The mountains rose above the other side of the wall. Grass inched its way up the sides, thinning out as it climbed higher between the rocks. Not even—*oh wait, there's a tree.* A crooked, skeletal tree.

And more rocks. So boring.

Dag's body loosened, and the tension in her shoulders drained away. Five minutes later, they'd completed a mile. She couldn't see the castle anymore, but they'd circle around and head toward it soon.

Cows to her left woke up and jostled each other. A servant stood among the herd, blending in with his brown wool shirt. The grounds were a convenient miniature farm, keeping fresh food on the table.

Another mile, and the mountain on the other side of the wall became a steep cliff; the start of the fjords, where they'd compete in the Sonne.

Karsten gestured to Dag to move toward the wall, which seemed to be getting shorter. She hadn't noticed a height difference when they'd arrived yesterday, but her window was on the opposite side of the castle. She could hear the steady waves, though.

As they continued, the servants' quarters and the trelleborg came into sight, and the castle rose behind them. The outer wall continued to shorten, and soon she could see over it. No, the walls weren't shorter—the land was just higher on this side.

She looked out over the orange-tinged landscape, the cliffs around the fjords rising mightily from the calm waters against the burning sky. Here against the ramparts, with the waves hitting the beach, her mind calmed.

The castle was now directly to their left. Karsten slowed down, distracted. She dropped her pace to match and followed his gaze to one of the windows, noting a flicker of light.

"Another lap?" she asked. "We've only gone a few miles."

Karsten slowed to a walk, his eyes focused on the castle. "Sure. It's about five miles around."

A blond head appeared in one of the upper windows.

Ah.

SOFIA TAPPED THE WINDOWSILL and breathed deeply through her anxiety, her gaze meandering along the fjord. Swaymark and the events surrounding the Sonne had kept her awake most of the night. She'd stared at the ceiling for hours until she'd fallen into a fitful sleep. At least the ceiling was painted with one of her favorite stories.

The Fairest Feet.

A quarter of the ceiling featured gods lined up behind a curtain, only their toes showing below. The giantess Skadi stood in front of the line-up. She was allowed to choose any one of the gods for a husband, but she had to choose by their feet alone. She assumed Baldur would have the fairest feet, since he was most attractive.

Lo and behold, the fairest feet belonged to Njord, worn smooth by the wind and the waves. When Njord stepped out, Skadi was surprised, but the second quarter of the ceiling depicted their magnificent wedding. The last half followed Njord and Skadi as they walked from the sea—their home for three days—back up the mountain, where they would spend three days before returning to the sea.

Back and forth, back and forth, never truly settling.

Just like her father, during the wars.

Just like the victor who was about to ascend, who would be thrown into battle.

And her role was to support them, no matter what.

A princess must serve her kingdom wholeheartedly.

Sofia took another deep breath. Skadi and Njord had a good life together, even if it wasn't the one Skadi had planned. With the summer's end, they'd venture back up the mountains. Their three days at sea were almost up, like Sofia's three months of sunshine.

Motion at the base of the ramparts caught Sofia's eye. Karsten was waving to her. Her stomach fluttered as she waved back. He gestured for her to join. She quickly grabbed a cloak from her closet and rushed to meet them, Max trailing behind.

Karsten and Dag waited for her near the front step. Karsten smiled at Sofia as she stepped out. "Good morning."

"Would you like to run with us?" Dag asked, shifting her weight. Her pale green eyes radiated energy beneath her thin, arched brows. Dag was two inches shorter than Sofia, almost a foot shorter than Karsten. Her light wool tunic was tight against her body, showing off her form far better than the loose shirt from the night before.

Sofia hesitated. "Sure, that might be fun." She glanced at Karsten; he'd keep her safe. "I thought you would be running outside the walls, though."

Dag sighed. "Not this morning. Security risk."

"King Eirik's request," Karsten added.

"Ah." Sofia frowned. There was nothing she could do to change the situation—unfortunately, even princesses had limits. But maybe running with the pair would cheer Dag up. "I'd like to run with you."

Karsten and Dag were still waiting for her on the step when she returned half an hour later, fully dressed in new clothes from the armory. Karsten nodded to Max, who stayed behind in the entrance hall as Sofia stepped into the fresh air.

Dag shifted her weight. "Ready?" Sofia nodded, and Dag grinned. "Off we go, then."

They took off toward the gate and the ramparts, moving at a slower pace to accommodate her. Within a couple of minutes, Sofia was panting heavily. They hadn't made it far; the sparring field was to her left, and the wall was to her right.

She caught Karsten watching her, and his expression was laced with concern. "Breathe in through your nose and out through your mouth. It helps."

Taking his advice, Sofia carried on. It did help—a bit.

Soon, her side started to burn. She pushed through until her legs started to burn as well, slowing her down further. Dag and Karsten slowed, sticking with her. The trio was barely past the sparring field. When the sores from the new leather shoes started, Sofia gave up. She stopped and curled over, clutching her knees as the stitch in her side pulsed.

"Go on without me," Sofia rasped. "I'm dying. Just let me die here."

Karsten's concern turned into laughter. "You aren't allowed to die under my watch. We'd better take you back to the castle. Then it will be Max's fault if you don't survive."

Sofia laughed through the burning in her legs and sides.

"Oh, come on," Dag chided. "You've barely made it a mile."

Sofia's stomach dropped. Dag wasn't impressed, and she needed to be. Sofia straightened, meeting Dag's eyes. "My strengths lie in running the kingdom, not running along the wall. Stepping up to lead after my mother died didn't leave much time for physical training. But it's okay, Dag. Go on without me. I'll see you later today."

Dag's forehead wrinkled slightly, and her eyes locked onto Sofia. She blinked, then looked at Karsten.

"Keep going," he said. "I'll walk Sofia back to the castle. We can run again tomorrow."

Dag nodded, then stepped toward Sofia and pulled her against her muscular body. Dag's hand rested against Sofia's lower back, and Sofia's breath hitched. Dag leaned toward her, then whispered, "Practice. If you run fast enough, they'll never see you coming."

"Noted." Sofia gulped, glancing toward Karsten. Fortunately, he was fast. She'd watched him run and spar for years.

Dag waved and ran off along the wall. Her strides were long and graceful.

"Hmm..." Karsten crossed his arms.

"What?"

"You don't watch me like that."

Sofia blushed a bright crimson. "You just don't notice."

Karsten chuckled. "I notice everything, Sofia."

She buried her face in her hands.

"Let's get you back to the castle," he said, holding out his arm to escort her. She took it gratefully, and they began their walk. The stitch in her side continued to prick.

"Did you sleep well?" Sofia asked.

"Like a troll. I'm glad to be back. I can tell you're tired, though."

Sofia laughed wearily. "Your *flattery* will get you nowhere. You aren't wrong, though. I had trouble getting to sleep."

"Anything in particular?"

She tripped on a rock, stumbling forward. Karsten steadied her, then pulled her closer, and the tightness in her chest loosened.

"The usual," she said.

Her entire future was up in the air, left to the next victor. What if the victor wasn't the wonderful man beside her? There was no backup plan. Who had time to make a backup plan when they were running a kingdom? There was barely time to make a first plan—and if it worked? Thank the fates.

But a princess doesn't break.

If only her mother were here to give her some guidance. She would have known what to do.

With the castle finally in sight, Karsten asked, "What did Dag say?"

"Wouldn't you like to know?" Sofia joked.

"That's why I asked." His jaw tightened. The Sonne—it was life or death. Clearly, he wasn't in a joking mood.

"If you run fast enough, they'll never see you coming."

Karsten gave a brisk nod. "Other than the sail, is it the usual schedule today?"

"Yes, along with last-minute preparations for Championsfest." Sofia sighed. "Victorsfest, too. I feel so behind."

"Well, I'm looking forward to both." Karsten smiled.

Sofia smiled back. "Hope you can make it."

"I'm sure I can carve out the time. A couple of things I have to take care of first." Karsten gave her a small nudge before pulling her close again.

They continued along the path. Servants crossed to the castle, starting their day. Warriors meandered around the trelleborg. A few walked in their direction, fully dressed, spears in hand.

Sofia leaned close to Karsten, speaking low. "We're still waiting on confirmation, but it seems Swaymark intends to hit Morge again. We received word yesterday from Sander. It's not looking good."

Karsten's expression gave away nothing. "When?"

"Two weeks from now. We will send guards to help protect Morge the day after Championsfest, but our warriors were already stretched thin, and with last week's attack..." Sofia bit her lip, taking a deep breath. Her side still pricked.

"It's a sound strategy, based on what we know," he murmured, then waved to the warriors, who were now a stone's throw away. "Morning, all."

"Karsten!" they chorused with enthusiasm, peppering him with questions until they split off for the gate.

At the front door, Sofia sat on the edge of the stone slab.

"Anything else on your mind?" he asked, sitting next to her.

"Well, I think running was a pretty horrible idea." Sofia wilted, curling her body forward to calm the stitch in her side.

Karsten leaned toward her and gently stroked her cheek. "You're tough. You can make it through anything."

NICO'S FOOTSTEPS ECHOED through the hallway. Tapestries and paintings covered the tall, wood-planked walls, but they didn't muffle much of the sound. Yawning, he stopped in front of a giant ship painted against a backdrop of glaciers that reminded him of home.

He didn't miss the sleeping mat—the mattress was far more comfortable—though he wouldn't mind having Elyse there to wake him up. But unfamiliar noises had interrupted at irregular intervals, keeping Nico awake half the night. It was nothing like his family's symphony. He hadn't fallen asleep until early in the morning, when the rain and wind had stopped.

He continued down the stairs. Karsten and Sofia's voices drifted in from just outside the open castle door. Sofia was sitting on the front step, her expression lively but her body hunched.

She looked up at him. "Good morning. How did you sleep?"

Karsten sat next to her protectively.

"Fine, thanks," Nico lied, averting his eyes briefly. "Heading to breakfast?"

Sofia shook her head. "I need to review some plans for the week, and I have a meeting with some of our Parliament. I'll be joining you at midday, though." Karsten's eyebrows rose, and Sofia met his amused expression. "I asked Pappa if I could come along for sparring."

Karsten smirked. "Are you sure the run didn't wear you out?"

Chuckling, Sofia's cheeks turned a light pink.

Nico leaned toward Sofia. "Are you going to spar with us?"

She turned back to him, her eyes bright. "I plan to. It'll be fun."

Karsten chuckled. "I'm sure it will be quite entertaining. I'll bring along some bandages."

"It's just sparring!" she huffed, reminding Nico of Elyse. "I won't need them."

"Well, they're not for you," Karsten quipped. "They're for your innocent victims."

"Karsten!" Sofia stood up, her heart-shaped lips pouting but her eyes still bright. She snaked her arm around Nico's. "Nico has confidence in me—don't you?"

"He hasn't actually seen you wield a weapon," Karsten said, smirking.

Nico's eyebrows rose. "Not all weapons are made of metal."

"Exactly." Sofia gave his arm a small squeeze before letting go. "On that note, I'll see you both later."

Karsten's eyes never left her as she entered the castle, her guard close behind.

"Breakfast?" he asked once the footsteps faded. Nico nodded, his stomach rumbling.

They made their way to the Great Hall. The gods painted on the ceiling welcomed Nico. Servants and guards lined the edges of the room, but only a few castle guests were scattered among the tables.

The king's wooden chair scraped against the stone floor as Nico pulled it out, then sat at the head of the table. Karsten sat on the bench beside him, saying nothing.

Nico pulled a plate from the stack, grabbed a fresh roll, and covered it with cheese and birch leaf jelly. The jelly tasted fresh and sweet, and it finished with a tang that left his mouth watering.

Wooden spoons and iron knives scratched against the wooden plates—mixed with chewing and slurping, taps of cups set on the table, and the beating of wings as a small bird flew around the hall, finally landing on the tall back of his chair.

Awkward, humdrum silence stretched on. When Nico became the king, he'd fill the hall with lively conversation. He'd fill it with his family.

Back outside, warriors were sparring on the field. Nico and Karsten crossed to the trelleborg, where the king was holding court with Dag and Jostein outside one of the four buildings—the armory, judging by the warriors walking in empty-handed and walking out fully equipped.

Heavy breathing and quick steps approached from behind.

"Just in time, Skip," the king said as Skip joined the group. "The first and only rule of sparring: don't kill each other. Save that for the Sonne."

All the champions shifted, fidgeting or adjusting their postures. To kill a fellow champion before the Sonne started would be poor sportsmanship—an undesirable quality in a leader.

King Eirik gestured to a pile of shields and spears, their tips wrapped in heavy wool tied on with leather. "Nico, Karsten. Jostein, Dag. Pair off. Have some fun. Skip, you can rotate in. A bit too much fun last night?"

Skip nodded and slumped on a bench, smiling gingerly. Even hungover, knocked flat on his rear end, he was still handsome.

The four picked up their weapons and moved to an open space on the sparring field. Stance firm, Nico braced himself, holding out his shield and keeping a strong grip on his spear; Karsten did the same.

Nico aimed his spear toward Karsten and attacked, the shield deflecting his blow. Karsten stepped away. Nico stepped forward and attacked again, pushed him back, kept him moving. After a few minutes of their dance, Nico stopped—Karsten was barely fighting. How this man had beaten anyone during Alderfoss's Championsmatch, Nico couldn't guess.

"Not going to fight back, Karsten?"

Saying nothing, Karsten shrugged, his movement small.

Dag wandered over, weapons in hand. "Spar, Karsten?"

He contemplated, then nodded, still a man of frustratingly few words.

She grinned. "Are you just going to stand there with your shield?"

Karsten put the shield on the ground, his eyes set and expression stoic. Dag accepted his silent challenge, putting her shield down next to his with a smirk. They walked toward an open space of the sparring field.

The king watched the pair from the side. A well-dressed group had joined him at some point, and they were watching too.

Skip sauntered over to Nico. "Do you think they will kill each other?"

"Maybe." Nico could hope. While it wouldn't be sportsmanlike on their parts, two fewer champions would certainly make the Sonne easier.

Jostein joined them, setting his spear down. "Should be a good fight."

"Looks like your sparring partner abandoned you," Skip joked.

Jostein shrugged, seemingly nonplussed. "I'm better with a sword."

"Win for Dag," Nico said. "Calling it now."

Skip's high-arched brows rose higher in surprise.

"Did you see him sparring with me?" Nico asked. "He didn't launch a single counterattack."

"Karsten was a guard in the castle, though," Skip said. "He was Sofia's head guard."

"Makes sense," Jostein said, his gaze on the pair.

"What do you mean?" Nico asked.

"Sofia is more comfortable when he's around."

Karsten and Dag raised their spears toward each other. They alternated between half steps and full steps, rotating and circling. It seemed all eyes were on them; warriors across the field had stopped their own matches to watch. The only sound left was a gentle breeze that tickled the grass.

Karsten observed Dag's every move. She was graceful. Strong. Practiced.

In a blink, Dag lashed out with her spear. Karsten dodged right. He lunged his spear behind Dag, sweeping it left and hitting the back of her knees, tripping her. She fell to the ground, her balance completely thrown off. He whipped around and stood over her, spear pointed at her chest, ready to take her out.

Nico paled as he crossed his arms, suppressing a desire to flee. Karsten could have easily taken him out.

This was what it meant to go up against trained killers.

Dag glared up at Karsten from the ground. If looks could kill, Nico would be hauling Karsten's body to the burial mound.

"Brilliant!" King Eirik shouted.

The group surrounding him clapped and cheered, and warriors across the field joined in.

Karsten bent down to help Dag up, and they rejoined the other champions as the rest of the field resumed sparring, the show now finished. Her expression was unreadable.

"Dag," Jostein said, "do you want to switch to swords?"

She nodded, and the pair aimed for the armory.

"Good show," Skip said once Dag was out of range.

Karsten opened his mouth to speak, interrupted by the king shouting his name. Karsten gave his spear to Skip, then joined the king's group. Shortly after, Karsten and the king walked toward the castle.

"Well, shall we?" Skip asked Nico, gesturing with the spear.

The pair took up a fighting stance. Happily for Nico, their match in height translated to a match in skill. While he'd grown up with a sword, a fishing boat on the open sea wasn't the best place to practice.

DAG SEETHED, sword in hand, Jostein on the field ten steps away.

Losing to Karsten was an embarrassing blow to her ego, but invaluable information had been gained. He watched, he waited, and he struck fast. She had to be faster. He couldn't see her coming.

During the Sonne, she'd be ready.

Sofia felt the excitement in her bones, eager to venture out on the open water that afternoon. She finished eating her strawberries at her desk while she organized the remaining plans for Championsfest. Inga needed the final menu, and the guards needed the final event timeline.

"Sofia," her father called from the hall. "Join us for a moment, please."

She rose immediately, then followed him and Karsten into her father's room. The rune-covered branch waited on the table.

"That's Swaymark's plan of attack, isn't it?" Sofia asked.

Karsten's eyes locked onto the branch, and his expression turned to ice.

The king handed the branch to her, then shared the details with Karsten. It appeared he had a favorite champion too. If her father was so confident in Karsten that he involved him in the plans...

Finally appreciating her tutor's persistence that she study the ancient languages, Sofia read over the runes, running her finger along the carved message. Even though she'd known it was coming, holding the message in her hands made everything feel real. "So it's as bad as we feared."

She handed the branch to Karsten.

"I spoke to some of the representatives and the captain of the guard this morning, out on the field," the king said. "They will send whatever warriors they can spare. Karsten, you probably heard we are sending reinforcements to Morge the morning after Championsfest—as soon as the champions leave for the Sonne."

Karsten nodded, then set the branch on the table. "And the victor will follow."

The king nodded once, sharply. "The victor will follow."

Sofia's stomach plummeted. She swayed, lightheaded.

Karsten's hand immediately grasped her elbow, steadying her. His ice-blue eyes scanned her. "Are you okay?"

No—but a princess doesn't break.

"Sorry, yes." She took a deep breath, then turned to her father. "We're sailing at noon. Is that all you wanted to cover?"

"For now. Enjoy the fjords. There's a nice breeze today."

Karsten let go of her elbow and followed her to the hall. He waited with Max while she grabbed the menu from her desk. Then the trio aimed for the kitchen and settled into a comfortable quiet.

In the kitchen, Sofia walked straight to the head cook. "Good morning, Inga."

"Sofia! Good morning." Inga put down her knife on the cutting board next to a bunch of half-chopped vegetables.

Karsten stood nearby, as did Max. Karsten was hovering closer than he normally did, not that she minded.

"I didn't mean to interrupt," Sofia said. "I have the final menu for you. For Championsfest."

"Nonsense, don't worry about it." Inga wiped her hands on her apron and took the menu, looking it over. "All this will be easy enough. Swayish pastries?"

Sofia nodded. "I'm assuming you're familiar?"

"Of course." Inga smiled wistfully. "I've been baking them since I was young. They're a holiday staple back home. In Swaymark, I mean."

"I imagine no one can bake a Swayish pastry better than you."

Inga straightened proudly. "They will be the best you've ever tasted."

"Thank you, Inga. Looking forward to it."

Nico swiped his spear at Skip. Muscles sore, he wasn't sure how much more fight he had in him.

Sofia appeared with Max and Karsten by her side, her eyes bright. "We've got a bit of time left before our sail. Who wants to spar with me?"

She looked around at all five champions, her smile fading as the group remained silent.

It was a losing proposition. Either Nico won but risked hurting the princess, or he purposely went easy on her and risked alienating her or losing her respect. His fellow champions' silence suggested they felt the same.

Karsten hesitantly picked up one of the spears and handed it to Sofia. "Okay, let's do it."

"Very brave of you," Skip joked.

Karsten laughed, picked up another spear, and turned to Sofia, who was too busy glowering at Skip to notice. "Come on, then."

Sofia grinned, and they wandered away from the group.

Dag and Jostein resumed their sword fight. She seemed far more content than she had earlier; the duo was an even match.

Nico and Skip went back to sparring. From the corner of his eye, he watched as Karsten guided Sofia through the movements and proper stance. Engrossed in his training, she focused on the motion of the spear in her hands. Jostein had been correct in his assessment. She was far more comfortable with Karsten than the others.

When the sun was directly overhead, a servant approached the group, calling out, "The ship is ready."

The group gave their weapons to the servant before setting off along the path.

Skip turned toward Sofia. "Do you know which vessel we're sailing today?"

Sofia shook her head. "I know it's smaller, though."

"What do you usually sail?" Nico asked.

"Well, anything and everything. The shipyard has spent the last couple of months building the largest longship in history. It's for the warriors, of course."

They wouldn't need it for fishing.

"How long will it be able to sail without stopping?" Jostein asked, finally engaging.

Skip's eyes lit up. "A well-prepared crew of a hundred? At least a week, maybe longer."

The group seemed impressed as they walked through the gate and aimed for the beach.

"My favorites are the smaller fishing boats, though," Skip said. "Easier to maneuver. Fewer people needed to crew. More fun."

Sailing with him would be fun. "I think most of our fishing boats are from Sander."

"They're the best. Entirely made of Fjordish oak."

Dozens of ships lined the shore and the small docks. All of them seemed new, unlike the ships in Fryse, which all showed signs of heavy repairs.

Their ship's hull was covered with a fresh coat of dark red paint. Red shields were perched on the sides, secured safely to the edges, ready for warriors to grab as they went to battle in a foreign land. The dragon figurehead carved along the stempost showed off the strength of Fjorden.

Two guards stood nearby. Skip jumped aboard, and Jostein climbed on next, holding his hand back toward Sofia. As she climbed on, she was breathless with excitement, barely containing her smile. Elyse surely would have had a similar reaction.

"Skip, do you want to be captain?" she asked.

He practically bounced off the boat. "Of course! Sofia, come sit by me. I'll teach you how to sail."

Sofia made her way back to the bench near Skip. Nico climbed aboard, followed by Karsten and Dag. They pulled in the lines, set up the oars, and unfurled the sail. Jostein and Nico sat near the front of the ship, oars in hand.

"Ready?" one of the guards asked from the shore. The other was already on board.

Skip beamed. "Absolutely."

The guard pushed the ship off the beach. It rocked in the waves, lurching as the guard jumped back in. Nico held the oar steady.

"Off we go!" Sofia squealed, just like Elyse would have.

Nico gripped an oar, prepared to lower it into the water. "Ready?"

Jostein nodded. "Ready."

They rowed together, keeping pace, bringing the ship slowly out into the middle of the fjord. Then they pulled the oars into the ship, laying them along the port side across the benches.

Waves lapped at the sides of the boat, and the wind hissed at a low volume. Seabirds called out overhead, creating a melody to go along with the thrumming of the ocean. Nico had missed the water, this daily piece of his life.

Karsten, Dag, and the guards worked together near the center of the ship, pulling the lines to raise the yard up the mast, dragging the sail higher with each pull on the halyard. The wool sail filled with wind, showing off its vertical red and yellow stripes. As they tightened the lines, the ship leaned and moved forward.

"Come on." Nico moved to the windward side and gestured to Jostein. "Movable ballast." Jostein followed, and their weight helped level the ship. "Have you been sailing before?"

Jostein settled along the rail next to Nico. "No. Fields of wheat don't make for easy ship crossings."

Nico chuckled. "No, I suppose not."

Jostein looked out over the water and toward the cliffs, losing himself to his thoughts. Nico could relate.

Skip had the steering oar firmly in hand and was pointing out pieces of the ship to Sofia, who seemed enthralled. Karsten and Dag tied off the last few lines and set the sail. The windward side lowered a bit more as the guards shifted up the deck toward the edge.

"So you got a second shift after guarding the wall today, huh?" Karsten asked the guards. Karsten seemed quiet and removed, but here he was, initiating conversation.

"This isn't too bad," the taller guard said.

Dag smirked, her skin paler than usual. "You could be back on land, Alexander."

He laughed. "I'm a Viking. Why would I want to be anywhere else?"

Nico agreed with him.

"Please loosen the sheet," Skip called.

Before Nico could assist, Karsten dropped down to the leeward side and adjusted a line, then shifted back to the windward side.

"Are you off for Championsfest?" Karsten asked Max.

"Yeah. But I have a feeling it's going to be a rough morning."

Probably. All the guards—all the people in the capital—had been invited to celebrate, and it was sure to be a late night.

"I am still on the night gate watch," Alexander said, "but I'll be joining before my shift."

"What about you, Geir?" Karsten asked.

"I'm not sure." Geir bit his lip uneasily. "It might be the only chance to visit my family before I ship out the morning after."

Why was he shipping out? Nico's chest tightened as he rubbed the back of his neck.

"Prepare to tack," Skip called.

"Get ready to move to the other bench," Nico said to Jostein as the rest of the group readied the ship.

Dag shifted down the deck hesitantly. She untied and released a line as Skip steered the ship in the other direction. Karsten pulled the line hard as the ship turned, tightening it quickly. The guards assisted with the lines as everyone settled back up on the windward side.

Smooth sailing. Skip was proving to be as good of a captain as he had drunkenly claimed.

Nico settled back onto the bench.

The empty bench.

No Jostein. Heart pounding, Nico looked around. He wasn't on board. He'd fallen off the boat during the tack, lost in the commotion.

Jostein was from land-locked Hamme. Nico was one step closer to becoming king. One step closer to—

No, he didn't want to win that way.

"Man overboard!" Nico shouted. He rushed to the stern and scanned the waves.

Sofia paled as she looked out over the water, wrapping her arms across her chest.

Jostein broke through the water's surface, coughing, struggling, fighting to stay afloat.

"There!" Nico cried.

"Tacking!" Skip shouted.

The crew scrambled to adjust the lines, swing the boom and get the ship turned back around.

"Helvete," Dag rasped, balancing awkwardly, almost falling out of the boat herself.

Hustling to the bow, Nico kept his eyes locked on Jostein's position. He knotted a rope to the bench, then tied the other end around his waist. At least the waters weren't filled with ice like they were in the north. Those rescues were always miserable.

Twenty feet away, Jostein went under the water.

Nico jumped, swimming hard and fast.

Down, down, down.

He clasped Jostein, then kicked toward the surface. As they broke through the water, Jostein coughed, then laughed, then coughed.

"We'll pull you in!" Karsten shouted.

The sail had been lowered to the deck.

The rope went taught around Nico's waist, and the group pulled them back into the boat. They helped Jostein over the side first, then Nico.

Jostein settled on a bench.

Sofia draped a blanket over his shoulders. Her face was lined with worry. "Are you all right?"

"Yes. My two brothers threw me in the lake all the time. Sink or swim." Jostein chuckled softly. "Sorry, all."

"No worries," Skip said, grabbing the steering oar. "Stay back here. Dry off. We'll head back to the castle."

Sofia grabbed a second wool blanket and brought it to Nico. "Good rescue."

"Fortunately, it doesn't happen often." Nico took the blanket and dried off as the rest of the crew prepared to set sail again. "Thanks."

She nodded, then settled back in next to Jostein, who watched the waves in silence.

By the time they were back on the beach in front of the castle, the sky had darkened, threatening rain. Thunder clapped as lightning streaked across the horizon.

"Right on time," Dag said, jumping out onto the beach first. *Thank the gods that's over.*

"Enjoy our day of sailing?" Nico asked.

Not particularly.

Voice low, Dag said, "I enjoyed Sofia enjoying our day of sailing."

"You sound like Skip," he whispered back.

That wasn't something she wanted to hear.

Karsten jumped out, then helped Sofia to the ground. Max flanked her other side.

"Looks like Thor is trying to ruin our day," she said.

"He just wants to join in the fun," Jostein said.

Dag could think of hundreds of far-more-fun things than being rained on.

"Maybe you'd like a tour of the castle before middag?" Sofia asked.

"I'd like to change, lie down." Jostein removed the blanket from his shoulders and draped it over the rail.

Fair enough. He'd almost drowned after hours of sparring.

"I'd also like to dry off," Nico said.

"Dag? Skip?" Sofia asked.

"Sure," he said.

Dag shrugged. *Might as well.*

"Karsten?" Sofia asked, turning around.

"I'm going to help with the ship. I'll catch up." His hand grazed her arm.

Don't touch my things.

Dag bit the inside of her lip, then walked back to the castle, followed by Sofia and the other champions. Jostein and Nico went upstairs, leaving the trio in the entrance hall with Max on guard.

"Skip, you've already seen my favorite." Sofia gestured to the maritime war painting behind her. "And you know the history."

Dag studied the painting, searching every inch. Her eyes landed on the fierce dragon gracing the bow. *The craft involved...* "She's beautiful."

Sofia smiled radiantly. "The ship was a tribute to my mother."

Fitting.

"Do you have any other favorites?" Skip asked.

"The tapestry of Yggdrasil." Sofia took off, leaving the rest to follow blindly. In the library, they passed dozens of bookshelves and walked straight to the end of the room. Sofia gestured behind her with a flourish. "Behold!"

The tapestry stretched from floor to ceiling, the colors faded but the image distinguishable. The mighty ash tree Yggdrasil grew around all nine of the world tree's realms. Midgard—the realm of the people, directly in the center of the tapestry—was covered in mountains and oceans and surrounded by Jormungand. An eagle, Vidofnir, perched on the top. Nidhogg the dragon curled around the base, chewing the roots, surrounded by snakes slithering along the trunk. Ratatosk the squirrel was running up the tree.

A fitting backdrop for Parliament.

"It's beautiful." Skip gazed at the tapestry, mouth agape. "What message do you think Ratatosk is delivering today?"

Dag shrugged. "He probably wants to gossip with Vidofnir."

"How well do you know your geography?" Sofia asked, looking right at Skip.

He smirked. "Certainly not as well as you."

She chuckled. "No one does—my tutor was relentless. But you must be able to point out Asgard."

"Easy. It's at the top." Skip sat on the tabletop. "Odin would never stand for anything less."

Dag pulled out a chair and sat down, getting comfortable. "Don't worry, Skip, you'll be on top soon. Valhalla's up there, you know."

"I prefer the bottom." Skip suggestively raised his eyebrows.

Of course you do. Dag rolled her eyes.

"And the rest?" Sofia asked.

"Well... Vanaheim is up there... Helheim—"

"Is part of Niflheim." Dag snickered. "Keep going."

Skip frowned. "Jotunheim and Muspelheim... You know, I'm not the best with geography."

He's really not...

Sofia chuckled. "You only missed Nidavellir, Alfheim, and—"

"Svartalfheim!" he shouted. Sofia burst out laughing, burying her face in her hands.

Dag placed her elbows on the table as she clasped her hands together, leaning forward with raised eyebrows. "You're a sailor, Skip. You should know the maps like the back of your hand."

Skip dismissively waved the back of his hand her way. "I'm not exactly sailing out of Midgard, Dag."

Pulling herself together, Sofia asked, "Are you versed in the twenty-two gods?"

He groaned. "Not even going to try. I'll offend half by forgetting them, and they'll smite me in my sleep before my twenty-two-year reign even starts."

Not if I get you first.

"Fair enough." Sofia grinned, her eyes glittering. "Would you like to see the Royal Wing?"

Excitement jolted through Dag. "Definitely."

In the upstairs hall, Sofia stopped in front of a gilded portrait. "Most of the paintings up here are of family members or ships. I'm sure you can guess who this is."

An image of Sofia, but not quite... "Ah. Ana-Sofia herself. You look just like her."

The door at the end of the hall opened, startling the group. The king peeked out. "Sofia, would you please join me for a moment?"

"Of course."

He disappeared into his room again. *My room, soon.*

"Sorry to cut our tour short," Sofia said. "I'll see you at middag." She stepped into the king's room, closing the door behind her.

"When you meet with Hamme's representatives, tell them to divert extra resources to Morge. We need to make sure all the warriors are well-fed."

Sofia nodded, watching her father. Waiting. "Was there anything else?"

"No. You can go back to Dag and Skip."

"Oh, okay."

Dag and Skip were already gone, but she found Karsten chatting with Max in the hall.

Finally, the gods were smiling upon her.

"Karsten, I'm glad you're here," Sofia said. "A minute?"

He nodded, then followed her into her room. She closed the door, her stomach in knots.

"Are you cold?" he asked, eyeing her trembling hands. "Let me start the fire."

She crossed to the nightstand and pulled out the handkerchief, then sat on the bench and watched him. Focused on his task, he only stopped to drape a blanket across her lap. Once the fire roared, he sat next to her.

"Your hands are still shaking," he said, clasping them.

Sofia swallowed, well aware it wasn't the cold affecting her. "I hoped…"

"I'm not helping you sneak anywhere," he said, rubbing her hands between his. "You're old enough to eat all the sweets you want anyway."

She laughed, thinking back to Filip knocking on her door in the middle of the night. He'd beg her to go with him to the kitchen after Mamma was asleep. They would tiptoe downstairs in their stockings—but wood carried sound far too well. Their mother always knew. So did all the guards.

Taking a deep breath, she said, "I hoped you would accept my favor."

He blinked, then nodded once, no longer moving his calloused hands. No longer moving at all. Hardly even breathing.

She placed the handkerchief—so small and delicate—in his palm.

Karsten looked at it reverently, then tucked it into his pocket. "I'm honored, Princess. Sofia. Thank you, Sofia."

He hugged her, resting his chin on the top of her head. Her tension eased as she snuggled against him. She closed her eyes and listened to his heartbeat, wrapped up in this safe space—the arms of this wonderful man.

Who would be fighting to the death in the fjords in three days.

And if he came back alive, then he'd be fighting in Morge against Swaymark.

She gulped, her body tense.

Karsten let her go, his eyes full of concern.

Full of understanding.

"Middag?" he asked. He kissed her cheek, then helped her up.

Nico, Jostein, Dag, and Skip waited in the Great Hall. Sofia and Karsten finally joined them. King Eirik walked in shortly after, much to Nico's relief.

Servants brought out fresh rolls and hot fish soup, the herbs mixed into the yellow cream. He scooped a bowlful and put one of the fresh rolls on his plate. The smell of the fiskesuppe brought him back to Fryse. His mother's soup had the same faint fishy scent when she cooked the fish in milk, but that was only on days they didn't need the goat's milk for cheese. On days they had to use water for the soup, the whole house smelled of fish. That wouldn't be a problem here.

Happy conversation and a good mood carried through middag. Once they finished and the king retired for the night, Nico pulled out his hardingfele. "Sofia, would you like to sing?"

"Sure." Sofia rose and stood behind Nico. "What song?"

"What about 'The Song of Ragnarök'?"

"Chipper choice, Nico," Skip joked. "Feeling dramatic?"

"Maybe a bit," he joked back.

Nico played the tune, sad and melodic, feeling the notes in his soul. Sofia sang along:

Vitality, the troll drinks,

from men sentenced to death.

The home of the gods,

he paints with blood.

The summer after,

the sunshine turns black,

and the weather mightily storms.

Do you know enough?

For much, I know,

and wide, I behold.

See, Ragnarök will come.

It's the fate of the gods.

As he played the final note, his fellow champions clapped.

"You played beautifully." Sofia sat back down, waving a servant over. They brought more ale with them.

Nico played another song, and another, losing himself in the music as the champions continued to drink and laugh around him. Eventually, only Nico and Skip were left. The ale continued to flow.

Skip took another swig. "You got to hear all about my family last night. Tell me about yours."

Their stories could never compare, considering how worldly Skip was.

Nico shrugged. "Two parents, two brothers, and two sisters. All my siblings are younger."

"So they look up to you?"

"I pretend they do, but one of my brothers is actually taller."

Skip chuckled. "Would your family want to move to Aldersfoss? If you win?"

"One of my sisters certainly would." Nico pictured Elyse's grin the moment she stepped into the library. The thought warmed him. "The youngest..." His heart sank. "She cried when I left."

"I'm sure she misses you." Skip took another drink. "I'm glad you're here though."

Nico realized he was glad too.

DAG STEPPED OUTSIDE THE CASTLE into the cool night air. Her footsteps on the gravel shattered the silence. She slipped into the armory, still seething from her loss to Karsten. After picking up a spear, she brought it outside to the training area.

The sharp iron blade gleamed in the moonlight, the molding graced with a simple cast of Yggdrasil, the socket connected to a heavy oak shaft meant to drive those on the wrong end to death.

She aimed at her invisible target, piercing the air repeatedly, going faster and harder and faster and harder and faster still, her arms burning, her breathing labored. She refused to quit until she was past the point of exhaustion.

There was one goal: victory would be hers—in the Sonne, and against Swaymark.

When her entire body felt beaten, she put away the spear and walked back to the castle.

Rustling bushes? An animal?...no, just my imagination.

She snuck up to her room and closed the door silently behind her, then crawled into bed, falling asleep immediately.

Two Days

Dag shifted on her mattress and rolled over, her muscles sore. The good kind of sore, though. The best kind of sore. The kind of sore that only hit when training hard.

The fire in the hearth had burned out again during the night, but the moon dimly lit her room. She placed her bare feet on the floor, more comfortable on the unfamiliar wood. She wondered if the floor in the king's bedroom was well-worn. Only another week until she would find out.

A soft knock interrupted the quiet. Dag grabbed her dagger from underneath her pillow before approaching the door and cracking it open.

"Did I wake you?" Karsten whispered, three feet away, his sword at his side.

"No."

"Ready to run?"

"Just a minute." Dag dressed and tucked her dagger in her right boot. Then they crept through the entrance hall and slipped out the door. The world remained silent, bathed in moonlight.

"Shall we run the opposite way today?" Karsten asked.

Dag sighed. "I don't think it will make much of a difference, considering we're still stuck inside the walls."

"No, I suppose not." Karsten's tone was neutral, but the corners of his mouth turned down.

He's my competition. Why is he trying to help?

"Well, let's switch it up, then," she said with all the enthusiasm she could muster. She walked toward the ramparts overlooking the beach. Karsten walked beside her, matching her speed in half the strides. *To Hel with his height.*

Minuscule waves lapped at the shore, the sound a balm. As the servants' quarters came up on their right, the wall grew tall enough to block her view of the water. *Oh well. It was enjoyable while it lasted.*

Dag increased her pace, ready to run. Karsten matched it, so she continued to ramp up until they were moving along at a decent speed. She thought one of the bushes moved, but as they ran past, it was motionless. *Clearly, I'm on edge.*

Yesterday's laps gave Dag a good feel for the route. She navigated the terrain easily—not that running along a wall was particularly taxing. The constant switch between flat and rocky terrain mixed with holes hidden by darkness had the potential to do damage, though. Damage she couldn't afford. She had to be in top form for the Sonne, thanks to her current companion.

"What is it like—running through the city?" Dag asked, her breathing slightly labored.

"It's usually just as quiet this early," Karsten said. "Even the servants aren't up yet. They will be soon, though."

"I like the quiet. I'm used to being the first one up."

"Me too. This was the only time I had to myself during the day."

"Same," Dag said, realizing she was an interloper. Karsten had knocked on her door that morning, though, so she brushed the thought aside. He didn't have to run with her, considering there was no risk she'd get lost on castle grounds.

Running along the wall.

The boring wall.

The wall is a cage.

Dag pushed away the feeling of entrapment. Allowing the champions outside of the castle grounds was a risk, especially after Swaymark's attacks.

This is the new routine. This giant circle along this circular wall. She'd either win the Sonne and become the victor, where the security risk would mean this was her permanent daily route, or she'd be on her way to Valhalla, where she would never need to run to maintain her stamina. Her body would maintain its muscular form permanently.

Nonsense. This was her new route.

The sparring field was empty of bodies, but smoke rose from the trelleborg's kitchen. As they approached the gate, Karsten called out a greeting to Geir and Alexander. The guards waved as Dag and Karsten ran past.

Back along the beach, Dag gazed at the orange streaks—creeping up the sky, reflected in the water. The light breeze pushed along small waves, but the fjord was otherwise motionless.

They continued in silence, running past the servants' quarters, past the fields, past the cows just starting to wake up. A third time, then a fourth.

Her stomach growled, the volume startling her.

Karsten chuckled. "Hungry?"

She missed the unlimited food from the always-open kitchen back at camp. "Ravenous."

"Let's head back to the castle. Breakfast should be ready soon."

The sparring field stretched before her. She accelerated across the grassy terrain, her legs flying, her body free. The flat expanse felt like home—her old home.

The comfort was short-lived. On the gravel path, they slowed to a walk and aimed for the castle. The carved dragons along the roof were silhouetted by the orange sky.

Back in the Great Hall, they sat on opposite sides of the king's table, the unoccupied throne between them. Dag grabbed a plate from the stack. The kitchen doors opened, and a servant brought out a platter full of meat, fish, cheese, and vegetables, and set it on the table. *Finally.* Another followed with a basket of bread and rolls, much to Dag's delight. She pulled out a still-warm rye roll, slicing it in half before putting it on her plate, then covered both halves in cheese and topped them with smoked salmon. In only five bites, she devoured the entire thing. Still hungry, she pulled more meats and cheeses onto her plate. Karsten smirked as he did the same.

Footsteps sounded from the entrance hall, throwing Dag into high alert. Nico walked in shortly after.

"Good morning." Dag took another bite of goat cheese. *Thank the gods for hearty sustenance to keep me strong...*

"Morning, Dag. Sleep well?"

"Yes. You?" Dag wasn't interested in a response. Karsten didn't seem interested, either.

"Well"—Nico sat on the bench across from her—"it's certainly quieter here than it is at home."

"This is home now," she responded, her tone matter-of-fact.

Nico's eyebrows rose, his jaw slack. "Of course."

Karsten finished his last bite and stood up. "See you both outside on the field." He waved and left the hall.

"Bastard," Dag and Nico muttered at the same time.

At least we can agree on something.

"I hope your sword work is better than your spear work," she said.

He scowled. "I'm not that bad."

Dag bit back a laugh. "You need to loosen up. Be more fluid. Otherwise, you won't take anyone out."

Nico's eyes widened. "Aren't you concerned I'll use that tip to take you out?"

"No." *Why would I be?*

Nico stared at her. She stared back undauntedly as she finished the last bite of her breakfast.

"See you outside." Dag stood up and walked toward the door.

"Bastard," he mumbled under his breath.

"Yes." Dag smiled back at Nico, then exited the hall.

"Hejhej, Jostein," Sofia said, meeting him in the entry hall. He didn't seem close to any of the other champions—not a surprise, since they were competitors—but he had a kindness within him. She breathed a sigh of relief, ready for a quiet morning walk with no expectations.

"Did you sleep well?" she asked.

"The rain kept me awake."

More than a lack of sleep hid behind his weary eyes, but Sofia didn't press. She tightened her cloak, appreciating the soft fur lining that protected her against the chilly morning. "Yes, it can be loud. And it never seems to end, does it?"

"Ah, but there's beauty in consistency and met expectations." Jostein pulled his cloak on, and they stepped into the cool, fresh air, Max close behind.

The smell of fauna mixed with dirt and saltwater reminded her of summers with Filip. Fluffy clouds layered across the gray sky promised heavy late-summer rain. Nico was riding Apple around the horse paddock, and Lars stood by. Sofia's heart warmed. She and Jostein turned toward the ramparts and walked along the edge of the grounds. Her pink silk dress was just far enough off the ground to avoid the dew on the grass.

"I was impressed with your sword work yesterday."

"Thank you, Princess." He straightened proudly, although his lips pressed together in a grimace.

"It seems like you've been training for a long time?"

"Every evening, after I helped my adoptive parents on the farm," he said, tone melancholy. "Kept me busy."

Sofia gave him a half-hearted grin before looking down at the grass. "When Mamma and Filip were killed, I had to take over Parliament immediately. Mamma had led the meetings, and she'd only just started training me." She twisted her ring around her finger. "I was still expected to be just as effective as her, and I was reminded every day. I never felt like I measured up."

She'd never admitted it to anyone, but there it was—the truth of it all. Her father should have remarried, should have found a new partner to run the kingdom, but he was too heartbroken. No one questioned it or pushed him, not even Tomas. And any possible political alliance forged by Sofia's marriage? Thrown off the table. Her father wouldn't let her go, stopped wanting to travel, even cut visits to the regions. Instead, she'd been assigned a guard at all times, and all the responsibility of running the kingdom had fallen to her. A permanent bandage to a festering wound. *But a princess doesn't break. A princess serves her kingdom wholeheartedly.* Sofia was born into this life. All she could do was her best, to protect her people and be what they needed. At least, until the end of her life string...

The quiet stretched between them.

"I felt the same about my brothers," Jostein murmured.

"Tell me about them?"

He smiled sadly. "Well, when I was little, I would follow them everywhere. It drove them crazy."

"Filip did the same, and I secretly loved it. Don't worry. Your brothers probably did too."

Jostein's expression softened. "Were you close to Filip?"

"Yes. He was six years younger, but it was always the two of us."

"What is your favorite memory of him?"

"Every morning, I'd go to grab him for breakfast, and I'd find him on his ride-on sheep."

"A ride-on sheep?" Jostein's head tilted slightly, and his eyes crinkled with laughter. "The prince had a ride-on sheep?"

"Yes! It was a gift at his naming ceremony. One of the local woodworkers carved it and covered it in sheared wool."

"I imagine it was twice his size."

"Four times his size when he was born!" Sofia laughed. "Every morning, he asked for just another minute, without fail."

Jostein grinned. "To ride the sheep? Into baa-tle?"

Sofia covered her mouth as laughter escaped between wheezing breaths, nodding vigorously. "Yes! It was so silly. He'd be swinging his wooden sword and charging into battle against the wind. The wooden sheep didn't move, of course, so there he would be, just swinging away on the sheep, his battle cry raging." Sofia wiped her eyes of happy tears as Jostein laughed heartily along with her.

She caught her breath, feeling lighter. "Filip loved to ride horses, too, in case that wasn't obvious. He named his horse Apple after her favorite snack."

"Did you ride with him?"

"Only sometimes..." She hesitated, not sure if she wanted to continue. After a moment, she soldiered on. "Mamma had taken him out riding when they were ambushed and killed."

"Oh," Jostein whispered.

Throat choked, she swallowed. "It felt like part of me was ripped away. I'd give anything to have them back."

They walked on in silence, continuing along the edge of the ramparts, both lost in thought. Sofia could only hope Jostein would find what he was looking for.

Thunder roared, shattering her reverie.

"Sofia," Max said, "we should return to the castle before the heavy rain starts." His tone left little room for discussion.

They followed the path toward the castle, picking up their pace. It was still no match for Dag or Karsten.

Thunder cracked again.

"Let's cut across the sparring field," Jostein said.

She scanned the muddy expanse. Agneta would not be pleased if she ruined her new dress. She contemplated whether she'd rather be muddy or rained on; neither sounded appealing.

"Do you want to jump on my back?" Jostein asked. "I'm faster. And bigger, and stronger, and all around more wonderful."

Sofia chuckled, grateful her dress would be spared. "You're not wrong. Thank you."

She placed her hands on his shoulders and hopped, Max assisting a bit as she got settled. As they raced back, another crack of thunder sounded. Jostein sped up, and Max kept pace.

They made it to the stone landing, leaving a muddy set of tracks behind. Jostein let Sofia down, then took his shoes off and picked them up before following her across the threshold.

"Better than a sheep?" he asked.

"Certainly faster. Thanks, Jostein." Sofia studied the landing. "We made a bit of a mess."

"But you can always count on the rain to wash away our marks on the world."

Jostein gave Sofia a half smile, then quietly walked up the stairs to the guest wing.

She stood in the doorway, gazing at the gray sky.

Nico slid off the horse's back, relieved to be back on solid ground. At least he could say he hadn't fallen off when the thunder spooked his mighty steed. "Thanks for the lessons, Lars."

"Apple can be a little skittish, but she's a great horse." Lars took the reins and guided her back into the stable. Nico followed, hit with the smell of fresh hay. Lars started to unstrap the saddle. "Two more days until the Sonne?"

"Yeah. Tomorrow is Championsfest." Nico rubbed the back of his neck, his mind churning with all the things he could do to help Fjorden when he returned. To help Fryse. To help his family.

He walked over to the dog and scratched behind its ear, earning a lick. "How long have you been here? In Aldersfoss, I mean."

"I think... sixteen years. I stuck around after the wars." Lars lifted the saddle from the horse's back and hung it on a wall rack. "Hey, Nico, can you go in the back room and grab an apple from the pile? They're her favorite."

"Sure." Nico slid open the barn door to the back room, eyes bulging at the vast supply. There was enough to help every family across Fryse, at least a little bit. Piles of dry goods, wool and silk, axes, pots and other kitchenware... and it was all being hoarded by the capital. Nico's stomach soured. Apple in hand, he went back to the stall.

"All the supplies..." Nico trailed off.

Lars took the apple. "They will be sent up to Fryse with the representatives after Championsfest."

"Really?" The capital was making good on their promises? But the representatives had said—

"Yeah. We've been sending supplies north for years, ever since the wars ended. I help load the ships." Lars gave the fruit to the horse, who took it happily. "Fryse's boats bring down amber. Leather. Ivory. Dried fish, too, sometimes. We send all this back with them. This pile's smaller than usual, with Championsfest and all."

The pile was massive. This many goods couldn't just disappear.

"My family never received anything," Nico said. "Neither did my crew."

Lars looked around, then leaned in, keeping his voice low. "My sister, she's with the gods now, but she never got any supplies either. Parliament said they were prioritizing those in need, but my sister, she... well, we weren't well-off. Nothing worth anything for her there."

"Sounds like she could have used some help," Nico murmured. "Our family does well, but some of the supplies would have been a relief, for us and our neighbors."

"Don't I know it. You can't exactly farm the frozen tundra."

The dog's sharp bark announced their chat was over. A warrior rode in, jumping quickly to the ground.

"Welcome," Lars called to the newcomer before turning back to Nico, whispering, "I expect great things from you. May the gods be on your side."

Dag sent her spear through its heart.

The straw man has been pulverized.

Her stomach rumbled with the pangs of hunger. She had no interest in a third day without more than two meals. Her body would riot from the mistreatment.

She tucked the spear into the corner of the armory and headed up to the castle. In the Great Hall, the servants ignored her, rushing about to prepare for Championsfest. *Not helpful.* Shouts sounded from behind the kitchen door as Dag approached. She hesitated, intimidated by the yelling—harsher than even the chiefs back at camp. *Someone's running a tight ship.*

With a deep breath, she bravely pushed the door open. She needed food.

"Get that pot on the fire! We'll be late if we don't start the soup!"

Dag approached the counter, greeted by the delicious smell of cooking meat, a sweet salvation for her stomach—which rumbled louder.

"Hello," Dag said to the woman who had shouted. *Clearly the head cook.* "I was wondering if there was something I could eat?"

The cook barely glanced at her, instead continuing to measure out ingredients. "There's food in the guards' quarters. Out with you."

"Sorry, I didn't know."

The cook stopped chopping to study her. "Haven't they shown you around the trelleborg?"

She straightened. "I'm Dag. One of the champions."

"Oh, I'm sorry. I thought you were one of the new warriors. I'm Inga. Let me—*GET THAT POT ON!*—get you a plate of food. Sit down."

"At camp, we could eat whenever we were hungry." Dag settled comfortably on the chair as Inga put together a plate. "I usually had four to five meals a day."

"You can always come down, or servants can bring food up. I'm only here from breakfast through middag, but anyone can help you." Inga gave her a full plate of freshly cooked pig.

Dag thanked Inga as her stomach rumbled again.

Inga laughed. "Since we only prepare two meals, there might be a bit of a wait to get something hot together in the off time. With Championsfest tomorrow, though..."

"Don't let me distract you."

"Not at all." Inga put a spoon and knife in front of her.

"Thank you." Dag took a bite. "This is delicious, Inga."

"There's plenty of it." She gestured to the giant roast. "So you're our champion from Morge?"

Dag nodded, digging into her meal.

"Did you grow up there?" Inga asked.

"Yes. My father was a warrior. I followed in his footsteps."

"He must be so proud of you."

Dag frowned. "He would have been. He was killed in the wars."

"Ah... Fjorden lost so many... I was still in Swaymark at the time."

"Oh?" The hair on Dag's arms rose. She resisted the urge to shift, taking another bite.

"I moved to Sander a few years back with my husband. I was just hired in the castle, so I'm new here too."

"Running the kitchen?"

"Forty-two cooks to mind between the castle and the guards' food hall. It keeps me busy." Inga returned to her chopping. "You should ask Karsten to take you. They have food available almost all the time, even at night. Probably more like what you're used to. He still eats there, so I'm sure he wouldn't mind."

Of course... So that's where he disappears to.

"Good idea," Dag said. "I'll do that. Thanks."

Inga smiled. "I'm always happy to help."

A MAP OF FJORDEN was spread across the king's table. Sofia glanced at her father's painted ceiling. Odin watched her from his throne in Valhalla. His ravens—Hugin and Munin—were perched on his shoulders. Surely they'd informed him of the events in Midgard as they unfolded.

What did Odin think of all this? Would he side with the victor? Sofia sighed. Only time would tell...

The rune-covered branch sat on the map, mocking her.

"Since Swaymark would be coming from the south," Sofia said, "it is likely they will hit the southeast coast. If their goal is more resources, though, they'll avoid Sander." She pointed to the east corner of Fjorden. "Probably here."

The king nodded. "To squeeze Morge from the north and the south... they can't go too far north now without risking damage from the icebergs."

"That means they have a limited area of attack. Probably here, then." Sofia slid her finger north along the coastline. "That would allow them to squeeze Morge tight and pinch toward the center. Should we move some warriors to the north and south camps?"

The king scratched his neck as he looked over the map. "Hard to say, but we will bring it up with Parliament. More troops could stop the attacks from progressing inward. On the other hand, it leaves the center of Morge vulnerable. Since we haven't confirmed the source... The southern camp has always been the best fortified, though."

"It's also the largest."

"And has the toughest warriors." The king straightened next to the table, grinning.

"Of course, you would say that," Sofia choked out through a laugh. "You and Dag."

"Correct." Her father smiled. "She'll be right at home if she wins the Sonne. As would Karsten."

Sofia glanced at Odin. He already knew the fate of everything... if only she could ask him...

"Sofia?"

"Hmm?"

"Are you okay?" Her father was watching her closely. "You looked a bit lost."

"Sorry, Pappa. Yes, I'm fine... Is there anything else we should cover for Parliament?"

"Not right now. I need to oversee the sparring."

Sofia grabbed her notes, then exited into the hallway, almost crashing into Karsten. His eyes lit up and his conversation with Max ended abruptly, leaving her stomach fluttering.

"Good morning," he said. "Are you sparring with us today?"

Sofia forced a smile, though her shoulders dropped. "I have some notes to prepare. I'm sure Jostein or Dag would make a better sparring partner, though. I'm still sore from yesterday."

"Did you spar?" her father said, his tone betraying his surprise. "I thought you just wanted to watch."

"I was a bit rusty, but Karsten and I worked on technique. It was fun." Sofia blushed, turning back to Karsten. The pride in his eyes filled Sofia with confidence.

"Come on down for a bit." Her father wore the biggest smile she'd seen since Mamma and Filip had been killed.

"Okay." Sofia would have picked up a spear years ago if she had realized how happy it would make him. "Max, is Agneta up here?"

He shook his head. "She went down with dishes and laundry a few minutes ago."

"Anything I can help with?" Karsten asked.

"Do you know how to braid?" Sofia flicked a bit of her hair.

"Haven't the slightest. I can find Agneta, though." He scurried down the hall.

Once he was out of sight, Sofia went straight to her desk and scribbled down notes from the morning's conversation, planning to expand them later.

Her father's footsteps echoed down the hall, stopping at the threshold of her room. He crossed his arms. "You haven't been particularly interested in sparring for quite a while..."

Her cheeks burned; her crimson face was betraying her.

He laughed. "Thought so."

"You aren't wrong, Pappa. A certain champion certainly made it more enticing."

"I'm glad." His arms dropped to his sides. "I'm sure all the champions are waiting. Come down as soon as you're ready."

Agneta appeared behind him with a pile of clothes in her hands. "Karsten sent me up with these."

Sofia stepped into her closet and changed out of her silk dress and into the wool shirt, pants, and boots from the armory. It was unfamiliar—but still comfortable.

"Two days in a row." Agneta gestured to the bench. Sofia settled into the furs as Agneta began to braid. "Should we braid your hair tomorrow too?"

"I'd like to wear it down for Championsfest."

"We should still do something to match your dress." Agneta tied the end and laid the braid against her back.

Sofia hustled eagerly to the sparring field, Max in tow. Guards and warriors were spread out around the field sparring, but the five champions were clumped near the king.

"Good morning, all!" she called.

They chorused greetings back.

"Skip, Dag. Jostein, Karsten. Nico, Sofia. Pair up!" The king gestured to a pile of weapons on the ground in front of him.

Sofia's heart dropped—she hadn't touched a sword in years. She pictured Filip's broken body, and her palms began to sweat. She tried to focus on her quickened breathing, but it only elevated her anxiety. Each of the champions stepped forward to pick up their weapons. Sofia would look dumb if she didn't join, but her feet were frozen in despair.

Nico appeared by her side, pulling her mind back. He held out a sword and shield. "Here you are, Sofia."

She grabbed the shield and held it close to her body, then inhaled a deep breath and took the sword cautiously, grateful he had saved her from approaching the sword herself. The metal was cold in her shaking hands. "Thank you."

Nico grabbed a sword and shield for himself. "Ready?"

"Yes," Sofia said.

No, she wasn't ready. She'd never be ready. She took another deep breath, calming her body's shakes.

The pair found an empty spot on the sparring field. Max stood guard, only ten feet away.

She lifted her sword to shoulder height and tucked the shield close to her body, safely between her torso and the sword.

Nico faced her, his sword pointed her way. "Shield out. Faster to block."

She stretched her arm out, feeling anxious and exposed, her chest tight. She wanted to throw the sword on the ground and run far away, leaving it behind.

But her father had been so happy for her to join. She couldn't let him down. His eyes were on her.

Stepping toward her, Nico aimed his sword at her shield. She flinched, stepping backward automatically.

This would never stand. She needed to pull herself together.

Sofia took another deep breath and swung her sword at Nico's, taking a step toward him. The metal vibrated, ringing out from the hit. She cringed from the blow.

If the sword didn't kill her, her anxiety would finish her off.

NICO MOVED TOWARD SOFIA, slowly flicking his sword at hers. He appreciated the weight in his hands. The hammered-metal blade, from pommel to tip, stretched the length of his arm. The hilt, the thin grip, and the guard were plain, and the edges were dulled for training, but it was still a higher-quality sword than he'd ever held in Fryse.

After stepping back, he moved forward again, allowing Sofia to block. The iron of their swords clanged. She was decent, though her nerves made him uneasy. They continued sparring for a few minutes.

He glanced at the other pairs. Jostein's graceful footwork and strong gait had Karsten on defense. Dag had Skip cornered, though she wasn't particularly energetic in her swings. King Eirik grinned, watching the champions alongside other Parliament members.

Nico frowned, noting Sofia's lack of enthusiasm. "You don't seem happy to be sparring."

Sofia sighed. "You're right."

Nico lowered his sword. "We don't have to be out here. It's just for fun, and you're obviously not having fun. How about you join me in the library instead? Maybe you can help me find maps of the area."

She brightened, then faltered. "Don't you want to continue sparring, though?"

"While I appreciate a beautiful sword, I'm not passionate about sword play. I've always preferred snowball fights." Nico chuckled, thinking back to the wars between his brothers. "And there's more to fighting than weapons, you know."

Sofia's shoulders relaxed. "Let's go find the maps."

The other pairs continued as Nico and Sofia brought their swords and shields back to the armory, then walked to the library. Max followed closely behind the entire way.

"Thank you for providing a valiant escape," Sofia said. "Which maps are you looking for?"

"I've been thinking about strategies out in the fjords. I'd like to see where we will be fighting. Get a lay of the land."

Her brow furrowed. "The sail wasn't enough?"

"Well, it was cut a bit short. And I want to be prepared. After all, knowing is half the battle."

"What's the other half?"

"Not dying." That seemed rather obvious.

"Fair enough," Sofia choked out through a laugh. "Don't worry. We'll find you the maps you're looking for. And if we don't, I can draw a new one for you thanks to the merciless insistence of my tutor that every stroke of every map in every last corner of the library be memorized." Sofia rolled her eyes, and Nico laughed along with her.

In the library, Sofia walked over to a huge oak chest carved with runes and patterned designs. It creaked as she opened it. "The maps are mostly in here."

"Is there one for Aldersfoss?"

"Yes, this one." Sofia spread the map out on the table. The ink was pale and faded, and the parchment smelled of oak.

"We're here." She pointed to the mouth of the fjord, close to the open ocean. "You'll be dropped off along here, twelve miles apart." Sofia slid her finger along the path. "There are freshwater streams and plenty of berries and animals. Survival should be easy."

His eyebrows rose. "Sure, easy."

She neglected to mention the four other champions who were far more skilled at wielding weapons than he was. Nico couldn't match them, even with practice. Not with only two days until the Sonne.

"There are even cairns to help guide you back to Aldersfoss," Sofia said. But she wouldn't be out in the mountains. She was the princess.

"How do you know that?" he asked.

"I helped pile the rocks to make them."

Nico blinked, stunned. "You... were camping?"

"Princesses can camp. Don't look so surprised." She crossed her arms, biting her lip.

"Sorry. You just seem... like you fit better indoors?"

"I suppose I do now," she said, relaxing. "I haven't actually been camping since Filip was alive. Pappa would take us." Her gaze drifted, just for a moment. "I can forage among the best. Though I wasn't particularly adept at catching animals."

"Fisherman. Not a problem." He grinned. "So find food and

water, follow the cairns, and then I just have to kill everyone else along the way. Doesn't seem too bad."

Sofia chuckled. "Yes, that's all. Nothing to it."

Definitely not nothing. "I've always thought there was more to being a good king than physical strength."

"After ten years leading Parliament, I agree. We focus on battle strategies to protect the front, especially now with Swaymark's latest attack, but there's so much more—training to build up the warriors, camp locations and movement, trading with partners, and making sure everyone has the resources they need to thrive."

"Does that include Fryse?" Did she know how some of the families struggled through the winter?

"Of course. We send resources north after every Parliament."

How far should he push? "My family never benefited. Neither did my crew."

Sofia's eyes narrowed, and her head tilted slightly. "I... never?"

Nico shook his head.

"I'll bring it up at the next Parliament. *Tomorrow.* I'll bring it up with Karl tomorrow," she declared, straightening her wool shirt. She looked rather out of place without a fancy dress.

"That would be a good start."

She fidgeted with her ring. "I am here to help, at least through Victorsfest. After that, it's your partner's job."

He hadn't even considered who he'd choose, if he even made it that far. "Would you stick around to train them?"

"Of course." She swallowed, then straightened. "I have to change and finish up my notes for Parliament tomorrow. Is there anything else I can help you find?"

"No. Thank you. I'll put things away when I'm done."

Sofia smiled, though the corners of her eyes didn't crinkle like they usually did. "I'll see you at middag, then."

DAG WENT THROUGH THE MOTIONS with her sword, blocking and dodging Skip's attacks. *This is not fun.* It seemed like the king wanted to help them get a feel for the other champions' fighting styles, but she already knew how Skip fought. *Poorly.*

He had quick reflexes, but he hadn't spent nearly enough time with a sword in his hand, and he lacked the control needed to even come close to matching her. It was like sparring with a new recruit. Never her favorite activity, since new warriors were often fragile—fresh-faced and unscarred.

Karsten seemed to enjoy training Sofia yesterday, though. If only Karsten had been paired with Skip instead, and she and Jostein could go at it. Jostein was more fun, a much better match than Skip—at least with the sword.

The other pair was swiping and dodging, and Jostein had Karsten on defense. Still, after hours of sparring. *Interesting.*

Skip's sword came down. She threw the shield up instead, letting his sword bounce off the iron center with a clang. The quick change in strategy startled Skip. *It will be easy to pick him off during the Sonne.*

Across the field, Jostein knocked Karsten's sword out of his hand. Maybe she could switch—

"Come on, Dag, is that all you've got?" Skip flourished his sword.

Don't take the bait.

She counted to four. She'd love to go at it, work off some of the pent-up energy. How she *hated* Skip at that moment. He wouldn't stand a chance against her. "If I had given it all I've got, your body would already be cold."

His eyes widened. "That's some big talk for someone so small." *Don't take the bait.*

He faked left and drove the sword right. She knocked it away.

Beginner. You fake left, then go left the second your opponent thinks they know...

Skip backed up, preparing to attack again. "I know you've got more than that in you."

"Yes."

"Come on, Dag. I can handle it." Skip moved toward her again, and she knocked his sword away easily.

"Doubtful."

He stopped moving and stared her down, his expression cold. Dag frowned uneasily as she stared back.

"You come in," Skip said, "judging all of us as lesser, ignoring our thoughts, even rejecting our compliments, but we're all just as worthy of being here as you are. Any half-decent future ruler would see that."

Her ears pounded as her head screamed in white-hot rage. *Half-decent? I will be the best ruler in Fjorden's history.*

She raised her sword and slammed it down, barely giving Skip a moment to defend himself with the shield. The harsh crack of the shield's wood echoed along the fjord.

Dag raised her sword again and came down harder. Skip threw the broken shield and dodged, barely evading her sword. He tripped and fell to the ground, and she kicked his side hard, raising her sword again.

A sword was coming right at her. She swung hers hard against it, blocking the attack.

Karsten.

She fought back, the clang of iron against iron ringing out. Hit, block, hit, block, smash, crash, push, and push. She was pushing him back.

He favored his spear training. She had him.

Suddenly, Jostein was beside them. Dag threw up her shield to block Jostein's sword. She kept pushing Karsten back, close to breaking through his defenses.

"Drop your weapons! Now!"

Dag jumped in surprise.

"NOW!" the king yelled again, his angry voice echoing louder than the metallic reverberations.

She dropped her blade to the ground, keeping her shield on her arm. Jostein dropped his as well. Karsten put his sword back in its sheath and dropped his shield. His training sword lay further down the field, still resting where Jostein had knocked it from his hands. *Helvete.*

Skip was curled up on the ground, his sword resting a few feet away, his face ashen.

Well, that was fun.

"Sparring is over! Get back to the castle!" The king stormed off the field, leaving them behind. All the other warriors around the field went back to sparring, the show now over.

Karsten held out his hand to Skip and helped him up, then escorted him back to the castle slowly.

"Dag," Jostein called, "grab the swords. I'll grab the shields, and we'll take them back to the armory."

She picked up the swords and followed. Inside the armory, Dag felt calm—right at home, since it was a smaller version of the armory in Morge. A giant table stood in the center, and weapons and protection covered the surrounding walls. She put the training swords back in the basket with the others as Jostein piled the shields in the corner.

"Dag," Jostein said, "what happened?"

Fair question. A training sword doesn't often crack a shield.

"Skip was goading me."

He frowned. "But you seem to keep a level head."

"I..." She thought back to the field, to Skip implying she wasn't worthy. Anger mixed with disappointment.

"Obviously something happened," Jostein said. "You don't have to tell me. Either way, it wasn't a good look."

"I know."

Jostein sighed. "Shall we head back?"

Dag nodded, and they walked to the castle in silence.

Back in the guest wing, she passed by Skip's open door. He was curled up on his bed in a fetal position. Her stomach twisted with guilt. Considering his background, it was probably the worst pain he'd ever experienced. She hadn't heard a crack when she kicked, so hopefully, he'd...

Well, he's still competition.

She entered her room and left her door ajar, worried Skip might call for... she didn't know what. And surely it wouldn't be her that he wanted help from. She left the door ajar anyway. Not that she needed to, since she could hear him through the wall. The wooden walls of the castle carried every single sound.

I'm glad Skip doesn't snore.

Light footsteps ended with a light knock; it was on Skip's door, not hers.

"Hey, Skip." Nico's voice carried a hint of concern. "How was sparring?"

"It was rough," Skip rasped. "Dag was barely fighting, and she seemed so bored. I egged her on, trying to show her I could take more."

Dag cringed with shame. She had almost broken the only rule of the Sonne. And Skip had only been trying to help.

"She came down so hard," he continued, "cracking my shield before kicking me while I was down. Then Karsten went after Dag, and Jostein went after both of them. You missed a spectacle, Nico. The three of them were unconquerable."

The wooden doorway creaked as Nico leaned against it. "At least tomorrow is Championsfest."

"You're right." Skip sounded perkier. "Look at you—always seeing the bright side. We'll drink the night away."

They deserve friendship before they die in two days.

"Hang in there," Nico said. Then his light footsteps faded down the stairs.

A while later, Jostein opened his door and walked past Dag's room. The middag migration was beginning. She was certainly ready to eat, though she didn't want to sit in awkward silence any longer than required.

Dag stared at the ceiling until she heard Skip stirring. His bed creaked as he stood up. She listened to him as he walked out of his room and down the hall. Her guilt increased with every one of his slow, uneven steps on the wooden floor.

Once he hit the stairs, she quietly exited her room, surprised to meet Karsten in the hall. They slowly walked down together, keeping a good distance behind Skip while still listening to his echoing footsteps.

The music of Nico's hardingfele carried out, welcoming them somberly into the Great Hall. It was slow, so he'd caught on to the group's mood. *Not that it took an expert...*

Skip winced as he sat down, then took a deep breath. Dag took her place next to him and Karsten sat across from them, just like their other middags. Karsten kept his expression stoic, and Dag copied. Jostein looked aloof after everything that had happened, which was fair. Today wasn't his fault.

Sofia entered the hall and sat in her usual space next to Karsten. She nodded to the champions but was otherwise silent.

The tension was palpable as Nico played on. When the king entered, Nico put his fiddle down immediately.

Glowering, King Eirik walked to the head of the table, then slammed the chair back and sat down. "Would someone like to tell me what happened today?"

The champions and Sofia remained silent.

"Spar, not slaughter!" King Eirik banged his hands on the table, his voice booming in the hall, startling the servants around the room. "You all have one rule, and that's *don't kill each other until the Sonne.*"

Dag's shame grew. She lowered her eyes to the table.

Across from her, Sofia shifted. "Pappa, they—"

"Should have known better! They're five of Fjorden's best!"

Sofia closed her eyes, turning her face downward. Since arriving at the castle, Dag had watched Sofia try so hard to please her father. To please the champions. To please the kingdom.

The king took in Sofia's expression. His eyes betrayed his shame. Shame, shame, shame. Plenty to go around, for all of them.

He settled back in his chair, his expression subdued. "I expect better from champions. You all know the value placed on respect and unity among all people, even during competition."

A little more than competition, considering we're all about to kill each other in two days...

The servants brought out the platters of food, and the group ate their meal in silence. As soon as the king finished eating, he left the hall. Some of the tension left with him, but the group remained on edge. Nico pulled out his fiddle from below the table and started to play.

"Still running tomorrow?" Dag asked Karsten.

He nodded, just once, wrapped in his usual stoicism. *Great.*

She slipped out and headed to the armory, then grabbed a spear and aimed for the sparring field, ready to clear her head the best way she knew how.

CALM HAD DESCENDED the moment Sofia's father left the hall.

She pushed aside the guilt she carried. She imagined her hand severed, her body broken, trying to stop the champions from fighting.

Champions. The best of Fjorden. She was no match for any of them.

Her cheeks flooded with embarrassment when she thought about her father yelling at her. His day had been stressful, but she wasn't the cause. It all sounded like a mess. He'd stormed back early and slammed his door so hard the paintings shook. And the situation with Swaymark...

Not that her day had been much better, between handling the sword and learning Nico didn't want her as a partner. She'd lose her home if he won.

What a mess.

But up against Karsten and Dag... well, Nico didn't stand a chance. No matter what, Sofia had to keep it together.

A princess doesn't break.

Jostein wandered off to bed, the circles under his eyes darker.

"I should check on Pappa," Sofia said to the group.

She walked up to her father's door, took a deep breath, and knocked.

"Come in."

Sofia entered and closed the door behind her. She took another deep breath. "Pappa, I'm sorry about middag. I didn't mean to question you in front of the champions."

Her father shook his head. "No, Sofia, I'm sorry I yelled at you. I was just as stressed as they are, twenty-two years ago."

Sofia clasped her hands together and nodded.

"Should I have paired you with Karsten instead? I thought Nico would be an easier match for you."

Sofia looked down. "Oh..." Tears started to well in her eyes. She tried to blink them away. "Mamma and Filip... the sword... and I just..."

"Of course." Her father rose, crossed the room in a heartbeat, and wrapped his arms around her, rubbing her back. "You took on so much when Mamma died." He paused, his face lined with grief. "I'm sorry I couldn't protect them."

Sofia took comfort in the shared silence. In the shared sadness they never talked about. Neither one of them had been able to protect two of the people who mattered most.

"Today wasn't easy." Sofia let go of her father.

There was a hint of mist in his eyes. "No, it wasn't."

"But tomorrow will be better." She dried her eyes on her sleeve.

"Yes. Tomorrow will be better." He gave her a sad smile.

Once she'd pulled herself together, she went back to the Great Hall, the mood tense. Nico's music echoed, a lovely, haunting melody.

Karsten's presence was a balm. She shifted closer, tucking herself directly against him.

"Enjoying the evening?" she asked the group tentatively.

"We need more ale," Skip joked.

"Problem-solving—my specialty." Sofia waved the servant over from the edge of the room, determined to turn the group's evening around.

"When was your last voyage?" she asked Skip. Surely that would get him talking.

"Just last week. Final trip to Tunland for the year before the northern waters freeze over, at least for our crew."

Sofia crossed her arms and leaned forward on the table. "Skadi and Njord are probably packing for the mountains already."

"I bet he's trying to convince her they should stay by the sea." Skip smirked in his usual charming way.

Karsten chuckled quietly as Nico started a new song.

"Endless summer?" No more frigid winters? Sofia closed her eyes, just for a moment. "That's actually a lovely thought. I hate the snow."

"Sofia, you're a Viking." Karsten nudged her, leaving his hand on her thigh. Her heartbeat quickened.

"Our ancestors were extremely misunderstood," Skip said. "Clearly, they spent all their time searching for sunny shores."

All four laughed.

Karsten circled his thumb against her, and she relaxed into his touch.

"Might I borrow you?" Karsten asked.

He rose and allowed Sofia to take his arm, then led her out to the ramparts by the shore. Her guard followed behind them, farther away from her than he was supposed to be.

The silence between her and Karsten felt comfortable, as always. They stood at the edge, overlooking the beach below.

"I'm sorry about sparring earlier," he said. "I thought you'd have fun, like yesterday." He glanced at her before looking out over the waves.

"I was excited that you wanted me to join in." She bit her lip. "It was just... the sword. And I—"

He tentatively held out his arm, and Sofia curled into him. She didn't need to explain. He wrapped his arms around her and pulled her close, making her feel safe and cherished.

She fidgeted with her ring. "Are you ready for the Sonne?"

"It's always easier to be brave when you have something worth fighting for."

He watched her, his eyes wandering over her features and ending on her lips. They stood in silence.

"Are you ready?" he asked.

She took a breath. "No, I'm not."

But Dag was the only real competition, and she had to hope...

Sofia blinked back moisture in her eyes, then gave up and closed them, listening to waves hit the shore.

Thoughts of the past six years filled her mind. This man, who would do anything to protect her, who would be anything she needed, might be blazing a trail in Valhalla soon without her.

A tear fell down her cheek. Karsten brushed it away delicately. She opened her eyes and looked back at him.

He bent lower, whispering, "You and me, Sofia."

His lips were mere inches away from hers. He was leaving the choice to her, looking out for her, like always. He would walk away if that was what she wanted. He would jump off the cliff if that was what she wanted. He would fight for her every single day he was in this realm. He'd fight all the way to Valhalla, and even then, he still wouldn't stop.

For six years, he'd kept his distance, the closest person to her in proximity—but always an ocean away. His strength and dedication were unmatched. He was her safe space, and she never wanted to let that go.

She just wanted him.

Sofia met Karsten's lips with hers, wrapped her arms around his neck, and pulled her body flush against him. He tasted like the summer honey ale he'd been drinking. He tensed, but she nipped at his lower lip, coaxing him on. Karsten returned her enthusiasm, matching her speed and meeting her tongue with his. He shifted his hands down her back, pushing into her with apparent desire.

The sun continued to set as darkness wrapped around them.

With a loud creak, the castle door opened. Karsten pulled back, instantly alert. He stepped in front of her and whipped out his sword in the span of a breath. Sofia blinked, dizzy.

"Good reflexes," her guard said. "It's just Dag heading in."

Karsten's eyes narrowed, just for a moment. He sheathed his sword, then wrapped his arm around Sofia's waist and pulled her close.

"You and me," he whispered again.

It felt like a promise.

With a kiss on her cheek, he gestured for her to lead the way. She took his hand, and he laced his fingers through hers. Sofia didn't let go until they arrived at the base of the stairs to the guest wing. Nico's music continued from within the Great Hall.

"Goodnight, kjære." Karsten kissed her again. "I'll see you in my dreams."

"How are you feeling?" Skip asked.

Nico wasn't sure. Calmed by the music. Soothed by the ale. He imagined Elyse running through the halls, filling the castle with life. He hoped to bring his family here. And he planned to win. "Determined, I suppose. It isn't worth worrying."

"I suppose that's true."

The smell of charred wood made Nico feel like he was back in Fryse. Like he was home, instead of knocking on the door to Valhalla.

"Do you recall the second verse of 'The Song of Yggdrasil'?" Nico asked.

Skip nodded. Nico played, and Skip sang:

Out come three maidens,
from Urd's endless well,
found under Yggdrasil.
Urd always comes first,
then Verdandi and Skuld.
They measure the fate,
of all children born.

After the final note, Nico put his hardingfele back on the table. "My life string was cut when I was born. My path was decided by the fates. As was yours."

"You're right." Skip sighed.

"I'm going to fight hard, and I'm determined to win, but I also acknowledge that it may not matter. My fate has already been decided. When it comes down to it, if I'm going to die anyway, I might as well do it with a sword in my hand, headed to Valhalla as a champion."

"That's quite poetic."

"It's just honest," Nico said. "What would you do as king?"

Skip smirked, raising his eyebrows. "Bed Sofia, to start."

Nico ignored a small stab of jealousy. "And then what?"

"Expand trade. Travel the world. Lord it over my brothers, mostly. What about you?"

"I'm going to make things better for our people. If we all weren't so worried about resources…"

"That's a nice dream, Nico." Skip hesitated. "I hope it happens."

Nico hummed in agreement. "I was wondering… You don't really seem like a fighter, and—"

"You think I can't take on Dag?" Skip's tone was sharp.

Shocked, Nico gaped.

Skip's eyes brightened. After a moment, he dropped his scowl. "Probably not, but I'll enjoy Valhalla."

He already knew he didn't stand a chance. He was still here because it would be cowardice, poor sportsmanship, to leave.

But Nico could offer them *both* a chance.

Not all weapons are made of metal.

He leaned toward Skip, looking him directly in the eye. "I think we should partner up during the Sonne."

Skip's eyes went wide. "Why? You basically just admitted you don't think I can win."

"Our best bet is to let Dag and Karsten kill each other first. Then we take on whoever's left once they're weakened, two on one."

Skip looked down at the table, tracing his fingers along the wood grain. "Makes sense. They'll either kill each other or die trying."

Nico nodded.

"What about Jostein?" Skip asked.

"I think either one of us can take him down—as long as we can get his sword away from him."

Skip continued to trace the wood grain. After a minute, he stopped, then looked up. "What happens when it's just us?"

"Then we battle it out." Nico shrugged. "The fates will decide whose time it is. Hel, they already decided. Not sure what else to say."

"So we have to trust each other not to kill each other."

"Yep."

"And then we have to kill each other."

"Yep."

Skip looked Nico right in the eye and raised his glass. "Well then, cheers. Let's do it."

One Day

Dag's footsteps pounded against the ground in a comfortable rhythm, faster on the now-familiar terrain. Her new routine.

Rustling bushes... Just the wind, just on edge...

As she passed by the castle, Karsten caught up to her. He ran beside her along the ramparts, and they circled the castle grounds for an hour as the sun rose, staying along the wall. Once they'd finished a second lap, they slowed to a walk.

She stretched her shoulders back, feeling relief in her muscles. "I want to grab a bite in the guards' food hall. Ready for breakfast?"

His eyebrows rose. "Missing camp?"

"Just missing four meals a day." *Since you've been holding out.*

"I'm not hungry yet. I'll see you later though."

He walked off, aiming for the front gate. The *closed* front gate.

Dag walked toward the trelleborg, keeping an eye on him. The guards at the top of the wall climbed down and helped him slip out—exactly where he wasn't supposed to go. *Of course they did... Where's he off to?*

Annoyed, Dag entered the food hall, engulfed by the delicious smell of a roasting sheep. Just like at camp, long wooden tables stretched down the room with benches on either side. At least two hundred could comfortably fit. The walls were covered in weapons and shields, as they should be.

Some of the warriors greeted her by name, welcoming her to their table. She ate her fill, enjoying the easy camaraderie. *Easy to get along when you're not about to kill each other...*

At changeover, she went to the Great Hall. There, she found Nico and Skip locked in conversation.

"Good morning, Dag," Skip chirped.

What has him so happy? Certainly not my presence...

"Morning." She sat in her usual spot.

Nico pushed a bowl of strawberries toward her. "Compliments of Sofia. She just went upstairs to prepare for Parliament."

No wonder she can barely keep up with us. She needs to eat better...

Dag pulled the bowl in front of her. "Thanks."

"Looking forward to the feast?"

"I'm sure it will be quite the celebration." *What you remember of it, anyway...*

"And in our honor," Skip said, eyes bright.

"I'm looking forward to the music," Nico said.

How expected.

"Our private concerts have been great too," Skip said. "Last night's was the best yet. You missed out, Dag."

"But I slept well." *If not for very long.* Every last muscle in her body felt sore after her late-night spear work.

"Of course you did." Skip's voice had a hint of an edge. Their rooms were adjacent; he must have heard her come back last night.

The two men looked at each other, then rose.

"Have fun today, Dag," Nico said. "See you this evening."

Dag grabbed a handful of strawberries and watched them walk out, thinking back to the prior day. *Something's changed. But what?*

An empty-handed servant approached the table. "Hi, Dag. I'm Agneta." She had brown hair, light skin, and bright blue eyes. "Sofia asked me to make you a dress for tonight—if you didn't already have something to wear."

Dag tried to remember what was in her closet. She failed. "I just have the clothes Tomas gave me."

"Well, we have plenty of fabric, so anything you want, we can make it happen." Agneta's eyes sparkled with excitement.

When in Aldersfoss... Dag gestured to Agneta to lead the way.

In the armory, they walked straight past the weapons to a door in the back. Agneta opened the door to a room full of shelves piled with fabric, a giant loom, and tables covered in scissors and needles and thread. Four substantial piles of goods of all manner of wood and metal sat on a table in the center. Iron plates and platters, glasses, silver coins, carved wooden animals, new leather boots...

The goods for the four grave mounds.

Dag paled, her head light.

"We have options." Agneta gestured to a section of the wall of fabric, drawing her attention. "New silk was delivered last week.

We also have some linen and lighter wool. Anything that catches your interest?"

The colors hit every shade of nature, from blood red to a wheaty ocher to blues more vibrant than the sea. "What would steal Sofia's attention?"

Agneta ran her hands over the silks, stopping over a deep pine green. "This is one of Sofia's favorite colors, and it will highlight your green eyes."

Dag nodded, nonplussed.

"Hm... That's Sofia's face when she is doing something out of obligation." Agneta put it back on the shelf. "What do you *want* to wear?"

"That." She gestured to the green silk.

"Are you sure?" Agneta asked, eyebrows raised.

Dag bit the inside of her cheek. "No."

"I didn't think so." She smiled. "So what do you want to wear?"

She wanted to look like a ruler, impress the people, steal Sofia's attention... but she didn't need a green dress to do that.

"I want to feel like me." It was the most honest Dag had been since she'd arrived at the castle.

Agneta stepped over to a pile and picked up a bolt of ivory linen. "This was just delivered yesterday. It's still raw. We haven't dyed it yet."

"Yes."

Perfect.

Agneta brought the bolt over and unwrapped it, draping it from the floor to Dag's shoulder and hanging it back to the floor, then picked up scissors.

Dag stared anxiously at the volume of fabric around her legs. "I like to be able to move quickly."

Agneta thought for a moment, then cut the fabric level to Dag's chest. She pulled the cut fabric forward over Dag's shoulder, and the adjusted length hit Dag's knees.

Much better. "Thank you."

Agneta cut the hole for Dag's head and fashioned short sleeves with a twist that would leave Dag's shoulders and neck bare. With impressive efficiency, she started pinning the dress together. "Sofia wanted to come, but she's still preparing for Parliament."

"How long have you worked for her?"

Agneta pulled on the fabric, smiling wistfully. "Since before she was even born."

"When did you come to the castle?"

Her smile dropped, though her hands continued to fly along the fabric. "I was only fourteen. Taken from my family. Brought to the mainland on a ship—from one of the isles."

No survivors left behind. Pillagers were ruthless.

"I understand," Dag murmured.

"I ended up here when the old king wanted a companion for his daughter. He bought me from the market. Ana-Sofia refused to accept me as a slave, though. She insisted on paid wages."

"That was kind of her."

Agneta didn't acknowledge Dag's statement. "She respected all of us as humans. Her death was a devastating blow."

Fascinating, to be so loved...

"Sofia... she takes after her mother." Agneta secured the last needle in the fabric. "She will always do the right thing for her people." She lifted the fabric and placed it on the table, seeming pleased. "Okay, Dag, you're free to go. I'll bring the dress to your room this afternoon."

"Thanks." Dag started to leave, then hesitated. "Sofia is lucky to have you."

She'll get to keep you. I'll make sure of it.

With a slight nod and a wistful smile, Agneta settled in at the table and started stitching.

Dag walked out of the armory, spear in hand, and continued to the sparring field. She stabbed at her invisible target, faster and harder and faster still. Victory would be hers.

Sofia fidgeted with her ring, wishing she were anywhere except here in the library. Nico wasn't interested in her as a partner, and any help she offered him raised the risk of losing her home. But he'd find help elsewhere, and Karsten's life string was cut. Her helping Nico wouldn't change either of those things.

"What about here?" Nico pointed toward the turn of the fjord and traced his finger along the map stretched across the giant table.

Sofia moved Nico's hand gently before pointing to an area about forty miles north of the castle. "The biggest falls are back here. They're breathtaking." She and Filip had spent hours at the beach nearby, playing in the sand and dancing in the waves as the mist of the falls floated through the sky.

"Then I look forward to seeing them soon. The falls in Fryse are frozen for over half the year."

"I don't remember our last visit to Fryse. Do you miss it?"

Nico nodded. "Home is home..."

And didn't she know it. "What do you miss most?"

He smiled softly. "I love reading to my sister. We only have a Book of the Gods, though. It can feel repetitive."

"We should send some books north with Karl for her."

"She'd love that."

A pair of Hamme's representatives strode into the library.

"Parliament starts soon," Sofia said. "Anything else?"

Nico shook his head, then put the maps back in the chest. "I'll see you tonight."

Parliament members trickled in, the overall mood jovial despite Swaymark's impending attack—only a week and a half away. Sofia sat at the head of the table, her notes in front of her. When Karl entered, Sofia waved him over.

"Princess Sofia," he said. "How is our champion?"

"In good health and good spirits. You'll surely see him tonight."

"And how does he stack up?" he asked, voice low.

"Nico's a plotter. I wouldn't be surprised if he won."

Karl remained silent, shifting a bit. Surely he wanted to get settled before the meeting.

"I wanted to check with you," Sofia said. "Does Fryse have enough resources to get through the winter?"

"Well, we could always use more." Karl's brow furrowed. "Why do you ask?"

"Nico mentioned his family hadn't received anything from the capital."

"Oh, they haven't." His face relaxed. "We provide for people with the highest need first. Nico's family has three strong brothers. Well, two brothers now."

"Of course," Sofia said. "Let's talk to Sander about extra supplies for this year. Maybe we can send more north before the freeze."

Sofia's new guard walked into the library, taking Max's place. She gestured for Max and, once he was close, asked, "Would you please stop by the front gate on your way back and confirm they've posted the extra guards?" She lowered her voice. "And check if Karsten has returned."

The king entered, taking his place on her right, filling the last of the twenty-one chairs.

"Velkommen, welcome, welcome," Sofia said. "First order: the attack on Morge. Source confirmed?"

Sander's representatives nodded, and one rose. "The branch is Swayish birch. Green shirt under their chainmail. No other bodies, but we found a boat less than a mile away."

"Small enough for one to sail?" Sofia asked.

"Yes," he said. "And we found fresh food in the deck box. Gave it to the birds."

"Thank you," Sofia said. "So—" He remained standing. "Was there something else?"

His forehead wrinkled. He bit his lip, then said, "The boat was new. Built with Fjordish oak."

Hushed whispers broke out around the room. Fjorden hadn't sold their boats to Swaymark in years.

"Find out which shipyard built it," Sofia said. They'd continue from there. "Tomas, are Morge's camps ready for the additional warriors?"

"We are. And we're ready for the victor to return," he boasted.

Sofia cringed. Debating the will of the gods wasn't in today's plans—nor should it be.

Hamme's newest representative jumped from his seat, smashing his fists on the table. "Bold statement!"

Tomas met his expression calmly, then said, "Watch."

"You didn't see Jostein conquer our Championsmatch. He has *real* fight in him. That can't be trained."

"They've been sparring." Tomas faced the king, then said, "You've watched. Who will be the victor?"

The king's expression remained neutral. "We'll know after the Sonne."

"Really, Eirik?" Tomas's eyebrows raised slightly. "Have you been asleep on the field?" There was an unfriendly edge to Tomas's tone. While the pair had challenged each other for years, this time, tensions were high all around the table.

"Pappa, we should move on," Sofia urged quietly.

Ignoring her, the king stood, his narrowed eyes locked on Tomas. "Karsten."

The entire room broke out in chatter.

Another day, another stack of notes for the trolls.

NICO PERCHED ON THE BENCH next to the king's throne while servants bustled about the Great Hall. One walked over to the far wall, unhooked a chain, and slowly lowered the iron chandelier from the center of the ceiling.

Skip entered the hall, crossing to the center. "Should we go somewhere quieter?"

"No," Nico said. "The noise will drown out our conversation. And if we stay here, it looks like we're just watching the setup for tonight."

"Smart," Skip said, then wandered to the kitchen.

A group of servants exited the kitchen with rags and began to wipe down tables. A few pushed a couple tables toward the walls, clearing an open space on the floor. The servant working on the chandelier carefully placed fresh candles in each arm, then lit them, slowly making his way around the circle. He still had at least a hundred candles—and four more chandeliers—to go. The glow of the candles against the painted gods would look beautiful during the feast.

Skip returned with two ales. "Here you are. No one will suspect a thing." Skip grinned, eyes bright. "Now, tell me about this plan of yours."

"Sofia and I—"

He flinched. "Hold on—she's in on it?"

Nico's forehead furrowed. "No."

"Okay." Skip relaxed onto the bench, then took another swig of ale. "Because if she's helping anyone, it's Karsten. Not that I blame her," he said with a smirk.

Nico ignored his handsome smirk.

"She was showing me maps in the library. I don't think she'd draw new ones just to mislead me."

"No, not likely."

"Besides," Nico said, "she's a terrible liar anyway."

Skip's eyebrows rose. "What did she lie about?"

"Nothing. That's the point. She knows she's a terrible liar, so she doesn't bother. And do you see how red her face gets?" Nico laughed. "She literally buries it in her hands."

"I haven't." He rolled his eyes, shaking his head. "We've sailed off course. Going back to the maps?"

A group of musicians entered the hall. Nico peered at them, trying to see what instruments they had brought.

"Nico?"

"Right." Nico refocused. "There are lakes in the mountains, meaning lots of fresh water and plenty of waterfalls."

"So it's a standard fjord." Skip's tone was flat.

The chain of the chandelier rattled. The servant was back at the wall, hauling the chandelier toward the ceiling.

"Ideally, we'll be dropped off last and can head toward each other. We could hide in one of the caves behind the waterfalls." Nico took another swig of ale. "We just have to wait out the others. They're all pretty fast, and they'd all be together. When the last champion comes to find us, they won't be expecting two on one."

Skip blinked, then leaned forward and rested his elbows on the table. "That actually makes sense. Good thinking."

One of the servants came by, wiped off their table, and moved on to the next. The chains of the second chandelier rattled as the fixture lowered.

"What if we're dropped off first?" Skip asked.

"Then it will be easy to find each other before any of the others. We should head inland and travel north. We can let the three battle it out. Then we circle back, take on whoever's left—catch them off guard."

"A surprise—I like it." Skip grinned. "If we're in the middle?"

"Everyone would be heading toward us. We'd want to head toward each other and then head inland. We don't stand a chance if they all find us at once."

Skip downed the rest of his glass. "So two on one. We take them down."

Heavy footsteps approached. Nico gestured a stop motion with his hand. Jostein appeared in the doorway—looking cheerful and energetic, his eyes bright. Skip waved him over, then offered him ale. When Jostein nodded, Skip wandered to the kitchen, taking his empty glass with him.

The iron chains sang a repetitive melody as the servant heaved the second chandelier up toward the gods on the painted ceiling.

Skip carried two full glasses of ale back to the table and slid the second glass in front of Jostein. "Here you are, my good fellow."

"Thank you," Jostein said. "When's middag? I could smell it cooking from upstairs."

"Soon, I hope," Nico said. "My baby sister Elyse would love this. My whole family."

"Mine too. I'm excited to tell them about it."

To have Jostein's level of confidence...

A servant brought a giant platter of fresh meats and vegetables to their table, setting it in the middle. Between the sight and the smell, Nico's mouth watered.

Skip grabbed a plate and a slice of ham. "Dig in!"

"Are you sure we shouldn't wait?" Nico asked.

"This feast is for us!" He downed the rest of his ale.

Nico helped himself to a slice of fresh reindeer. More servants swarmed the hall with platters of food and pitchers of ale. It was more food than Nico had seen in his life. The servants rushed to light the last of the chandeliers before hoisting them back to the ceiling. The soft, warm glow of the candles lit up the final corner of the gods above.

A loud commotion broke out in the entry, and laughter echoed through the Great Hall, followed by the boisterous members of Parliament. Sofia and the king were markedly absent, but Nico recognized the faces of Fryse's representatives.

The musicians began playing, drawing Nico's attention away. The hardingfele had mother-of-pearl inlay along the tailpiece that matched his own. Two musicians flanked either side of the fiddle player. One had a bone flute, and the other had a horn. A fourth musician sat in front with a drum. Their lively melody elevated the mood of the room.

Chants from outside the hall grew louder by the second. A wave of guards washed into the room and filled it quickly, followed by people from Aldersfoss. The cheers and chants mixed with the music, bringing the Great Hall to life.

The king strolled through the doors, and the energy of the room heightened. Championsfest had officially begun.

"Ready?" Agneta asked Dag from the bedroom's doorway. The new dress was folded over Agneta's arm.

Dag nodded, mentally preparing for a new kind of battle. The fabric fell against her skin. A slit along the leg left her movement unrestricted. She sighed in relief. Agneta pulled a natural leather belt around her waist and secured it with a shield-shaped bronze strap mount, cinching the dress at the base of her ribcage. The neckline showed off her iron spear pendant, filling her with pride.

"Agneta, it's perfect." Dag beamed. "Fit for the victor."

Eyes bright, Agneta asked, "Would you like help with your hair?"

"Yes, please." Dag sat next to the window, watching the people meander toward the castle. Agneta braided a crown across the top of Dag's head, then pulled a gold hairpin out of her pocket. *The metal of the gods.*

"Sofia won't mind." Agneta winked, then tucked the pin along the braid. "Besides, she'll be wearing her crown tonight." Clasping her hands together, she said, "I need to assist Sofia now, but you're welcome in the Great Hall whenever you want to head down." She started to walk out the door, then turned back. "May Odin be on your side tonight."

Dag put on her leather boots. She was relieved once her dagger rested in its usual spot. She counted to four, then walked down to the Great Hall.

Hundreds of unfamiliar faces crowded the noisy room. She scanned the room quickly but thoroughly, keeping an eye out for weapons or potential threats. Across the room, the king mingled with Tomas and other members of Parliament. Dag wandered over to them, grabbing a glass of ale along the way.

"Dag!" Tomas said warmly. "Cheers to Morge's champion and soon-to-be victor. Hip hip!"

"Thanks, Tomas. King Eirik." Dag nodded his way in greeting.

"Not for long." He raised his glass toward her, then drank. His crown—hers soon—glittered atop his head.

Dag considered his past strength—now weakened by time.

Fjorden is ready for a new ruler. No, I take that back—Karsten would throw over the kingdom for Sofia, Jostein would be useless without his sword, Nico couldn't handle the physicalities of war, and Skip would be too busy feasting to actually run the kingdom. Fjorden is ready for me.

"How are you enjoying the castle?" Tomas asked.

Dag smiled. "It's starting to feel like home."

"Don't get too comfortable, Dag. We'll have you back out in Morge leading the warriors against Swaymark soon enough."

She liked the sound of that.

Straightening with pride, she said, "Looking forward to it. How was Parliament?"

"Long and loud, like always." Tomas glanced toward the king as his fingers began to tap at his side.

King Eirik raised an eyebrow. "Our victor will hear all the details after the Sonne. For now, let's enjoy the evening."

"Don't worry. He'll be a great mentor once the Sonne is over." Tomas leaned toward her, keeping his voice low. "Did you hear warriors are being sent east?"

"Tomorrow," she whispered back.

"Warriors spotted a couple of Swayish ships off Morge's coast. They haven't approached, but we think they're part of an attack planned for a week and a half from now."

Dag nodded. The sooner she won the Sonne, the sooner she'd crush her enemies.

Tomas straightened. "Dag, I look forward to seeing you soon in Morge."

"Sofia," Karsten said, entering her bedroom.

She rose from her desk, rushed across the room, and threw her arms around his neck. "Did you bring your parents for the feast?"

"My father would have disowned me if I hadn't." Karsten winked. "He's living vicariously through me this week."

Sofia chuckled. "Your mother never wanted this life. She would have killed him if the Sonne didn't."

"She threatened to kill me today if I kept chopping her garden." He let Sofia go, then swung his bag around and opened it, revealing fresh pink blooms. "She didn't mean it, though."

Warmed, Sofia clasped her hands in front of her. "Thank you."

The corner of his lip turned up. He brought the flowers to the desk and began placing them in the vase.

Possibly for the last time if Dag won. Sofia's stomach churned.

She sat on the bench and reminded herself to be brave. "Did you know, Pappa told me he never would have won against your father."

"And that's why I spar with him every day. We got in a good three hours this morning." Closing the empty bag, he left it on the chair before joining her. "How was Parliament?"

"One for the books." Tension crept up her shoulders. "The intelligence surrounding Swaymark's planned attack is legitimate. And ships have been seen along the coast of Morge, though they remain far off. There aren't many yet, but we expect more soon enough."

Karsten frowned. "So a week and a half."

"A week and a half." But only a day until the Sonne.

Footsteps from the hallway put Karsten on alert, though he relaxed when Agneta appeared in the doorway with Sofia's new dress in hand.

Her head tilted slightly. "Karsten, I wasn't expecting you up here. The feast has already started."

"I'm heading down now." He stood, then helped Sofia up. "Save the first champion's dance for me?"

"Always," Sofia said.

He smiled shyly, then grabbed the empty bag and strode from the room, closing the door behind him.

Agneta helped Sofia into the silk dress—ice blue, the same shade as Karsten's eyes. She slipped on her beaded, navy silk slippers.

"Let me grab your mother's crown," she said.

"Actually," Sofia started. "Well... I'd like to wear a different crown tonight."

NICO POURED ANOTHER GLASS OF ALE, then passed the pitcher across the table to Jostein.

Dag appeared beside the empty throne, almost like magic.

"Looking sharp," Skip said, eyeing her unabashedly. "You clean up decently."

A pang of jealousy hit Nico, but he tamped it down.

"Decently? Just *decently*?" She sat down next to him. "Skip, if I was looking *decent*, then you wouldn't be looking at me like *that*."

"Sorry, Dag." Skip raised a cup of ale her way.

Nico tamped the jealousy down harder.

"I'll let you keep your head tonight—in exchange for the ale." Her tone was light, unexpected.

Skip handed her his cup immediately, laughing and gesturing to the servants to bring another. With ale flowing so freely, Skip's morning was sure to be slow. That didn't bode well for their plans. But they'd be hiding to start, so as long as they found somewhere safe…

The musicians started a new song.

"I'd love to be playing tonight," Nico said.

"You're better than them."

Nico started, mouth agape. "Dag, was that a *compliment?*"

She crossed her arms, her eyebrows raised. "It was a statement. Completely objective."

"I think that was a compliment." He grinned.

"The ale is getting to you, then." She smirked. "Go up there."

"What?"

"Go up there," she said again. "You're a champion. Surely they'd love to meet you."

Maybe she had a point.

"You should," Jostein said.

"I'll go with you," Skip said. "Come on."

The musicians finished their song. Fidgeting with excitement, Nico approached the group. "Beautiful playing, all! I'm Nico."

"It's an honor to meet you," the hardingfele player said with a smile.

Up close, Nico noted the Swayish serpent carved on the scroll of the fiddle. "Your hardingfele is beautiful."

"Do you play?"

"Does he ever," Skip crooned, nudging him.

"Since I was five," Nico said.

"Oh!" The fiddle player held out his instrument. "Play for us, please."

Nico looked at the beautiful fiddle; it called to him. And this might be his only chance in front of this many people… "Are you sure?"

"Absolutely."

He took the instrument. The Swayish birch was lighter than the Fjordish oak he was used to. Stepping into the center of the group, Nico placed his hand at the top of the neck, wrist straight, and put the chinrest under his jaw, aligning the fiddle with his arm. He pulled up the unfamiliar bow, gently but firmly.

The room had quieted—and all eyes were on him.

Nico rested the bow on the strings and pulled it down with the weight of his arm. The familiar tune washed over him. Hauntingly melodic notes filled the entire hall, reverberating differently with all the bodies. The other musicians began to play along with him. He tapped his feet as the crowd danced to the quick rhythm, Skip included. If only Nico's grandfather could see him…

He finished the final note and handed the fiddle back to its owner, enjoying the cheers from the crowd.

"Beautiful playing, Nico. May the gods be on your side."

A CHEER BROKE OUT NEAR THE DOOR. Guards welcomed Karsten, swarming around him with excitement.

Dag's eyes narrowed as she took in the scene.

When Karsten deigned to join them, Nico asked, "Where have you been all day?"

I'd rather know how he convinced the guards to let him off the grounds.

"Sparring." Karsten filled his plate with food, barely glancing Nico's way.

Inga carried a tray piled with fresh Swayish pastries to the five champions. "Congratulations, all. Good luck tomorrow." With a cheerful smile, she bowed her head, then set the tray on the table. The group chorused a thank you.

Skip pulled the tray toward himself. "I haven't had these in ages!"

"Going to share?" Dag asked, eyebrows raised.

Skip didn't meet her eyes.

Jostein laughed, a deep belly laugh that caught her off guard.

Yeah, we're all about to kill each other, but this is still fun.

Another cheer rose from the crowd, and the entire room stood, Dag included. Sofia entered the Great Hall. Her long-sleeved dress and the navy belt around her waist emphasized her feminine shape.

The embroidery along the neck and sleeves was sewn into a dark blue pattern reminiscent of the ocean. Her long hair cascaded down her back, and her head was topped with a crown of pink wildflowers pinned in with gold. Turtle brooches with long chains fell below her chest, the glittering gold declaring her the princess.

A fitting partner for the future victor.

Dag abandoned the other champions, quickly appearing at Sofia's side. "Might I pull you in for a dance?"

Sofia glanced toward her father, then nodded, grasping Dag's hand and following her to the open floor.

Taking the lead, Dag held Sofia's left hand with her right. They bowed to each other and began the steps, moving together in a large circle along the floor. Dag pulled Sofia in, spun her twice, and led her backward. The crowd joined in, and Dag continued to lead Sofia in the steps of the Springdans.

"You look flawless. I see why you've been hiding all afternoon."

A light blush colored Sofia's cheeks. "Sure, since Parliament ran itself today." She spun along with the other dancers.

"How did it go?" Dag asked.

"Could have gone better, but at least plans are in place to address Swaymark. They can wait until after the Sonne, though."

Not really...

Dag hummed. "Thank you for sending Agneta to find me."

"Of course," Sofia said as they continued their steps. "I hoped you'd enjoy the attention. I want you to feel at home here."

Thoughtful.

Sofia curtsied low as the song came to its conclusion. "Thank you for sharing the first dance."

Dag nodded, then kissed her hand before letting it go. "Sofia."

Mine, along with the rest.

"I need to stand with my father for the formal greeting. I'll see you later." She walked toward the king.

Dag returned to the champions' table, and Karsten scampered off to a group of guards. *Helvete, his wolf-pup eyes every time Sofia walks into the room.* Dag would end them tomorrow, then be back in Morge next week to end Swaymark.

She eyed the empty platter in front of Skip. "Couldn't save a single pastry? There were a dozen."

He grimaced. "Sorry."

She rolled her eyes. *Oh well, I'll ask Inga to make more before I leave for Morge next week.*

"Welcome to the Championsfest!" King Eirik's bellowing voice greeted the guests. The entire room cheered loudly. "Tonight, we celebrate our five champions, the best in their regions."

Another round of cheers rang out across the room, and Dag lifted her chin with pride.

The king raised his glass. "I've enjoyed getting to know all of you, and I hope to celebrate with all of you in Valhalla one day. To the champions!"

The crowd went wild, toasting and drinking heartily. King Eirik turned to Sofia, offered his hand, and together the pair began a dance.

Skip and Nico clinked their glasses together, then drank.

Dag started. *They're planning something.*

Tomorrow, she'd know exactly what.

"QUITE THE STATEMENT." The king's mood was in contrast with the lively music swirling around them.

Sofia gave a single nod. "It was rather forward. Dag surely didn't know she was stealing the first dance from you."

His eyes narrowed. "I'm not feeling particularly forgiving."

"I let her steal it, though. That makes it partially my fault."

"It would've been poor form for you to turn down a champion."

Stumbling slightly, Sofia refocused on the steps of the dance. The champions had far more grace with their swords than she'd ever have with her own two feet. "We still have plenty of feasts left. You aren't going anywhere."

Her father spun her around and pulled her back. "Not as the king, though."

"One more, Pappa, at Victorsfest. You're still the king until the coronation."

"The victor opens the dance for Victorsfest." Her father sighed. "No, I wouldn't want to take that away from him."

Sofia bit her lip. "You've written Dag off."

He lifted her in a quick turn. "I don't think she has the victory in her. Arrogance can be deadly."

"Only the fates know."

"Did something happen?" His eyes narrowed and his head tilted slightly, confusion written across his features. "Has your favor shifted?"

"Just... trying not to hope." Trying to hold herself—and the kingdom—together.

Her father nodded and spun her once more. "I think you'll be fine, kjære."

The song ended, and she curtsied low as he bowed. The entire room broke out in applause. She latched onto her father's arm and scanned the room for Karsten.

Crossing back to the Parliament members, the king grabbed a glass from a servant's tray. "Cheers, all!"

Tomas moved beside her. "Sofia, you look beautiful tonight. Just like your mother."

"Thank you," she said. Lowering her voice, she asked, "Do you have a moment?"

He held out his arm. With her guard following, they escaped to the library. Her guard closed the door behind them, muffling the music.

"What's on your mind, Mouse?"

Sofia hadn't heard her old nickname in years. She looked up at the painted stars, then took a deep breath. "You're so confident in Dag." Tomas nodded, watching her closely. "Well... is it just because she's from Morge?"

"No," Tomas said without hesitation. "Karsten or Jostein could knock out most of Morge's warriors. Neither one would have any trouble establishing themselves as king." He paused. "Sofia, I've learned a lot out on the battlefield. One of the most important lessons is this: when you have something to prove, you fight twice as hard."

Didn't she know it. "Pappa thinks she's arrogant. He thinks it will cost her."

"She is. Extremely arrogant. But it's earned."

"Is it?"

"Lucia and I arrived at the south camp the day after the battle. We asked Chief Ragnar if we should still hold a Championsmatch. Then Dag flew through the gates, barely out of breath from her run. The chief said there was no need for a match. When he called Dag over and told her we were canceling, she was livid. Everyone else was still asleep, and here's Dag, ready to go, bruises and all. She's a force."

"That's..." Sofia fought against the weight threatening to pull her under.

"Dag's a fighter, and glory drives her. Don't underestimate that."

Sofia glanced at the floor before meeting his eyes. "I'm nervous,

Tomas. This is the only life I've known." Karsten was the one she wanted to share it with.

Tomas raised his eyebrows. "What's most important?"

"Fjorden," Sofia answered immediately.

"And if Fjorden goes to war, who will best protect it?"

Sofia hesitated. "A fighter."

"Yes, *our* fighter." Tomas placed his hand on her shoulder. "Winning drives Dag, and she won't settle for less. She's the ruler we need." His expression brightened, his eyes twinkling. "Plus, she's from Morge."

"I knew it," Sofia joked—though her heart sank. She hoped Karsten would be ready.

"It's no use worrying. The fates cut their life strings already. And if Dag wins, you can train the king consort and become a representative for Aldersfoss, or you can go live with the mountain trolls if you like. Remember them?"

Sofia couldn't forget. She put her hands on her hips and pouted her lips in jest. "Mamma was ready to kill you for telling me those stories. I didn't sleep for a week, so neither did she."

"Smart of you to stay awake. They're creatures of the moonlight, after all." Tomas chuckled. "We should get back to the feast, little Mouse. Although I suppose your old nickname doesn't quite fit anymore..." He smiled wistfully.

The nickname hadn't fit since the moment her mother was killed; since she'd been forced to step up and lead with a strong voice, thrust into a life she didn't ask for. Or maybe it did still fit, since here she was, putting everything and everyone else first.

Back in the Great Hall, Sofia meandered toward the champions' table, stopping to welcome guests along the way.

"Ingmarie," Sofia squealed. "How's maternity leave?"

"Wonderful. Mostly." She looked happily exhausted, cradling her new baby in her arms.

Sofia held the baby's hand. "We'll be happy to have you back after Jolablot. Enjoy the time."

Progress through the room was slow, but she hadn't seen her constituents since Midsommer. She greeted a local farmer, but they only stared over her shoulder, uninterested in her.

Moments later, a hand brushed her arm. "Sofia." Her favorite voice, deep and low. "Would you like to dance?"

Sofia happily took hold of Karsten. He led her to the open floor, and they joined in with the dancing circle.

As the next song started, Sofia leaned in. "I'm glad you found me. I was headed your way."

Karsten spun her out before pulling her back, keeping her at arm's length.

She swallowed the lump in her throat. "Sorry about our dance. I didn't want to upset Dag by turning her down."

He spun her and pulled her back, a bit closer this time.

"Pappa was cross with her," she said.

"I'm sure he was. I was surprised you didn't say no."

She relaxed into a turn. "I'm just trying to stay on her good side so she doesn't kick me out of the castle."

He stopped breathing, stopped moving.

"Karsten?"

"It's nothing." He spun her around, his expression blank.

She missed her step. "It doesn't seem like nothing."

They stopped dancing, stepping off to the side.

"Sofia," he said, voice low, "who do you hope returns?"

She paled, ice flooding her veins. "I'm... I can't..." She took a deep breath, chest heavy, throat choked. "Whatever happens, the gods chose this life for me. I've strived to meet every obligation to the kingdom and my people."

"That's not an answer," Karsten said as the song ended. He kissed the inside of her wrist, then walked toward his parents, leaving her behind.

Her heart cracked, but she pushed her feelings into a box and locked them away with a key.

A princess doesn't break.

She just needed fresh air, to hold herself together.

Sofia pivoted, aiming for the exit. She just needed the exit.

Just fresh air. Her heart pounded.

Exit.

Dag followed Sofia immediately. As she stepped into the entrance hall, a swish of blue exited the front door.

She walks faster than she runs...

Outside, guests milled about the grounds and along the path, but no one paid attention to her. Their voices mixed with the sounds of the wind and the rustling leaves under the moonlight.

"Princess," Sofia's guard murmured.

Pivoting toward the sound, Dag climbed over the waist-high bushes. Mumbling an incoherent response, Sofia rested her hand against the castle wall, then leaned against the wood. Shoulders slumped, she slid downward.

Dag caught her, barely. "Sofia, what's wrong?"

Her breathing heavy, she didn't respond. Six feet away, the guard's ashen face twisted in horror.

"Get water," Dag said to him, then helped Sofia settle in the grass and sat next to her, keeping her fingers on Sofia's wrist. *Heart racing.*

Through labored breaths, Sofia choked out, "I'm fine."

"Really?" Dag's eyebrows rose. *Because I'm pretty sure you're panicking.* "Head between your knees. Deep breaths—slow them down." *Can I actually leave you in charge when I'm gone?*

Sofia nodded limply, closed her eyes, and followed directions, so that was something. Her heart rate came down, albeit slowly. Dag listened to the people mingling on the grounds, their conversations loud and surely influenced by an inordinate amount of ale.

The guard returned with the water. *Took him long enough.*

Dag let go of Sofia's wrist. She reached for the water, thanking the guard.

"Does this happen often?" Dag asked.

"I..." Sofia took a drink of water. "Not often, but yesterday was close."

Helvete. Where can I find a new partner this late...

Sofia closed her eyes, then leaned against the wall. "A sword killed my mother and my brother. And holding one in my hands was difficult. Which is why I usually avoid them."

Okay, that's fair. Misguided, but fair. "A *human* killed your mother and brother, wielding a sword. The sword wasn't to blame. Don't be afraid of it."

The silence stretched between them.

"Some scars are more visible than others," Dag said.

Sofia's gaze went straight to Dag's neck, though she remained quiet.

"Are you curious about mine?"

"Yes." Sofia blushed, looking down.

Dag lifted Sofia's chin. "You can ask."

She hesitated, then seemed to find her courage. "Where did it come from?"

"Swaymark had come to pillage. One of the bastards waltzed right into our house, stabbed my mother, came for me—slicing his dagger along my neck, calling me a pretty thing." Sofia gasped as

Dag continued. "I wrestled away the dagger and stabbed him with it. Seven years of training were put to good use."

She tried to sound nonchalant. The reality of the fight was far more bloody, a struggle that had painted the floor red. She had barely survived—but she didn't want to think about that.

Sofia smiled weakly. "Tomas said you're a force."

As he should.

Dag straightened, chest out. "Most people have underestimated me. Considered me too weak to be a threat. They quickly realized it would be the last thing they did before I sent them to Valhalla."

Those reunions will be fun.

"Was it the same at camp?"

"No," Dag said quickly. "At camp, they place value on the best fighters. I proved myself a thousand times over."

Sofia hummed. "I can't remember the last time a woman won the Sonne. I expect some will not be happy when you win."

Finally—real confidence.

"It'll be done. What can they say?" Dag relaxed against the wall. "They could have fought in the Sonne. Hel, they can challenge me every day for the next twenty-two years if they want to, but they're guaranteed to lose. The gods will be on my side."

"That's true."

Besides, Odin values women warriors. All his Valkyries are women, and becoming a Valkyrie is one of the highest honors. Sofia knows that...

"I have to ask—are you prepared to lead alongside me?"

Sofia's eyes widened. "Well, it's up to you, of course."

"You've been trained since birth to help run the country, and you've spent half your life running Parliament. I'd be an idiot not to make you my partner, regardless of my feelings for you, physical or otherwise. But that wasn't what I asked."

She swallowed, took a moment, then said, "Yes."

Good. Done. Dag rose from the grass, brushing her dress off before holding out a hand to Sofia. "Have you ever used a dagger? They're far more useful against any trouble you'd be in."

Sofia shook her head.

With practiced ease, Dag pulled her dagger out of her right boot. The guard flinched, then thought better of it. *Don't mess with a champion.* "This is the dagger that gave me my scar. Do you want to learn how to use it?"

Sofia nodded, and Dag moved away from the wall, pulling Sofia with her.

"Daggers are small and fast, just like me." She placed the dagger in Sofia's hand. "You hold it like this," she said as she wrapped Sofia's hands around the grip, the blade pointing down. "There are a couple of ways to protect yourself. Let's start with the most obvious."

Dag stepped behind Sofia and pulled her arm back above her head. "Pull it back up here, allowing for the most force when you bring it down." She pushed her body against Sofia's back and placed her hand on Sofia's stomach. "Back straight, entire body engaged."

Sofia's heart raced. *Not panic this time...*

She guided Sofia's hand down in a snapping motion. "Just like that, aiming for the neck. You can aim for the lungs, too, but you might hit ribs at this angle."

Dag held on a moment, then let go of Sofia. Sofia's breath hitched, but she remained silent.

"Another trick is to hold the dagger low, getting behind them and stabbing them in the lungs..." Dag ran her hands over Sofia's rib cage, enjoying the silk of her dress. "Or belly..." Dag touched her just below her ribs. "As long as they don't have chainmail on. Stab hard and fast as many times as you can. Keep yourself behind them. They'll bleed out quickly, dead in a minute."

Sofia shivered, then turned around bashfully and handed the dagger back to Dag, her cheeks pink. "Thank you for the lesson."

Hopefully, she won't need to use it...

"Shall we head back in?" Dag held out her arm, and Sofia took it. They wandered back around the bushes toward the front, the guests still chattering merrily.

Back in the entrance hall, Sofia let go of her arm. "I'm going to head upstairs. Goodnight, Dag."

Dag nodded, then watched Sofia walk toward the Royal Wing, her guard close behind.

I'm done too. I can feast after I win.

THE SONNE

Disoriented, Nico rose from the soft bed. The dead fire, the quiet room... the morning of the Sonne, his last in the guest wing. He packed his bag.

In the Great Hall, he filled his plate—plenty of salmon and cheese to keep him full in the fjords, at least for today. Guests were scattered throughout the hall, though everyone moved slowly and spoke at a low volume. Servants scurried around, still cleaning from Championsfest.

Jostein joined him, though he skipped breakfast. He had deep circles underneath his eyes. At a quarter to seven, he and Nico walked out to the sparring field. After all the rain that had fallen during the week, the sunshine felt unsettling.

Skip sat beneath a tree, his pallor deathlike.

"Hey," Nico said. "You okay? What's going on?"

Skip twisted forward and vomited in the grass. The smell sent Nico's stomach lurching. Wiping his mouth, Skip said, "Rough morning."

Nico sat next to Skip and gave him his waterskin.

"I'll go grab a towel." Jostein dashed toward the armory.

"Hang in there," Nico whispered. "We'll lay low for a bit. You can sleep it off."

Skip leaned against the tree, thanking Jostein once he returned. Dag joined them, dropping her bag and helmet on the ground. Her sword rested on her hip. The chainmail hugged her small, muscular body; it looked like it was made just for her.

Karsten exited the trelleborg, fully dressed in his armor. Why wasn't he coming from the castle?

"Where have you been?" Dag asked once he was within earshot.

"I went back with the men last night."

She blinked at him, then cocked her head. "Slept through your morning run?"

His eyebrows rose. "I didn't realize you'd miss me."

Karsten turned toward the castle. Nico followed his gaze. Sofia stood in the window, watching the five of them. Had she talked to Karl about the supplies?

King Eirik came out promptly at seven. "Good morning, all." The champions chorused it back, but it was half-hearted. He frowned, looking over the group. "I understand you're anxious, but look at the bright side: it will all be over soon."

The flippancy didn't feel appropriate, though sending the five strongest of Fjorden to kill each other did seem like a joke. There were better uses for all the blood than coating the rocks.

"Come on." The king walked toward the trelleborg, gesturing for the group to follow.

Nico helped Skip up, and they tailed the group into the armory.

Skip's brow was coated in sweat. He'd had plenty of ale every other night... Didn't he know his limits?

"You can leave your bags here by the door," the king said. "They will be brought back to the castle or your burial mound."

"That's reassuring," Skip muttered, low enough that only Nico could hear. Nico chuckled in response.

Taking in the walls of weapons, Nico's hands started to sweat, his shoulders slumping.

King Eirik grabbed a large leather bag from the table and held it up. "Five backpacks. Each has a full waterskin, a knife, and an axe. The land will provide for the rest of your needs."

Animals and berries for eating, caves for shelter, branches to build a fire, and three other champions out for his blood. Four, once Skip turned on him. Nico gulped.

Each champion grabbed a bag.

"Skip, Nico, Jostein," the king said, "there's armor back here if you want any."

Jostein put on a chainmail shirt, picked up a helmet, and walked back to Dag and Karsten. With the pair decked out in full armor, Nico decided to follow their lead. He put on a tan padded shirt and a half-sleeve chainmail shirt over his tunic. It was loose around him, the weight heavy and unfamiliar. He grabbed a helmet—simple in design, with a crossbar nasal guard jutting down—and tucked it into his bag.

Skip seemed perkier, now that he was up and moving. He copied Nico, putting on the two shirts and tucking a helmet in his bag.

King Eirik moved toward the wall of weapons. "You're each allowed a spear, a sword, a shield, and a dagger. You can use your own or take them from the armory."

Nico took one of each, as did Skip. Karsten already had all his weapons. Dag grabbed a shield and spear, then returned to her spot. Nico realized with a start that she'd likely had a dagger the whole time they'd been in the castle. Jostein had his sword, grabbed a shield, and that was that—but he preferred his sword, so it made sense.

They were a formidable group, but Nico was ready. He had a plan; he just had to follow it.

"Guards in big red cloaks will be patrolling the area via boat," the king said. "Do not attack them if you see them. They will not help you unless you're dead, at which point they will bring your body to the mounds for burial."

The group walked across the sparring field.

"Not so great, then, eh?" Skip whispered to Nico.

"No, I suppose not."

Sofia was still watching from the window.

King Eirik stopped at the gate. "Before the boats take you up the fjord, I want to show you something. Come this way."

They cut left toward the forest, the world becoming quieter the further they walked. Wind whispered through the trees. Critters chirped in the tall grass. The ground sank softly under the weight they carried.

After a few minutes, the king stopped in front of four identical mounds surrounded by stones placed in the form of a ship, the scene framed with patches of trees. "These four warriors were the best in their regions during the last Sonne. All of them brought strength and bravery with them into the fjords. It was determined by the fates that their time in Midgard was over, but they continue to live in glory in Valhalla. Four of you will have the opportunity to meet them soon."

The group stood in silence. His point was made.

Nico could only trust Skip, but that partnership was built on melting ice that would ultimately crack. There could only be one victor, and they both knew it.

The champions began the walk back to the boats.

Skip sidled up next to him. "Sticking to the plan?" he asked in a hushed voice.

Nico nodded. "Sticking to the plan." Though he wasn't sure it would be enough... "Feeling better?"

"I'll feel better after a nap," Skip said.

At the beach, three guards in red cloaks waited on the deck of the same boat they'd taken out three days ago.

Nico shuddered at the fierce dragon gracing the bow. Dag and Karsten boarded first. They moved to the back of the boat, sitting on opposite sides with as much distance between them as possible, considering they were sharing a bench. Jostein sat in front of Dag; brave of him, since she'd stab him in the back without a second thought if it didn't break the rules. She might do it anyway. Skip and Nico sat in the front of the boat, separated from the other champions by the guards, the mast, and the furled sails.

The king watched from the shore. "I wish all of you the luck of Thor's hammer. May we all dine together again, feasting on the bounty of the gods."

The champions shouted out a last "hurrah," but it sounded hollow.

One of the three guards jumped out, the bottom of his cloak dipping into the water. He pushed the boat into the waves and leaped in, leaving a trail of water behind as he crossed the deck. "Right, then. Let's begin."

HANDS CLUTCHING HER WINDOWSILL, Sofia watched the ship carry the five champions away.

After a sleepless night, she'd crept across the castle, her guard in tow. Karsten's room had been empty. Her guard didn't know where he was, and Max was late for shift change, and now the champions were sailing away. She couldn't tell Karsten she wanted him, needed him—not unless he returned.

He had to return.

"Thanks for covering," Max murmured from the hall. The guards whispered together, then traded places.

Sofia looked out the window again, but the ship was gone.

Releasing the windowsill, she padded to her doorway. "Did you and Karsten have fun at the feast?"

"We did." His hand clenched his spear. "Princess… Karsten bunked with me last night. That's why you couldn't find him this morning. He was"—Max averted his eyes—"devastated."

And it was her fault. Because she'd been trying to protect herself. She hadn't let herself hope.

Eyes closed, Sofia took a deep breath. "I'm going to lay down."

"I'm sorry," he said, voice low.

She closed the door, then leaned against it and slid to the floor. Tucked her head between her knees, the way Dag had told her to. Slowed her breathing.

And hoped the gods knew what they were doing.

Seabirds called out overhead, their caws a calming music to Nico's ears. Waterfalls of melted snow cascaded down the sides of the cliffs, carving shallow trails, slowly altering the formations. The air smelled fresh and salty, a reminder of home. The guards brought down the sail and turned toward land, rowing toward the beach.

Without warning, Dag stood—her backpack still on, her shield strapped to her back, the spear in her hands, and determination in her gait. She jumped into the shallow water with a small splash, her chainmail jingling. One of the guards eyed another, but they shrugged in return. No one else seemed surprised. The guards reversed their rowing.

At the base of the cliff, Dag assessed the rocks, then found her footing and climbed. There was hardly a path on the sheer cliff face. Dag was better suited for the climb, and Nico was glad she'd made the decision for all of them.

Chest lighter, Nico watched the guards raise the sail, and they continued the journey.

"This weather feels more like home." Jostein gazed at the sky, his expression thoughtful. "I missed it, with all the rain this week."

"We're used to rain, but not this much of it," Skip said. "Sander gets more of a break."

"It's prettier here, though. Lovely flowers." The mountains were covered in bright pops of color, the blossoms stretching toward the sun. The cold would wipe them out soon, but for now, at the end of summer, they were thriving.

A mountain goat wandered down the cliff face along the ledges, letting out a bleat like their goat at home, just meandering and eating grass, with its curving horns pointed toward the sky and its gray coat blowing in the wind. The goat's confident footing reminded him of Dag. He hoped he wouldn't be next off the boat.

With a start, Nico realized he'd left his needle case behind. There was no need to carry it around the castle. He'd broken his habit. Now, if one of his layers ripped, he'd be unable to repair it. At least there wasn't a risk of freezing to death. It wouldn't be like camping in Fryse.

Waves lapped at the boat, a soothing hum as they traveled along. The guards pulled down the sails, turning toward the shoreline, where tall rocks rose above the water. "Jostein, you're next."

Nico sighed in relief. He and Skip still had a chance of being dropped off last. And they would be farther from Dag—not that Karsten was much better...

Once Jostein was settled on the shore, the guards carried on. Nico watched as Jostein shrank in the distance, hopefully for the last time. Dag was out for blood.

EXHAUSTION TOOK OVER, pulling Sofia down into the depths of her anxiety. Her restless sleep had helped pass the time, slowly.

Max stood directly in front of her door, where he had denied the servants access all morning. He'd even intercepted Agneta when she brought up breakfast, bringing the bowl of strawberries in for Sofia himself. She hadn't wanted it, but she'd thanked Max anyway.

Her father's footsteps approached her door.

"Apologies, King Eirik," Max said. "Sofia isn't feeling well. She's sleeping."

Sofia's gratitude toward Max increased as the silence stretched on. Finally, she heard a muffled acknowledgment, and her father's footsteps started again, then faded.

Sofia rolled over. Rolled back, burying her head in her pillow.

And let sleep take her.

DAG SCALED THE TOPS OF THE CLIFFS, following the trail of the boat. Fast and strong, she kept up her pace.

Jostein sat on the rocks along the shore. His sword was on his belt, tucked safely in its sheath. His shield lay on the ground next to him. *Easy killings.*

She ducked below the cliff line, thinking back to all her sparring with Jostein. She knew the steps of his dance as he moved with his sword. She would have to be fast and deadly.

One chance for an easy blow. He could force her on the defensive, but she was confident she'd win either way.

She peeked out again, eyeing his exposed neck. Both his helmet and his chainmail sat on top of his backpack.

Jostein was giving her an opportunity to pick him right off. *A sitting seabird, an embarrassingly easy win.* He would be sent to Helheim immediately.

She carefully started the journey down the steep cliff.

Mere steps from the bottom, she accidentally kicked a rock off. She stopped, cringing as it fell to the water with a plop. Jostein flinched, but he kept staring out at the water. *Did he…?*

"Hi, Dag."

Yep. "How did you know?"

He continued to stare up; his gaze followed clouds that drifted along in the wind. "Lovely sky, isn't it?"

"Why aren't you getting up?"

"The blue is beautiful." He remained with his back to her, his neck completely exposed.

An easy kill.

Her jaw clenched. "Jostein."

"Skip isn't nearly as quiet, and he partnered up with Nico. Karsten would have killed me by now."

She stepped off the cliff and onto the rocks. "Okay, but why aren't you getting up?"

"Dag…" His tone carried nothing. "I never wanted to be king."

"But don't you want to go to Valhalla when I kill you?"

Jostein turned around, his eyes empty of life, the circles under his eyes dark. "I don't deserve to."

"What are you talking about? Jostein, you're a champion."

"I'm not brave enough," he murmured.

"Jostein—"

"I am not enough!" he shouted, his eyes blazing.

Dag held silent, her eyes wide, her mouth agape. A look of realization came over his face. His eyes glazed over, and he hunched his shoulders, turning back out toward the water.

"Enough for what?" she asked.

Quietly, he said, "I wasn't brave enough to defend my family. I didn't stand up for them as they were attacked." He shuddered. "I ran, and I ran, and I let them fight alone. I let them die," he choked out, leaning his upper body over his knees. "I don't deserve to be rewarded by the light of Valhalla. I don't deserve to be with them. I'm a bloody coward."

This is nonsense. "Pick up your shield."

Jostein ignored her.

"Pick it up."

"I don't deserve it, Dag." His breathing was unsteady, but it was evening out.

This is such nonsense. "Jostein, you *were* a coward."

"A bloody coward."

"Yes, a bloody coward who failed to fight."

"Exactly." He turned to face her.

"Now fight. Prove you're not a coward, you're a *champion*."

A single tear ran down his cheek.

"Jostein, get up. Don't fail your family a second time."

"Just kill me, Dag. Just end it." He wiped his eyes with his tunic. His voice was quiet, his tone matching the emptiness in his eyes.

He just... "No."

"What?" His sad eyes met her gaze.

"No. Get up and fight."

"Why?"

"I'm not going to let you die a coward. You're a champion."

He turned back out to the water. "Dag... I don't care..."

This conversation is going nowhere. Should I just... but he'd...

She sat on the ground, completely flummoxed.

Jostein continued watching the clouds.

Dag watched the clouds with him. "You're right—the blue is beautiful today."

He nodded, remaining silent.

"What was your family like?" she asked.

Jostein bit his lip, hesitating. "Why?"

She shrugged. "I'm just curious."

With narrowed eyes, he said, "My pappa was a farmer. He grew up in Hamme. He and Mamma met in school. There weren't many options—small village, middle of nowhere."

"What about your brothers?"

"They were both older. We all helped with the farm."

"Tell me about them?"

"One of them was quiet, shy." Jostein scratched at his arm, then rested his hands at his sides. "The other was a talker. He loved sitting in the taproom with the other warriors in the village. He struck up a courtship with the barmaid, and they married and had a baby within a year."

Dag hesitated. "They're all dead?"

"No... the wife and baby were in town when the attack on the farm happened. They moved back to her parents' home. He's an adult now—just turned sixteen. But everyone else died fighting. The neighbors too."

Sixteen... "Why did you run?"

He looked back toward the water. "My brother pushed me and told me to go. I wasn't thinking."

Dag let it all sink in. "You were a child. You've become a man, who fought bravely and became a champion—willing to risk death in the face of becoming a king." *Sixteen years...* "It was so long ago... Do you want to see them again?"

"Yes," he whispered, nodding almost imperceptibly.

"Don't you think they want to see you again?"

He remained silent.

"They told you to run—to save you. They loved you."

This is going nowhere.

She stood up, readying her shield and sword. "If you don't fight now, you'll never see them again."

Jostein looked at her, then looked down.

You will not walk away from this alive.

The silence stretched.

"You're right." He stood up, a new light in his eyes.

"Of course I am."

He reached for his shield. *The fight is on.*

Dag attacked, bringing her sword down. He raised his shield, blocking her, but barely. The shield smashed into pieces.

Throwing the remnants to the ground, Jostein whipped his sword from its sheath. Dag's blade smashed into it, the clang of metal echoing across the fjord. He blocked, then stepped toward her, striking hard. His blade hit her shield. She blocked, then swiped back, forcing him toward the water.

Dag drove her sword toward his midsection. He jumped back nimbly, his footwork graceful. But she'd watched him for days, knew where he'd step next. She hit again, cutting through his tunic into his chest, drawing blood.

He grunted, jumping back. His eyes blazed with fight, shooting fear through Dag. The slip gave him a moment to push her back toward the wall.

End it fast, or you'll lose.

She dodged left as he stepped right, adrenaline coursing through her. She gained momentum in her swing, slamming her sword through his neck, severing it clean.

His body tumbled to the rocks, the sword clanging. Blood poured out—its scent engulfed her.

One down.

Catching her breath, she watched his blood coat the rocks. She pulled out his waterskin and drank the rest of it before tossing it back onto the bag.

And then she watched the clouds drift across the sky.

They are rather beautiful...

She pulled Jostein's leather cord from around the stump of his neck and put it on. The small iron Thor pendant dangled next to her iron spear. *That feels right.*

Dag climbed back up the cliffs and continued walking.

Three to go.

"Feeling better?" Nico asked Skip—though with the rocking of the ship, it was doubtful.

Skip took a drink from the waterskin. "Too many pastries."

"You should have shared."

"Yeah, I should have." Skip chuckled, clutching his stomach.

Karsten ignored them, looking out over the water instead.

The guards pulled down the sail and rowed toward the shore, aiming for the beach. "Skip, you're up."

Not ideal. Nico kept his voice low. "There are turns up ahead where the water bends, and there are some lakes and streams a few miles inland from there. We should be able to find each other and some shelter before nightfall."

"So water and food?"

"We'll fill the skins from the waterfalls before we head in. We can easily find berries along the way. Maybe hunt. Let's see how much time we have before dark."

Skip grabbed his bag and his weapons.

"I'll jump out next, the way Dag did," Nico whispered. "Stick to the shore. We'll meet in the middle."

Skip jumped onto the shore, waved, and walked toward the cliffs. The boat went back out, the sailors silent. Nico remained at the bow, watching the waves lap at the cliffs, appreciating the soft rhythm. The wind whistled along, nipping at his cheeks. Twelve miles later, they turned toward the shore.

The moment the guards pulled down the sail, Nico stood. They nodded to him. He put on his backpack, ready to go, waiting for them to row the rest of the way to shore.

Seabirds walked along the beach, but they didn't fly off as Nico's feet hit the sand. They seemed to know he wasn't hunting for birds; he would be hunting humans.

The Sonne had officially begun. It was now a free-for-all, and the last one standing won the crown. The last one standing would shape Fjorden's future. It would be him.

Karsten's expression was one of steel resolve. He nodded to Nico, sending a shiver down Nico's spine. The boat pushed off and left Nico behind as it sailed down the fjord for the last drop. He walked toward Skip, hoping to put as much distance as possible between himself and Karsten. He couldn't take him down alone.

Sofia pulled herself out of bed, placed her feet on the floor, and took a deep breath. Looking at the notes on her desk, the plans she still had to finish... She didn't have it in her.

Body ice-cold, she put on a heavy, blue wool dress. Deep down, she knew the chill had nothing to do with the end-of-summer weather.

When she opened the door, Max immediately stepped aside. His eyes were full of concern. "How are you holding up?"

"Could be better."

Max gave her a half-smile. "Keep it together, Sofia. Karsten will kill me if you're not in one piece when he gets back."

When he gets back...

She went to the library, Max in tow, and found the Book of the Gods. Settling at the head of the table, she opened to the story of Odin and Freja. *She allowed him to come to her bed, but she guarded her heart zealously from him...* Was it a mistake to guard her heart, even though Freja had done the same?

Sofia gazed at the tapestry of Yggdrasil, hoping Thor was looking out for Karsten. With his pendant and handkerchief...

Her father entered, startling her. "Sofia, the first champion has fallen."

Sofia clasped the arms of the chair, her heart pounding. "Who?"

"Jostein, kjære."

Relief washed over her, chased by heavy guilt. She didn't want Jostein to die; she didn't want anyone to die.

She just wanted Karsten to come back to her.

"His body's already on the way to the burial site." The king's tone was urgent.

Sofia rose immediately, following him upstairs. Max switched out with another guard—it was already three o'clock.

Agneta was waiting for her with a mourning dress.

"You heard, then," Sofia said.

"Let's get you changed," Agneta said. "I'm sorry you're going through this, Sofia. Your mother never wanted you to face it. The Sonne just about broke her."

Sofia's eyes widened, and her frown grew. "Really?"

"She mourned every life lost. She had hoped... Well, let's get you changed. We need to hurry."

Sofia finished dressing, then shrouded herself in a dark cloak. "Could you please bring the white röggvarfeldur blanket over from the first room of the guest wing?"

Agneta's brow furrowed, but she nodded.

The king returned, his chainmail covering his dark leather padding underneath. He and Sofia exited the castle.

With an entourage of guards, they continued down the path, past the gates, and into the forest. The farther they walked, the more muted the sound of the waves along the beach became. The smell of saltwater faded, replaced by the fresh scent of the forest. Eventually, the only sounds left were wind rustling through the trees, birds calling and cackling above them, and bugs buzzing in the grass and among the reeds. Sofia's feet sank slightly when they crossed the cushy, damp moss patch. Their quiet walk calmed her thoughts for the first time since she'd watched the champions depart. They wandered along the dirt path past small hills—burial mounds, built around all the tall trees, wholly covered in thick, green grass. A large pile of dirt sat next to four freshly dug holes.

Four graves—for four champions.

Sofia followed the king to the first grave. Two guards stepped into the hole and emptied their bags. Out came iron cups and plates and bowls, silver jewelry, tapestries, linen and wool clothing, leather shoes, and a variety of other things Jostein would need as he traveled to Valhalla. They carefully laid the items against the first walls, leaving space for the body. When they finished, they climbed out and took their places at the foot of the grave.

Wind rustled the leaves of the treetops. Sofia watched them sway, ignoring the graves, pretending she was tucked in her room.

Finally, three guards cloaked in red carried Jostein's body down the path. They laid it out in the grave, then pulled his head out of a bag and placed it on his neck, his face turned east to watch the sunrise. A fourth guard followed with Jostein's weapons and bag, passing the items down to the guards, who laid them out with Jostein's body and moved the other goods closer, allowing for easy access during the journey. Once the guards had the grave settled, they picked up wooden shovels and piled up the dirt until it reached Sofia's waist.

The king stepped toward the mound. "May Odin welcome Jostein to Valhalla."

The guards cheered, per protocol. Hands clasped together, Sofia stood silently by, hoping Jostein would find what he was looking for, thankful it wasn't Karsten.

"Only three more to go, kjære," her father whispered somberly, offering his arm. She grabbed it, and together they walked back to the castle.

In the Great Hall, Sofia draped her cloak across the empty bench—the space Karsten had taken up.

A couple of Parliament members had congregated at a table in the corner, but the hall was otherwise empty.

Her father joined her once he'd removed his armor, taking his seat at the head of the table. "I'd like to say this all gets easier, but I don't think it will."

Servants brought out two glasses of wine and two plates of bread, chicken, and roasted vegetables. No point in bringing out full platters now that the champions were gone. Sofia took a few bites, but it had no taste.

"Are the plans for Victorsfest and the coronation finished?" the king asked.

Guilt tightened Sofia's chest. *A princess serves her kingdom wholeheartedly.* "Not quite, but I've reviewed the menu with the kitchen. And most of Parliament will be here already."

He frowned. "We can't have any delays. I let Chief Ragnar know the victor would arrive with reinforcements next week, in addition to the warriors who left this morning."

"We'll be ready."

She glanced up at the gods, thinking back to quiet nights curled up with her mother. Mamma would cradle the key to the castle, always keeping it in her pocket, as the temporary head of the household. They both hoped for Pappa's speedy return, so she could give the key back. So he'd be home.

Next week, Sofia would be looking for a new home or holding the key, worrying about her partner's new battle—though she barely knew how to get through this one.

After middag, she returned to her room, determined to serve her kingdom.

The white röggvarfeldur blanket lay on her bed, waiting for her. She ran her hands across the soft fleece, then wrapped it around her shoulders, inhaling what was left of Karsten's scent.

Outside, there wasn't a cloud in the sky; the ground was dry for the first time all week. Instead, the floor inside became wet as a tear fell silently to the wooden floor.

NICO MADE HIS WAY ALONG THE FJORD, hopping across the falls, scaling the boulders, looking for Skip. He was over halfway back to where they'd dropped Skip off, but there was no sign of him. Was he hiding, waiting to attack? Was he more confident than he'd let on? Maybe he wanted to get a kill in before Valhalla…

The wretched sound of vomiting came from around the bend.

"Skip," Nico called, climbing to where his partner lay, curled into a ball on one of the flatter rocks.

Skip wiped the vomit from his mouth, his brow coated in sweat. "Sorry, I didn't quite make it to—"

"No, it's fine, Skip. Let's find shelter, and you can sleep it off. We will worry about the Sonne in the morning." They weren't on a timeline. Some of the past champions had dragged out the Sonne for weeks, camping out and plotting their attacks carefully. Dag wouldn't let it go on that long, but one day wouldn't hurt. All the pair needed was a safe place to spend the night.

Ignoring the stench, Nico helped Skip rise to his feet and wash off in the water.

"Let's leave the heavy stuff here and grab it tomorrow," Nico said. They piled their equipment—chainmail, helmets, shields, and spears—safely behind the rocks, then began their ascent.

While it wasn't easy, the climb was beautiful. The mountains in the distance were tinted blue through the haze. The tallest peaks were capped with hints of snow, reminding him of Fryse.

When Skip lagged, Nico slowed to match his pace. At the precipice, they found a cairn. Nico approached the rock pile and studied the markings on its base. "I wonder if this is one of the piles Sofia helped stack."

Skip's eyebrows rose. "What was Sofia doing out here?"

"Camping with her father and brother."

"She doesn't seem outdoorsy."

"They stopped camping after Filip's death. It sounded more like her father was preparing Filip for the Sonne." None of them would stand a chance if Filip had been alive. Nico definitely wouldn't have competed. He scanned the fjord. "Dag was crossing the tops of the cliffs, so we should probably go a bit further, just in case."

Skip nodded weakly.

"You okay?" Nico asked.

"Sure." He wiped the sweat from his brow. "I could use water."

They walked away from the fjord. Small birds called out from the sparse trees that populated the mossy landscape, and wind rustled the leaves. White baby's breath reached above the grass, but purple bellflowers hid within it.

Nico listened closely. Through the light breeze, burbling water caught his attention. He moved slowly toward the sound, jumping back when the ground gave out beneath his foot. "Found some."

Barely two feet wide, the stream was half-covered with brush and moss. He pulled the foliage away, then fished the leather waterskin from his backpack and filled it.

Skip sat on the grass. Nico took his waterskin, filled it, and sat next to him. Skip gulped the water greedily. Nico took a few more sips of water, losing himself to the melody of the stream mixed with the whispers of the wind, brushing his hand along the tops of the reeds. Once Skip had drunk all the water, color slowly returned to his cheeks. He chuckled quietly.

Nico followed his gaze, but all he saw was a boulder covered in moss. "What's so amusing?"

"The pile of rocks. It looks like a giant."

When he squinted, Nico could see it. "I suppose. But why is it funny?"

"Four of us are leaving Midgard, you know?"

"But for Valhalla, not Jotunheim."

Skip shrugged, remaining quiet.

Nico took his axe out of his backpack. "I'm going to pile up a few of the tree trunks against the rocks. We'll take advantage of the overhang." It would be a fine shelter, just for the night. Enough to protect them from the creatures and the other champions. "You can supervise. I'll get this sorted."

"Sounds good." Skip lay back in the grass, entertaining Nico with stories of his travels as Nico built their shelter.

Soft cries, clicks, and barks called out from behind him. Two baby foxes hid in a small den in a hollowed-out tree, calling out to their mother.

"Skip." Nico moved to him, then pointed toward the den.

He smiled when he saw the pair. "They sound like my brothers."

"Mine too. My mamma used to send all three of us outside when they complained. In the winter, we'd build fortresses in the snow and throw snowballs at each other for hours."

Skip rolled to his side. "My brothers and I did that too."

"A rite of passage."

Once Nico deemed the shelter acceptable, he helped Skip inside, setting up the backpacks as pillows.

"Are you hungry?" Nico asked. "I'm going to find some food."

"Not really. I probably can't keep it down anyway." He looked rather pale again.

"Get some sleep. We can wait until late morning to head back. Karsten and Dag should have found each other by then. If the fates are on our side, maybe they'll have killed each other."

"Oh, to be so fortunate."

Nico left him to rest, finding blackberry bushes near the stream. He ate as he picked them, enjoying the tart, earthy taste as the sun painted the sky with its fire. A light wind blew the grass and reeds across the darkening landscape. The air was getting chillier. Was a fire worth the risk? No—Jostein would probably sleep tonight, but Karsten or Dag would see the flame if they were out hunting.

Back in the shelter, Nico crawled next to Skip and settled in. Skip didn't stir; light snores escaped from his throat. Warmth emanated from him, and his brow was coated in sweat again. This wasn't just a sickness from imbibing.

Nico closed his eyes uneasily. He finally admitted to himself that his worry wasn't just because he needed Skip to help take down the other champions.

THE DARKNESS WEIGHED HEAVILY ON DAG as she meandered along the moonlit fjord. Her sharp eyes caught motion along the edge of the cliff, sending a rush of adrenaline through her.

A fox.

Hungry, Dag pulled out her dagger and hit her mark effortlessly. The fox fell with a guttural bark.

If only it had been another champion...

She pulled her dagger out, wiped off the blood, and tucked it back into her boot.

Raw fox meat sounded tough and unappetizing after being spoiled by the food from the castle. She looked around, debating whether to start a fire. *No signs of motion, other than the fox. But Karsten, Nico, and Skip are still out there...*

Nico and Skip were together by now. If they were smart, they'd find camp for the night, and one of them would guard. Sitting birds, if she just had the energy to find them. No risk of them stumbling on her fire. *Karsten, though...*

She was confident she'd traveled at least twenty-five miles along the fjord, although every step of the last half had seemed twice as long. That would put her in line with the third drop, but they must have gone north. Probably safe, but she'd keep watch.

Dag climbed partway up the cliff, grabbed a small, dead tree, and pulled it back to the beach. She snapped it apart as quietly as she could, piled the branches, and broke a few apart for kindling. She listened closely, but all she could hear were the waves and the wind.

After carving the end of a branch into a point, she lit a small fire; it caught with practiced ease. As her eyes adjusted to the light, Dag was keenly aware the fire gave away her position.

She sliced meat from the fox, stabbed it with her knife, held it over the flames, and thought about Jostein. Dag had sized him up as the second greatest threat, yet he'd never intended to be the king—he'd become a champion, intending to die.

To feel so low; so empty; so useless, with no one left to care for.

Still, he had been patient and understanding. He'd made an effort to connect with her, even when he was rejected. Even when all the champions had ignored him.

Dag knew the feeling of victory; this was not it. This was not conquering enemies and grinding their bones to dust. Jostein's death seemed senseless. She had made her first kill and was one step closer to becoming the victor—but it was not worth celebrating.

His empty eyes. His invisible scars.

She'd re-lived their conversation a dozen times during her walk, confused by how much the emptiness weighed. The heaviness resided deep within her.

Once the fox was cooked through, she finished off the tough meat, then stomped out the fire and listened closely as her eyes adjusted to the moonlight.

Still just the wind and waves.

The world felt empty. She wished her thoughts would follow.

Dag shook her head. *Focus.*

She couldn't stay on the beach. It would make her an easy target come first light. Dag grabbed her bag and climbed the cliff. A quarter mile in, an oak tree braced itself against the wind. She climbed up the branches and settled in. There, she allowed herself to drift toward sleep, her thoughts pulling her into deep dreams.

THE CASTLE FELT EMPTY.

Sofia finished writing the last of her correspondence by the light of the fire. Seven missives for camps in Morge, eleven directives for farms in Hamme, three quick notes for shipyards in Sander, nineteen memos for Parliament members, and...

Her shoulders slumped. She set her pen down on her desk. There was no filling the gaping hole her mother and Filip had left behind, and ten years had taught her that. But here she was, trying to fill the void left by Karsten's departure, as though it could be any different this time.

The last few wildflowers in the vase—the ones that hadn't been braided into her crown for Championsfest—brought her back to ten years ago, the first time Karsten had snuck flowers into her room. She'd noticed the blooms after stripping off her mourning dress and throwing it angrily to the floor. They were the sole bright spot when everything else was dark, when nothing could be fixed. But Karsten had tried anyway. For weeks after the funerals, he had continued sneaking in flowers from his mother's garden, blushing a bright crimson the day Sofia caught him filling the vase. He'd said it was nothing, but since that moment, he'd been helping heal a piece of her. Karsten was everything.

She blinked a tear away and changed into a wool nightshirt before crawling into bed. Buried beneath the white röggvarfeldur blanket, Sofia watched the fire crackle.

RUSTLING LEAVES STARTLED DAG FROM HER SLEEP.

Her adrenaline spiked. Her palms began to sweat. The rustling stopped, but it had come from the bushes fifteen feet to her left.

Focus. She hadn't moved, so they probably hadn't seen her in the darkness. Moving too fast might alert them to her presence.

Weapons. Her dagger was in her right boot, easy to access. Her sword was sheathed at her side. The shield was strapped to her back. Her spear was hidden in the grass near the tree.

Plan. Her dagger never missed its mark, and she was a Valkyrie with her sword. Throw dagger, jump, sword out, smite down hard.

Karsten will die.

Dag pulled out her dagger. She listened carefully, but the world was silent. Motionless.

Was I just imagining the rustling?

She watched the moonlit bushes closely.

There! Her dagger flew toward the rustling leaves. She launched from the tree, landed hard, and whipped her sword out.

"Oof!" came from the bushes, the voice low.

She raced toward the sound, ready to take them out.

They're surprised—this is my shot!

She raised her blade, circled the bush, and—

"A troll?" Dag stopped.

Lowering her sword, she stared at the little rock creature. He was barely up to her knees. His head was as big as the rest of his body. Dark, round eyes watched her from beneath dark, fuzzy eyebrows that matched his dark, fuzzy hair. His nose was long and large on his wrinkly face, and his pointed ears were as big as his hands.

"Hi. I think you…" The troll looked down at the dagger sticking straight out of its mossy coat. "You might have dropped this?" He gestured to the dagger, watching her closely. "Do you, maybe, want it back?"

Dag gaped, blinking. "Right. Sorry. Yes, sorry. Please."

Well, I hit my mark…

She sheathed her sword quickly, grabbed the dagger's handle, jerked the weapon out of the troll's mossy coat, and tucked it back into her boot. "Sorry about that."

The troll shrugged, like it was an everyday occurrence. Maybe it was.

Dag bit her lip. "Aren't you a bit... small for a troll?"

The troll glared back at her, baring its teeth. "So you attack me, then insult me?"

Her jaw dropped.

The troll chortled. "I'm teasing. You're probably thinking of the giants. They were banished from Midgard ages ago—back to Jotunheim. So you don't have to worry."

Dag nodded. "Right. Of course."

Because I didn't even know trolls were real, so of course I was worrying about the giants. Gods, am I even awake right now?

"Wait," she said, "have you been following me the last week?"

The troll averted his eyes and shifted uncomfortably.

All those rustling leaves—it was you.

"The spirits brought me to you." The troll's head tilted. "Why do you look confused?"

Reasons.

Dag rubbed the sleep out of her eyes. "What spirits?"

"The gods have angered them with silly games, and Yggdrasil is no longer in balance."

Dag eyed him warily. *I really just wanted to sleep.*

He sighed. "Come with me."

She grabbed her spear from the grass. The little troll grabbed her hand.

"Where are we going?" she asked.

"You'll see."

The little troll carried on silently, pulling her along. They were moving inland, away from the fjord, passing trees and brush, padding quietly along the mossy ground. Finally, they entered a small clearing.

Dag studied the empty space. *Nothing of note.*

The little troll walked into the middle. "Come out!"

Another small troll poked her head out from behind a tree, barely lit by the moonlight.

I'm losing my mind.

Dag waved to her, and she hesitantly stepped into the clearing. Six more trolls crept out of hiding, and soon Dag was surrounded.

"It's her!"

"It's Dagny!"

"She's here!"

Dag took in their excited faces. "How do you know me?"

How do you exist?

One of the trolls pulled on Dag's tunic, then pointed up. "Look."

With a dreamy hum, wisps and crystals of light slowly filled the sky above the clearing.

"What's this?" Dag asked.

"Watch," the little troll demanded.

The lights formed a scene of ships storming across seas of blue light, surrounded by Jormungand. The sailors attacked each other ruthlessly.

A shudder ran through Dag. The trolls began circling around her and singing "The Song of Ragnarök" in round, their voices creating layers of a terrifying harmony. *Vitality, the troll drinks... He paints with blood... And the weather mightily storms...*"

Turning orange, the scene morphed into a fiery hellscape. The lights grew brighter and brighter, the ruthless fighting stark against the black sky. Dag trembled, her hands shaking.

The lights continued to paint scenes of brutality.

As the first hints of the sunrise climbed over the horizon, the spirits began to fade, though the trolls kept singing in round.

"Keep fighting, Dagny," one of the trolls squeaked, "so you can become the queen you were meant to be."

The rays of the sun began to turn the trolls back to stone, until only one voice remained. *"See, Ragnarök will come. It's the fate of the gods."*

Nico stirred, his eyes closed against the morning sun. It was only beginning its journey across the sky, brightening the world slowly. He missed his bed in the castle, missed the piles of blankets against the chill—but the quiet delighted him. No loud family, no creaky wood of the castle, no snoring... No snoring? "Skip?"

Nico opened his eyes, blinking away the sleep.

Skip lay next to him. He hadn't moved since last night.

He wasn't moving. His chest didn't rise. His lips were tinged blue.

Ice flooded Nico's veins. "Skip!"

Nico shakily placed a hand on Skip's forehead. It was cool, no longer feverish. Skip had died in the night. His body wasn't yet stiffening, but it wouldn't be long.

"No," Nico whispered, biting his lip. "No, no, no..."

His partner was gone—and he hadn't died fighting. Skip hadn't earned his place in Valhalla. There would be no glory for him—the sickly were sent to Helheim. Nico would never see him again. Hel would never let Skip go, not after she had him in her clutches.

Nico punched the ground, then slumped in defeat.

Skip would still get his grave. Nico could see to that. He'd carry Skip's body back to the fjord and make sure the guards brought it back to the castle for a proper burial, fit for a champion. Then he'd face whoever remained in the fjords—alone. He couldn't give up; he had plenty of time to figure out a new strategy.

Nico put on his backpack and hoisted Skip's body over his shoulder, then carried it back across the mountain, every step heavier than the last.

At the precipice near the cairn, Nico scanned the fjords. Other than the waves, he didn't see any motion. Slowly, sliding along carefully with Skip's body, he made his way down the side of the cliff, checking around the bend for the other champions. Still no one, to his relief.

He laid out Skip's body on the rocks, then gathered Skip's weapons from where they were hidden and laid them nearby. The guards would see the body as they traveled the fjord; they'd be looking for it.

Exhausted, Nico washed off in the cool water. His safest option was to climb the mountain and figure out a new plan.

He gathered his weapons, strapped them on, and returned to Skip's body. Were Fryse's burial rites appropriate? "Well, Skip…"

Footsteps sounded from around the bend. Nico hid behind the rocks, his best chance of survival. Hopefully they'd walk on.

Karsten came around the bend, his eyes widening when he saw Skip's body. He looked around, but Nico ducked before he could catch sight of him.

Rocks grated against each other—Karsten was kneeling. "I've been looking for you all night. Where's your partner?" After a beat of silence, Karsten said, "Skip… you should have chosen better."

Anger nipped at Nico. He was a good partner. He'd carried Skip across the—

The stones scraped again. Karsten was rising. His footsteps approached Nico's hiding space. If Nico didn't do something, Karsten would find him—and end him.

Nico had the element of surprise. Could he take on Karsten alone? He swallowed, adrenaline coursing through him.

Clasping his shield and spear, Nico darted out and raced toward Karsten.

Eyes wide, Karsten raised his spear and deflected Nico's attack, shifting left and hitting back with a grunt. He thrust his spear toward Nico, then pulled out his sword and sliced the tip of Nico's spear clean off, leaving a deep cut on Nico's arm.

Karsten's eyes raged with an icy fire, terrifying and godlike.

Nico threw the useless shaft down, his fist clenched around the shield. Without a plan, he'd never take Karsten down. He needed a new strategy if there was any chance of winning.

He turned around—and ran.

Ran like his life depended on it. His arm throbbed, but he couldn't stop now.

Adrenaline pushed him forward. He risked a quick glance back. Karsten wasn't following; he was watching from beside Skip's body, his look cold and calculating. Nico sped up, eager to put distance between them. His lungs screamed; his throat cried for water; his arm needed stitches.

When he felt safe with the distance, he filled the waterskin at a waterfall and drank desperately. The iron smell of his own blood left him lightheaded. After washing off, he reached for his needle case, grasping at air—the case was back in the armory. Clenching his fists, he let out a breath of frustration. He'd have to stitch his arm back at the castle. He couldn't let the Sonne go on too long then...

With his knife, he sliced some fabric from the bottom of his tunic, then wrapped his arm tightly, taking a moment to think. He needed a plan. Fjorden needed him.

Without Skip, he didn't stand a chance against Karsten or Dag. And Karsten hadn't chased him.

Karsten... hadn't...

Dag was still out there. He had to move.

Grabbing his things, he sped along the edge of the water, moving forward as he glanced behind.

Dag appeared directly in front of him—like magic.

Nico raised his shield, ready to fight. Her spear blasted through his chainmail.

NICO'S BLOOD SPILLED INTO THE WAVES at Dag's feet, his dead body splashing in the water. *Slow and stiff, like always.*

And alone... what happened to Skip?

Dag washed her hands of Nico's blood and pulled her spear from his body. *The sheer terror on Nico's face... Karsten is close.*

She continued along the shore, lulled by the alternating crunch of rocky beach and the pad of her shoes against the boulders. Despite being exhausted, she had this. *The trolls agree.*

She considered everything she knew about Karsten. He was fast, so she had to be faster. He was strong, so she had to be stronger. He was brave, so she had to be fearless. And he was consistent, though he'd skipped his morning run yesterday...

It was no secret that Karsten would do anything for Sofia, but he still had to send Dag to Valhalla to win—and she wouldn't make it easy. Dag would be the victor, and she'd live a long and glory-filled life before taking her place in the Royal Circle of Valhalla.

A mile down the fjord, she stopped at the base of a roaring waterfall, cupped her hands, and drank deeply, relieved by the slight respite. Once she'd had her fill, she gathered her things, then noticed Karsten walking her way. *Surely he'll stop for water too...*

Dag ducked behind boulders next to the falls, peeking out. She'd get him while he was preoccupied. *My timing has to be perfect.*

After looking around the falls, he set his spear down, then moved toward the water. With slight hesitation, Karsten pulled something out of his pocket. A scrap of fabric—small, white, a brown border...

Her eyes narrowed. *The princess's favor.*

But it didn't matter. The kingdom would be hers, Sofia would be hers, and the other champions would be dancing in the halls of Valhalla. She had this. *And Karsten's distracted.*

Dag readied her shield, gripped her spear, and rushed forward, leaping across the rocks at the base of the falls to the other side. Too fast, Karsten whipped his sword out, shifting and putting a forceful hit directly on her shield. The clang of the metal echoed in the fjord. *Helvete—not fast enough.*

He avoided her spear, landing another powerful hit with his sword. She stabbed at him with the spear again, but it grazed off his chainmail. He ducked to the side and swung back at her.

I'm better with my blade.

She threw her spear in the water—where he couldn't reach it—and whipped out her sword in the same breath, slicing it at him. Dag aimed for Karsten's neck. He raised his sword to block. She smashed through the metal, but he dodged a direct hit. Karsten tossed the remnants to the ground, falling back hastily. She had him on the—

Ducking, he picked up his spear, aiming it at her. She narrowly evaded, his spear grazing her shield. Anger seared through her. She had pushed him to the weapon that made him the deadliest.

He stabbed at her repeatedly and pushed her back toward the slippery rocks of the waterfall. She aimed her sword at him—but he had the advantage of attacking from a distance. She couldn't get close enough for the kill.

Dag slid on the wet stones, and her head hit the wall of the cliff—she tasted blood. Karsten knocked her sword right out of her hands. She threw her shield at him, aiming for his face. He raised his arm to block; it bought her precious seconds.

She couldn't outrun him—but she could climb.

Dag scurried up the cliff. Karsten followed, but he was slower, less agile.

Raindrops began falling through the sunshine, increasing the slippage, slowing Karsten down. She made it to the top of the waterfall and pulled out her dagger.

This ends now.

Karsten climbed over the ledge, his spear aimed at her.

One chance to win.

Thunder crackled, shaking the world.

Dag lunged for Karsten's neck as he plunged the spear into her side. She forced her dagger down, her weight throwing him off balance.

He fell into the water below while she tumbled onto the rocks. Her side continued to bleed. She watched the red puddle grow beside her.

The clopping of horse hooves echoed in the fjord, the sound unexpected. Moments later, the creature stood in front of her, its hooves a light gray and its legs a bright white.

The rider dismounted, their feet clad in golden leather sandals with wings at the tops. Their red dress billowed out. Sienna skin covered the well-defined muscles of their legs. The sword at their side had wings along the guard.

Suddenly, Dag found herself lifted up, looking out over ivory wings, her feet dangling in the air.

"Let's get you back to Valhalla."

WITH A PEN IN HER HAND, Sofia sat at her desk, the plans for Victorsfest and the coronation laid out in front of her.

"Sofia," her father said from the doorway. "Come downstairs for middag."

Her stomach in knots, Sofia glanced at Skadi and Njord crossing the ceiling above. "I've still got some work to do."

His frown deepened. "We can't have you wasting away."

Sighing, she rose and followed him to the Great Hall. They settled in at the head table. Servants scurried over with plates of fresh fish and vegetables.

"Day two for our champions," her father said.

Sofia swallowed the lump in her throat. Between the four, it would surely come down to Karsten and Dag; but the pair were a close match, and Dag was out for blood...

A guard entered the hall and walked straight to her father. As they whispered, her father's face fell. With sad eyes, he studied Sofia, his expression strained.

And her heart shattered into a million shards.

She let out a choked sob. Her hands covered her mouth as her father flew to her side. She hadn't told Karsten how much she cared, hadn't said goodbye—and now she couldn't.

Karsten was gone.

He'd been the cairn guiding her, the balm soothing her, the ropes tying her together. Now he was gone, wiped from Midgard.

You and me, he'd whispered. It felt like a broken promise.

Her father's arms were around her—he'd picked her up and started carrying her upstairs. She wrapped her arms around his neck and buried her face in his shoulder, soaking it with tears. He held her close, rocked her. "Sofia... my kjære daughter..."

Keening, she could barely breathe through the pain. Her tears streamed like a waterfall for all she'd lost. "I knew," she choked out, sobbing harder.

Seconds, minutes, later...

Her breathing steadied. *A princess doesn't break.* She needed to help run the kingdom for...

"Has Dag returned?" she whispered.

Her father swallowed, then shook his head. "All five champions are dead."

Sofia's heart broke all over again, splitting into pieces smaller than she knew possible.

SOFIA WOKE TO DARKNESS, wrapped under her blankets, still dressed in her day linens. She reached for the röggvarfeldur blanket and pulled it closer to her. The tears continued to fall as she drifted in and out of consciousness. When tendrils of orange snaked across the sky, Sofia abandoned her restless sleep. She breathed through her pain, grasping at reality. There was no option except to face the day—even though the gods were putting her through Ragnarök.

"Max," her father said from the hallway, his voice muffled by the closed door.

He opened it, then entered and sat beside her. Taking her hand, he held it gently. "We buried Dag, Skip, and Nico last night. It would have been disrespectful to delay their send-off to Valhalla as champions."

She'd failed in her duty to be there. "Karsten?"

"The servants started preparing a fifth mound late last night, but we need to pull items for the grave. Do you want to help?"

Sofia didn't want to, because the Sonne wasn't supposed to go this way. She took a deep breath. "Yes."

"Okay. The guards can take items from the castle. Tell Max what to bring." Her father hesitated. "We have an order of business as well, kjære. No victor... well, it puts Fjorden in a bad position. I tried to delay until tomorrow, but Parliament called an emergency session for two o'clock this afternoon."

And she needed to run Parliament. It was her responsibility. "Of course, Pappa. I'll prepare this morning."

"Thank you, Sofia." He sighed and closed his eyes, rubbing the bridge of his wide nose. "I might have to go to Morge myself."

"Right." Sofia took a deep breath, blinking back tears. "The king should be there."

"There's often unrest when a new ruler takes the throne, but now with no one in line..." Her father stood. "I'm sorry, Sofia. I don't know how to fix this. Any of this."

Sofia nodded, then looked out the window. Light raindrops tapped on the glass—Thor announcing his presence. Why hadn't he been looking out for Karsten? Karsten had been carrying his pendant and her favor. Thor's hammer had been with him.

Agneta entered with a bowl of strawberries. "Are you hungry?" she asked tentatively.

Food wouldn't fill the emptiness. "Thank you. You can put them on the desk. I'll be out of bed soon."

She placed the strawberries near the vase of wildflowers and left with the laundry—a stark reminder that life went on.

Sofia studied the wilting pink buds, then forced herself to focus on her task. "Max, let's start with the röggvarfeldur blanket." She crawled out of bed, then folded the blanket with painstaking care. "Does Karsten need weapons?"

"The guards were able to retrieve all of his..." Max drifted off, his expression somber.

One thing settled. "And his backpack had clothes, so no need to visit the armory."

Sofia crossed the hallway under Max's watchful gaze, stopping in front of the door that had remained closed for ten years. She took a deep breath, then opened it, the iron hinges creaking.

Filip's wooden sheep stood by the window, ready to charge. She walked over to it, petting the soft wool on its back. The only enemy that could have reached Filip in his room was the wind—but he fought against it valiantly.

On top of the shelves, she found her target. "Max, would you please pull down the hnefatafl game?"

He retrieved it, then resumed his post in the hall. She blew dust off the wooden box, admiring the ships carved into the top. Inside, she found the old ivory pieces. She picked up the king, held the weight in her hand.

"Why hnefatafl?" Max asked.

"War strategy. Karsten loved it." Sofia swallowed. "He played with Filip sometimes, when he was off duty." She put the king back in the box and closed it. "Most of the guards didn't want Filip tagging along, but Karsten never seemed to mind."

Max smiled sadly. "It was always amusing when Filip swung his wooden sword around. The prince had better form than most of the warriors in the trelleborg."

"Sounds about right." Laughing wistfully, she stepped out of Filip's bedroom, closing the door behind her. "We need items from the kitchen."

With the blanket and game in her hands, Sofia greeted Inga, then set the items on the counter. "We need a few things for the burial. Cups, spoons, knives, plates. Solid iron, please. The decorated set."

"I'm sorry for how everything turned out." Inga found a basket, then moved toward the cabinets. "You know, I had hoped Karsten would win—after I actually met him. He seemed like he would be a thoughtful partner for you."

"You mean when we bumbled around the cellar together?"

Karsten's last day as her guard—the day she decided to move the Sonne forward a month, rather than risk her father, all for nothing. The king would be on his way to Morge soon anyway, leaving her with the castle's key. Her chest tightened.

Inga shook her head. "No, when he brought in almonds."

Sofia's jaw slackened. "When was this?"

"The day the champions arrived. He'd found almonds in the market for the marzipan cake and brought them to me first thing in the morning."

Sofia stared silently as Inga continued to gather the items and fill the basket, the hollow space inside her heart growing. Once Inga finished, Sofia and Max went to the library, items in hand. Fighting back tears, she stopped in front of the tapestry of Yggdrasil and studied Asgard, hoping Karsten would enjoy Valhalla.

"I want to add the tapestry to the pile." Sofia tried to pull it off the wall, but it didn't budge.

"Princess, the servants or the guards can take it down."

Sofia pulled harder—Karsten needed it.

"Princess, they can help." Max's voice cracked.

Sofia pulled with all her strength. The nails popped out of the wall, and the tapestry came down on her. She fell to her knees, the tapestry covering half her body as she clung to it.

"Max, what's wrong?" The king's voice pulled her back, his footsteps fast approaching. Her father's arms wrapped around her, pulled her out from beneath the fabric. "Max, take it out."

Through tears, Sofia watched Max remove the tapestry from the library.

"We need to head down for the burial," her father said.

Sofia allowed him to help her up. He guided her back to her room, where Agneta was waiting with a shift and cloak. Once she was dressed, he collected her, steadying her on the walk.

Light rain left a sprinkling of water over the grass. Birds chirped, leaves rustled in the breeze, and the forest welcomed them. At the burial site, four fresh mounds of dirt waited for time to cover them with grass and reeds. Two guards stood by a fifth grave, watching over Karsten's body. The rest of the guards circled the gravesite. Max stayed close, his presence a small comfort. Sofia and her father stopped at the head of the grave.

While pale, Karsten could have been asleep on the tapestry, washed clean of blood. Dag's dagger had pierced his neck, the way Dag had taught her. His death would have been quick—Sofia's only solace.

"Do you want a moment?" her father asked her.

Sofia nodded and put on a stoic face, and her father helped her down into the grave. She touched Karsten's hand, then reared back—it was cold and stiff.

The handkerchief was tucked into his belt. She folded it and placed it on his chest, letting her hand linger, kissing his cheek.

Her father helped her up, and she held onto him as the guards filled the grave with dirt.

King Eirik stepped forward when they finished, shouting the customary, "May Odin welcome Karsten to Valhalla."

The guards cheered half-heartedly. Sofia watched in silence. As she gazed at the five fresh mounds, the reality of the situation hit her: This would throw the kingdom into turmoil.

In silence, they walked back to the castle.

Sofia went directly to her desk and scribbled down an agenda for Parliament—the priority was establishing a new ruler. She nibbled on strawberries while she focused on her work. The sky outside darkened, threatening heavy rain.

At a quarter to two, Sofia stacked her notes and walked to the library. Half of Parliament was already seated when she entered. As they argued about the best course of action, she took her place at the head of the table, watching quietly as the rest of the members trickled in. Finally, the king entered and took his place.

Sofia rose, saying, "Velkommen, welcome, welcome."

No one turned. Instead, their voices became louder, speaking over each other, the concern for Fjorden clear.

The king stood up, his chainmail jangling. "Time to begin!"

The room quieted. The only sound left was the tapping of the rain against the windows. He sat back down.

Sofia nodded a quick thanks. "Now, as you're all aware, the Sonne didn't turn out—"

Thunder interrupted her, shaking the castle.

She blinked away her surprise. "Apologies." She straightened her dress. "The Sonne didn't turn out as expected. In an effort to move forward, let's—"

Thunder crashed again, and a guard slammed the library doors open. "Attack from the water!"

Chairs scraped against the wooden floor, chainmail clinked, and footsteps pounded as the Parliament members scrambled to their feet. "Get to the boats!"

Feet stuck to the floor, Sofia couldn't move. Cold metal pressed into her trembling hand.

"Sofia, take this," the king said.

"What?"

"Get upstairs," he demanded.

"Pappa?"

"I'm going to fight." He rushed to the wall of the library and pulled down a helmet and a spear.

"What?" She couldn't blink, couldn't breathe.

"Max! Take her upstairs!"

"Wait, Pappa!" she cried out.

Max grabbed her arm and pulled her toward the door. "Princess, we have to go."

Sofia stumbled out of the library and up the stairs, entering her room in a daze. Max urged her forward, guarding her from behind while the thunder roared. She opened her hand, looking at the castle's key. Its handle ended in a circle full of Yggdrasil's branches.

"Take this." Max placed his dagger on top of the key, the weight snapping her back to reality. "Listen to me." He gripped her arm and looked her in the eye. "Lock the door and do not open it."

Unable to speak, she nodded. Max stepped back into the hallway with his spear at the ready. She set the dagger on the bench, then closed and locked the door.

Rushing to the window, she clenched the key in her hand. The fjord was being taken over by green sails as far out as she could see. Swaymark had tricked them with a false message planted on a dead body, luring the warriors away, leaving Aldersfoss weak and exposed.

Fjorden's warriors scrambled along the beach and the docks, preparing the ships. The first launched—filled with warriors. Two more ships quickly followed and aimed for Swaymark's fleet. The red sails rose mightily, and they took off at full speed.

Sofia dared to hope.

Warriors hustled from the trelleborg, their number depleted by the fortifications sent to Morge.

The first of the ships neared Swaymark's fleet, the warriors preparing to attack. Swaymark's ship tried to tack around, but Fjorden was ready. Fjorden's ship sailed next to Swaymark's, and warriors jumped ships, spears ready for blood.

Pounding rain drowned out the battle cries. Sofia's heart sank as bodies fell into the water from both sides, turning the fjord red. More of Fjorden's ships launched, aiming to cut off Swaymark's fleet. Fjorden was holding them off.

From among the green sails emerged a giant ship—the Kronan. Swaymark's flagship. Prince Magnus was leading the attack.

Sofia's blood ran cold. Dread pulsed through her as she watched helplessly, unable to find her father in the melee.

Two of Fjorden's ships steered for the Kronan, their warriors launching onto the deck. Green sails broke through the line of red, aiming for the shore at full speed.

Warriors on the beach readied their line, preparing to fight. When the ships landed, Fjorden's warriors fought back. They held the shield wall, spearing their attackers, but Swaymark's warriors broke the line and aimed for the castle.

With all her might, Sofia pushed the bench in front of the locked door, then clasped the key.

She caught sight of her father on the deck of the Kronan—a head above the rest of the warriors. Releasing a breath, she locked her eyes on his towering form. He pushed his opponent toward the water and charged forward with his spear.

Footsteps sounded from the hallway. As she faced the door, Sofia's heart pounded with every clang of metal against metal. A grunt was followed by a thud, another grunt, and a sharp crash. A shout. Another thud. Then quiet.

"Max?" Sofia called.

"Shh. Don't come out."

Relief washed through her. She ran back to the window, looking for her father on the deck of the Kronan. The rain obscured her vision. Waves rocked the ships, and bodies continued to fall to their watery graves.

Her father's form was locked in battle against a warrior who equaled his stature. The opponent smashed their sword down, breaking the spear in her father's hand.

Sofia screamed, her throat raw.

Whipping out his own sword, her father fought back.

Multiple sets of footsteps pounded, echoing from the hallway. Metal clanged against metal, and a heavy crash shook the door. Wood splintered, followed by a hard thud against the floor—Max.

"She's in here!" yelled an unfamiliar voice.

They rattled the doorknob violently, but the lock held. Sofia's heart thrashed in her ears. There was no way to escape. With heavy battering, the door shook—and the bench with it—over and over, as loud as the thunder.

She scanned the body-strewn field. The Kronan was almost to the beach, and more ships had broken through Fjorden's line.

"Harder!" the voice yelled from the hallway.

Sofia clenched the key in her fist, terror pulsing through her. The metal bit into her skin.

The door cracked open with the next bang, knocking into the bench. Another bang sent the bench flying across the room. Four of Swaymark's warriors entered, stepping over Max's bloody body. "Take her alive."

Outside the window, the Kronan landed. Her father remained

locked in battle. His opponent's sword came down swiftly, slicing her father's head from his body.

Sofia cried out.

The key fell to the floor.

Part III

Freja collected her fallen herself,

and she welcomed them with generosity.

ALDERSFOSS

"Fight! Push! Take what's yours!"

The crowd's screams were loud, but Karsten focused on his father's voice. He held his wooden sword the way his father taught him—with a firm grip and a strong gait. His challenger ran toward him, taller and broader, but Karsten held his ground.

Raising his shield, Karsten blocked their strike with ease. He swung his sword at his challenger, getting in a hit on their shoulder and another on their arm. The crowd went wild, his father's cheers drowning them out.

Karsten pushed his challenger back, hitting their sides, getting around their shield. When they were backed against the fence, Karsten pointed his sword at their chest, looking up at them with a grin. He had won.

His father rushed to his side, picked him up, and hugged him. "Good job, son."

Karsten hugged his father back. "Can we eat now?"

He chuckled. "Sure. Let's find Mamma."

"Hey, Kjell," someone from the crowd said, "that was a great fight. How old is Karsten now?"

"Three and a quarter."

"He's going to be a Hel of a fighter."

His father grinned. "Takes after his old man."

Karsten held onto his father, smiling. He would make his father proud. He would prove his father right.

Twenty-two Years Later

The wind whipped around Karsten as he fell down, down, down, then splashed at the waterfall's base. The fjord pulled him under, and water filled his nose and mouth—but he didn't feel a thing.

Waves brought him to the base of the cliffs, pushing him gently onto the rocky shore. Birds called out from above. Motionless, he stared at the sunny sky.

His spear was missing from his hands. *Today, the overgrip,* his father had said all those years ago. *Arms bent, palms out, fingers curled. Shift your full body forward, and attack!* They'd practiced until he fell asleep on his feet, barely moving. Then his father had carried him to bed and tucked him in. It was the same routine the next day.

Karsten had relied on his exhaustive training and the practiced technique instilled by his father. But here he was, unable to move. His technique had failed him.

Had he given away his advantage, back on the sparring field?

Are you just going to stand there with your shield? Dag had asked—so nonchalant, but so arrogant. He'd waited for her to make the first move, watching her grow impatient. Her glare when he'd stood over her, poised to take her out... The day after, when she'd almost bested him with a training sword...

The sunlight warmed his skin; intrinsically, he knew this. Yet an icy chill gripped him, refusing to let go.

Karsten's mind drifted to Sofia; to her warm body, tucked against his. She was waiting back at the castle. It was supposed to be their home. He needed to get back to her.

A cart approached, rocks crunching below its squeaky wheels. But Karsten couldn't turn his head toward it. Soft purrs rumbled in his ear as the wagon stopped beside him. The rider jumped out, knelt beside him, and caressed his arm in a soothing motion. Their blond hair blocked the sun.

"Karsten," Sofia said.

No, not Sofia. She wasn't here. It wasn't her.

"Karsten," the woman said again.

A nose poked his cheek, turning his head toward the woman. Although her hair was the same shade as Sofia's, the similarities ended there. Sofia's blue-green eyes were wide and trusting, but these green eyes were narrow and sharp. Chiseled like a warrior, she was tall and proud in stature.

He knew her.

Karsten attempted to swallow, then tried to say *Freja*, but the sound was trapped in his throat. His loss washed over him; there would be no returning to the castle now.

"You can sit up," she said. "Do you want help?"

He flexed his fingers, then pressed his palms to the ground and pushed himself up slowly. The waves hummed along in the fjord, surrounded by the cliffs. He tried to swallow again, failing.

Freja reached for Karsten's neck. Eyes wide, he reared back.

"Hold still, and we'll just—" She grabbed Dag's dagger and yanked it from his neck, then handed it to him. "That's better."

"Thanks." He grimaced, tucking it into his belt. At least he could speak again.

"I realize that wasn't the most pleasant." Freja rose, ruffling the dark brown feathers along the collar of her cloak. She held her hand out and helped Karsten stand.

Her giant blue cat nudged him again and pawed at the ground. A second cat mewed, its snout covered with gray hair. Freja patted their heads and snapped her fingers. The harnessed pair stood at attention, ready to pull. Their yellow eyes studied him.

Freja stepped into the wooden chariot. Two shields rested on the edges, one on either side. Lined with gold, the chariot could comfortably hold two.

Karsten hesitated, gazing back at the fjord. He'd had Thor's hammer—both around his neck and on his handkerchief.

I hoped you would accept my favor.

I hoped, Sofia had started, as though there was any possibility he wouldn't. The neat, even stitches were the work of an artist. Brown thread lined the edges, and Thor's hammer rested in the corner, surrounded by pink wildflowers. Holding it, he'd stumbled over his response, couldn't correctly form words, could barely even remember to breathe. All he could think was, *It's me she wants.*

She cared for him, though she'd tried to protect herself—with all her loss, all her pain, he could understand why. But she'd shown him she was with him. She'd wanted Thor to be with him. She'd wanted him to return, even if she couldn't say the words.

"Time to go," Freja murmured.

Swallowing, he asked, "Wasn't Thor on my side?"

She scowled, a fierce rage in her eyes. "After he helped Eirik return to Ana-Sofia during the last Sonne, he tried to steal my thunder and call himself the god of lovers! Some *god of lovers*—that idiot was too busy stealing my favorite dress so he can break into Jotunheim."

Karsten stepped into the cart beside her. "What—"

"Don't ask." Freja cracked the reins, and with that, the chariot soared into the sky.

Clinging to the side, Karsten gazed back at Aldersfoss. The wooden castle he'd protected and served in, the trelleborg he'd called home, the fields he'd sparred in, the surrounding fortress wall, the city sprawling outside of it—it was all supposed to be his. The higher they climbed, the further Karsten could see. Hamme, full of farms that kept the people well-fed. Sander, where their best ships originated. Fryse in the north, the coast already covered in ice and snow. Morge, where they were fighting to protect the country, where he should be heading. Everything he knew was disappearing behind him.

"Who won?" Karsten asked.

"None of the champions survived. You killed Dag when she killed you. And she killed Nico and Jostein too."

Leaving Fjorden's future unknown.

Karsten inhaled sharply. "We have to go back."

Below them, Midgard was shrinking, Jormungand asleep along the edges.

"It doesn't work like that." Freja cracked the reins, steering the chariot toward a giant tree trunk—the mighty Yggdrasil. The white ash tree stood proudly against the black expanse.

But Sofia... He'd promised to return to her, promised he'd never stop fighting.

His calm, put-together princess had questioned if he was ready for the Sonne. He'd been honest, saying, *It's always easier to be brave when you have something worth fighting for.* But leaving her had worried him, even though he knew winning was the only way to be worthy of her hand, worthy of his father's pride. And then she'd cracked; a tear ran down her cheek, and he'd been desperate to stop it, to say anything to take away her pain. He'd brushed the tear away as her wide, trusting eyes had begged him, *stay*. And he'd promised—*you and me.*

You and me, no matter where she went. He'd follow her to the ends of Midgard, to the ends of Yggdrasil.

When his lips had met hers, he had delighted in the taste of strawberries. Her playful nips had invited him to join her, to be brave. For years, he'd waited for that moment.

He couldn't give up. He couldn't stop fighting.

"Freja, we need to turn around. Sofia needs me."

"She'll figure it out. Midgard always moves on without us."

He pictured Sofia at Championsfest, her silk dress falling all the way to the floor, a train trailing behind, her shoulders and neck exposed. Pink wildflowers formed her crown—the flowers he'd brought from his mother's garden.

Yet he'd walked away from her, left her standing alone, when she couldn't say she wanted him to return. *The gods chose this life for me, and I've strived to meet every obligation to the kingdom and my people.*

She'd shown him, over and over, that she wanted him. He only had to pay attention. Instead, he'd gone to Max, raised his glass, and pretended everything was fine—but he'd seen Sofia cracking, trying to keep herself together.

Be careful, guard-turned-champion, Inga had said when he brought her almonds. *She could fall in love with you.* He hadn't been careful; he'd walked away.

The chariot was halfway to the tree trunk and approaching Svartalfheim or Nidavellir; both were grassy plains, so he couldn't be sure which. Jotunheim was in the distance, recognizable by the rocky mountains covered with ice. He looked down, where the fires of Muspelheim raged against the ice of Niflheim along the roots of the tree. But Urd, Verdandi, and Skuld were down there.

"What if we go to the fates? They can repair—"

"Your life string was cut at birth, and it can't just be repaired." Freja gave him a soft smile. "You'll enjoy Folkvangr, Karsten. You'll fit right in. And a friend is waiting for you."

She took half the dead; plenty of his friends were probably there. But they weren't Sofia.

Freja shifted the reins, turning the chariot up toward the treetop, toward Folkvangr—where he'd be stuck forever, if he didn't think of something.

He considered the first moment he saw Sofia, at her naming ceremony. The queen had held her up in front of the castle and welcomed the crowd to meet her. *Mamma, I'm hungry*, Karsten had said, clinging to his mother's skirts. She'd chuckled, ruffling his hair, asking, *Don't you want to meet the princess?*

He'd give anything to go back. There had to be a way. "Please, Freja, you're the goddess of *lovers*. Is there any way to get back?"

She sighed, then looked directly into his eyes. "I'm willing to make you a deal."

"Anything." No hesitation. He'd do anything, go anywhere, to get back to Sofia. He'd made her a promise.

"I want a day named after me, just like Thor. I'm as good—no, better than him. But I was passed over for that stinky, thieving troll."

Karsten blinked, twice. He could surely convince Parliament; they would never deny a request directly from a god. "Consider it done."

Eyes brightening, Freja cracked the reins, turning the cart around gleefully. "I can't wait to see Thor's face once he finds out."

His chest loosening, Karsten glanced back at Asgard, Dag's new home. Nico's and Jostein's too. Skip, though... Something wasn't quite right with Skip's death. It wasn't a surprise he was sickly all morning, considering he'd overindulged on the ale and hogged the pastries, but he should have been fine after some sleep. His lips had been blue, and there were no signs of a struggle. He and Nico had whispered all morning on the boat, planning something... Had Nico won his trust, then poisoned him?

They flew quickly along the giant white branch, back to Midgard. Jormungand snapped at them as they crossed, but Freja glared at him. He slunk back, letting them pass.

"Overgrown serpent," she mumbled, rolling her eyes. "Ratatosk is worse—such a gossip."

The entirety of Midgard stretched out before them. Tunland, the massive tundra making up over half the land mass, bordering Kiniska, Stantland, and Romiska. Marrocs and Swaymark. And Fjorden. *Home.*

Soon he'd be home. With Sofia.

They picked up speed, flying downward. He could finally make out the regions.

"I..." Freja started, her brow furrowed. "I have some picking up to do after I drop you off."

"What do you—" His body went cold. Swaymark's green sails filled Aldersfoss's fjords, though red sails dotted the water. The largest ship was perched on the beach, empty of its crew. "Drop me on the front step of the castle."

Freja turned the chariot, her cats running harder through the air. She pulled her sword from its sheath, then handed it to Karsten. "Take Mardöll."

Eyes wide, he gingerly took the golden sword. It was heavier than he was used to.

"Don't die again, Karsten. I want my name day."

Sofia glared at Magnus, her nails biting into her palms. He'd attacked her country, beheaded her father, sent his men to capture her, and now—across the table in the library—he sat in *her* chair. She had lost her love and her father, but she refused to lose her kingdom too.

Swaymark's guards lined the room; they had unceremoniously dragged her here along with the Parliament members who had survived the attack, all smelling of sweat and blood.

Gold light filled the room from outside the giant windows—but no, she must have imagined it. Rain was still pounding outside.

Magnus narrowed his eyes, pushing his floppy, black hair off his forehead. "We learned last night that all five champions are dead."

Sofia started. Who'd told him?

"So you took advantage and slaughtered my people," she hissed.

The fire crackled in the hearth, the only sound in the room.

Clasping his hands on the table, Magnus said, "On the contrary, our ruse sent a goodly number of warriors away from the capital to protect them. We need them—to take on Tunland."

Weakening Aldersfoss in the process.

"It's time to step up," he said. "We've protected Fjorden from the Tunish for years."

"Yet *you* killed our king." She was hit by a sharp pang of loss.

"Your father refused to assist, refused to ally. But I'm aware of the love your people have for you. They'll rally behind you."

Sofia narrowed her eyes. "Why would we ally with Swaymark, when you ask with weapons instead of words?"

"The words came first, I can assure you," he growled. "For years, we have pulled out all the stops to help your people, with little reciprocation. But without more of Fjorden's resources, we'll lose our country to Tunland, and Fjorden *will* fall victim shortly after."

More...? Fy faen, the goods for Fryse.

She straightened, her frustration increasing. "You have been commandeering our ships."

His eyebrows rose. "Not at all. We've been purchasing them *cheaply*, but it's not enough."

Sofia scanned the table. Karl and the other representatives from Fryse hadn't survived the attack. The region would be better for it, though, considering they'd stolen resources from their own people.

Underhanded deals, infiltration, slaughters... this was not a partnership Fjorden wanted. "We—"

Commotion sounded from the hallway—shouts and cheers mixed with clashing metal. Sofia turned her head sharply toward the door as it slammed open.

Karsten strode in, a glowing golden sword in his hands.

But it couldn't be. She had buried him that morning, touched his stiffening hand, pressed her lips against his cold cheek. The pile of dirt covering his grave had risen to her waist. Her heart stuttered.

His ice-blue eyes locked onto Sofia. She knew those eyes, loved them, loved him. She let out a breath. *Karsten.* Here, in the library.

Magnus leaped up and sent the chair toppling to the floor. He ripped out his sword. Gold glinted on the hilt, but the blade was iron. Karsten sprinted across the room and positioned himself between Magnus and Sofia—always protecting her.

Their swords clanged, the vibrations jarring. Over and over, they hit, dodged, shifted, attacked, but Karsten didn't give an inch.

The guards around the room scrambled. Parliament members rose, and some of them picked up chairs and broke them over the heads of their captors. They yanked weapons away from some of Swaymark's guards, turning the tides.

"Leave no survivors," Magnus shouted.

Ice flooded Sofia's veins. Weaponless, she moved closer to Karsten. Sweat glistened on his brow, his breathing heavy. Magnus got a hard hit in, pushing Karsten toward the wall, but Sofia stayed with him.

She pulled books off the shelf, throwing them at the guards, though it saddened her to treat the precious texts disrespectfully. Although they were too light to do damage, the books created a distraction for Parliament members to get real hits in. More of Swaymark's warriors fell to the floor, coating the wood in blood.

While Magnus and Karsten remained locked in their sword fight, she pulled off a mounted shield and passed it to Karsten, then grabbed a second for herself.

"Sofia!" Karsten yelled.

She spun around as the guard behind her swung his sword at her. Filip's broken body flashed before her eyes. Terror pulsed through her, freezing her in place.

Like magic, Karsten was beside her, fighting back against the guard. Their swords clanged, shocking Sofia into action. She raised the shield and held it out, blocking Swaymark's warrior; the shield vibrated heavily on impact. Her arms shook violently, but she kept the shield firmly extended.

With Karsten distracted trying to protect her, Magnus closed in on them. Sofia threw her shield at him, but he blocked it, letting it clatter loudly on the ground.

Karsten stabbed the guard with the glowing golden sword, then slipped a dagger into Sofia's hands and locked swords with Magnus again, pushing him away from her.

Sofia knew this dagger—it was Dag's.

She could *use* this dagger. Dag had guided her hand down in a snapping motion, saying, *Just like that, aiming for the neck.* Sofia could protect her kingdom from Magnus, from Swaymark.

Parliament members were fighting off Swaymark's warriors, who continued to drop. Karsten distracted Magnus, turning him around, giving her the opportunity to take him out. This was her chance. With the dagger in the folds of her dress, Sofia moved stealthily toward the—

She tripped over her own two feet, but she managed to keep hold of the dagger. Karsten caught her, giving Magnus a chance to slice his arm. Blood trickled from the fresh cut.

Anger pulsed through her. She wouldn't lose her love again.

In a rush of adrenaline, Sofia raised the dagger, then thrust the blade forcefully into Magnus's neck, just like Dag had taught her. His blood spurted from the wound, coating the dagger and splashing her hand with the warm liquid. Horrified, Sofia let go of the weapon as Magnus dropped his sword, clutching his neck. He gasped for breath, blood spewing from his mouth to the floor of the library.

Karsten raised his sword one last time and sliced Magnus's head off, ending his suffering.

Swaymark's warriors retreated from the room, calling out, "To the ships!" Parliament members chased after them.

A Swayish warrior came toward Sofia. Defenseless, she gasped, her heart pounding in her chest. He raised his spear, aiming at her.

Clangs rang out as Karsten blocked him, then fought back and stabbed him with the golden sword. Shoulders sagging, Sofia let out a sigh.

Just like that, only the two of them were left in the library. Blood was splattered across them both.

Her father was gone, but her kingdom was safe, and her love...

Hands shaking, Sofia stared at Karsten. His eyes blazed with fire as he gazed back at her. But it didn't make sense.

"I buried you," she whispered, biting her lip. "This morning."

He sheathed the sword and moved toward her, stopping when she flinched. Hurt flashed across his face.

"How are you here?" she asked. The only way back to Midgard was to be reincarnated—reborn as an infant from the womb of a family member. And yet, here was Karsten.

"I made a promise, kjære. *You and me.*" Though he watched her sadly, the corner of his lip quirked. "And Freja took pity on me."

Freja—goddess of lovers.

Karsten took a hesitant step toward her, then another. "There was nowhere else on Yggdrasil I wanted to be, not without you."

Her heart sped, her breathing became shallow, but she couldn't move.

"I made a deal with Freja. To return to you." He pulled white fabric out from his pocket—the handkerchief. The same one she'd placed carefully on his chest earlier that day. Karsten held it out to her, then swallowed, watching her with his ice-blue eyes. Eyes she adored and knew intimately. Eyes she'd known most of her life.

Sofia took the favor from him, tangible in her hands. "You're... here?"

Karsten nodded silently.

She rushed to him and wrapped her arms around his neck, crying into his shoulder, feeling his presence. He was warm, sturdy, strong, brave—and *with her*. Physically with her. With all the loss, with all the pain, he was *here*.

Relief replaced every emotion she had felt since the end of the Sonne. Her family was gone and Fjorden had suffered immense losses, but her kingdom would be safe, and Karsten was *here*.

Amid the carnage, he held her tightly, squeezing her close, until her tears stopped, her heart rate slowed, and her breathing returned to normal.

"You and me," he murmured into her neck. "Marry me, Sofia."

Standing in the middle of the bloody mess, there was nothing she wanted more.

Karsten sat in the king's seat at the table. He'd watched King Eirik occupy the space for years; it felt foreign, undeserved. But it was next to Sofia, and he refused to be anywhere else.

The remaining Parliament members settled in—for a third time that day, according to Sofia. Torches and the fireplace lit the library, offsetting the threat of darkness outside. Sofia sat in her usual spot with a fresh, clean dress on.

Covered in blood, Karsten had helped take the bodies outside for burning. Servants were already stoking fires for the pyres on the beach. Taking out Max's body had been particularly painful.

"Tomas," Sofia said, her voice low. He sat on her left. "I realize it's late, but could you stay after?"

He nodded. "What do you need?"

Sofia glanced at Karsten, then said, "As the senior Parliament member, we were hoping you could perform a small marriage ceremony."

Tomas grinned, saying nothing more. Tension released from Karsten's shoulders. Without her father's approval, Tomas's would be second best for Sofia; he'd silently given it.

"Velkommen, welcome, welcome," Sofia said to the group. "I apologize for the late meeting, but I know many of you want to get home first thing tomorrow. We'll be fast."

The members around the table nodded.

"Some of Swaymark's ships departed before we could lock their warriors up, but thank you to everyone who wrestled those left behind into the dungeons."

A weak cheer came from some of the men. Karsten didn't blame them for the lack of enthusiasm. He was just as tired.

"About half of Swaymark's ships were made from Fjordish oak." Sofia bit her lip. "None of Fryse's representatives survived, but Nico let me know his family wasn't receiving supplies we've been sending north—for years. It seems they were the source."

Some of the members banged their fists on the table, though there wasn't anything to be done.

Sofia continued, "Second order of business: the new king."

"Cheers for Karsten—the victor," called a representative from Aldersfoss. If anyone should be named the victor, it was Dag. Surely, she had already taken Valhalla by storm.

"There was no victor," Tomas said. "All five died."

"Then how's he here?"

"Freja brought me back. We must honor her with a name day." Karsten definitely couldn't forget their deal. A couple Parliament members shrugged, and the table agreed to Freja's day—to follow Odin's day and Thor's day—before they circled back to the topic at hand.

"The deaths mean the gods found all of you lacking," an old representative said. "Clearly, we need to hold another Sonne."

To Karsten's dismay, the room murmured in agreement.

Sofia paled beside him. If there was another Sonne, she could lose her home and her kingdom to the victor. Worse, *he* could lose *her* if she felt obligated to partner with the victor. She was willing to give up everything for her kingdom. Would she give up *him*? Would he have to fight again? No, he wouldn't let that happen. He couldn't. He would never leave her, never let her go.

With a start, he realized *she* was the answer.

He rose, capturing the attention of the room. "We should end the Sonne and—"

"Nonsense," a representative shouted. "The Sonne has found us a strong ruler for hundreds of years."

"You're just sore because you lost," another said.

That wasn't a good start to his cause. But he couldn't give up, not when he'd come this far.

"There are other ways," Karsten said. "Sofia has been trained to lead since she was born. She stabbed Prince Magnus, protecting Fjorden in the attack. He'd still be alive if it weren't for her. She should take the throne."

Beside him, Sofia dropped her pen, and her eyes widened with shock. "Karsten, I'm not worthy."

"That thinking is exactly why you *are*."

She swallowed, but she didn't argue.

He turned back to the room. "She's been leading our kingdom for over ten years."

The remaining representatives looked around, remaining silent.

Tomas rose. "I've watched Sofia grow into a strong leader, and I second the motion. We should hold a vote."

She blinked at him. "Okay then." Sofia wiped her hands on her dress and took a deep breath. "All in favor?"

All the hands rose around the room. Karsten raised his, too, even though he wasn't part of Parliament. He smiled at her with encouragement, silently sharing his confidence in her.

"Huzzah!" Sofia shouted, hiding her nerves well, and all the representatives chanted it back, officially closing the vote. "With that, you're all welcome to stay in the castle tonight. Have a safe journey home tomorrow."

As the last Parliament members dispersed, Karsten turned to Tomas. "Thank you."

"No need to thank me," he said. "If the gods don't like it, they'll smite Sofia, and we'll end up with another Sonne anyway."

Sofia's jaw dropped, though she closed her mouth quickly.

"So, a small marriage ceremony?" Tomas said.

She looked at Karsten, then Tomas. "Yes. Meet us upstairs in an hour. Just enough time for Karsten to wash off all the blood."

Karsten kissed her cheek, then hustled upstairs.

Emotions had overwhelmed Sofia during Parliament,

leaving her shocked, humbled, and desperate to care for her people in the wake of the tempest. She would start with Fryse.

On a blank piece of paper, Sofia wrote *Elyse—Nico wanted you to have these*. She grabbed *Fjordensaga*, her favorite history book, and a couple of storybooks. Then she tucked the note securely into one of the books, belted the stack together, and found Lars in the stables.

"I'm worried about the supplies for Fryse," she said. "I was hoping you could go with the ships to drop them off. Make sure they arrive safely."

"Of course," Lars said.

She held up the stack of books. "I want to send these along too—for Nico's little sister. He wanted her to have new bedtime stories."

He nodded, then took the pile. "I'll give them to her myself."

Nico would have appreciated that.

Back in the Royal Wing, Sofia stepped into her old bedroom. The bench was still flung halfway across the room, and the key was still on the floor. She picked it up. It was hers now.

Agneta entered, stepping around the bloodstain on the floor, the space where Max had given his life to protect her. With a heavy heart, Sofia hoped Max was enjoying glory in Valhalla.

Hugging Agneta, Sofia said, "I'm so glad you're safe."

Settling in, Agneta braided a crown across Sofia's hair and helped her into the wedding cloak, its white fox fur brushing

Sofia's cheeks. Sofia traced the oceanic pattern along the sleeves, embroidered by her grandmother.

"Thank you, Agneta. For being here, when Mamma wasn't able to be."

"She'd be so proud of you," Agneta said. "Good luck. I'll bring up a small meal from the kitchen."

Sofia went to the king's chambers—now hers—and found Tomas and Karsten waiting near the fireplace. A simple braided rope was draped over Tomas's shoulder.

Karsten smiled, extending an arm toward her. He'd washed off all the blood and put on clean clothes. His new golden sword was sheathed at his side. She curled into him, appreciating his warmth; his presence; his comforting, woodsy scent.

"Thank you for coming up, Tomas," she said. "I'm sure you're exhausted."

"Your father would come back from Valhalla to kill me if I didn't." He smiled sadly; he'd lost his best friend. "He'd be so proud of you, Mouse."

Rubbing her back, Karsten murmured in agreement.

Her father certainly wouldn't have expected this outcome. He would have been happy, though. And she'd see him and her mother in the Royal Circle once her time was over, and Karsten would be with her too. The thought warmed her.

"Shall we?" Tomas asked, his voice choked with emotion.

Karsten kissed the top of Sofia's head, then took her hands in his.

They were the same warm, callused hands she had held four days ago. There was no hint of the coldness from the grave.

"Sofia Eiriksdatter," Tomas started, "do you take this man to be your husband?"

"Yes." She felt it in her blood, in her bones. He had literally fought against death for her, and there would never be anyone she wanted more. There hadn't been—not since the first day he snuck flowers into her room. Karsten's hands tightened around hers. His thumb caressed her knuckles, silently promising, *You and me.*

"Karsten Kjellsen," Tomas continued, "do you take this woman to be your wife?"

"Yes." He gazed at her, a shy smile playing on his lips.

"I will now tie the knot." Tomas pulled the rope off his shoulder. He enthusiastically wrapped it around Sofia's hands, then circled it around Karsten's wrists and knotted it with a flourish, officially joining the pair. "May your lives be forever intertwined—and your life-strings long."

"Huzzah," the trio chorused.

Karsten carefully pulled the rope from their hands, leaving the knot securely tied. He placed it on the mantel.

Tomas said goodnight as Agneta entered with plates of roasted lamb and vegetables. Two days of barely eating had taken its toll. The delicious smell had Sofia's stomach rumbling. She ate every bite as Karsten recounted his tale with Freja, sparing no detail of the glories of Yggdrasil.

"As much as I appreciate what she did," Sofia said, "Thor was supposed to protect you before it got that far."

Karsten chuckled. "I'm with you, kjære. We will make sure to celebrate Freja's day with twice the excitement every week."

Once she had changed into her soft wool nightshirt, Sofia crawled into bed beside Karsten. She tucked herself against him, embraced in his warmth, and listened to his heart beat steadily. It was a relief, a comfort—her safe space. And he had been her safe space for so long...

With his hand against her lower back, his thumb caressed her.

"What if I'm not enough?" Sofia whispered.

His brow furrowed. "For what, kjære?"

She swallowed, then continued, "For the kingdom."

He stopped moving. "You are more than enough. Your people don't need you to be perfect. They've never needed you to be perfect. They just need *you*." He kissed the top of her head. "All I need is you."

Nodding, Sofia snuggled against him. She didn't know if she could believe him—but she'd try. She would serve her people wholeheartedly, the way she had her entire life.

Her limbs grew heavy, and her eyes drooped; she fought back against sleep, though she was losing her final battle of the day.

Squeezing her close, Karsten took her hand and kissed the inside of her wrist. "Whenever I storm the gates of Valhalla, whether it's tomorrow or a lifetime from now, know that I did it loving you."

"I love you too," she said fearlessly. He was hers; he was here; and with the help of the gods, they had made it through together. The longest day of her life had finally ended.

Karsten held Sofia, her sleeping body curled next to him. She'd sleep well past sunup. She always did, and after yesterday... He'd finish a morning run and still be waiting hours for her to wake up. His routines had always served him, kept him in top form; Karsten wanted to get back to them.

Careful not to wake her, he slid from beneath the covers. The hearth had burned out, leaving behind darkness. He relit the fire and put another blanket on the bed, hoping she'd stay warm enough. She'd awoken during the night, cold and trembling.

He exited the castle, then walked the path to the gate, greeting Geir and Alexander. Continuing along the inside of the wall, he passed the quiet dungeons, their Swayish inhabitants fast asleep. They'd have to be dealt with later.

Thoughts drifting, he ran the same route he and Dag had taken. Her death was at his hand—but she had killed him too, so they were even.

The castle, the Sonne, Swaymark's attack, his precious Sofia... When he went hard enough, fast enough, far enough, he finally outpaced the cacophony in his mind—though he knew it would return once he stopped running. He turned back when the first rays of sun snaked over the horizon.

Karsten ascended the stairs to the Royal Wing, where hurried footsteps echoed down the hall. He rushed into their bedroom and was attacked in full force, the air knocked out of him. Stumbling, he caught his balance against the wall, his precious Sofia clinging to him.

"I thought it was a dream," she choked out, her eyes threatening tears. With her arms around his neck, she held tight, making it hard for him to breathe.

This was the true cost of the Sonne. Karsten would spend his life helping Sofia heal, reassuring her, putting the pieces back together.

"Kjære," he said, "I'm not going anywhere. I'm right here."

Caressing her arm, Karsten stared into her beautiful, blue-green eyes, the pupils lined with flecks of tan and brown, round and wide-set behind long, dark lashes. Eyes that made him feel safe, at home, and whole. He hoped she'd feel the same, in time.

Shifting closer, she fisted his shirt, tugging on it, asking for more of him. He pulled the shirt over his head, tossing it aside, and met her lips with his—confirmation that he was there, he was staying, he was hers.

He lifted her and carried her to the bed, setting her down gently before removing Mardöll from his belt. Lying next to her, he kissed her temple. When she trembled, he pulled the blanket over them and let her share his warmth, thinking, *This. I want this, forever.*

With light pressure, Sofia's hands dragged along his body and stopped on his shoulders, giving him permission to do the same. Karsten's heartbeat increased and desire swelled within him. His breathing shallow, he affectionately kissed down her cheeks.

After years of wanting, after months of fighting, all he needed was here in this bed.

With the rest of their clothes cast to the floor, he lowered himself between her knees, his hands light against her legs. He pressed his mouth against her, murmuring her name, taking care of her until her muscles clenched and a small, breathy moan of satisfaction escaped her lips. He would always take care of her. Their life-strings were tied.

Grasping his hand, Sofia pressed her lips against his palm, giving him silent confirmation. Settling in between her hips, Karsten slowly pushed into her, letting her adjust, enjoying how well they fit in every single way.

She pulled him closer, their chests flush, and kissed him. He deepened it, slowly moving inside her. "Karsten," she begged, pushing back against him, rocking into him, writhing beneath him. He increased their pace, giving her what she wanted.

They didn't need words, had never needed words. But he gave them to her anyway.

"I've got you," he whispered in her ear. "You and me."

Together, they both let go.

ONE MONTH LATER

SOFIA ENTERED THE STABLES, her guard following behind. "Welcome back, Lars."

"Your Majesty," he said, bowing his head.

"A few hours left." She grinned. "How was Fryse?"

"Unexpected. The crowd was ecstatic, celebrating in the streets. Elyse thanked you for the books—I gave them to her myself."

"Thank you for making sure everything arrived safely." Sofia crossed the stable to Apple, petting the horse's nose and offering a snack. Apple munched with enthusiasm. Sofia whispered, "I hope you'll have a rider soon."

She walked the path to the castle, welcoming the guests that were milling about before the coronation. Additional guards, freshly returned from Morge, stood at the doors and along the halls.

Pink flowers waited for her at her desk, their floral scent filling the room, though Karsten was missing from the Royal Wing.

Sofia flipped through a stack of correspondence; most of the letters could wait until tomorrow. An old letter from Magnus waited at the bottom of the pile: *Tunland attacked again...* She skimmed it quickly, then threw it into the fireplace, watching it curl in the crackling flames.

At her new desk beneath Odin and his ravens, she reviewed her lines for the coronation. *A true ruler is always brave; a true ruler will always fight for her people...*

An hour later, Agneta entered with a cream-colored dress. "You'll look stunning."

Sliding into the silk shift, Sofia's heart soared. She glanced at the painting of her parents, their absence palpable—but surely they were celebrating in the Royal Circle of Valhalla. She'd join them after a long reign with Karsten by her side.

His footsteps echoed down the hall; he entered shortly after. "Kjære."

"There you are. Where were you hiding all day?" Sofia asked.

"I'll tell you after dinner." Karsten wrapped his arms around her, putting his hands on the small of her back and pulling her against him. "I can't be late for my wife's coronation."

She placed her hands at the nape of his neck, nipping at his lower lip, kissing him playfully. "You're up to something."

"Of course I am." He kissed her forehead, then let her go. "That's all you get until later. I already have to sneak in through the kitchen." In a whirlwind, he changed his clothes and was out the door, calling back, "See you in the Great Hall, Your Majesty."

Sofia blinked, staring after him. *You and me*, he'd promised, and he'd kept his word even through death. Her heart warmed.

"The coronation cloak," Agneta said, the fabric draped across her arms. She helped Sofia put it on and pinned the sleeves. Her father had worn it last. Made for the victor—usually someone taller and broader than her—the cloak was too big, trailing behind her. She'd have to be careful not to trip.

She attached her turtle brooches to the cloak, their long chains dangling. They matched the crown her father used to wear, which she'd be wearing soon.

"That's it, Your Majesty." Agneta smiled, her eyes misty.

With one last glance at the portrait of her parents, Sofia walked downstairs, passing by the paintings of her elders—the many kings who came before her. She'd earn her place beside them.

Tomas waited in front of the closed double doors, wearing a fatherly smile. "Your Majesty."

Sofia hugged him, then took a deep breath. This was it. The commitment to serve her people had been made in her heart years ago; but today, it would be written into their sagas.

A servant handed Tomas a pillow with the gold crown resting on top. Jormungand was cast into the circlet, and twenty-two bits of ivory, one for each of the gods, were set into his back. Spaced evenly, five palisades reached the same height, representing her commitment to serve the five regions equally.

Guards swung the doors open. Hundreds of people cheered inside the hall, drowning out the musicians playing "The Song of Yggdrasil." They filled the space, eagerly waiting for her.

The first guard walked down the aisle carrying her father's shield and spear. After the ceremony ended, the set would be hung in the castle. Another guard followed him, carrying a new spear and shield made by the people; they would be Sofia's soon and would protect her during her reign. Tomas went next. Once on the stage, he set the pillow with the crown on a simple wooden plinth. There, it waited for her.

Mouth dry, with the cloak dragging behind her, Sofia strode forward. Parliament members both old and new sat on benches near the stage. Karsten watched from beside them, his expression stoic but his eyes bright. Sofia gave him a small wave, then ascended the steps onto the platform.

"Velkommen, welcome, welcome to all," Tomas said. The room cheered again, the applause thunderous. "We are here to recognize Sofia Eiriksdatter as the rightful ruler of Fjorden."

"May the gods protect her," the crowd chorused.

Sofia's heart swelled with love for her people. They had been beaten, battered, almost broken, but they'd made it through.

"Your vows," Tomas said to her.

Sofia straightened, well-prepared. "I vow to always fight for my people, to uphold our laws, and to serve the entire kingdom of Fjorden to the best of my ability." She continued on, delivering each promise with the solemnity it deserved. Her vows to Karsten paled in comparison.

After she finished, the guard gave her the new spear and shield—freshly painted Fjorden's red, with bits of gold to garner the protection of the gods. Tomas picked up the crown, then held it an inch above her head. Per tradition, he let it drop, forcing her to feel the full weight of the country resting on her head—a burden she eagerly accepted.

The entire crowd rose to their feet, applauding and shouting with joy. Finally, the feast could begin. Servants filled the tables with smorgasbords and distributed the ale.

Karsten joined her on the stage, kissing her cheek.

"I don't think I'll be dancing in this cloak," she whispered.

He smirked. "Don't worry. There are plenty of things I'd rather do with you tonight."

Her cheeks heated. "Sounds like a plan."

Karsten took the shield and spear, then helped Sofia down the steps. Blessed by the gods, she didn't trip on the fabric as they made their way to the head table, greeting guests along the way. Karsten helped her settle into the king's chair, then sat beside her in what used to be her space.

In what was once her father's seat, wearing what used to be her father's crown, she held back tears, her throat choked with emotions. She blinked them away, focusing on the activity around her.

Inga approached them, carrying a small marzipan cake on a platter. "Your Majesty."

Sofia squealed with delight as Inga set it in front of her.

Karsten chuckled. "I thought you'd appreciate it."

"This is where you were all day?" She picked up the spoon.

"Six different vendors to find the almonds. Though Inga baked the—" He frowned, eyes darkening, and took the spoon right out of Sofia's hand, extending it to Inga. "Will you taste it first?"

Inga gulped, her smile crooked. "I already had a taste in the kitchen. It's delicious."

"Karsten, what's going on?" Sofia tried to take the spoon back.

His eyes narrowed, locked on Inga. "You didn't try this piece."

Her gaze flicked to Sofia. She turned and ran toward the kitchen.

"Stop her!" Karsten yelled. He flipped the platter onto the table, laying waste to the perfect cake, then chased Inga through the hall. The guards apprehended Inga as she tried to escape through the kitchen door.

Scooping the bottom of the cloak, Sofia crossed to the group, pushing through the sea of onlookers.

"What's going on?" Sofia demanded.

"The cake was poisoned," Karsten said, voice low and tone deadly. "Just like the pastries Skip ate at Championsfest."

Sofia dropped the cloak, her hands shaking. "Is this true?"

Inga paled, glaring, pulling against the guards. "Unhand me."

Karsten placed a hand on the small of Sofia's back. "When I saw Skip in the fjord, his lips were blue—no injuries. I thought Nico did it, though I couldn't figure out why. But it was Inga, *from Swaymark.*"

Sofia's chest was heavy. Her first official act... "Take her to the dungeon to await a fair trial."

The guards escorted Inga from the hall and the crowd dispersed, focused again on the feast, though the gossip was spreading. She'd address it at Parliament next week. Tonight was for celebrating.

"Can I help, kjære?" Karsten asked, crossing their bedroom.

Sofia nodded, shrugging out of the coronation cloak and letting him take it. He draped it across the table before helping her take off the crown, which was heavier than he expected. They could be returned to the Royal Treasury later.

With his hands on her hips, he lifted her onto their bed. He'd almost lost her tonight. He wanted to feel her physical presence, feel her beneath him. Everything else could wait.

"I was thinking..." she started.

Sofia swallowed, biting her strawberry-stained lip. She hadn't wanted to eat anything else after the cake, but he'd retrieved the berries himself from the kitchen stores. He tucked her hair behind her ear and sat beside her. "What is it?"

"Well, about Filip."

Karsten sat beside her, resting his hand on her thigh. "Anything specific?"

"He never became the person—the king—he was meant to be. He never had a chance to fight for a spot in Valhalla. And I thought, since you came back... maybe Filip could too."

His heart dropped. He couldn't fix this. "We can't leave Midgard, and even if we could—"

She shook her head. "No, I know we can't get him back as he

was, but... I mean, I want to name our firstborn Filip. So that he could... well, have the chance he never had."

Karsten started. Filip's spirit would be reborn, brought back to Midgard, his life string extended by the fates. And he'd be here, with them.

"But it wouldn't exactly be him," Karsten said hesitantly. "He wouldn't remember..."

"I know," she said, "but I didn't know how you'd feel? And if you don't..." She bit her lip again.

His heart filled with so much love for her. "I want that, too, kjære. Let's bring Filip home."

FOLKVANGR

"COME ON, FILIP. MOVE YOUR PIECE."

Filip picked up the king, feeling the weight in his hand. The hnefatafl board sat on the wooden table in front of him.

He thought back to the hours spent strategizing in his room, forming a plan to beat Karsten. A win meant something back then. He was preparing to lead the kingdom, to make his father proud. Now, the endless rounds of hnefatafl were getting boring.

Setting the piece down, he said, "You know, I don't feel like playing anymore. Someone else can."

He rose from the bench. A few of his friends fought for his seat.

Torches along the walls threw a dim light, casting shadows across the longhouse. The red walls were covered with rosemaling, nothing like the Great Hall at home. No shields, no gods along the ceiling; but in some spots, there were painted scenes from Midgard—lots of places he'd never seen before. He liked those.

He was allowed to paint, if he wanted to, but that didn't sound like fun. Or he could read, although that didn't feel exciting. No one wanted to spar—not here in the home of the lovers and the artists. So he'd played hnefatafl, a lot, over the last four months.

At least there wasn't a tutor chastising him and Sofia for not studying enough. There wasn't really a point now.

Striding down the hall, Filip glanced at the painted scene of Aldersfoss's castle before exiting the longhouse. He climbed the exterior wall, his fingers and toes finding purchase between the giant logs. Laying back, he settled on the grass-covered roof, staring at the sky.

A speck in the distance caught his eye. It grew, approaching him.

"Freja!" he shouted, rising.

Her cats ran through the air, pulling Freja's wooden chariot toward him. She landed on the roof, her smile wide. The wheels of the chariot squeaked until the giant cats came to a stop. Filip bounced over to the cats and cuddled them fiercely. They mewed in response, always happy to see him.

"Do you have a new story for me?" Filip asked.

Freja chuckled. "I just had a delightful visit with Thor. I'll tell you all about it on our journey."

His brow furrowed. The last time they went on a journey, he ended up *here*. But... maybe it would be fun?

Hesitantly, he circled the chariot, then asked, "Where are we going?"

Freja helped him up, then hugged him tight. "Do not worry, little one. This is the will of the gods."

Acknowledgements

I'm grateful for August 16, 2022, the day I wrote Sofia's first words onto the page. It's been a long journey. This is the book of my heart; it made me a writer and will forever carry a piece of my soul.

Thank you to my husband. If you weren't around, this story would have never been finished. *You were right.*

To my family and friends who supported me along the way, I appreciate each of you. Your encouragement keeps me going.

Huge gratitude and the sincerest thanks to my beta readers and my amazing critique circle, who read every chapter and considered every last detail of the story many times over. This book wouldn't be half of what it is without each of you.

A special thanks to the amazing team of people who helped bring this book to life and gave it that final polish.

Booksellers, librarians, and the fabulous individuals who help connect people with books: thank you for all you do to make the world a better place.

Most importantly, thank you to each reader who has given this book a chance. I hope you find what you're looking for.

Writing Playlist

"Beautiful Now" – Zedd ft. Jon Bellion

"Die Young" – Ke$ha

"Fighter" – Christina Aguilera

"Ice Storm" – Lindsey Stirling

"If I Had a Heart" – VioDance Hardanger Violin Cover

"I'm Feeling It (In the Air)" – Sunset Bros ft. Mark McCabe

"Into the Unknown" – Idina Menzel ft. Aurora

"Iris" – Goo Goo Dolls

"Love Is Gone" – SLANDER ft. Dylan Matthew

"Loving You Is a Losing Game" – Duncan Laurence ft. Fletcher

"OK Not to Be OK" – Marshmello ft. Demi Lovato

"The Only Exception" – Paramore

"Show Yourself" – Idina Menzel ft. Evan Rachel Wood

"Warriors" – Imagine Dragons

"When You're Gone" – Avril Lavigne

"Where Are You Now" – Lost Frequencies ft. Calum Scott

"Willow" – Taylor Swift

"Wolves" – Selena Gomez ft. Marshmello

About the Author

Kriss Dean is a hopeless romantic and an obsessive reader. By daylight, she puts her BA in Mathematics to use in the financial services industry. Come nightfall, she can be found writing books in the dark corners of coffee shops. She lives in Florida with her husband and their two golden retrievers.

Growing up, she spent three months in Norway every year with her father. Two decades later, she finally appreciates the quantity of museums he dragged her to each weekend in an effort to instill a love for her heritage. She considers Oslo her second home.

"What are your plans?" he asked.

"I need to check in with my executor at the bank tomorrow. I need to ensure my finances are in order. I only allowed him to access funds from a separate account designated to maintain this place. The rest is safe in two different Swiss banks, and I'm the only one with access to them." I paused and added, "I plan to continue your financial support."

Jax smirked. "It must be nice to have been married to a rich Danish prince."

His comment stung. "I would rather him still be alive."

"Yeah, I know. Sorry. I didn't mean to be insensitive," Jax said.

"I still think about Lars every day." My voice was crackly and I felt tears fill my eyes again. "You know, after he died, I kinda went crazy and that's when I went into modeling. And my life spun out of control."

"You were pretty crazy all right… *Raven*." He glanced at the large oil portrait that hung over the fireplace with a crooked grin across his face.

I turned to study the painting, and instantly recalled the day I'd shamelessly sat nude with my back to the painter and looking over my left shoulder with my waist-length black hair cascading down my back. I felt a knot in my stomach, remembering how I used to feel so proud of that piece. "I'm probably going to take that painting down."

"Why?" Jax asked.

"I don't recognize that person anymore."

A long and awkward silence followed. Jax's previously relaxed posture now stiffened and there was a deep furrow on his brow.

I stood, anxious to change the mood. "I'm probably not going to be much company until I check out the rest of my place, take a shower, and try to get presentable."

"I understand. Do what you need to do." Jax uncrossed his legs and put both hands on his thighs. "The kitchen is well stocked, so you can easily get something to eat. I'll stop back this evening and we can go out to dinner. How does that sound?"

"It sounds perfect." I smiled. Jax stood and gave me a warm hug and a kiss on the cheek. "Feel free to bring Mick if you want. I would love to meet him."

His face instantly brightened.

* * *

Walking the twenty-five steep wooden stairs to my second floor felt good. Even the touch of the shiny lacquered banister on my hand made my smile widen. I'd dreamt of finally being home for what seemed like an eternity.

I turned the corner while on the top landing. passing the second set of stairs that led to my third floor and the three guest bedrooms. I opened the two wooden doors and walked inside my master suite, an area I'd hired a designer to produce the dream space I'd imagined. I scanned the room, studying the details of my king-sized mahogany bed, the filmy white canopy fell from the ceiling and surrounded the crisp linen bedding. Fresh flowers sat on a round wooden antique table beside one of the chairs in front of my fireplace. I walked over to smell them—no doubt Jax arranged for the cleaning lady to put them there. I walked to the built-in bookcases beside the fireplace, studying the books and framed pictures neatly placed on the shelves. One particular photo caught my eye and I picked it up—an eight-and-a-half-inch by eleven-inch portrait of Lars.

Tears filled my eyes as I kissed Lars' picture and hugged it with both arms close to my heart. He was the love of my life. I know I'll never love another man as deeply as I loved Lars.

"Lars, my love," I said out loud, something I hadn't been able to say for many years, "I really screwed up my life, and now I've got to fix it."

CHAPTER 2

Charlotte

Eight hundred and fifty square feet of walk-in closet pleasure welcomed me when I flipped the light switch of my antique crystal chandelier that hung from a bronze chain ten feet down from the twenty-foot-high plastered ceiling. I felt myself smile at the fragrant cedar shelving that housed the three hundred and twenty-five pairs of designer shoes. I felt goosebumps when I picked up a pair of red Jimmy Choo stilettos. I blew off the dust. I carried the shoes to the pink velvet upholstered bench with the bronze-painted legs—an art deco piece positioned in the center of the room. I sat down and pulled off the distasteful sneakers, throwing them in the trash can against the wall. A pair of strappy satin and rhinestone stilettos spoke to me, so I put them on, then stood.

"Oh my God, these feel great," I said. My body and spirit lifted higher as I stood and pranced towards my full-length mirror at the far end of the room, passing the built-ins that housed my clothing and accessories. I felt every bit the princess Lars said I was.

* * *

At seven sharp, the doorbell rang. I strutted to the door to answer, enjoying the feel of my black Gucci stilettos and matching leather pants with the blush-pink Stella McCartney blouse. The large golden geometric-tiered earrings clanked together like wind chimes beneath my cascading blonde waves. The fresh scent of Chanel's *Coco Mademoiselle* tantalized my senses when I opened the door. I could also detect the jasmine from my shampoo, so different from the institutional stuff I was limited to using while incarcerated and had caused my signature black color to rinse right down the drain. The makeup, clothes, hair, and perfume truly metamorphized me, making my spirit lighter and brighter; my true soul came back to life.

A tall and slender silver-haired man with heavy black-framed glasses stood beside my brother. The man appeared to be at least sixty years old, attired in stylish designer jeans, reptile-skin cowboy boots, and a solid white silk shirt that was unbuttoned to display several gold chains. His skin was darkly bronzed and contrasted against his bright white smile.

"Good evening and welcome." I stepped aside to allow both men to enter.

"Charley, you're looking good," Jax said, using the childhood pet name as he gave me a warm hug.

"You must be Mick." I offered a handshake, which he accepted.

"Yes, that would be me," he said. He had a slight Eastern European accent.

"It's great to finally meet you, Mick."

"Likewise." He flashed an even wider smile.

I sensed him checking me out as I led the way to my living room.

"I thought we could eat at Vinnie's down the street," Jax said as he took a seat on one of the sofas. Mick sat down beside him.

"Sure." I fondly remembered the gourmet Italian restaurant. "Is it still owned by the Valentis?"

"Gino's in charge now. His dad passed the place on to him and retired." Jax used to wait tables there when he first moved to the city from San Diego. "The food's still the same. Marcella continues to micro-manage the kitchen." Marcella was the eldest Valenti daughter.

"I wonder if anyone will remember me," I found myself mumbling.

There was a painfully long silence. Mick cleared his throat and shifted in his seat.

"Sorry. I wasn't trying to make anyone feel uncomfortable."

"Charley, it's okay," Jax said.

"We all have histories," Mick said.

I gave a feeble grin. "Some have a darker history than others."

"I also served time," Mick said and glanced at Jax. "Spent fourteen years behind bars for armed robbery of a jewelry store."

I refrained from asking for details of Mick's crimes but said, "I guess Jax told you about my issue."

"He didn't have to. It was all over the news. But I have to tell you. I don't think anyone would recognize you now. You look totally different without all the long and straight black hair and heavy makeup." Mick gave another soft smile.

"Thank you for not saying I look old."

"Hey," Mick raised both hands and gave a wink, "from where I'm sitting, you certainly look like a child."

All three of us laughed at that one. I noticed Jax looking at his watch. "We should probably get ready to leave," Jax said. "I made our reservations for seven-thirty."

"Okay. I just need to run upstairs and grab a purse."

* * *

The evening air was brisk and I was grateful for having grabbed my Chanel blazer with gold brass buttons. The clear sky featured stars I hadn't been able to stand underneath for years. I smiled, inhaling deeply. Even the exhaust fumes from passing cars seemed sweet as I took in the sights of the two blocks from my house to the Old World-style restaurant. My brother and Mick were deep in a private conversation as I trailed behind on the narrow sidewalk. I was grateful for the respite of silence. Excitement ran through me as I drank in the scenes of every ordinary activity. In truth, little of the topography had actually changed—I was merely viewing my neighborhood with fresh eyes.

A towering digital billboard on the left caught my eye. A buxom blonde in lacy white lingerie was seductively posed on a chaise lounge. She had a set of wings behind her and the words VICTORIA'S SECRET panned across the bottom of the screen. A knot formed in my stomach at the memory of being on that same billboard—also sporting angel wings and racy undies.

"Hey, Charley," Jax said, pointing towards the entrance of the restaurant. "Isn't that your old modeling agent?" My brother had also briefly modeled for the woman's agency.

I spotted a stout woman with short curly gray hair wearing a solid black pantsuit. She was at the door, about to go inside. Hilda Reicher, the last person I wanted to see on my first evening home. She visited me once during my first month of incarceration only to ream me out over how much money I'd cost her in broken modeling contracts. I was scheduled to be exclusive with a major cosmetics company, but then I ended up in prison. Hilda tried to send another model from her agency, but the client rejected the model. That was Marilee Jenkins, the one I believed framed me.

"Jax." I got closer to my brother and slowed my pace. "Any chance we can eat someplace else?" I pointed to the doorway where I saw Hilda.

"Come on. This place has great food, and I got lucky in getting us reservations."

I inhaled deeply, straightened my posture, and glanced again at the open doorway. Hilda was out of view, so I figured if we waited a few more minutes, maybe she would miss us.

I saw my brother whisper something into Mick's ear, then Mick stepped forward and went inside. "Mick's going to make sure we're seated away from Hilda," he assured me.

"Thank you." My brother put his arm around my waist and planted a quick kiss on my cheek.

Mick then reappeared, motioning for us to go inside. I walked behind him through the tiny front foyer and into a dimly lit packed dining room. I glanced around the large room checking for any sign of Hilda. So far, so good.

Red velvet-upholstered chairs were around circular dining tables with white linen tablecloths. An olive tree in the center of the room towered halfway towards the thirty-five-foot-tall ceiling. Smaller saplings dotted the room. Intimate dining alcoves lined two walls. A maître d' led us to a back-corner alcove.

"Madam." He pulled out a chair and I sat. Jax and Mick seated themselves across from me.

With a menu in hand, I again scanned the room. All clear.

"Stop worrying, sis," Jax said.

"Yeah. Just let it go," Mick piped in. "What's that bitch gonna do anyway?"

Jax gave an embarrassed laugh.

Now I gave an embarrassed laugh. "You're right, of course."

Dinner was nice. Jax and Mick both ordered balsamic salmon and I ordered scampi. That first bite was delectable; I closed my eyes as I savored it—the first decent meal I'd had in six years. The bland stuff in prison was barely palatable, and there wasn't ever much of it. This plate was piled high, more than enough for two inmates to eat. I momentarily wondered if I should feel guilty.

Conversation was light, mostly Jax and Mick chatting on and on about their friends and parties. I just nodded and smiled as if interested, when I'd tuned them out, lost in my own thoughts.

"Raven?"

I heard a high-pitched voice behind me and I turned to see who it was. I recognized a former model I worked with once. She was still anorexically thin, but now sporting long, straight black hair and heavily kohl-lined eyes. She appeared intentionally similar to my old look, right down to the dark mole above her lip. The last was obviously fake.

"Hi, Jenna." I was grateful I remembered her name. Then I saw her—Hilda. Standing right behind Jenna, wearing a stern expression.

"We need to talk," Hilda said.

CHAPTER 3

Charlotte

Hilda's nuts if she thinks I'm going to check in with her! I thought about the evening before as I poured a steaming cup of hot coffee. I carried my mug to the back door, opened it, and walked on to the red brick floor of my private patio. I was grateful my brother had maintained the foliage that lined the perimeter in front of the tall black wrought-iron fencing giving full privacy from my neighbors, and thus allowing me to wear a silk robe. I placed my mug on a luncheon-sized black wrought-iron table, pulled out one of the matching chairs, and sat. I pulled out another chair to put my feet up. My thoughts flashed on Lars, who created this patio garden. In one corner, Lars had planted a blue Chinese wisteria tree. I was impressed with how tall it had grown in my six-year absence. The opposite corner had a most fragrant yellow Carolina jasmine tree. Various flowering shrubs lined the lower bed.

Near the door were my lavender plants. Lars had planted those for me after our baby died. The fragrant smell reminded me of how he and I had longed for the day we would meet our son. But our dreams were dashed when our baby was stillborn. I was crushed, but Lars was shattered. Our son would have been heir to the Bjorn dynasty in Denmark, where my husband was the crown prince. Erik is what we named him. We decided on a private funeral; just him and me with a few close friends. Erik's tiny body was flown to Copenhagen, where he was entombed in the Bjorn family burial cathedral. Lars was later entombed beside Erik.

We had planned to move permanently to the family residence in Copenhagen as soon as Lars had finalized arrangements for the Château de Cahors wine distribution in the US. He'd inherited the winery when his grandfather died. Lars was on his way back to New York City to get me when his private plane exploded in mid-air.

"You're sure up early." It was Jax, barefoot in striped blue pajamas, who'd insisted on spending the night, claiming I shouldn't be alone. He held a steaming cup of coffee.

"Good morning." I put both feet on the ground and Jax took the chair.

"Did you sleep okay?" he asked.

"Not really. Maybe tonight will be different." I took another swallow of my coffee.

Jax's expression grew serious. "Just so you know, Lars' sister was here last week. I'd come in to water the plants out here."

Ugh. The woman hated me. "What did Adeline want?"

"I made the mistake of letting her inside. She'd tried to get inside before, but I never let her in. Don't know why I did this time." Jax slowly took another drink, then looked away. "Sorry."

"Don't be sorry. Just tell me what happened."

"Adeline was quick to scan the room. She pointed at your portrait and cursed. I won't repeat what she said. She tried to go upstairs, but I stopped her."

"Good grief! Why would she want to go upstairs?" The thought of Adeline in my house made me sick.

"She claimed you had a family heirloom that was rightfully hers. It was that diamond and emerald tiara."

"Lars gave that to me!"

"Yeah, I know. Your princess crown."

We both laughed.

"How did you get her out?" I was certain Adeline hadn't been easy to deal with.

"I threatened to push the security alarm. She was obviously high, probably coke."

"Quick thinking, but I don't have any security system."

"Yeah, but she didn't know that. Did you know she was friends with that Marilee woman you think framed you?" Jax raised an eyebrow.

"Oh yeah. Adeline wanted to be a model and she thought Marilee could help her. They were friends well before I even joined the agency. I think Adeline was jealous I got in and she didn't."

"I'm sure you're right." Jax scratched his head. "Do you have any plans for today?"

"I want to make a few business calls." I paused and took the final swallow of my coffee. "After that, I don't know. Everything feels like a time warp."

"I bet."

Jax had known to be silent to let me talk, and right then I'd wanted to talk. "I feel like such a screw-up, and I'm angry. I want to clear my name. No one believed me when I told them I was innocent. I feel like such a fool for leaving my purse behind when I went inside that hotel with Garth."

"It's history now. Better to move on," Jax said.

"Move on? You've got to be kidding! I won't rest until the person who framed me is behind bars."

"You may never know who that was."

There was a brief silence.

"I had recurring nightmares when I was locked up. Garth met Lars in heaven and told all. The look of disgust and hurt on Lars' face haunts me."

"You need to forgive yourself."

"I don't know how." My voice cracked as the tears came. I shook my head. "Sorry."

"Let it out. Cry till there aren't any more tears to come. It will help you heal." Jax sounded much wiser than I remembered.

I wiped the tears from my face. The practical side of me kicked in. "Is my car still in the garage downstairs?"

"Yeah," he answered. "But I doubt it will start. The battery is probably dead after sitting all this time. I didn't ever drive it. I just parked my car beside yours when I was here."

"You're probably right."

"I'll go downstairs and check it out if you want," he offered, standing.

"I'll go with you."

We both made our way back inside and took the stairs from the side of the kitchen down to the basement garage. He went first and I followed. And then I saw! My bright red Mercedes with the black convertible top. I'd always loved this car—even the shiny silver HyperVision rims. I put my left hand on my car and traced all the way around, noting my license plate with the name RAVEN still present. I walked to the driver's side, opened the door, and got inside. I couldn't help but notice the faint smell of cigarette smoke. I'd never been a smoker. The garage door remote was still on the sun visor. I pushed it and the garage door opened. The keys were in the ignition, and I turned the key. It started!

Jax's face was shocked. "Damn, that's some battery!"

I turned it off and got out. "Someone has been driving this car. It smells like cigarettes and I'm sure that's why it started."

"It definitely wasn't me," he said.

"Maybe it was someone doing the house cleaning."

"I wish we had the mileage so we could check. Or, for that matter, a security system. That would easily have solved the mystery."

"I'm still going to call a mechanic to come over and check it out. Also, that license plate has to go."

"Yeah, and the main reason I didn't take it for a spin while you were gone."

We both laughed.

* * *

I managed to convince Jax to go home to Mick's. Jax did phone a good mechanic at the Mercedes dealership who would stop by tomorrow morning to check out the car. I knew getting the license plate changed would take more effort. I walked to the back right of my living room and to a door that led to my home office library. I went inside and sat at the desk.

"This is Charlotte Bjorn," I told the woman on the other end of the line. "May I please speak with Oscar?" Oscar was my financial manager at the Vanguard Westend Bank. We'd been in communication the entire time I was locked up.

"Charlotte," he replied in his usual curt tone. "Glad to hear from you and learn you got home okay."

"Thank you. Any chance I can come to see you today?" The bank was two blocks away and an easy walk.

"Sure," he replied. "Can you make it at three? I have a board meeting until two-thirty."

"Sounds good. I'll see you then."

I glanced at the clock on the wall: eleven-thirty. I turned my chair around and faced the wall behind my desk. There was a framed oil painting of a garden: an original Vincent Van Gogh. I stood and carefully pulled the right side of the picture frame out, exposing a home safe. I punched in the thirteen-digit passcode, placed my thumb on the thumbprint reader, and opened it. My banking records were all there, including the records of the accounts in Switzerland. I pulled out all the documents and looked them over, then placed the Swiss account information back in the safe. Oscar only managed my local account while I was in prison. I hadn't yet purchased a computer to check things out myself. My previous computer was confiscated prior to my incarceration. I reached inside my safe and pulled out a stack of twenty-dollar bills. I counted out five hundred and put the rest back.

At the very far end of the safe was a cherry box with a brass front latch. I reached inside, retrieved it, and placed it on the desk beside the bank documents and cash. I opened it up and there it was, my most prized possession—the diamond and emerald white gold tiara. The tiara was insured for thirty million dollars. It was the "princess crown" Adeline was trying to snatch. I was surprised my former mother-in-law had allowed me to keep it. I wore it on my wedding day at the family residence in Copenhagen.

* * *

I was dressed in a navy Dolce and Gabbana pantsuit with my hair in a low bun as I walked the two blocks to the Vanguard Westend Bank, which was soon visible; a five-story renovated 1950s limestone that encompassed an entire corner. Upon entering the bank, I noticed the entire area had been renovated with lots of chrome and glass. It was nice, but the charm was gone. A tall and slender blonde with short hair in her mid-twenties approached. Her black stilettos tapped loudly on the restored white and burgundy mosaic tile floor.

She smiled wide, showing bright white teeth through her dark red lipstick. "May I help you?"

"I'm Charlotte Thoreaú Bjorn and here to see Oscar Bennet. He's expecting me."

"Sure. Right this way."

The sound of the woman's high heels echoed as she led me down a long hallway, where the brick walls were painted bright white. Framed pictures of various historical scenes from New York City's past lined the walls. At the very end of the hallway, there was a placard beside a heavy wooden door: OSCAR BENNET, VICE PRESIDENT OF FINANCIAL AFFAIRS.

The woman opened the door and we were in front of a receptionist, a twenty-year-old with short curly brown hair and black heavy-framed glasses. The nameplate in front of her desk said PATRICIA JACKSON. Patricia looked up from her computer and eyed me from head to toe. She nodded and motioned for me to sit on a couch across the room. She picked up her phone and dialed. The tall blonde who'd been my escort left without a word.

I was impressed by all the formality, as this was a dramatic shift from how I'd interacted with Oscar before. No doubt the title change on the door was telling.

Patricia rose from her seat. "Mr. Bennet will see you now."

I followed her to a side door, which she opened before stepping aside. Oscar sat behind a massive wooden desk. His white hair made him look older than his mid-sixties. He wore thick-framed black glasses and a black business suit with a white shirt and striped tie.

"Good afternoon, Charlotte." He smiled wide, showing bright white daVinci veneers. He rose from his seat and shook my hand. "So glad we can finally talk in person." I hadn't physically seen him since my incarceration, only spoken with him frequently on the inmates' shared phone line. His demeanor was stiff, but polite.

"Yes, thank you." I took a seat in front of his desk and he returned to his behind his desk.

"What can I do for you?"

I crossed my legs and found myself nervously swinging the top leg. "I need to review all my finances and come up with a plan. I also need bank cards so I can conduct my personal affairs. Basically, I have nothing right now except expired debit and credit cards."

"That's easy enough." He pulled out a drawer on the side of his desk and took out a folder. "I have already printed out statements." He handed me the folder; I leafed through the seven pages and noted it all looked fine. "I suggest you invest some of your funds. Six million dollars is a lot to keep in a savings account," he said.

I closed the folder. "I will think about it."

"I know you have a lot on your plate right now." His expression softened. "Take some time, and give me a call when you are ready to talk investing. Patricia will get your needed banking cards as soon as we are finished here."

I was back in the lobby, headed towards the door out of the building. The blonde I met initially was standing close to the door talking with a tall, middle-aged Black man in a security guard uniform.

"Goodbye, Raven," said the blonde with a smirk.

I ignored the comment and quickly exited the building, while a burning sensation stirred in my gut—shame, anger, guilt. It was abundantly clear as I walked the two blocks home that New York City wasn't my friend any longer. It was time to move on and begin anew someplace else. But where?

CHAPTER 4

Charlotte

I sat at my round oak kitchen table in my pink silk pajamas, eating Italian lasagna that had just arrived via delivery. It wasn't in me to go out grocery shopping for fear of being recognized again. The sting was still there from the bank incident.

I glanced around the modern kitchen with the polished dark granite countertops and the riverstone bricks backsplash that covered the wall behind the stainless-steel stovetop. The refrigerator, double oven, and dishwasher were also stainless steel and sat on an ivory quarry tile floor. I loved this kitchen and it had frequently been the focus of my thoughts while eating bland food in the Bedford Hills dining hall.

My thoughts drifted to Corey, my only friend in prison. Corey was tall and large-boned, with ebony skin and a massive Afro. The entire left side of her face was scarred from a serious burn she suffered during a burglary that landed her in prison the first time. Her left arm was completely covered with a dark tattoo of a nondescript design. She had a tough reputation but seemed to like me, which was a good thing. The inmates were cliquish and Corey always stood up for me whenever one of the bullies tried to harass me. It had been Corey's second time at Bedford Hills and she was in for life now, no chance of parole. Her crime: arson that had killed a man who was inside the house.

My thoughts were cut short by the sound of the front doorbell. I glanced at the digital clock on my stove and noted it was nine-thirty. I wondered who would stop by this late as I stood and walked to the door.

I glanced through the peephole. It was Jax.

I opened the door wide to let him in. "Hey, come on in."

"Mick and I had a fight," Jax said.

"Sorry." I hugged him. "Let's go to the kitchen. I was just eating my dinner and there is plenty for both of us."

"Just a glass of wine. I feel like getting drunk, but I won't." He followed me to the kitchen and went straight to my wine rack below the kitchen island. His hand reached for a bottle of expensive merlot, then he retrieved a glass from the upper cabinet. He poured himself a glass and made his way to the table where he say across from me.

"What happened?" I asked before putting another fork full of lasagna into my mouth. I knew he was ripe to talk.

"The short story—Mick has syphilis and it isn't from me." Jax took a large swallow from his wine glass. "Don't ask me how I found out."

I raised an eyebrow.

"He claims it was a one-night stand, but I don't believe him. There have been signs recently, but I ignored them. Didn't want to believe it."

"What do you want to do? You are always welcome to stay here." I walked the same kitchen cabinet, retrieved a wine glass, and filled it with wine. I returned to sit at the table.

"I appreciate that. Just for tonight." Jax finished off his glass and went back to the kitchen island. He grabbed the bottle and brought it back. "I don't want to be at his house right now. Mick left before I did. He always leaves when we argue and he knows I'm right. I have no idea where he goes and right now, I don't care."

"Sounds like you both need time to cool off." I took a final bite of my dinner, then pushed it forward out of the way. The wine was relaxing.

"Enough about me," Jax said. "Tell me about your day."

I described the banking experience and how the blonde woman treated me.

"You need to let that slide. It's bound to happen from time to time, at least as long as you are in the city."

"I love my place here, but I know you're right. Where do I go? The only relative you and I have left is Aunt Lydia and she's isolated on the edge of the Mojave Desert."

"It's not so bad," Jax said, now glassy-eyed from all the wine. "Her place might be isolated but it's huge. I went to a Pride rally there last summer and she easily hosted at least three hundred on her compound grounds. She and her partner, Pearl, are quite gracious and I know they would be happy to have you. The guest houses are quite nice too."

"Maybe." I took a final swallow of wine.

Jax's cell rang. "Hello?" He stood and walked out of the kitchen and into the backyard. No doubt it was Mick.

However, he had given me food for thought. Could I bear to leave my beloved home and live in the Mojave Desert? It seemed unthinkable as I'd always gravitated to the city lights. I decided to sleep on it.

I pulled back the covers of my massive bed and crawled inside. I stretched out, fully experiencing the comfort of the high-quality mattress and the luxury of the soft bed linens and plush comforter. I closed my eyes and was struck by the quietness and the pleasant scent of the fragrant flowers on my bedside table. It felt like heaven.

* * *

Metal banged against the steel bars of the cell beside me. It was dark, well past lockdown and lights out.

"Raven, baby, what ya doing?" said a voice from the next cell. It was Grace. "Ooooowe. I'd sure like to get me some Raven tonight."

"Go to sleep!" I yelled and pulled the coarse wool blanket from the steel-framed bunkbed over my head, hoping to dull the noise. I had the lower bunk. The banging on metal only intensified.

The cell door opened. It wasn't supposed to after lockdown, but it did. Grace came into my cell, and over to where I was in bed.

"You can't run from me now." Grace got on top of me and held down my arms. Another set of hands pulled off the covers and ripped open my top. Coarse, rough hands fondled my breasts while another person took off my pants.

I tried to fight them off me, but the strength of the other women was too much.

* * *

"Stop!" I screamed. I opened my eyes and sat up. I was covered in a cold sweat. I looked around for reassurance I really was in my own home. The nightmare haunted me. That rape was only the first of many from Grace and her cohorts. The abuse hadn't stopped until Corey became my cellmate.

Because Corey was the size of an NFL lineman and displayed a tough demeanor, it intimidated the other prisoners. Despite Corey's tough appearance, she was kind to me, not a predator. She never made sexual advances at me and instead kept Grace and her clique at bay.

I glanced at the clock on the nightstand. Three in the morning. I turned on the lamp and pulled off the covers, then got out of bed. Five hours straight of sleep, the most I'd had since intake into prison.

I walked down to the kitchen, flipping on lights along the way. I put a coffee pod into the coffeemaker and hit start. As I waited for the coffee to brew, my thoughts turned somber. Jax had gone back to Mick's last night, but he'd given me a lot to think about before he left.

I took my cup of coffee to my library office and flipped on the light. I placed my coffee mug on a table beside my favorite leather chair in front of the fireplace. I glanced around at the three shelved walls, which filled with leather-bound books from the floor to almost the ceiling. A floating ladder was at the farthest wall. Lars had been a rare book collector. I walked to the back wall and traced my fingers on a row of red leather spines: books of poetry in Danish. I pulled one out and placed it to my nose, inhaling the aging leather scent, recalling Lars reading aloud to me and translating. I opened the front cover. In blue ink he'd written, "*jeg elsker dig*, Charlotte." Danish for "I love you, Charlotte."

I hugged the book close to my heart and walked to the leather chair. Tears poured onto the front cover.

"Lars, my love. Will this aching for you ever leave me? Life doesn't ever seem worth living without you." I closed my eyes. "My God, I love you, Lars. My life is screwed up. I'm screwed up." The tears turned into bellowing sobs like I'd never cried before.

The tears did finally dry and I was numb. I knew my head wasn't where it needed to be, and I seriously considered ending it all. I didn't own a gun, but I did have a sharp knife in the kitchen. I imagined going to my bathroom, getting into the tub, cutting both wrists, and just… drifting away. A scene of that happening danced in my mind, over and over. I rose from my seat and started for the kitchen.

A compulsion overcame me. I reached for my phone and dialed Aunt Lydia's number.

The phone rang three times, then a familiar voice answered. "Hello?"

"Aunt Lydia, this is Charlotte." Then the waterworks started up again.

"Talk to me, Charlotte." Aunt Lydia's voice was calming and I felt comfort for the first time in many, many years. She waited patiently for me to regain my composure.

"I'm so sorry to bother you. I just now realized the time difference…"

"I've been waiting for you to call. Pearl had a vision about you last night. I want you to come stay with us for a while," Aunt Lydia said.

"My head is so screwed up right now."

Her voice remained calm and soothing. "Are you able to pack some of your things?"

"Yes, I can do that."

"Good. Now can you arrange a plane ticket?"

"Yes, I can."

"Very good. Text me the flight information and I will pick you up at the airport."

"Thank you. Thank you so much."

"You are always welcome at our place and you can stay as long as you want and need. Pearl and I are here for you."

I made flight arrangements as soon as we ended the call, then texted my aunt the information. I sent Jax a text. The flight departure was at ten the next morning. I made my way to my closet to pack.

CHAPTER 5

Charlotte

I stared out the window of the Boeing 737 flying from the La Guardia Airport in New York City to the small Palmdale Regional Airport. I'd been able to get the last first-class seat and was grateful. The privacy pods between each seat meant if I started crying again, it would be okay.

I kept my sunglasses on; my eyes were seriously red and puffy. The flight attendant had been kind when she offered a beverage. I ordered a white wine and sipped it slowly.

The flight was long, but after the second glass of wine, I was able to doze into a dreamless sleep. It was almost seven hours later when the pilot gave the "fasten seatbelt" announcement for the descent.

I spotted my aunt immediately as I descended the steps of the plane. I found myself practically running into her open arms. She looked so much like my mother, for a brief moment, I found myself thinking it was her.

Aunt Lydia appeared older than I remembered, with dark salt-and-pepper hair. Her eyes were such a rich dark brown that it made her thick eyelashes always look as if they were faux lashes. She was tall like me, but much thinner. Her full lips smiled wide, displaying perfect white teeth, a trait of the family my mother also had. She was dressed in her classic ankle-length floral skirt and a long-sleeved white cotton peasant blouse. Her brown Birkenstock sandals were the same style I remembered she'd always worn.

Aunt Lydia's dark blue 1999 Ford Expedition SUV was in pristine condition and the inside smelled like vanilla and lavender. The cushy velvet upholstery was most comfortable.

"How was your flight?" she asked as we traveled down the long road towards the Mojave Desert. Desert sand was on each side of the two-lane road and tumbleweeds were scattered. The traffic was sparse.

"It was fine. I was lucky and got the last first-class seat. It was a smooth flight."

"I'm really glad you called when you did. Pearl and I knew something was up. You know Pearl, she gets these visions."

"I'd forgotten about that, but now I do remember. Her visions were all quite accurate. I hope the one she got about me wasn't too terrible. I don't think I can take any more negativity."

"Do not worry. Pearl will give you a reading after you are settled in. We can also do a negativity release ceremony," Aunt Lydia said.

My lips turned into a smile for the first time in several days. "I hope it's not the one where we all dance naked around a campfire."

Aunt Lydia roared. "Not unless you want to do that one!"

"I think I'll pass on the naked firedancing. Though I do have so much inside of me I could probably start a bonfire."

"We'll release that. Don't you worry. Now, tell me how Jax is doing?"

"From what I can tell since I've been home, he seems to be the same as he always has. Still fledgling with regards to employment. I've been giving him financial support every month. My executor at the bank took care of that while I was in Beford. Jax and Mick seem to have a lot of highs and lows. I don't think they have a stable relationship."

"That's too bad. I was hoping he would find someone. Maybe he will someday. I got lucky with Pearl," Aunt Lydia said.

"You sure did. She's an angel. You're lucky to have each other."

"I wish I'd been able to visit you more frequently than I did when you were in prison. The distance posed a problem," she said apologetically.

"I completely understand. I'm grateful for those times I got to see you. You were my ray of sunshine—my *only* ray of sunshine. I wouldn't wish that hell hole on anyone."

A wrought-iron archway gate with Sunshine Oasis at the top came into view. Aunt Lydia turned and drove underneath the archway. The long driveway led to a white mansion-sized farmhouse, with a large porch across the entire front. There were rocking chairs and a porch swing on each end. Twenty colorful tiny houses stood to the far right of the house lined in two neat rows.

She stopped the car on the left side of the main house. "Here we are," Aunt Lydia said.

We both got out. She went to the back of the car and grabbed my suitcase as I carried my heavy carry-on bag.

Two large basset hounds ran to meet us.

"Meet Bessie and Ralph." Aunt Lydia bent down to pet each.

I did the same. "They are sweet."

"Hello, hello, hello!" Pearl called out as she walked through the front door towards us. She was a beautiful woman of Native American descent and her long black hair was in a single braid down her back. She wore an ankle-length denim skirt, a white t-shirt, and suede moccasins. The large turquoise jewelry around her neck and both wrists contrasted with her white top. The matching long dangly earrings almost touched her shoulders and pulled at the piercings in her ears.

"Pearl!" I went to her, and she gave me a tight hug and a kiss on the cheek.

"Welcome to our home," she said with a wide smile and led me inside.

The generous-sized foyer had hardwood floors with a Navajo rug. A wide staircase was visible in the far back. All the walls were off-white and eclectic artwork was displayed on every visible wall. Some were oil paintings of colorful desert scenes. Dreamcatchers with bright feathers hung between several of the paintings.

"We thought you might want to stay in our guest room on the upper floor rather than in one of the guest houses," Pearl said.

"Yes, I would like that very much." I followed Pearl up the stairs, Aunt Lydia tagging behind with my suitcase.

The sturdy wooden stairs wound to a wide landing. Four doors to the guest bedrooms were on the back wall. Another set of stairs was in between the four doors that led to the uppermost floor. The weather outside was an arid ninety-five degrees and expected to be down to fifty-six tonight. The air system inside made the house quite comfortable. At the top of the second set of stairs was another landing that led to a double-door entry. We went inside.

The fifteen by-twenty-five room was quite welcoming, with a king-sized bed and a lovely colorful quilt on top. The walls were a pale beige with paintings of various desert scenes lining two walls. The exposed beams gave the room a rustic appearance and added to the homey feel. A full wall window on the back gave a view of the outside front yard.

Aunt Lydia placed my suitcase in front of a closet. "Pearl and I have said prayers and blessed this room. We placed crystals in each corner to hold that energy. We want you to heal," she said with a soft smile.

I went to my aunt and gave her a huge hug, then Pearl.

I felt tears of gratitude fill my eyes. "I can't thank you two enough."

Aunt Lydia's pragmatic approach to things always gave me a sense of security. "Okay, enough of this. Let's go downstairs and have a glass of whiskey."

Pearl and I nodded.

We were seated outside on the front porch in rocking chairs, sipping whiskey from small glasses. The whiskey helped me relax. Bessie and Ralph made appearances and demanded pettings from each of us. Bessie plopped at my feet and gazed up with loving amber eyes.

"Pearl made some killer Irish stew for our dinner and fresh brown bread," Aunt Lydia said.

I continued rocking. "That sounds wonderful."

"I call it comfort food," Pearl said. "Just what you need."

When all of our glasses were empty, Pearl stood. "I'll go inside and get our dinner finished up. You and Lydia stay here and talk. I'll let you know when to come inside." She disappeared into the house.

My voice was quiet. "I was close to ending it."

"Go on," Aunt Lydia prodded gently.

"The high I felt finally getting out of prison and back into my home quickly disappeared after a few days. My home is filled with memories of Lars and the pain of his loss swallows me up. The memories of modeling and keeping busy with that flood my mind too. It had only been a diversion, a way to stave off all that pain. I didn't really like modeling and hadn't made any close friends. None that would visit me in prison at least. The realization of all that came at me full force while I was sitting in my library holding one of Lars' leather books. He'd written a special message inside for me and I kept reading it over and over and over. I cried all over the leather front cover till it was so wet I think it damaged some of the inner pages. I kept calling out to him and of course I didn't hear anything back.

"The tears dried up. I don't think there were any more left. I sat there staring at the fireplace. Images filled my mind of how I could just end it all and I planned the way I would do it. I imagined a specific knife from the collection in the kitchen to take with me to my bathroom. I would get into the tub, slice my wrists, and wait to fade away."

"What stopped you?" Aunt Lydia asked.

"A strange power came over me, a force that walked me to my desk. It was outside of my control. Then, I found my hand picking up the phone and dialing your number…"

"That must have been when Pearl had her vision. We stopped and prayed fervently for you."

"Your prayers were heard. Now what?" I asked.

"It will all be clear in due time. I can guarantee that."

Our conversation was cut short when Pearl appeared. "Dinner is served," she announced, her voice cheerful.

* * *

Dinner had been wonderful, the conversation light. Feeling emotionally drained, I was grateful for that. Both my aunt and Pearl joked around and told stories of happenings around the area, though the area of Boron is quite small, with a population of only twenty-two hundred. Both my aunt and her partner frequented friends in the neighboring town of Desert Lake, where an eclectic community of artists lived.

The Blue Moon Festival was scheduled to happen at Aunt Lydia and Pearl's place in two days. All the tiny houses had been spoken for and the event was apparently a big deal. I wasn't sure what exactly to expect, but I knew if Aunt Lydia and Pearl put it together, it would be grand.

I prepared to retire for the evening and put my pajamas on. Bessie had nosed her way into my room and refused to leave. I was happy to have her there.

There was a tranquility to this room. Whether it was Bessie or the crystals, I'd never know. But it felt nice, like

I was being cocooned in love. I easily fell into a dreamless sleep with Bessie at the foot of my bed.

CHAPTER 6

Charlotte

Two days passed and I mostly slept. Pearl and Lydia were busy around their property and insisted I needed to rest. Tonight was the Blue Moon Festival and I wanted to help with getting things set up.

I put on a pair of tan cargo shorts and a bright yellow t-shirt. My brown sandals were slide-ons. I put my long hair back into a single braid down my back. Glancing in the mirror, I knew I certainly looked the part for being here.

I found Lydia and Pearl in the front yard setting up the lighting for tonight—solar tiki torches and fairy lights and lanterns—around the property. Welcome baskets were lined up on the front porch with fruits, nuts, and cookies.

I descended the stairs. "Can I help?"

"Good morning!" Pearl called out. "Yes, you can help. How about grabbing the fruit baskets and placing one inside each guest house."

"Will do." Bessie stayed at my heels. She was growing on me.

As I walked, holding two baskets, I heard Pearl singing in her native language. It was a lovely song.

All the front doors to these tiny houses were wide open. I entered the first house and was astonished at how lovely it was. The walls were painted a soothing pale green. There was a seating area with white canvas-upholstered chairs, a small kitchenette, a tiny bathroom, and a loft with a king-sized bed with a colorful quilt on top. There was a small wooden coffee table in front of the seating area. I placed the basket there, took a little white welcome card, and placed it visibly in front of the basket. Fluffy white towels were in the bathroom and the kitchenette was fully stocked with bottled water. *Impressive*, I thought.

I soon learned each of the tiny houses was appointed the same, only the quilts differed.

I walked to Aunt Lydia, who was placing a tiki lantern in front of each of the guest houses. "I'm ready for my next task."

"Over here!" Pearl called out. She was carrying a large box filled with tambourines.

"Come with me to the drumming circle around back. Not everyone has a drum so these are for them to make some sound."

"Cool." I followed her to the back of the house where there was a stack of folding chairs on the ground. There was a large circular area that designated the burning pit.

She pointed to an area on the far left, away from the burning pit. "Let's set these folding chairs up over here."

"Sure. Do you want them in a circle?"

"Yeah, go ahead with a circle. There will be those who want to be outside the circle, but they can move the chairs to suit themselves," Pearl said.

The next three hours were spent finishing up all the preparations for the evening. Tables of food would be on the front porch and since it was a potluck, there wasn't anything more to do but have drinks available.

I went inside to change. I chose a simple yellow-print sundress and slid on some strappy white sandals. I let my wavy hair fall loose around my shoulders and back.

Five o'clock finally came and the guests began to trickle in. They were a lively and friendly crowd, bringing food and drums of all shapes and sizes. It was an eclectic group of all ages with married couples, life partners, and even a handful of children. Most everyone was attired in hippie-type clothing. Many first went to a tiny house, no doubt to claim their space before returning to the gathering.

Music from the seventies and eighties played in the background and people were already in the food line. And what a spread it was! The tables took up the full length of the front porch. Meats, cheese platters, cut-up fruits, veggies, and breads. There was pasta, cold and hot, with meatballs and sausage. Crockpots lined one side of a table filled with main courses. There were salads of every possible variety, and even a table full with nothing but delectable desserts.

A young couple invited me to join them to eat, and I felt quite welcomed. Introductions to others kept coming. My spirit began to lighten and by the time the first drum sounded, I was ready to walk back to where the circle was.

All the chairs had already been taken, so I grabbed one of the tambourines from the box and stood in the back with the others.

The volume of the drums began to grow as others joined in. I was fascinated by how a pattern began to take hold and the drums seemed to harmonize. There was a space in the center where many decided to dance in a primitive style. Pearl was among them and danced in a traditional Navajo style. It was so beautiful, I marveled as I continued to play my tambourine.

The drummers would come and go. When one left, another stepped in. This went on for several hours. It was one continuous sound until a loud gong rang out. It was Aunt Lydia; she stood on a chair.

"It's time to get the firepit going. Tonight is the blue moon and we will do a ceremonial ritual to release those things in our lives that no longer serve us. All are welcome to participate—releasing silently or out loud. Whatever you choose," she explained.

The burning pit was initiated without much fanfare. Once it was blazing, people trickled towards the perimeter, becoming quiet, and soon the only audible sound was the crackling of the fire.

There was a small table outside of the burning pit area with pieces of paper and pencils on top. I grabbed one and walked away from the crowd, finding a place on the ground to sit. I began writing. I poured my heart out, releasing all my pain, suffering, and shame. I went on and on till my paper was full on both sides. I wrote for quite some time. I folded up the paper and rose from the ground.

I made my way back to the burning pit, noting the number of people left was less than half before. I stepped to the spot I wanted. With my eyes closed, I took my piece of paper and held it to my heart. I then opened my eyes and threw the paper into the fire. I watched it burn and imagined everything on that piece of paper burned out of my life.

I left the pit and made my way back towards the house.

CHAPTER 7

Charlotte

The festival was still going full steam when I quietly made my way to my bedroom. Once there, I closed the door and lowered the blinds. I wanted to be alone.

I took off my shoes and grabbed my iPhone, a recent purchase. I went on to Amazon and found a romance novel from one of my favorite authors and purchased the eBook. I propped up the pillows and began to read.

It wasn't long before I heard scratching at the bottom of my door, followed by a single bark. I opened the door for Bessie; she rushed inside and jumped onto the bed. I closed the door, returned to my reading position, and Bessie put her head on my feet. I instantly felt better. Maybe this dog was an angel. Why not?

I must have dozed off because when I opened my eyes, the time on my phone said five in the morning. I was still in the same reading position, the phone in my lap and Bessie at my feet.

I went to the window and opened the blinds. I wanted to see if there was any activity still going on. There wasn't. I closed the blinds and changed into an oversized t-shirt before returning to bed. Sleep came quickly.

* * *

It was one-thirty in the afternoon when I heard a light knocking at my bedroom door.

I blinked a few times to focus. "Yes?"

"Charlotte, it's Lydia."

I sat up. "Please come in."

"I thought you could use this." Aunt Lydia walked in carrying a tray with a steaming mug of coffee and a cinnamon scone. She set it on a small side table beside the bed.

I picked up the coffee, blew lightly on the top, then took a swallow. "Yes, you're right. Especially that coffee."

Aunt Lydia pulled up a chair from the side of the room and placed it close to the bed. "How are you doing?"

"I should get dressed and help with clean up outside."

"Nah, you stay here and finish your breakfast. It's about all cleaned up anyway. Those that slept in the guest cottages cleaned up. There's just a few guests stacking those folding chairs and taking lights back to the barn," Aunt Lydia said.

"I can't thank you enough for taking me in on such short notice. I feel so much better being here. And Bessie is my new best friend." Bessie peered up then put her chin back down at the foot of the bed.

"Bessie is our intuitive dog. I'm not surprised she latched on to you." Aunt Lydia reached down to pet Bessie, then bent down and kissed her on the top of her head.

"You said something earlier about how Pearl got a vision about me," I prompted and Aunt Lydia nodded. "I would really like to get a reading. I'm hoping to get insight on how to move forward in my life. I'm feeling a stirring inside, a fire really, and I'm not clear about it."

"I saw you participating in the New Moon Ritual Burning Ceremony. That is a powerful ritual. Part of what you are now feeling could be related to that. It's all good," she explained. She patted my feet and then stood. "Bessie, I bet you need to go outside, don't you?"

Bessie's ears perked up. She jumped down to the floor and followed Aunt Lydia out of the room. My aunt shut the door behind them.

I continued to ponder my situation as I sipped coffee still in bed. There was a definite renewal in my mindset following the paper I'd thrown into the fire.

I began to reflect on the items I'd written. The first was to clear my tarnished name, then for the guilty party to be caught. Another was to forgive myself. The final and most important was to heal from all the pain of losing Lars and our baby.

* * *

Three weeks later

Time flew by quickly at Aunt Lydia and Pearl's. There wasn't anything to do and yet everything to do. Riding horseback in the desert with Pearl was fun and energizing. There was sand as far as my eyes could see. Many Salsola tragus, once green little shrubs, had broken off and formed tumbleweeds that rolled gently across the desert sand. Joshua trees, some close to a thousand years old, were scattered, and in the far distance were the mountains.

Pearl wasn't much for conversation and I was grateful. The desert sun and heat were unforgiving, but there was a stillness there. It was as if both the sands and sun were keeping guard of secrets. There was a mighty and healing energy only the desert could share. I absorbed it.

We were once again back at the house, and the horses happy in their stable. Aunt Lydia had offered me and Pearl glasses of whiskey, which we both accepted. We were all seated in a cozy library tucked away on the second floor.

"Are you ready to return home tomorrow?" my aunt asked.

"Yes, I really am. I feel like a different person now. My head is clear."

Both older women gave knowing smiles. Aunt Lydia pulled Pearl close and put her arm around her, then kissed her on the lips.

"I promised you a reading. I think now is a good time," Pearl said. Aunt Lydia nodded.

I instantly felt a nervous twinge in my belly but said, "I would love a reading."

Pearl slid to the floor, sitting with her legs crossed on a Navajo rug. She motioned for me to do the same and I sat across from her. Pearl raised her hands high and lifted her head upward. With her eyes closed, she began to chant words in her native language. Song came next and when she finished, she blew out a deep, guttural breath, lowered her arms, and opened her eyes.

The temperature in the room seemed to change—or was it merely full of loving energy? I couldn't be sure, but there was a definite *something* present. Pearl smile, contented, when she held out both her hands and I knew to place my hands into hers.

Pearl again closed her eyes and there was silence for what seemed like half an hour; it was probably only half that time.

"Lars is here," Pearl said. Her smile brightened even more.

I felt his familiar spirit and knew what Pearl said was truth. "Oh Lars, my love. I miss you so."

"He asks that you close your eyes, and he will talk to you directly," Pearl said.

I did as she told me. Instantly, Lars' beautiful face appeared. His lips came to mine and when he kissed me, waves of love filled me like never before.

"You must go on living. Our time together was only meant to be brief. You may not understand that now, but someday you will. The same is true for our baby." He gave me one final kiss, then disappeared. I opened my eyes.

Tears streamed down my face. "Oh God!"

Pearl's hands began to shake.

"What you are searching for will come to be. Hold on to faith like you've never done before. The tides are changing. Great Spirit is showing favor on to you."

* * *

I sat in my first-class seat on the flight back to New York City. I reflected on the past three weeks in awe. I was a changed woman.

CHAPTER 8

Charlotte

It was ten on Monday morning. Much had been done to get up to speed with current society still, including getting my driver's license ready and finances secure. Almost everything was in order but me. I needed to schedule a hair appointment, and go shopping. I wanted some new makeup and perfume. All the items in my vanity were long past the expiration dates. I also needed hair products, but figured I could easily get what I needed at the salon.

I was still in my silk pajamas when I made my way from the kitchen to my library office. I sat my half-full mug of coffee down on my desk, then pulled out the tan leather chair and sat, careful to slide my fuzzy white bunny slippers underneath. I opened the right-side drawer and found my old brown leather address book. I thumbed through the pages till I found the number of the salon I used to frequent. It was the salon my old modeling agency had sent me to. I dialed the number on my new iPhone.

"Carlyle Salon and Day Spa," answered a high-pitched woman's voice.

"I'd like to make an appointment with Olivia."

"I'm sorry, but Olivia no longer works here. She left two years ago. Can someone else work with you?"

"Okay, but I want someone who isn't fresh from beauty school." I gave a light laugh.

"I hear ya," the girl replied. "When would you like to be here?"

"This afternoon, maybe?"

"Three o'clock good?"

"Yeah. Perfect. Thanks." I was grateful for such a quick appointment; this salon had always been booked out.

"Name?"

This was the moment I'd been dreading. What should I say? Certainly "Raven" was out.

"Name?" the girl repeated.

My heart raced. "Charlotte Bjorn."

"Hmm. Okay." There was a brief silence. "Can you hold for a minute? I need to check something."

"Sure." What else could I say?

"Charlotte, unfortunately that three o'clock has already been taken. I suggest you phone another salon." The girl hung up quickly.

Shame, humiliation, and hurt filled me—emotions I knew were undeserved. The encounter with the snide woman at the bank, now the refusal of an appointment at the hair salon. What next?

I picked up my phone and dialed Jax. He answered after two rings. "What's up?"

"Any idea of a really good hair person who will take me?" I told him the entire scenario about the hair salon.

"Wow! That sucks!" Jax said. "It's probably because Hilda sends all her models there. Maybe another place wouldn't even care."

"Any ideas?"

"I know someone. Let me make a call and get back to you," Jax said.

"Thanks." I hung up and stood. I glanced around at the shelved walls filled with leatherbound books. I remembered the last time I picked up one of those books, the most special one, and vowed not to do that again.

The phone rang. "I found you a great hair person and he can take you today," Jax informed me.

"That's great. You say he's good?"

"Oh yeah. Mick and I go to him, and I've seen a lot of his work."

My mood brightened. "Sounds good. When can I get in?"

"Deuce said four today is open," Jax said.

"Perfect. I'll take it," I said, relieved and excited.

"Want me to pick you up and take you?"

"Sure. Where is it?"

"It's in Queens. It'll take us thirty minutes to get there. Are we good?" he asked.

"Very good," I replied.

* * *

Jax pulled up in front of my townhouse promptly at three-thirty. I'd been watching from my front window. I grabbed my purse and made my way out to his Mustang.

"I really appreciate this. I'm anxious to get some of this hair cut off." It had grown past my waist.

"Are you dyeing it black again?" Jax smirked.

"Nah. Raven is dead. I want to move on."

"Good idea." Jax weaved in and out of busy traffic. It wasn't long before we were on the edge of the Queensbridge neighborhood—a well-known ghetto.

I was now worried. "Are you sure we're going to be safe?" I'd avoided this area for years as it was known for harboring gangs.

"Don't worry. We're fine." Jax turned into a small parking lot behind an old red-brick building. We both got out of the car and Jax led the way down a sidewalk to the front of the building. A solid black sign beside the door said THE DUNGEON—HAIR, INK, AND PIERCINGS.

"Don't let appearances scare you," Jax said. "Deuce is good."

I grimaced. "I'll take your word for it."

We walked up the cement steps to the landing and opened the heavy black metal door. The four windows on each side of the door had ornate black wrought iron burglar bars. Jax went inside and I followed. There wasn't a reception or waiting area. Heavy metal music blared. Six stylists—four men and two women—lined the walls; all were working behind black leather chairs with chrome. The walls they worked in front of were mirrored. All remaining wall space, as well as the ceiling and floor, were painted black. Black-encased spotlights hung from the tall industrial ceiling and were aimed at each stylist's work station.

One tall and muscular woman had patches of purple, yellow, and red hair. She wore a solid black top and ankle-length skirt with heavy black combat boots. Her arms and neck were heavily inked in red roses, Sanskrit symbols, and a dark blue lattice design. The woman beside her, petite, with long and wild bushy purple hair, wore an orange jumpsuit that reminded me of my old prison garb. One platinum-haired man of medium height had a long white beard; he was wearing a red paisley Nehru shirt and faded jeans. A dark-skinned man, well over six feet tall, had a full Afro. He had a solid black t-shirt and black leather pants. An attractive, clean-shaven Black man of average height with short hair, wearing a white silk shirt and dark-wash jeans, looked out of place next to the previous man and the other one beside him—a slight built man of five foot seven, with a shaved head covered with dark blue and red tattoos. He had piercings that circled both ears and two in his nose. He too wore a black t-shirt and black leather pants and had rings on all his fingers with his nails painted black.

"Is Deuce in the back?" Jax called out to no one in particular.

The platinum-haired man nodded. I followed Jax to a backlit hallway and then opened the double doors on the right. We walked into a brightly lit twenty-by-twenty room where all the walls were painted white; its design was the inverse of the outer room. I blinked a few times as I adjusted to the change in light.

"Hey, Deuce," Jax said to a towering man of six feet four inches.

"Deuce" wore his wavy medium brown hair to his shoulders and had a full beard. His bright, gray eyes squinted at the corners as he beamed. He was dressed in faded jeans and a tan t-shirt, showing well-defined muscular biceps. I sensed I'd met him before, though couldn't quite place it.

"Hi, beautiful," he said in a deep voice and with a slight New York accent. "You must be Charlotte."

"That I am." I smiled crookedly, shy, positive he knew all about me.

He winked, then pointed to the chrome and white leather stylist chair. I sat, staring at myself in the mirrored wall.

"I'll make my exit now," Jax said. "I'll be next door at Buck's. Haven't talked to him in a while."

"Who's Buck?"

"He's the best tattoo artist in Queens. Call me when you're ready to leave."

"Sure." I watched him walk out.

"Now," Deuce's expression turned serious, "what can I do for you?" He studied my face and ran his fingers through my wavy long hair.

"I'm thinking a cut. Maybe twelve inches. That will bring it to just below my shoulders."

"Okay," he said. "Let's do it."

He opened a drawer and pulled out a solid black drape. He guided me to a sink; I sat and leaned back. His hands quickly went to work; they felt wonderful washing my hair. I hated it when he finished.

"I appreciate you taking me on such short notice," I said, breaking the silence once back in the chair.

He began sectioning my hair. "Your brother and his partner are clients."

"I guess he told you my situation."

"Yep, but your release date was in the newspaper. Sorry."

"That sucks!" Now I understood why I'd been getting cold receptions virtually everywhere I'd gone to take care of business. "Seems like I should leave the city, go someplace else for a while until I can clear my name. I never did what I was accused of."

His face was expressionless but he said, "I understand."

"What is it about sitting in a hair stylist's chair that makes one want to talk?" At that, he laughed, so I kept with it. "I'm sure you've heard it all."

"You would be right. I've been told I'm a good listener."

"I won't dump on you." I gave a nervous laugh. "How long have you been at this salon?" I wanted to change the subject—get him to talk about himself so then the focus wouldn't be on me.

"I bought this building last year."

It was clear Deuce was a man of few words and I wasn't going to get much out of him. An uncomfortable twenty minutes of silence passed.

"You know, Deuce, I didn't do what I was sent to prison for," I blurted. I felt compelled somehow. "Really."

"I know," he replied. "I was there."

CHAPTER 9

Dmitri

People call me Deuce, but my name is actually Dmitri Zhukov.

I was cleaning up my space at the salon and preparing to leave for the day when I glanced at the floor and noticed a large hoop earring—Charlotte's. I picked it up, placed it on the counter, then continued sweeping, and put the detritus into a trash bin. The black nylon smock she'd worn was draped on the back of the chair. I picked it up and put it to my nose. The scent of her perfume was still distinguishable. I inhaled deeply.

Scenes began to flood my mind from six years ago. I had planned to approach her at that party. I wanted to get to know her. I'd been watching her for several months—ever since my father had deeded me the building. The bulk of business was special events, predominately fashion shows. I spotted her when she walked through the front door, with her long and straight shiny black hair, head held high, and a most purposeful gait as she disappeared backstage with the other models. I was instantly attracted to her and learned her name was Raven.

The party was held at a hotel across the street from my building. I never attended any of the fashion show afterparties before, but decided to this time because I knew Raven would be there. A stocky man with white hair and

"

attired in a black suit was quick to open the front door. I walked inside.

I was clean shaven, had short hair, and dressed conservatively in a black suit with a light blue dress shirt. I wore with the first two buttons undone. My footsteps echoed on the white and beige marbled floor. I passed beneath a fifteen-foot crystal chandelier, which hung on a brass chain from the three-story high ceiling. I navigated the ballroom-sized lobby, making my way to the check-in desk, passing conversation areas with upholstered couches and chairs. A petite blonde sat there.

"My name is Dmitri Zhukov and I'm here for the Damara Conner party."

She pointed to a hallway behind her. "Take the elevator to the eighteenth floor. You'll see it."

I nodded and made my way to the already open door of the elevator. Once inside, I hit the eighteenth-floor button and traveled there nonstop. The door opened to a large, dimly lit banquet room buzzing with caterers and an open bar. Patrons occupied some of the nearby round tables with long white tablecloths. Outside the far glass door, loud dance music and voices indicated where the real party was. I went there.

A pool was in the center of this roof garden. There was a DJ in the very back, the dance floor full. Raven was there in a long, form-fitting red dress. Her long black hair covered the cut-out back of the dress. I ordered a beer from a bartender I spotted to the right side of the entry. I took a large sip and kept my eyes on the dance floor. Her dance partner was clearly intoxicated and she appeared to be the same. When the music stopped, they walked to a table between the pool and the dance floor, and sat. I was within easy view of the couple, but couldn't hear anything they said.

A tiny red sequined purse with a long gold chain was on top the table. She opened it and pulled out some lipstick, refreshing her lips. When she tried to put the lipstick back in, she missed and the contents of her purse fell to the floor—a set of keys, driver's license, that tube of red lipstick, and a fingernail file. She attempted to put the contents back into her purse, but missed again, and the items scattered across the floor. The guy she was with retrieved the items from the floor. There wasn't anything resembling cocaine.

I watched as both Raven and her dance partner stood and walked to the door leading inside. She left the purse on the tabletop, so I figured they would be right back. Twenty minutes passed and there still wasn't any sign of them.

I decided to go inside. I planned to tell Raven about leaving her purse on the table, certain she wouldn't want it stolen. But when I got inside, I couldn't find them.

The food looked good and I was hungry. I walked to one of the buffets; a server placed sliced roast beef with gravy on a plate and added green beans and a French roll. I found a table in the corner of the room. I was near a full glass wall with an easy view of the table where Raven and her dance partner sat. The red purse was gone.

After I had finished my meal, I returned outside. I wanted to get another beer and have a cigarette. There was a different bartender behind the bar, a tall and slender Latino in his mid-thirties.

When I picked up the bottle from the top of the bar, I noticed the red sequined purse behind the bar on a table.

"How did that purse get on that table?"

"I don't know." The bartender shrugged. "It was there when I started my shift."

"I know who it belongs to."

"It's mine," a voice said from behind me.

I turned around to a tall redhead with long wavy hair. She stood beside another woman, also tall and quite striking, with ebony skin and shoulder-length natural hair

. The redhead was quick to snatch the purse and both women practically ran inside. Two men followed behind. I recognized them—Gustav and Polvalaski—two of my father's men. Gustav turned towards me and gave me a stern expression before going inside. I knew not to follow. Whatever was going down, I knew it wasn't my fight.

CHAPTER 10

Charlotte

"Hey, Jax, what's the story with Deuce?" I asked as we were driving on the highway back to my place.

"Deuce is someone Mick knew before he and I met. Why?"

"I don't know..." I paused, remembering the familiar feeling when I first stepped into his hair salon.

"Is there something wrong?" Jax said. "Your hair looks great, by the way."

I gave a light laugh. "Yeah, I really do like it. Huge change." I ran my fingers through my hair, enjoying its softness and shorter length. My mind again returned to Deuce. "I think I've met him before, but I can't say where."

"Maybe you did six years ago and he just looks different now. People change."

"Maybe you're right." I paused. "He said something strange."

"Like what?"

"He said he was at that party when I was arrested. He also said he knew I wasn't guilty. I wish he'd come forward when I was in court."

Jax's mouth dropped. "You're kidding?"

"I'm not kidding. Thing is, what can I do with this? I do want to clear my name."

"Why didn't you ask him to elaborate? You were right there!" Jax said.

"I definitely should have. I wish I had and I don't know why I didn't," I lied. I was attracted to him and it stunned me.

"Want me to ask Mick about him?"

"Yes, please do."

We traveled the remaining distance to my house in silence.

* * *

Jax wasn't able to get any information about Deuce. Jax said Mick acted like he didn't want to talk about it. I was disappointed. It would have helped to know more about Deuce before I placed this call. There was something about him I struggled to define. Somehow, he felt powerful—maybe even dangerous—very much out of place at that salon. When he handed me his business card, his hand brushed across my forearm. I felt tingling sensations run straight to my core. Why? Maybe it was because he was so good looking?

I was nervous about calling him, but I wanted to learn what he knew about the night I was arrested. He said he was there but I don't remember seeing him. But if he could help clear my name—get the real guilty party behind bars—then talking to him would be worth it. I picked up my phone, sat on my couch in the living room and dialed. The phone only rang twice before he answered.

"Hello, this is Deuce."

"Hi, Deuce, this is Charlotte. I hope you're doing well."

"Yeah, I'm good," he replied. "What can I do for you, or is this a social call?" He gave a light chuckle.

"Actually, I was hoping we could talk. Not on the phone, though. Maybe at the Starbucks on your street?"

"How about dinner instead?" He sounded eager.

I was momentarily stunned, not expecting this. Dinner felt more like a date. "Dinner? I don't know," I said hesitantly.

"I insist, and you can pick the spot," he said.

"Okay, if you insist." I knew I'd better take him up on this offer if I had any hope of learning what he knew. "There's a nice Italian restaurant on Perry Street. Alberobello. I can meet you there." I'd been wanting to go there, remembering how good the food was. It was also an easy walk.

"How about tomorrow night?" he asked.

"Sure. What time?"

"Six o'clock?"

"Sounds good. I'll meet you there."

"See you then," he replied.

* * *

The weather was mild and there was a nice breeze. I decided to wear a pale peach floral print dress that cinched at the waist and the skirt flared out. It hit right above my knees. I chose three-inch nude pumps as they were comfortable for walking. I also grabbed a coordinated shawl wrap in case the restaurant was chilly. My plan was to leave the restaurant before dark, around seven-thirty. The two block-walk went quickly, or perhaps my nervousness made it seem so. Soon, the door of Alberobello was visible. I was grateful there wasn't a line and I easily walked underneath the black awning to the brass handle of the shiny black door. Once inside, I spotted Deuce, standing close to the reception desk, though I hardly recognized him. He was clean shaven, hair short, and wearing a black Armani suit with a solid black shirt. He was quite handsome with chiseled features I hadn't been able to see beneath his bushy beard. His tall stature was commanding as were his broad chest and shoulders.

"Good evening," he said, showing bright white perfect teeth and the sides of his gray eyes squinted when he smiled.

"Hello to you too." I found myself blushing and didn't want that. "I almost didn't recognize you. Nice change." I managed to smile back.

"Shall we go in?"

"Yes."

Deuce motioned to the receptionist at the front desk that we were ready to be seated. "Please follow me," said the attractive middle-age Italian woman. I immediately noticed how the place had been renovated since the last time I was there. The dining room was elegant, at least double the size. The walls were tan stucco and the floor was inlaid stone tile. Five matching chandeliers were evenly spaced above an area that was longer than it was wide.

The hostess escorted us through the half-full dining room to a table in a far side private alcove. I sensed Deuce had spoken to the hostess beforehand.

"Allow me," he said and pulled out my chair for me. I sat. He took the seat across from me at the round table. The white linen tablecloth draped near to the floor.

"Shall I bring the wine list?" The woman glanced at Deuce, who looked at me.

"That would be nice," I surprised myself by saying.

The woman nodded and left.

"I'm glad you chose this restaurant," Deuce said. "It's been a while since I've been here. I remember their food was always good."

"I used to come here a lot before Bedford. There were different people working then."

An awkward silent came next. No doubt the word *Bedford* was the cause. I was grateful when a waiter appeared with a wine list.

"What are you in the mood for?" Deuce asked.

"I think a merlot would be nice."

"Do you have Basilica del Pruneto Merlot?"

"We do," the waiter replied. "Shall I bring a bottle?"

"Yes," Deuce said.

I recognized the name of that wine. It was over two hundred dollars a bottle. Deuce was pulling out all the stops, going way over the top. He was acting as if this was a date. I hadn't planned it this way, but I had to admit it felt good.

The waiter quickly reappeared with the bottle of wine. He uncorked it and poured some into a wine glass. He handed it to Deuce, but Deuce handed it to me instead.

I took a swallow and loved the smooth rich taste. I smiled at him.

"I believe she likes it. Go ahead," Deuce said.

The waiter poured the wine, and sat the bottle on the table beside Deuce. The waiter presented each of us with a menu and said he would return shortly.

"I propose a toast," Deuce said. "May you find the answers you're looking for."

"I will drink to that." We clinked our glasses to the other. I took a swallow of the smooth and full-bodied wine. It was decadent and I immediately wanted another swallow, but held myself back.

The waiter reappeared for our food orders. Deuce ordered shrimp fra diavola and I chose the balsamic salmon.

"Charlotte," Deuce said after the waiter left. *I loved how he said my name.* "You said you wanted to talk to me. I'm all ears." He took a swallow of the wine.

"I think you know what I want to talk about."

"Yeah, I believe I do." He took another swallow of the wine. A large one.

CHAPTER 11

Charlotte

We were both feeling quite relaxed—no doubt due to the wine, especially since he ordered a second bottle after we'd finished our meal and the plates had been removed. We talked about everything *but* what he witnessed at that party. He was quite the jokester and I found myself laughing much of the time.

There was a heavy pause before I said, "You still haven't told me what you know about my arrest at that party."

"I will. After you dance with me," Deuce said with a crooked, mischievous grin. He motioned to the small dance floor where a piano player had been playing dinner music. A young blonde woman with a flute joined the pianist. After a brief intro, the piano player began singing "Moon Dance," an old Van Morrison song. One couple was already on the dance floor.

"You're kidding, right?"

"Nope," he replied, then stood, walked to where I was sitting, and offered me his hand.

"Okay." I accepted his hand and we walked to the dance floor.

Deuce was a smooth dancer and his lead easy to follow. It wasn't long before I found I enjoyed dancing with him. Maybe it was the wine. Or perhaps I enjoyed his company. Maybe both. One song led into another—a Latin piece

Deuce was quick to lead in a rumba. I found it fun and moved right along. He pulled me close; I could smell his cologne. It was nice.

Before the next song began, Deuce took my hand and led me back to our table.

"You can certainly dance."

He grinned broadly. "So can you."

I was gazing into his gray eyes, which seemed brighter somehow. His smile was sweet. "Please tell me what you know about that party?"

"First, I have to tell you we've met before. I was the owner of the building where all those fashion shows were held. We saw each other in passing—as you were entering the building and then later walking to the back stage," he said.

"Dmitri Zhukov?" A cold rush fired through me. It had been rumored the building was owned by a Russian crime family.

He nodded.

I studied his face as I leaned back. "Should I be afraid of you?"

"No," he said. "I can help you."

"Are you in the mafia?"

"Why did you ask me that?" His expression was blank and I felt it was intentional.

"Rumor had it backstage that the building was owned by a Russian crime family—the Zhukovs."

He raised an eyebrow. "Do I look like mafia to you?"

"No. But I've never known anyone who was in the mafia."

"My father owned the building first," he said. "He deeded it to me before he returned to Moscow. I managed it for a while, but decided to sell it."

I was curious. "Why?"

"I have other interests."

"Is it the salon?"

He laughed. "No."

An awkward silence followed. I took another swallow of wine. I wanted to ask what those *other interests* were, but decided not to.

"Please tell me what you know about the night I was arrested," I implored. He didn't flinch as I studied his eyes.

"I saw you return to your table from the dance floor. You had a small red sequined purse and it fell to the floor. All the contents fell out. You picked it up, but it fell again. Same thing; all the contents fell out on the floor. There weren't any vials of cocaine," Deuce said.

"I forgot my purse on that table when I went inside with my date. I never saw Garth do anything besides drink champagne. But clearly, he did. I just never saw it."

"I'd gone inside to get something to eat," Deuce continued. "When I returned outside, the purse was behind the bartender on a table. I told him I knew who the owner was, but before I could say anything else, a woman behind me told the bartender it was hers and grabbed it. She all but ran back inside with another woman. I remember seeing that woman at my building for a fashion show. I assumed the other woman was also a model."

"What did the woman that took my purse look like?"

"Tall, long, wavy red hair, heavy makeup," he said.

"Marilee. Who else was with her?"

"An attractive Black woman with shoulder-length natural hair."

"Zahara. I don't get it. Why would they frame me? What could have possibly been their motive? I know Marilee was jealous, but I don't think that would be enough for her to frame me for murder."

"Are you sure it was them?" Deuce said. "Sometimes things aren't as they seem."

"You're right, of course." I fixed my eyes into his. "Why didn't you come forward at my trial with this? It may have prevented me from having to spend all those years in hell."

Deuce's eyes remained fixed into mine. "I couldn't. I wanted to; believe me, I did want to. I wish I could tell you why, but I can't."

I was suspicious. Why couldn't he tell me? The notion of mafia sounded plausible.

"But I can help you clear your name if you will let me," he said.

I turned my eyes away as I felt tears welling up. Deuce noticed. He reached over to my hand and held it in his. I became quiet as tears ran down my cheek. He let go of my hand, pulled out his handkerchief, and handed it to me. I wiped my eyes.

I attempted to regain my composure. "You know, it would be simple to sell my house, change my name, and move far away. Just start over."

"Is that what you want?"

I thought about it before answering, "I don't know." I took another swallow of wine. "I have an aunt who lives in the Mojave Desert. She's my mother's sister. I've thought about moving there."

"It would be more difficult for you to prove your innocence that far away from here. Your brother told me both your parents had passed away. Do you have any other family members besides your brother and aunt that are still living?"

"Not blood relatives. My late husband's family used to keep in touch until I was incarcerated. They're in Denmark." I glanced down at my watch. It was nine. "I should probably leave for home."

"Of course," he said. "Did you drive here or take a cab?"

"Actually, I walked."

"It's sure to be dark outside. Please allow me to walk you home," he said.

"That would be nice. Thank you."

Deuce motioned for the waiter, who was prompt. He gave his credit card—a black one.

The air was brisk and the slight breeze felt cool. I wrapped the shawl around my shoulders as Deuce and I began the walk to my house.

"Thank you for dinner," I said, breaking the silence. Deuce wasn't chatty.

"The pleasure was mine," he said with a slight smile and a wink. "I'm glad you called me."

"You have to admit you knew that when you dropped the bomb and said you were at that party, I would want the details."

"I understand," he said.

"I want to prove my innocence and what you told me is helpful, but I don't believe it's enough to take to court. If I'm going for it, I need to have more."

"I can help you," Deuce repeated.

"How can you help me?" I asked, uncertain.

"Trust me," he replied.

I raised my eyebrow. "Trust is earned, not expected."

He smiled. "Fair enough."

I pointed to the shiny red door. "This is my house." We stopped on the sidewalk in front of my steps. I opened my purse and pulled out my house key.

"I'd like to see you again. May I call you?" Deuce asked.

"That would be nice." Dinner with him had been pleasant. Actually, just being around him felt wonderful—something I'd not felt in a long time. "I guess you have my number from my hair appointment."

"I do. I almost forgot. I have something of yours." He reached into his jacket and pulled out a hoop earring. "I found this on the floor in my shop."

"I wondered what happened to that. Thanks." I put it inside my purse. "I enjoyed dinner with you. I was afraid I wouldn't but I really did." Our eyes met.

"Me too." He then took my right hand in his, lifted it to his mouth, and lightly kissed the top of it.

I felt myself blush. "You know, I should be mad at you for not stepping forward at my trial."

"Are you?" he asked.

My eyes fixed into his. I felt so drawn to him. My inner knowing told me he was a good person. There was something he couldn't tell me about that night. I sensed he wanted to.

"No." I tried to shake off my longing for him to touch me. "Good night." Our eyes remained fixed on each other. I was the first to look away, before I climbed the steps to my front door and went inside.

Inside, I flipped on the front foyer light, leaned on the closed door, and took in a deep breath. *Oh God, why do I feel this way? I just can't. I must stay focused on getting my life back together and clearing my name.*

I walked through my house, flipping on each light before I made it to the office library. The message light was flashing on my answering machine. I put my purse on top the desk and retrieved the message.

"Charlotte, this is Jax. I tried to call you on your cell, but you didn't answer. Give me a call back. We need to talk."

I pulled out my phone from my purse. Sure enough, he did try to call. I'd put the cell on silent while out to dinner. I dialed Jax's number.

"Hi, Charley." Jax sounded anxious.

"What's going on?"

"Mick's been shot. He's in the hospital in critical condition." Jax began to weep.

"Oh my God. What happened?"

"We were at Bread Sticks, a new nightclub. We'd gone outside to the back alley to smoke. A black sedan with darkened windows drove by, someone rolled down a backseat window, aimed a gun at Mick, shot him in the chest, then sped away."

"Did he have any enemies that you know of? That couldn't have been a mere drive-by; otherwise, you would have probably been aimed at too."

"No enemies that I know of. Mick has always been super guarded about his business dealings and past. I'm surprised he told you about being in prison. He never even shared that with me," Jax said, defeated.

"Wow." I wondered why Jax knew so little about his partner. "I'm guessing the police have done a full report?"

"I told them all I knew at the hospital. I rode with Mick in the ambulance. The police mentioned two other witnesses whom they got statements from, but no clues about the shooter."

"This is awful. Is there anything I can do?"

"No, I don't think so. Once I know more, I'll let you know. He's still in surgery. I'm waiting in the lobby till they call me."

"I'm so sorry. I know this hurts."

"Yeah."

* * *

I awoke the next morning in the midst of a dream. Deuce and I had been dancing. He held me close and I relished every second of it. But those images became clouded at Jax's news about Mick. I was worried about my brother.

I walked to the kitchen, put a K-cup in the Keurig, and as the coffee was brewing, decided to flip on the small television sitting on the corner countertop. I searched through several channels till I got to the local news. A young blonde anchor sat behind a news desk. A picture of Mick was displayed with the caption, RUSSIAN BROADWAY DIRECTOR, MIKHEIL LEVINOWSKI, SHOT AND IN CRITICAL CONDITION. NO SUSPECTS AT THIS TIME. INVESTIGATION IN PROGRESS.

I was stunned! I never suspected Mick was Russian! I grabbed my cup of coffee and cell. I dialed Jax's number. He answered on the first ring.

"Hi, Charley," he greeted flatly.

"Just wanted to check in. How is Mick doing?"

"Not good. He made it through surgery, but now he's in the ICU. Unconscious. He's on a respirator and they had to defibrillate him twice." Jax began sobbing.

"Can I do anything?"

He didn't say anything, only continued sobbing.

"Do you want me to come to the hospital and sit with you for a while?"

He sniffed. "No. I'm going back in there when the medical people are finished, and if it looks like he's stable, I'll go home, shower, then return here."

"I'll call you in a couple of hours to check back in. Of course, call me before then if you want."

"Okay," he replied.

I grabbed my cup of coffee and went to the back patio, pulled out a chair, and sat. The morning breeze was chilly but still pleasant. I took a sip of coffee and looked around my patio, admiring and appreciating all the lovely flowers and foliage. In the farthest corner, I noted a medium-sized rock, approximately eight inches wide. I knew it hadn't been there before. I walked over to inspect it. When I picked it up, there was a shallow hole underneath, with a small square package inside a clear baggie. I picked it up and opened the plastic bag. Inside was a four-inch square wooden box. It looked like something from Pier One Imports. I took the whole thing back to the patio table, sat down, and opened the box. A black flash drive was inside. Chills ran down my spine. *What was on it? Who put it there? Why my backyard? What should I do with it?*

I wanted to see what was on it but didn't have a computer. My previous one had been confiscated by the police prior to the trial. Jax was the only other person who had access to my place—or so I thought. I regretted never installing security devices, and vowed to do that as soon as possible. The thought of Jax doing something nefarious made my stomach burn. I decided not to tell him about this until I knew what it was.

I returned the rock to where I found it. I took the other items inside, tossing the baggie into the kitchen trash can underneath the sink. I put the flash drive back in the box and made my way to the library office so I could put it inside the safe. I phoned Best Buy and ordered a laptop to be delivered. Then placed a second call to arrange for Wi-Fi to be installed. I was about to phone a home security company when the front doorbell rang.

Still attired in pajamas, I made my way to the front door. Peering through the tiny peephole, I noted a young woman holding a vase with roses.

I opened the door. "Hello."

"Charlotte Bjorn?" the woman asked.

"Yes, that's me."

"These flowers are for you." She handed me the vase, then turned around and walked back to the delivery van.

I took the two dozen roses to the kitchen and placed them on the table. There was a small envelope attached and I opened it. The card inside read, ENJOYED LAST NIGHT. DEUCE.

I was touched by this gesture—pink roses, at that—my favorite. Making my way to the library office, I placed them on a table beside my favorite leather reading chair. I sat in that chair and reflected on the evening before. There was definitely chemistry.

Grabbing my cell, I sent him a text: *Thank you for the roses. Pink roses are my favorite. I enjoyed last night too.*

His response was quick: *I'm glad you like them. I would like to see you again.*

My heart raced as I replied: *I would like that.*

How about this Sunday? A picnic in Central Park, he wrote.

Yes, that would be fun.

Pick you up at 4?

Perfect. In three days, I would see him again. Brightness filled my soul.

CHAPTER 12

Jax

I paced in the lobby of the intensive care unit at Mount Sinai. Two physicians and three nurses were in Mick's room. I'd been sitting in a chair beside Mick's bed when suddenly the cardiac monitor began to screech; there was a flat line on the monitor. I ran out of the room and screamed for a doctor. Medical staff were quick to respond and I was made to leave the room.

God, I wanted a cigarette—bad—but knew to stay close by. I wanted to be in the lobby should a doctor or nurse come out. There was a coffee machine by the back wall of the room with disposable cups. Caffeine was probably a bad idea given my current state, but I got a cup anyway. It was a diversion and I needed that.

The waiting room was sparsely occupied, just one other person in a far back corner; an elderly woman reading a soft leatherbound book. Probably a bible. I sat on a beige leather couch that faced a picture window with an outside view. Sipping my coffee, I reflected on the past two weeks.

Things had been tense. Mick was distant and preoccupied on his computer. There had been numerous phone calls he insisted be private. The door of his home office remained closed much of the day. I'd heard loud conversations in Russian numerous times coming from inside the office. I was anxious to know what Mick was hiding. It had to be serious. I wondered what might be on the computer, and vowed to find out. Opportunity presented itself when Mick needed to be at the theater for auditions. I knew Mick would be gone several hours, and fortunately, as odd as he had been acting, the office wasn't locked.

With a fresh flash drive in hand, I went into Mick's office and powered up the computer. As expected, it was password protected. I was a pretty good hacker and found it easy to get into. There were numerous folders on the desktop. Two were labels I recognized as theatre related. But three jumped out among the rest. All were labeled in Cyrillic. I pulled out my cell and Googled the single word on a folder: Moscow. I slid the flash drive in and copied that folder as well as the other two. I planned to read the whole thing on my laptop. Once everything was fully copied, I removed the flash drive and shut down the computer, making sure to destroy any trail.

I put the flash drive into my pants pocket. I was paranoid and wanted to put it somewhere safe—where Mick or anyone else couldn't find it. I knew Charlotte was out to dinner with Deuce, and which gave me the perfect opportunity to gain access to her place. There the drive would be safe.

I grabbed my laptop on the way out the door, checking my watch on the way. The folder transfers had taken twenty minutes.

The drive to Central Park was uneventful and within minutes, I found a parking spot in a mostly empty lot. I powered up my laptop and inserted the flash drive. The first file in the Moscow folder was in Russian, but the content was clearly financial. It was cryptocurrency and the numbers were high—over seventeen billion dollars. I closed that file and opened another. This one was also in Russian, and I used Google to translate: SURVEILLANCE. The third folder was labeled TRAVEL.

There wasn't time to translate anything else. My most urgent need was to hide the flash drive at Charlotte's before she got home, and immediately return to Mick's place. Keeping it in my space at Mick's would be risking discovery. There was a whole lot more going on with Mick than he led me to believe. Better to protect myself now.

Burying the flash drive in Charlotte's backyard happened a day ago, just hours before Mick and I had met up at the night club where he was shot. Still seated in the hospital lobby, I worried about what to do. What if Mick didn't make it? Who else knew about these documents?

Two hours passed and still no information about Mick. I walked to the ICU desk clerk, a little elderly woman with short white hair wearing a floral dress.

"My partner is in room twelve. Do you have any updates on his condition?"

She scanned several locations on her computer before glancing back to me. "I'm showing that the doctor will be here to talk with you shortly," she said.

"Thank you." I knew this couldn't be good.

Back at my seat on the couch, I continued drinking my coffee, which had turned cold.

The receptionist's phone rang. She picked up the receiver, said something I couldn't hear, then stood and walked towards me.

"Sir, I just received a call from the doctor about your partner. I was asked to take you to a family room. The doctor will speak with you there."

The woman led me to a steel door in the far-left corner of the lobby. As I trailed behind her down a brightly lit corridor to an open door on the right, my stomach was in knots. A twenty-by-fifteen-foot room was painted a light green. It was a spartan space, furnished with only a couch and two upholstered chairs There was a coffee table in the center with a black King James bible on top.

"Go ahead and have a seat on the couch. I'll wait with you until the doctor gets here."

A short and stocky middle-aged man appeared. He wore green scrubs and had a mask on that couldn't hide the deep furrow in his brow.

"Mr. Thoreaú?" he asked.

"Yes?"

The doctor went to the chair across from me and sat. "Your partner Mikheil has passed away. We tried everything we could to save him, but he didn't respond. I am sorry."

Sobs rushed out of me. "Oh God, no!"

The physician remained quiet and reserved until I regained composure. "Would you like to see him?" the doctor asked.

"Yes, please."

The doctor led the way down the long hallway that curved to the right and then to a room on the left. Mick was lying on the hospital bed. All the medical equipment had been removed and a quilt was placed over his body.

"I can leave you alone with him for a little while if you want."

I nodded.

"When you're ready to leave, just stop at the nurses' station to let them know." He left.

I walked to the side of the bed. I put my hand on Mick's forehead, stroking it, and gave him a kiss on the cheek.

"I've never loved anyone like I've loved you. Life will be empty without you." Tears poured out. I picked up his hand, kissed it, and put it back on the bed. I gave one last look, then left the room.

It was clear I needed to quickly get all my things out of Mick's place. Since he and I had never married, I had no right to anything. Mick had a younger sister, Dasha, who was sure to be the executor of the estate since there weren't any other close family members. She and I had never gotten along. Actually, she and Mick couldn't stand each other. Regardless, they were blood. Dasha would want all of Mick's money and anything worth cash. I knew she would want me out immediately. I was listed in Mick's medical records as the person to call in an emergency. Dasha would have created drama at the hospital, so I didn't call her. The woman at the nurses' could make the contact. A house key would be in his belongs so Dasha would have that. There wasn't any need for me to see the woman. It was time to move on. Dasha would make a big production of the funeral and wouldn't allow me to be there. I could visit the gravesite alone afterwards; grieving would be private. Mick knew he was loved; that's all that mattered.

I got to Mick's house in record time. I quickly gathered up my few things and loaded them into the car. I walked back inside for the last time when I remembered an item of Mick's I wanted to keep—a star sapphire ring. I'd given it to Mick on our one-year anniversary. He hadn't worn it on the day he was shot. I put the ring on my right hand; my left hand wore the black onyx ring he had given me on the same occasion.

CHAPTER 13

Charlotte

Jax and I were in my office library, sitting in matching leather wingback chairs beside each other. The fireplace had burnt to mere embers as we faced it.

I took another swallow from my wine glass—chardonnay—and asked, "What do you want to do?"

"I wish I knew," he replied. "I've wrestled with calling Aunt Lydia to see if she can put me up for a week or two till I can figure things out." Jax took a sip from his drink, a dark German beer.

"If that's what you want. Aunt Lydia's a welcoming soul. She reminds me so much of Mom. They even look similar."

"Yeah, I know what you mean."

"You know you're welcome to stay here with me. This place is certainly big enough for both of us."

"I appreciate that," Jax said. "It just seems I need to go someplace to get a fresh perspective. I realize now how little I really knew about Mick." He paused and took a final swallow of his beer. "I have a confession."

"Okay…?" I said, curious.

"I found something on Mick's computer that concerned me. I copied it on to a flash drive and buried it in your backyard." He placed the empty beer bottle on to the round wooden table between us.

"Oh, so *that's* what I found!" I said excitedly as I studied him for a reaction.

"I should have known you'd find it. Where is it now?" he asked.

"I put it in my safe. I don't have a computer yet and wasn't sure what it was. To be honest, it scared me. I worried who put it there." I took another sip of wine, then walked to the fireplace and grabbed the poker to use on the embers. I grabbed a small log and put it in the fireplace.

"I should have told you about that before I did it. Guess I panicked when I saw what was on it," Jax said.

"What did you see?"

"Just enough to worry. All the files were in Russian, but I translated one folder label that said Moscow and another with the caption Surveillance. The third one is labeled Travel. In the Moscow folder, I opened one file. The text reads in Russian, but I could clearly see it was a financial statement. It showed an ungodly amount of money in crypto—seventeen billion dollars."

My jaw dropped. "Wow!"

"I plan to use a translation software on the whole thing." He stood. "I need another beer."

I nodded and he made his way to the kitchen. It worried me that Jax might get in way over his head should he go prying into Mick's affairs. Even if all that money was Mick's, Jax still didn't have any right to it. Then there was that surveillance folder. Surveillance of whom or what? I wanted to know.

"I need another drink," I decided, so I joined Jax in the kitchen. "Do you have your laptop?"

"Yeah."

"How about powering it up and let's take a look? I'll get the flash drive from my safe while you get your laptop."

He nodded and went to the locked garage where he'd parked his car next to mine. He retrieved the computer from the trunk, and came back inside. I was already back in the library office and the flash drive was on top my desk.

"It will take me a little while to retrieve that Russian translation software, and then get the whole thing translated. Did you ever get Wi-Fi?" he asked.

"Yeah, it was installed this morning. I know it works because I've been able to connect to the internet on my phone."

Jax put his laptop on my desk, pulled out the chair, and sat. I walked back to my chair in front of the fireplace and observed him go to work. Staring into the fireplace, my mind drifted to Deuce. The scent of the pink roses he'd sent filled my senses. Tomorrow we would be picnicking in Central Park. Falling for him wasn't what I wanted. My life was already complicated, and I sensed his was far from simple as well.

Twenty minutes passed. I glanced at Jax. His face was beet red as he stared at the computer. Clearly what he found worried him.

"Jax, what is it?"

"It looks like Mick was into some deep shit! Apparently, all this money belongs to two Russian oligarchs—Igor Smirnoff and one other person, but there isn't any name. It appears Mick was in the process of having it all converted into gold. I can't tell if it was already done or he was just working on it. At the bottom of this spreadsheet are access codes. I'm guessing to get into that crypto. There's another name on a following page with details about the gold. It seems both were going to actually get the gold and physically put it somewhere. It doesn't say where, though."

"Holy crap! That Igor guy has the same last name as Garth."

"Garth?" Jax asked.

"The guy I went to prison for 'killing.' I wonder if there's any connection?"

"Maybe?" he said.

"Do you recognize that other name?"

"No." Jax paused and took a deep breath. "Some guy named Sergei."

"I wonder what all this means. Do you think he's responsible for Mick's murder?"

"I wonder," Jax said.

"What do you want to do?"

"I don't know. If I leave town, which is what I want to do, then it might look suspicious to this Sergei guy. I covered my tracks on Mick's computer. So I should be fine. But you never know."

"If you go to the police with this, then what can they do? It appears to be Russian related. Maybe even political. What's in the folder labeled Surveillance?"

"I'll open it and see." Jax did a few clicks and a list was visible. He clicked on one and a video appeared. I stood behind him to see.

"My god! That's Deuce!"

"Shit! Let's keep watching, maybe we can figure out why he was taped."

The video merely showed ordinary things: early morning runs in Central Park, getting out of his car with groceries. The tape was over an hour long.

"I don't get it. Why?" I said, clearly confused.

"I don't think we're going to know by watching only one video. There are sixteen videos in this folder."

"I hope Deuce isn't in any danger." A burning sensation filled my gut. "I want to tell him, but I don't think I should until we've watched all of those videos. Or maybe something in a file in the other folder would prove insightful."

"Definitely don't tell Deuce. I know you have a date with him tomorrow. Promise me you won't say anything," he said.

"Yeah, I know. I promise. Let's watch another one."

Jax clicked on another video. It showed a scene in some tavern. Deuce was sitting with others at a brown rustic-looking rectangular table. All six men had large mugs of beer.

"I know that place!" Jax said. "It was in Queens but burnt down last year. The land is still vacant."

"Let's keep watching."

One of the men at the rustic table looked like an older version of Deuce, who sat beside him. His father, maybe? Two middle-aged men were Asian. One man was burly with coarse features and receding light brown hair. The sixth man was Black and appeared to be in his mid-thirties. About twenty minutes into the video, Deuce stood up and said something to the others. The outside door was visible and Deuce walked out. The man that could have been Deuce's father pulled out a large manilla envelope and discretely handed it to the Black man, who nodded. The video ended.

"It appears that whatever business was happening, it didn't take place until Deuce left," Jax said. "I don't think Deuce was involved."

"Who is Deuce's father? If we knew that, perhaps we would have some clues."

"Let's watch another one," Jax said with a few more clicks.

This video was taken outside of Bedford Women's Correctional facility. I watched with horror as the scene unfolded: my release day from prison, and everything that occurred until I got into Jax's Mustang.

Chills ran down my spine. "Shit!"

Jax's mouth dropped. "Damn."

"Let's watch the next one."

This video showed the same tavern as before, only this time they were sitting at corner booth. The man who could have been Deuce's father sat at the table with two rough-looking men who appeared to be approximately mid- to late forties. The video appeared to be a security feed as it was grainy, but it did have audio. It wasn't all clear, but the three men were speaking Russian.

"I need to find an audible translation program," Jax said.

Jax clicked on another video. It was of Deuce again doing random things, just like the previous one of him.

"I am scared to death! I don't get it. Deuce is in danger and it looks like maybe I am too."

CHAPTER 14

Charlotte

It was Sunday and at four o'clock, my doorbell rang. I glanced through the peephole in the door. It was Deuce.

I opened the door and gave a wide smile. "Good afternoon. Please come in."

He wore Levi jeans and a black t-shirt that displayed large biceps. The scent of his deep woodsy cologne reminded of the evening I danced with him. Delicious! He glanced around my entryway and into the living room. I led the way there.

"Please have a seat."

"Raven," he said, standing in front of the oil portrait over the fireplace. He turned to face me.

"I need to take that down. It's a terrible reminder. I'm not her anymore." I wished I'd said something different.

"You're more beautiful now," he said.

For a moment I was lost in his eyes. They were tender and penetrated to my soul. A warm tingling sensation filled me. "I need to go upstairs and grab my purse. I won't be long."

He gave a knowing smile and sat down on the sofa.

I studied my reflection in the full-length mirror in my dressing room. The white button-down blouse just barely touched the waistband of my dark beige wide-legged trousers. I slid on tan leather sandals, ran my fingers through the loose curls, and smiled. I felt beautiful.

I descended the front steps of my home. Deuce was right behind me; he stepped forward at the bottom of the stairs and pushed a button on his keychain. The passenger door opened upward on the hinge of a dark caramel Lamborghini sportster with shiny silver double-spoked wheels. My jaw almost dropped. I glanced back at him. He was clearly attempting to hold back a grin.

"If you're trying to impress me, you just did." I winked before getting inside. The new car smell hinted at a recent purchase.

"Mission accomplished then." He gave a hearty laugh before closing my door, and then going to the driver's side and getting in. He started the ignition. "I just got this baby out of the shop and I wanted to give it a spin. It's mostly just parked in my garage so the battery goes dead."

"No picnic basket?" Clearly there wasn't room in this car for one.

"Better than that," he said. "You'll see."

The twenty-minute drive brought us right into Central Park. He drove until we were close to the pond, then took a slight right turn into a heavily wooded area and onto a dirt road. Within a couple minutes, an entry gate with barbed wire fencing was visible. There was a Private Property sign posted and the gate was already open. He drove a quarter of a mile to a rustic stone picnic shelter, then parked the car to the side of the shelter beside a white van.

Deuce glanced at me, smiling, and announced, "Here we are."

"My gosh. I didn't know this area existed."

"It's actually just outside the park and privately owned." He pushed the button to open both car doors. He got out and then went to my side of the car and offered his hand to help me climb out.

The stone shelter was fully open along the front wall, but all three other walls were enclosed. I guessed it could easily accommodate a large family gathering. There was a small brick fireplace in the farthest wall and a blaze was already glowing, which was most welcomed as the breeze had become rather chilly. A dark crimson Persian rug was on the floor in the center with a low round whicker table in the middle. Two place settings were on top of the white tablecloth. Large square pillows were placed on the floor across from each other at the table. The large wooden picnic tables had been moved against the two side walls.

A young Latino man in a white chef's shirt stood when he saw us approaching. "Sir, madam."

Deuce nodded and led to the low whicker table. "Shall we?"

I smiled, kicked off my sandals, and sat cross-legged on a square pillow. The waiter stood behind Deuce with a bottle of wine and two glasses in hand. Deuce took the pillow seat across from me.

The waiter stepped forward. "Madam?" he asked before pouring wine into my glass.

I nodded.

He then filled Deuce's glass, put the bottle on the side of the table, and walked back to the area where a stainless-steel rolling cart had prepared food on the top and second shelves. The server stood silently beside the cart.

"I propose a toast," Deuce said and raised his glass. "To beginnings."

"Yes." I raised my glass to touch his. Swirling my glass first to infuse it with air, I closed my eyes and took a swallow. It was smooth and decadent—the same wine we had on our first date.

"Hungry?"

"Yes, I am."

Deuce glanced at the server and nodded to him. The server reached underneath the second shelf of the cart and produced a platter of assorted cheeses, sliced baguettes, grapes, and tiny finger sandwiches. He placed them in the center of the table, then returned to his station at the cart.

"This looks yummy," I said as I took a slice of the brie and a piece of bread. Deuce helped himself as well.

"Derrick," Deuce addressed the server, "I believe we are fine by ourselves now. I will text you when we're finished."

"Yes, sir," the server replied before leaving us alone.

Deuce smiled. "I don't think we need a chaperone."

I giggled and took one of the grapes from the platter, popping it in my mouth. "Yum, these are good!" I took another one. "Tell me about yourself. I really don't know all that much about you."

"What would you like to know?" he replied.

"I want to know everything. You know so much about me already."

"Where to begin?" He took a grape from the platter and popped it in his mouth. I watched as he briefly paused and his eyes looked into the distance and his jaw tightened. "The shortened version: I was born in Moscow, and when I was three, my parents split up. My mom and I immediately flew to New York. She's an American and I got my US citizenship when I was twenty-one. My dad and I stay in contact."

"Do you have any siblings?"

"No. My mother never remarried and I seriously doubt she had any lovers. Right now, she lives in London."

"I'm guessing your father never remarried?"

"He did but there weren't any children," Deuce said but then added, "but my father is a most worldly man so who knows?"

"I have to know. Why the hair salon? You don't resemble the man I met who did my hair."

"That's a story for another day," he said. "Care for some more wine?"

Both our glasses were empty. I was trying to relax and I sensed he was too.

I nodded; he filled each glass and then sat the bottle back on the table. He took a piece of the bread, a wedge of the brie, and a small sandwich on a small plate, then handed it to me.

"Thank you."

He filled his own plate. "I wanted to see you when you were incarcerated." He took another drink of his wine, a large swallow.

"Why didn't you?"

"Guess I wondered if you would even remember me. After all, I was just someone at the building that you glanced at on your way backstage."

"Please forgive me. I was 'Raven' then: rude, arrogant, and ego driven. I hate her!" I took the final swallow of my wine.

Deuce refilled my glass. "Nothing to forgive. You probably had to be that way to do your job."

"I don't know. I wonder why I even did the modeling. Maybe it was because I didn't feel I *could* do anything else." I was definitely feeling the effects of the wine. "So much had happened prior to that and I was a mess."

"Tell me about it?" he asked.

"When I was married, I became pregnant and we were both so happy. But all that changed when I delivered our son. He was stillborn. Then, a month after that, my husband was in a plane crash and died. It was horrible! I didn't think I could go on. I spent months holed up in my house. Mostly in bed. When I wasn't sleeping, waves of sobs came. I refused to answer my door unless I knew it was food delivery. But one morning, the tears dried up. I got brave and walked a couple of blocks to Starbucks. It felt good to be out of the house, so it became a regular morning routine. One day as I was sitting alone, a woman walked up and introduced herself. It was Hilda Reicher—owner of a modeling agency. The rest you already know." Tears filled my eyes at the overwhelming memories.

Deuce reached for me, placing his large hand on top of mine. It was warm; it felt safe. My eyes traveled to his and I wanted to stay there. He didn't look away.

CHAPTER 15

Dmitri

We finished eating and moved the pillow seats away from the table to face the fireplace, very close together. The embers crackled and there was the fragrant scent of burning wood. I watched her inhale it and close her eyes. I placed my hand on top of hers. She opened her eyes and turned to me.

"May I kiss you?"

She said nothing, but moved closer to me while her longing eyes fixed on mine. My hand was gentle as I lifted her chin and kissed her softly. She kissed me back. Passion ignited. We both wanted more of the other.

I picked her up and placed her onto my lap. I knew she could feel my rigid shaft through my jeans and was certain her own arousal grew. Our lips met again with more passion. She ran her fingers through the back of my hair and I pulled her closer. My hand glided down her back as tongue went into her mouth, then traveled down the side of her neck. The warm scent of her body was intoxicating, sending sensations through me that I ached to satisfy.

"Charlotte," I whispered.

I felt her melt right into me. My hand moved underneath her blouse to her breast. I gently flicked her nipple. She threw back her head and moaned.

My hand traveled to her sex and felt her moisture even through her clothes. I knew she wanted me.

"Make love to me," she whispered breathlessly.

"Not here."

"I don't care. I can't wait."

I picked her up and carried her, placing her on the rug gently. I laid beside her and unzipped the front of her pants, sliding my hand down to her wetness. I inserted a finger inside of her and traced my palm across to her clit.

She moaned so I inserted a second finger and began moving up and down. Her moans got louder and I felt her tighten around my fingers and she pushed up, guiding me deeper. I inserted a third finger.

She called out my name and I watched her ride the waves of ecstasy.

I was gentle when I pulled out my hand and traveled upward to her belly, her wetness still on my skin.

She put her hand on to my hard cock still inside my jeans. Her hooded eyes fixed into mine. "This isn't fair," she whined.

"My place?"

"Yes."

I pulled out my phone and texted the waiter. I stood and offered her my hand. Once she stood, I brought her hand to my mouth and kissed the top of it. "Shall we?"

Charlotte fixed her eyes to mine and smiled.

We drove out of Central Park, down 59th Street to Columbus Circle, to a high-rise building. I pulled my car into a well-lit underground private two-car garage. Once inside, the garage door closed. I pushed the button for the car doors, which opened, and rushed to her side of the car.

I offered my hand for her to get out. "May I?"

She glanced at my shiny black Aston Martin parked beside the Lamborghini.

I led the way to the back of the garage to an elevator. I placed my hand on the reader, pushed the button, and it opened immediately. We got inside. I pushed a lit round button, one of only three; we traveled upwards and stopped at the penthouse, seventy-five floors above the streets of New York City.

The elevator door opened and we walked directly on a shiny hardwood floor and into a tasteful modern-style living room with a fifteen-foot ceiling. Tan leather furniture was placed around a dark brown Persian rug. But the main focus was the full-wall, floor-to-ceiling window overlooking Central Park and the entire city, including the Statue of Liberty facing west over the Hudson River.

She put her purse on the couch and walked to the window, then slid open the sliding glass door to the patio. She walked outside.

"My gosh," she said. "I think you have the best possible view."

"I think so too." I joined her and put my arm around her waist. "I never get tired of staring out there."

"I can understand that," she said. She leaned her head on my shoulder; it just felt right.

I kissed the top of her head, my arm around her waist tightened. "To the bedroom?"

"Yes," she said.

We walked back inside. I held her hand and led the way down a hallway to the very end. Heavy wooden double-doors were open. I stopped right before entering and turned to her with questioning eyes.

"Yes," she said.

I picked her up into my arms and carried her to the king-sized bed and placed her in the center.

I got onto the bed beside her and put my hands on each side of her face. I kissed her softly on the lips. She put her hands around my neck and kissed me back. I deepened the kiss, my tongue going into her mouth. I began to pull back, and as she made a hungry moan, my tongue traveled down the side of her neck, eliciting another moan from her.

I unbuttoned her blouse and parted the two halves, exposing her sheer white lace bra and her aroused nipples. I carefully removed her blouse and placed it on a chair beside the bed.

My fingers glided to her hard nipple over the material of her bra. She closed her eyes as her arousal rose.

"Look into my eyes."

With half-open lids, she fixed her eyes onto mine. I unhooked her bra's front clasp and pulled down the straps to remove it. I guided her to lay down on her back in the center of the bed. I unzipped her pants and slid them off completely, exposing her white lace thong, already moist with desire for me. Our eyes remained fixed into each other.

"Lovely Charlotte."

I unbuttoned my shirt and tossed it onto the floor. Her eyes studied my body and I could tell she liked what she saw.

I bent down to her and when we were skin to skin, my arousal grew. Our lips met. I was gentle, but when she arched her back, I knew she wanted more.

"Patience," I whispered, taking both of her arms and raising them over her head.

My tongue traced the side of her neck and down to her breast. I circled her nipple, then sucked it. She moaned and I did the same to her other breast, then traveled my tongue down to her belly. My fingers hooked under her panties; I removed them and slowly opened her knees. My tongue went inside her folds and darted in and out of her wetness.

I put my tongue on her clit and sucked, then a finger inside of her. Primal sounds came out of her mouth as she rode the wave.

"I want you inside of me," she said.

I stood and took a step back. "Condom?"

"No, I have an IUD."

I undid my jeans and removed my boxer briefs, letting them fall to the floor. I took a hand and stroked my hard cock for her.

She moistened her lips with her tongue.

I put my hands underneath her knees and pulled her towards me. Then, I inserted my cock inside the first part of her, careful not to hurt her. I knew I was large and her passageway tight.

"More," she moaned, arching her back.

I went deeper.

"More." She arched her back again to get even more of me, pulling her arms down and wrapping them around my back.

I went all the way inside her and began pumping. Faster and faster. With each thrust, she met me. All I could think about was how beautiful and sexy she was. She was even better than I imagined. A raging fire stirred me. I wanted more of her but I forced myself to hold back. I didn't want to scare her.

Her inner muscles clenched around me so tight I knew I couldn't hold out much longer. I knew she was close and so was I.

"Come with me."

I was pounding faster and faster and she was clawing my back.

She screamed out my name.

We reached the same place together.

I stayed inside her, motionless—treasuring we were now one. I bent down and kissed her lips softly. I rolled her on top of me while I was still inside of her. A perfect fit. Her head now rested on my chest.

"I could stay like this forever," she whispered.

"Me too."

* * *

I grabbed a cup of coffee from my kitchen and walked to the sliding glass door in my living room. Sliding the door open, I stepped outside and sat in a wooden patio chair. I took a sip of coffee while staring at the skyline. Thoughts of yesterday and last night ran through my mind. Charlotte had rocked my world and I wanted more of her. I hoped she would spend the night; I knew she wanted to. But she said her brother would worry if she didn't return home as he was now living with her.

The entire afternoon and evening with her had gone beautifully as I'd planned, but I'd not intended on seducing her, planning instead to take things slow. I treasured her and didn't want to scare her away. But the chemistry was too strong between us and things just escalated. I wondered how she was feeling now.

I sat my cup on a side table and walked inside for my cell. Once back in my seat outside, I dialed her number. It was ten-thirty. The phone rang only twice before she answered.

"Hello?" she answered.

"Good morning, beautiful."

"Good morning to you too," she replied in the sweet voice I remembered from last night.

"I hope you slept well."

"I did, and you?" It seemed we were feeling each other out.

"I did." I wanted to say more—that I was totally smitten—but I didn't. "I want to see you again."

"Me too," she replied.

"I have a house on the beach in Long Beach Island in Jersey. I was wondering if you would like to go there with me today? The weather will be cool, but the view is great. We could spend the night if you are open to it."

"I would love that," she replied.

"Great. Can you be ready for me to pick you up at one?"

"Yes, I can." Her voice was light and eager.

"Perfect. I'll see you then."

CHAPTER 16

Charlotte

Standing in front of my full-length mirror in my dressing room, I studied my reflection. The Flannigan flare jeans from six years ago still fit perfectly. The white cotton V-neck pullover sweater hit just below the waist. I remembered the day I'd worn this top for an Anthony Thomas Melillo fashion show. I'd been allowed to keep it. The white Tory Burch lace-up sneakers were also a runway keep.

I got closer to the mirror and ran my fingers through my hair to give it a more tousled look and then smacked my clear lip-glossed lips together. Next was a spray of a light floral perfume that I gave a single spray high over my head and allowed to fall over me. Another glance in the mirror and my confidence rose. I knew I looked good and hoped Deuce would think so too.

It was now twenty minutes before one. My overnight bag was packed so I carried it downstairs and left at the bottom landing. I walked to the library office, grabbed a pad of paper, and wrote Jax a note to let him know where I would be. I walked to the kitchen and left on the table. He was sure to see it there. A text message would have been better, but I didn't want to engage in any dialogue. Jax had left earlier that morning before Deuce had called.

Promptly at one, the doorbell rang. I walked to the door and opened it.

"Hi." He gave a wide smile. He wore faded jeans, a black pullover sweater, and dark brown leather sneakers.

I couldn't help but smile wide in return. "Please come in."

Once inside with the door closed, he bent down and kissed me on the lips. I put my arms around his neck and kissed him back.

"Ready to go?"

"I am."

"Let me carry your bag," he offered.

"Thank you." I followed him out the front door to the black Aston Martin I'd seen in his garage last night. He put my bag in the trunk before going to the front passenger door to open it for me to get inside.

"The drive is just over an hour and a half," he said after he started the car and pulled out into the street.

"That's not bad, and the weather is beautiful."

"I thought we could stop at a grocery store once we're almost there. I know the kitchen isn't stocked. I haven't been there in over a month. Generally, I'm only there in the spring and summer."

I wanted to ask questions about the place, but decided against it. "If you want, we can cook dinner together."

"That would be nice," he replied. "I have a grill on the back deck. If you like steak, I can grill."

"Then maybe I'll make a salad and two baked potatoes?"

"Sounds good." He glanced briefly at me, grinned, and gave a wink.

I leaned back in the seat and couldn't help but smile. He was so charming, sexy, and damn good looking. How could I be so lucky to be with him? I knew if I focused on all my insecurities, negative dark thoughts would fill my mind and destroy what happiness I could experience now. Yesterday was history and tomorrow wasn't promised. The only sure thing is what's happening now, and right now feels pretty damn good.

* * *

It wasn't long after we went grocery shopping that we were back on the highway and traveling down Long Beach Boulevard. He pulled onto a stone-paved driveway lined with beautiful shrubs and tall trees, giving a sense of privacy. The driveway ended in a circle with more decorative greenery in its center. The house was breathtaking—an all-white two-story Cape Cod with a wrap-around porch.

We stopped in front of the garage. He pushed the button on his visor; the door rose up and he drove inside. There was a small Jeep already parked there. He got out, walked to my side, opened the door, and gave me his hand to get out. He put his hands around my waist and pulled me towards him. It felt so good to put my hands around his neck. Then our lips met. He broke the kiss and gave a soft smile before letting go of me.

"I'll open the door for you to go inside, then I'll come back out here for our bags and groceries," he said.

"Please let me help you."

"No, I want to do it." He walked to a door at the back of the garage. There was a combination keypad on the left side. He punched in the numbers and opened the door. I followed him inside as he flipped on the lights. We entered an impressive open-concept kitchen, where a dining area and a living room could be seen. Everything was quite stylish as if a professional had decorated it. There was lots of chrome and glass, with a royal blue sofa and two matching upholstered chairs. A sliding glass door in the farthest wall displayed a decking that overlooked the ocean. I walked to the glass door and opened it wide, then walked outside onto the wooden deck. I inhaled the cool salty air. The sight and sounds of the crashing waves were magnificent.

I felt his arms around my waist from the back.

I leaned my head against his chest. "This is so beautiful."

"You are the beautiful one," he replied.

I turned around to face him and gazed into his eyes. "Thank you, but I can say the same about you."

He pulled me closer, then bent down and kissed me. His lips were soft and his kiss gentle. I melted into his arms.

"Shall we go for a walk on the beach?" he asked.

I beamed. "Yes."

We silently walked hand-in-hand along the shoreline towards a lighthouse in the distance. It was slightly chilly and we each had on a hoodie sweatshirt. There wasn't anyone else on the beach. We passed a fisherman's pier but no one was there either. In short order, we made it to the lighthouse. Deuce led me to an open doorway.

"The view is really great at the top," he said.

I smiled, then followed him up a winding narrow stairway to the very top. There was an open viewing area. We walked to the railing and stared out at the endless sea.

I turned to look up at him. He wrapped his arm around me and kissed the top of my head.

"I wish I'd brought my phone so I could take a picture of you here. I want to remember this moment forever."

"Next time," he replied.

I loved the sound of his words, implying there would be another time. Being with Deuce felt so right—I was struggling to put logic and reason into my mind—reminding how sudden and new our relationship was. I didn't want to fall in love with him for fear getting hurt. The devastation would be too much. But maybe it was too late.

"What are you thinking about?" he asked.

"I don't know. Maybe how this feels so perfect."

"I feel the same way," he said. "About you and me." His eyes were dreamy when his eyes met mine.

"I can't call you Deuce anymore." My hand lightly stroked the side of his face. "You are Dmitri to me."

He smiled. "Let's go back to the house," he said.

I nodded.

We walked hand in hand back to the house and took the steps up the back deck. He'd led the way and the sight of his butt through his jeans stirred more longing for him. He was an incredibly handsome man. Once inside the house, he closed the sliding glass door and pulled me into his arms. Once again, our lips met. He pulled me close and I felt his hard shaft against me and my desire for him grew.

"To the bedroom?" he asked.

"Yes."

With his hand holding mine, he led the way through the living room down a short hallway to the master bedroom. Both our bags were on the floor between a closet and the master bathroom. A king-sized bed was against a wall and fifteen feet from a sliding glass door that led to the deck. I kicked off my shoes.

He stopped at the foot of the bed and turned me towards him. While looking into my eyes, he pulled my sweatshirt over my head and tossed it on an upholstered chair. His hands took the hem of my top and pulled it over my head, then tossed it on top of the sweatshirt. His hands traveled to the top of my jeans, and unbuttoned and unzipped them. I stepped out of them, leaving them on the floor, and moved as he guided me to the bed and laid me in the center on my back. My eyes danced when he took a step back and slowly removed his sweatshirt and t-shirt, exposing his smooth and chiseled chest.

He removed his jeans and boxers, allowing them to stay on the floor. I licked my lips as I feasted my eyes on his large, rigid cock. He walked to the foot of the bed and knelt onto his knees, then traced his hand at the soaked gusset strip of my barely there white lace panties. He hooked his fingers on to the side of my panties and slid them completely off.

He placed his hands on my knees and gently parted them, then traced the inside my thighs and up to my petals.

He thrust his tongue over that most sensitive spot, then entered me with his pointed tongue darting in and out quickly till I was on the edge.

I gave a breathless moan.

He inserted one finger.

"More."

He inserted two fingers and went in and out.

"More." My fingers threaded through his hair and my back arched.

He inserted a third finger.

I called out his name and rode the orgasmic wave.

He lifted me up and got into bed beside me, kissing my lips. Tasting myself on his tongue was wickedly erotic.

His tongue traced along the side of my neck, sending thrilling sensations to my core. He kept moving down to my breasts. I felt him unhook my bra from the front and remove it, exposing my stiff nipples, which he traced with his tongue before he sucked on, and then lightly rolled between his fingers. It was full of the contrast of pain and pleasure.

"Oh my God," I heard myself say as he circled my nipple with his tongue. He did the same with my other breast.

He got on top of me and my hand found his shaft. My thumb rubbed across the very tip where he was wet with pre-cum.

"I need you inside of me."

He took my arms and placed them over my head, stroking his cock while our eyes fixed on each other.

He entered me. Slowly. I knew he was making sure I was ready for him.

I arched my back when he began thrusting. I met each thrust as he went faster and faster, going as far as he could go inside of me.

"Oh God, you feel so good," he growled.

Beads of sweat formed on his brow and chest as he continued to go wild pounding into me. I clenched around him tight; I was on the very edge.

I screamed out his name.

He let out a primal growl and we arrived at the same place together.

I rolled over on top of him, resting my head on his chest. He kissed the top of my head and held me tight.

We lay that way for a while in silence. I could hear his heart beating and feel of his chest rising as he took each breath. Love for him filled me so full it almost hurt. I wanted to tell him, but was afraid.

CHAPTER 17

Dmitri

I was at my desk in my home office in Manhattan, my laptop open with my financial summaries displayed. I was set to close on the sale of the hair salon this afternoon. An investor who lived in Queens had offered to purchase it, and I was grateful for the generous profit I would make.

I hated having the place, as it was a cover for my father's money laundering. It had taken me six months of classes in a California barber school to get a license. New York required two years of schooling, but I didn't want to go to school that long for a profession I wasn't going to stay with. I hated the whole thing, but my father insisted and I wanted to please him. It had been a mistake—a huge mistake. This business was the last I owned where my father's unethical deeds included me. I would be free at last.

I'd been investing in property—both rental and commercial in New York and New Jersey. There was also a small vineyard and winery in Napa Valley I'd owned for only a year that was doing quite well. I'd amassed over two billion dollars, secured at the Union Bank in Switzerland, in addition to my substantial funds in the US. Financially I was quite comfortable. The only snag was my father, Andrei Zhukov, a prominent Russian oligarch with strong ties to Putin. I suspected my father of black-market arms dealing but I didn't have proof. I also suspected he was involved with drug trafficking alongside his brother Sergei. Since I was an only child, there had always been pressure on me to do my father's bidding. Regrettably, I had obliged, but I didn't want to anymore.

At eighty years old, my father's health was declining. No doubt his lifelong habits of heavy smoking and drinking contributed. I loved my father but resented his criminal activities. Always lurking in the background, it had the potential of jeopardizing my affairs. I was anxious to have all that behind me. Honesty and integrity were my goals, now more than ever since Charlotte was in my life.

It was now two in the afternoon and the meeting with the lawyer was at three. I closed my laptop and placed it inside my briefcase with all the paperwork for the closing.

* * *

I was back in my chair on the roof patio, with a slim cigarillo. I lit it up. The property deal was done and I felt more relaxed than usual; the attorney was to contact my father with all the details of the sale. I was avoiding talking to him as I was sure there would be another scheme he wanted me involved in. Given the political climate between the US and Russia, I didn't want to be red-flagged by either government. But now, at thirty-five years old, I was finally free.

My mind filled with thoughts of Charlotte. I wished I was a better man for her. Would she want to be with me if she knew my truth?

When I made my move from Russia to New York City permanent, my plan was to turn a new leaf. I'd been careful to walk that fine line between keeping my father happy while keeping myself free of wrongdoing.

There was one incident that haunted me. The images appeared in my mind of a shooting ten years ago. It was one in the morning, and I'd gone to get my father at a strip club. It was one he owned in a seedy area of the city. He was in a back room, gambling and drunk. The game was between my father and one other man. No one else was in the room. I had just entered the stuffy, smoke-filled room when the burly man accused my father of cheating. Then, the man stood, pulled out a gun, and aimed it at my father. The drunken man had been quick, but my reflexes were faster; I pulled out a gun. The bullet hit the man in the center of his chest, and he fell to the floor—dead.

I knew we had to get out of there. I locked the door where I'd entered. There was a side door that led to the parking lot. It wasn't lit—not from the building or in the parking lot. There weren't any security cameras.

Even though he hadn't been shot, I held my father up as we exited the building and walked to the parking lot. Once we were both inside my car, I drove out the back into a dark alley, then drove as fast as I safely could out of there.

My father was aware enough to phone two of his men to go back and dispose of the body and clean up the room. These were the same two men who had been at the party where Charlotte was arrested. I knew I had to tread lightly with them; they were close to my father and he was a powerful man.

But now I wished I had come forward and perhaps spared Charlotte all those years in prison. If I knew why the incident at the party had occurred, maybe it would all make sense. The only way to find out was to contact Gustav and Polvalaski. I wanted to help Charlotte clear her name. But how could I do this without exposing all the dirty secrets?

I had been trained early to handle a gun with skill. I'd also trained to fight hand to hand. I'd killed more men than I even wanted to count. But it never settled well with me. I knew my father expected me to be the Zhukov Bratva successor, but I never wanted it. I'd been free of violence since the incident in the strip club. If it hadn't been for me arriving when I did, my father would have been shot. Probably killed.

I pulled out my cell and composed a text to send to Gustav and Polvalaski, asking them if they could meet me for lunch the next day at my penthouse. Within minutes, they each replied they could meet. I phoned a restaurant and arranged for food to be delivered for the luncheon.

* * *

The food had been consumed and I sat with the two men at my dining room table. I'd been careful to guide the conversation, as these men worked for my father, not me.

"Shall we go outside to the patio and smoke cigars?"

"Sounds good."

Gustav said and Polvalaski nodded. We already had fine-label whiskey and we poured another shot to take outside.

Seated in one of the wooden chairs, I pulled out my pack of cigarillos and offered one to each man. Both accepted and lit up. "I'm sure you're wondering why I wanted to talk with you both."

Gustav took a draw. "Yeah."

"Remember the model who was arrested at that fashion show party?" Both men nodded. "Well, I know she was framed and I want to help her to clear her name. I saw both of you there and I was hoping you might have something useful that I could use."

"We didn't frame her," Polvalaski replied.

"Do you know what actually happened?"

"Our job was to get Garth Smirnoff out of there, put him on a plane to Moscow, and get him to his father, Igor Smirnoff," Polvalaski said. "Your father owed Igor a favor and that's how we got involved. The kid was dealing coke and hooked on heroin. Igor wanted his son back in Moscow to get him clean. The two female models got there first and had already phoned the police. When we saw what was going down, we got out of there."

I believed them. "Any clue why those two models would frame Charlotte?"

"Nah. You need to ask them yourself. But good luck with that. One of the models is the daughter of your father's attorney, Austin Jenkins. I don't know anything about the other girl," Gustav said.

"Fuck! What do you suggest I do?"

"You're on your own, dude," Gustav said. "That's way beyond my paygrade."

While I the information from these two men was enlightening, the real culprits would be difficult to approach. I knew the attorney well and had used the man for the closing of the property where those modeling events had been held. I was now grateful another attorney handled the sale of the salon.

"The obvious thing would be to go to that modeling agency and see if you can locate the other model," Polvalaski said. "You might get more information about the other girl. Maybe you can approach her."

"Thank you for the suggestion." I knew I wouldn't do that. A more subtle approach would work best. Not backfire. I'd hire a private investigator; I wanted to keep this information to myself.

Once their cigarillos were out, the men left. I thanked them for their help. When they were gone, I pulled out my cell and flipped through my contacts until I found the private investigator I used a few years back.

I sent him a text: *Would like to hire you again. Call me if you are interested.*

The phone rang shortly thereafter. "Hi, Bart. Thanks for calling me so quickly."

"Sure thing. What can I do for you?" he asked.

I described the situation and how I needed him to locate the attorney's daughter and find out anything he could about her.

"My retainer is ten grand," Bart said.

"Sure, no problem. Stop by tonight and I'll write you a check."

"Five o'clock good?"

"Good," I confirmed.

CHAPTER 18

Charlotte

Jax and I were in my library office and viewing the last of the surveillance videos from the flash drive. "I don't get it. Aside from just being creepy, there isn't anything incriminating on those tapes. I wish I knew why they existed," I said with a sigh.

"I did translate the Russian conversation from the second video at the restaurant," Jax said.

"What did they talk about?"

"The video was grainy and the clarity of what they said not much better. From what I was able to gather, they were talking about some arms deal with Sergei Zhukov and someone by the name of Igor Smirnoff. They were supposed to be paid in cryptocurrency. I didn't get an amount."

"The cryptocurrency that Mick had might be related."

"I wouldn't doubt it. Now, what—if anything—should we do about it?" he asked.

"I'm thinking that Sergei Zhukov might be Dmitri's father and that scares me."

"I can't see anything where your boyfriend is involved. It might be that his father is just a crook."

"I hope that's the case. Dmitri doesn't seem to be a crook at all. Actually, since a huge chunk of those surveillance videos are of Dmitri, then he can't be involved."

"Let's hope that's the case. It does seem so, but we don't know," Jax said, trying to be positive.

"What else is in those other files?" I asked.

"A log where Mick details travel arrangements to Ghana and how he'd planned to convert the crypto into gold. It looks like Mick had already initiated it, but it's not clear how far into the process he got. The final entry in this journal was two days before he was shot," he said.

"Is there anything that tells where the money came from? Like maybe drug trafficking, or arms dealing, or even political stuff?"

"No, nothing," Jax said.

"That video of me getting out of prison scares me. What could I possibly have to do with any of this?"

"I'm wondering if perhaps the reason you were *in* prison had something to do with it. Like maybe the person who framed you is responsible."

"Interesting theory." My heart was pounding hard enough and my head swimming already. "I want to tell Dmitri, then forget about the whole thing." Jax nodded. "Copy that entire flash drive for me." Jax pulled out a new flash drive and copied it all, then handed it to me. "Thanks. I'm going to call him now."

The phone only rang twice. "Hi, Charlotte," he answered.

"I have something you need to see. Are you available sometime tonight?"

"Of course," he said. "Are you okay?"

"I'm not sure," I hedged.

"I can come to your place."

"No, I want to come to you."

"Sure. I have a meeting at five-thirty and it should be over with by seven. I'll send a car for you then?" he said.

"Thank you."

"Of course," he said. "Looking forward to seeing you."

"Me too."

CHAPTER 19

Dmitri

I sat back in my desk chair, pondering what was going on with Charlotte. She sounded shaky. If it wasn't for the meeting with the private investigator in an hour, I would have driven to her place right away. I hated taking her home last night. It was difficult to be away from her. I'd never been smitten by a woman before—not like this. It was more than mere lust. I didn't want to admit to myself I was in love with her. It was too soon—or maybe it was too late.

* * *

I was in front of the building waiting when the limo drove up with Charlotte inside. I opened her door and helped her out.

"Thank you, Anthony."

The driver nodded and drove away.

"Hi." I embraced her and kissed her forehead. Her face was deep red and there was fear in her eyes. "Let's go inside." I put my arm around her waist and led her inside to the elevator. I punched in a seven-digit security code on the side keypad, placed my palm on the reader, and pressed the button displaying the seventy-fifth floor. The elevator door opened right in my living room. "Can I get you something to drink?"

"Sure, I could use something," she replied. She followed me to the kitchen and took a seat at the breakfast bar.

"Would you like the same wine we had before, or would you like a white wine? I have a nice chardonnay."

"Chardonnay would be nice," she said.

I went to a side cabinet and opened the door. Red wines in the slots above and in a small refrigerator underneath. I opened the refrigerator, pulled out a bottle, grabbed a corkscrew from a drawer, and opened the wine. Grabbing two wine glasses from a cabinet, I carried everything to the bar.

I placed the glass in front of her and poured the wine into it. "What's going on?"

Charlotte reached into her purse, retrieved a flash drive, and set it on the bar in front of me. Her hand was shaking. She took a swallow from the wine glass. "My brother found something on his late partner's computer and copied it on to this flash drive. There's a lot on here, including separate video footage of you and me."

This was shocking news. "What?"

"Yeah. There's quite a bit in Russian, so you can easily understand what's in the documents. My brother used translation software to understand what they said. Aside from some financial statements and a journal entry, nothing else makes sense. Since you are the prominent one in these videos, I wanted you to see them. I'm worried about you." Her eyes filled with tears as she finished speaking.

I walked over and put my arms around her. "Let's move to my office." I picked up the flash drive and my glass of wine. She followed me down a hallway; on the opposite side of the living room, the other hallway led to the bedrooms.

The large room had bookcases on three walls and an executive-size wooden desk in front of the bookcase on the right. There were two leather chairs in front of my desk. She sat on one of them and I took the seat behind the desk.

I opened my laptop, powered it up, and then put the flash drive in. She sat silently as I clicked away.

I pulled my chair back from the desk. "Interesting."

"If you look at the second video, it shows a group with you at some restaurant. Then, the fourth video is of three men at that same restaurant. There are quite a few videos of you just doing random things. It's like someone was keeping a close eye on you," she said, trying not to ramble nervously.

I clicked the mouse a few times and sat watched silently. Twenty minutes passed. She kept sipping her wine till her glass was empty. Mine was empty too.

"Shall I get us both more wine?" she asked.

"Yes, please."

She grabbed the bottle from the kitchen and brought it back to my office. She filled my glass, then hers. "Any ideas?" she asked.

"I haven't a clue." I pulled my chair away from my desk. "I do remember being in that restaurant and spotting my uncle. He was alone at that table so I left the bar and walked over to join him. We were only seated for about half an hour when those other men walked inside. I instantly felt the tension when they joined us at the table, so I decided to leave. The other video is of my uncle and two men I recognize—Viktor Polvalaski and Leonid Gustav. They work for my father. I can't really decipher much of their conversation on this video. There are only bits and pieces about a piece of property, but I can't tell where it is. The financial documents appear more concerning."

"I thought so too. I also saw one video of me," she said.

"Which one is it?"

"The third video," she answered. She watched silently as I then studied the video with her in it.

"This doesn't make any sense." I again backed my chair away from the desk. "It will take me a while to look at all of these. I need to study everything on this flash drive. Maybe there are clues. Do you have any ideas?"

"I'm suspicious of that cryptocurrency. I can't imagine it all belonged to my brother's late partner. From what I can tell the money belonged to some Russian oligarch—Igor Smirnoff. It appears that Mick was trying to convert it into gold bullion," she said.

"My father is friends with Smirnoff, and he's also residing in Moscow. I spoke with my father a few days ago. He mentioned seeing him."

"The guy I went to prison for murdering had that same last name."

I wished I could have told her all that I knew about that.

"I really don't think my brother has anything to do with this. He'd been suspicious of a few things with his partner, so he went snooping while Mick was at work. It's strange how Mick had been shot close to the time my brother got ahold of these files. Jax doesn't know what to do."

"I can understand that."

"I wondered if it would be best to just ignore the whole thing as if we'd never found it," she pondered aloud.

"I don't think that would be wise. I'm worried about your safety. I want you to move in with me. I know I can keep you safe." I also wasn't convinced Jax was totally innocent.

"What about my brother?"

"He isn't in any of these videos. Has he shared his plans with you?" I asked.

"Jax wants to move to my Aunt Lydia's in the Mojave Desert. Soon," she confided.

"He probably should. Where is he now?"

"He was at my place when I left for here."

"I think we should go there and talk with him. It doesn't appear your brother is in any danger, given he isn't in any of these files or videos. But it would be wise to be extra cautious." I was good at reading people and wanted to see Jax's reactions to the questions I was going to ask him.

"You're probably right," she said.

"While we're at your house, you could pack some of your things and then come back over here. Are you okay with that?"

"My new home security system is supposed to be installed tomorrow," she said.

"We can both go back there for that."

She nodded. "I'll call him now." She dialed his number, then after a pause said, "Dmitri and I want to talk with you. Will you be at my place the rest of the evening? Good, see you in a bit."

I walked to where she was.

She stood and came into my arms.

I kissed the top of her head. "It's going to be okay."

CHAPTER 20

Charlotte

Jax was in the den when Dmitri and I got there. A space across the hallway from the library office. He was sitting on a tan leather recliner and watching television. He had a glass of whiskey in his hand.

"Hi, Jax."

"Hey, Charley. Deuce."

"Nice to see you," Dmitri said and took a seat on the matching tan leather couch.

Jax turned off the television.

"Would you like a glass of wine?" I asked Dmitri.

"No, I'm good," he replied.

I sat on the couch beside him. It was obvious Jax had been drinking for a while. His eyes were bloodshot and glazed over.

"I wanted to talk with you about the information on the flash drive Charlotte brought over to show me," Dmitri said.

Jax returned the recliner to a full upright position. "Sure."

"What are your impressions of what's on there?" Dmitri asked.

"I'm trying to wrap my head around it," Jax said and took another swig from his glass. "I think Mick was into something but I don't know what."

"Did you notice anything strange about Mick's behavior in the weeks prior to his death?"

"Just a lot of time spent in his office with the door closed; I could hear him speaking on the phone in Russian. I don't know who that was with. Also, Mick was locking the office door whenever he went in there and he hadn't been doing that before."

"Besides that, did you notice anything else about Mick?" Dmitri asked.

Jax was silent for a moment and took another drink from his glass. "He froze me out of the checking account." His voice was flat as he stared across the room.

I was shocked at this revelation. Seems he was getting money from his partner as well as the allowance I was giving him. He hadn't had a job in over a year. "How long ago was that?"

"It was two weeks prior to his shooting," Jax replied.

I took a deep breath and glanced at Dmitri.

"I appreciate you allowing me to look over these files," Dmitri said.

Jax's voice was hollow. "Sure."

"I've only glanced at a couple of the documents and only a few of the videos. I will study each in a day or so to look for clues," Dmitri said.

Jax glanced at Dmitri. "Let me know what you learn."

"Of course."

I felt sick inside. I didn't know whether to trust Jax. Did he *really* not know anything about the items on that flash drive? Perhaps some of the items were a surprise, but others weren't. They couldn't be.

"I'm going to pack a bag and go back to Dmitri's." I chose not to elaborate. I purposely didn't share that Dmitri and I would be back for the home security installation.

"Have you been watching the Tampa Bay Buccaneers game?" Dmitri asked. "Looks like Brady might actually retire at the end of this season."

"I heard he would really retire this time. I missed the last game, but heard it wasn't one of their best," Jax slurred. He reached for the whiskey bottle and poured himself another drink.

I stood, turning to Dmitri. "Just give me about fifteen minutes."

"Sure, take your time," Dmitri said.

* * *

"Are you hungry?" Dmitri asked while behind the wheel of his Aston Martin.

"No."

"I know it's late, but we do need to eat. Do you like Mexican?"

I smiled wide.

He gave a grin. "I guess that's a yes."

"It's a definite yes."

"Have you been to Ernie's?"

"No."

"Their food is good. Let's go?"

"Sounds good to me." I relaxed my head back onto the headrest. His hand touched the top of my thigh. I glanced at him and smiled.

In ten minutes, Dmitri pulled into the parking lot of a restaurant on the bank of the Hudson River. The sign on the front said ERNIE'S FINE MEXICAN DINING.

I was grateful I'd worn my dark chocolate brown jeans with a pale pink cashmere pullover sweater and shortie boots. This outfit was dressy enough to pass for elegant as this restaurant was definitely high-end. I put my hand inside his arm and we walked to the entry of the restaurant. A hostess greeted and led us through a dimly lit dining room and to a table with a window view of the Hudson River. She took our drink orders and left us menus.

"What do you think about my brother?" I asked once the hostess left.

"It's too soon to form any strong opinion. Once I study everything on the flash drive, maybe something will jump out," he replied.

"Something feels off."

"Like what?"

"For starters, I didn't know Mick was financially supporting him. I've been giving him a generous allowance for years since I entered prison. I still am. I feel used."

"I can understand that," he said.

"Then there is the fact of how little he really knew about his partner. There were things Mick openly shared with me that Jax didn't even know about. Like the fact Mick had spent fourteen years in prison for armed robbery. It just seemed odd to me."

"It does seem that your brother's partner should have shared that."

The waiter appeared with our drinks: a German beer for Dmitri and a vodka gimlet for me. "May I take your order?" he asked.

"Chicken quesadilla for me," I said.

"I'll take the pescado zarandeado," Dmitri said.

"Sure, I'll get that right in," the waiter said and left.

"I want to know more about you," Dmitri said.

"What would you like to know?" I asked.

"You can start with where you grew up; what was your childhood like?"

"My childhood wasn't anything special, actually quite ordinary. Both parents were present. I had a stay-at-home mom and my father worked as an insurance salesman. We lived in the suburbs of Los Angeles. I was a cheerleader in junior high and high school. I was more the social butterfly than academic and I was the homecoming queen in my senior year. I should show you my yearbook so you can laugh."

"I wouldn't ever laugh at you," he said. "It sounds like you weren't ordinary at all. I would say extraordinary."

"Well, I can't claim that. If I was 'all that,' I would have gone to college rather than flight attendant school. I was with Delta. That's how I met Lars, my late husband."

"When did your parents pass away?" he asked.

"It was my first year as a flight attendant. I was nineteen. They were driving home from a New Year's Eve party and were on the San Diego freeway. A drunk driver was going the wrong way. Hit them head-on. Both were killed instantly."

"That's tragic," he said. "You must have been devastated."

"I was, but my brother was a mess so I had to stay strong for him. He was still in high school and we didn't have any relatives who could jump in and take over. Actually, we did have a single relative—Aunt Lydia was somewhere in Africa at the time. We didn't know where. I had to pick up the pieces: make sure Jax stayed in school, manage the estate, which wasn't terribly difficult as the house was already paid for and it was just the upkeep. Jax and I stayed there until he graduated from high school and left to attend college at UCLA. After he left home, I sold the house and split all the money with Jax."

"What did he study in school?" Dmitri asked.

"History, but he didn't get very far; too much partying and he flunked out."

"That's a shame."

"Enough about me," I said. "I want to hear about you."

He gave a light laugh. The waiter appeared with our food. Dmitri thanked the man, who immediately left. I sensed Dmitri was deep in thought, as if he was pondering what—and what not—to share.

"This food looks good." I took a bite. "Yum." He smiled and took a bite of his food; I sensed he was hoping to deflect. "Okay, please, continue telling me about you," I prodded.

"I attended Yale right out of high school, and earned my MBA. Then I moved back to Moscow and lived with my father."

"Very impressive."

"I enjoy business and decided New York City was where I wanted to be, so I left Moscow." He took another bite of his food.

Even though I knew he wasn't planning to elaborate, I raised my brow. "I have so many questions, but I won't squeeze the answers out of you."

He gave a crooked grin. "Ask away."

"How old are you?"

"Thirty-five. Is that too old for you?"

"It's perfect for me. I'm twenty-eight. Am I too young for you?"

"You are perfect," he replied.

I was feeling taxed by asking so many questions, but got the feeling he wouldn't volunteer anything if I didn't ask.

"Have you ever been married before?" This was a question I'd pondered numerous times but was afraid to ask.

"Yes, when I was in Moscow, right out of college. Her name is Tatiana and she was a prima ballerina with the Russian ballet. The marriage was doomed from the very beginning, a relationship made in hell. We divorced after only a year."

"I wouldn't be with you now if your marriage to Tatiana was made in heaven."

That got a smile from him. His eyes met mine. "I'm glad you're here."

"Me too." I wanted to say more but stopped.

Our meal was finished and we were in the parking lot.

"Want to walk to the riverbank?" he asked.

"That would be nice."

Given the late hour, the riverbank was deserted. There was a long cement bench facing the water. We sat. The city lights and the full moon reflected on the water.

"It's beautiful."

He put his arm around me and softly kissed my cheek.

"I'm in love with you, Charlotte." His voice was almost a whisper.

Our eyes met.

"I never thought I could love again, but you changed that. I'm in love with you too," I admitted. I poured my heart out to him. It felt good to finally say it. "We happened so quickly, it's almost frightening."

"Are you afraid?" he asked.

"I should be, but I'm not. I love you. That's all that matters."

CHAPTER 21

Adeline

"Oh Sergei." I let out a loud moan beneath the silk sheets of Sergei Zhukov's bed at his house in Frankfurt, Germany. "You feel sooooo good! Faster!"

"Yeah, baby," he said with a strong Russian accent as he pumped into me. His sweat dripped onto my bare breasts.

"Come with me, Sergei. I'm ready." I knew he was close and wouldn't stop pumping until he felt he satisfied me.

He made a loud primal sound, and I took that as my cue to fake it with an equally loud theatrical moan; I was anxious for it to be over.

I'd known our lovemaking would be quick and intense, as it always was, and I was more than okay with that. The man was easy to please and I made no demands of him, which caused him to shower me with more gifts. He liked flaunting his wealth at me. I could be quite the seductress, and Sergei was putty in my hands. He was part of my plan and so far, everything was falling right into my lap. The man was already married; his wife was in Moscow. I didn't have to worry about him wanting more from me than I was willing to give. While he was nice looking, he was thirty years my senior.

I was estranged from my family so they wouldn't interfere with all my fun. I enjoyed partying and if I wanted to do drugs, then it was my own decision. Cocaine was expensive and with my trust fund frozen, I needed a sugar daddy, and Sergei was the perfect fall guy. He liked cocaine as much as I did, so there was always a plentiful supply of it. The international travels in his private jet to his fancy homes was a plus, as was the nice apartment he put me up in. I was living on top of the world.

* * *

I was determined to ruin Charlotte once and for all—reduce her to the commoner she was. My brother had been a fool for the woman and now he was dead. If she'd not been in his life, he wouldn't have been on that plane going back to New York to get her. I believed the tiara was rightfully mine. After all, Charlotte was no longer in the Bjorn family, and the thing was worth a fortune.

I hated Charlotte for easily getting into the modeling business; I'd tried and was turned down—being told I was too short and weighed too much. That had been a slap in the face, particularly since I was at least as beautiful as Charlotte. I had the long and straight black hair and it was all natural; I looked more "Raven" than Charlotte. It turned out there were others who were also jealous of her. The two models I had befriended were eager to dethrone "Raven" and take her place. It had been easy to egg them on while drinking at a bar. I convinced them it would be easy to frame Charlotte for murder, and the agency would then fire her.

I hadn't expected the two would actually follow through. The whole thing had snowballed when no one came forward admitting the crime. I hadn't felt any remorse when Charlotte ended up in prison. Sergei knew about the whole thing and didn't care. After all, he didn't know Charlotte, and figured it was my problem, not his. He was happy to stay out of it and I was very okay with that.

"Sergei, you're looking mighty sexy tonight." I sauntered to where he was standing in the living room and planted a kiss on his cheek.

"Oh yeah?"

I gave him a wink. "Good enough to eat."

"Tonight, my sweet," he said, grinning, "I need to go out for a while to take care of a little business."

I pouted. "I will be so lonely while you are gone."

He pulled me close and planted a kiss on my lips. "Wear something sexy for when I get back. You know what I like," he said with a wicked grin.

"I sure do." I put my hand to his crotch. "Don't be too long."

He gave out a boisterous laugh. "You want it, don't you?" he said.

"I sure do." Then I gave him a wet kiss before he left out the front door.

I waited until Sergei was long gone, then picked up my cell and dialed.

"Hello?" Dmitri said.

"Hi, Dmitri. This is Adeline and I am here with your Uncle Sergei."

"Okay?"

"Guess you are wondering who has been watching you." I gave a dreadful laugh.

"Who are you?"

"I am your worst nightmare."

I was feeling wickedly elated. I knew Dmitri and Charlotte were an item, and the whole thing made me furious. I didn't wish Charlotte any happiness. It would be fun to ruin her.

CHAPTER 22

Dmitri

Charlotte and I were lounging in chair on my roof patio in Manhattan. "That was interesting."

"You seem troubled," she said.

"The person on the phone said her name was Adeline."

"I know someone by that name, but it might not be her," she said.

"Who is that?"

"The Adeline I know is the sister of my late husband. She hates me."

"Hmmm."

Charlotte looked troubled as she chewed the inside of her mouth. "What did that woman say?"

"She said she was with my Uncle Sergei. Mentioned something about 'watching' me, and then said she was my worst nightmare. I'm wondering if she is responsible for all that video footage on the flash drive."

"My God! That has to be the Adeline I know. I don't understand why she would do that to you."

"What exactly does this woman have against you?" I asked.

"For starters, she thinks I'm responsible for her brother's death. Because if he wasn't on that plane, and on his way to pick me up, then that plane wouldn't have crashed."

"That's ridiculous."

"Then, there's a tiara Lars had made for me to wear on our wedding day. It's worth quite a lot of money. It's insured for thirty million. I keep it locked in my home safe. Adeline believes I should give it to her since I am no longer in the Bjorn family. She knows her brother had it made for me, and therefore it's not part of the family jewels. But she doesn't care. She just doesn't want me to have it. The Bjorns are the royal family of Denmark."

"That tiara is yours to do with as you please," I reassured her as I took a swallow from my bottle of beer.

"My brother told me Adeline came over to my house several times while I was incarcerated and demanded to be let inside. He only allowed her inside once; she stormed through my place and tried to get upstairs. Jax was able to stop her and get her out."

I took another gulp of beer. "It's good you have home security now."

Charlotte took a sip of her wine and held it while staring out at the city skyline.

"I don't want to cause you any trouble. I couldn't ever forgive myself if something happened to you because of me."

"Or anything happened to *you*." I put my hand on top of hers and squeezed it. "I love you, Charlotte."

"I love you so much," she said, struggling to hold back the tears.

I put my beer onto the side table. "Come here."

She got out of her chair and came to me, sitting in my lap. I put my arms around her and held her tight. She put her head onto my shoulder. She felt perfect in my arms.

* * *

I hated the idea of having to phone my father about Sergei's girlfriend Adeline, but I knew I had to. It was important to address the problem right away. Charlotte was taking a bubble bath and I knew she would be there for a while. I planned to join her after the call.

I picked up my cell and dialed my father's number. It only rang a couple times before he answered.

"My son, it is nice to hear your voice," my father said.

"It's nice to hear yours as well. How have you been?"

"I've been doing okay since I saw a new doctor. He gave me some new pills and they seem to help." He started coughing, then wheezing.

"Papa, you don't sound good at all."

"I sound worse than I actually am. Do not worry."

"How is Marta doing?" Marta was my father's second wife.

"She's doing well. She keeps busy with her friends and still enjoys riding her horse on our property," my father said.

"That's good to hear." I paused briefly. "I need to ask your advice."

"Of course."

"This has to do with your brother Sergei. He has a mistress who phoned me and wants to cause me trouble."

"How so?"

"The woman's name is Adeline." I told the details of the phone call, but didn't say anything about Charlotte.

"I knew he had a girl, but I don't understand what this has to do with you."

"Neither do I. What do you suggest I do?"

"I suggest not doing anything. Just watch your back. Since you don't have any proof of wrongdoing, then that is all you can do. I've never met her. Sergei was bragging to me about her; said she was a young Danish princess and really hot."

I was now certain Charlotte was correct; this woman was her late husband's sister.

"Thank you for this advice. I will call you back if anything new develops."

"Yes, Son, please do."

* * *

I softly knocked on the bathroom door.

"Please come in," Charlotte said. She was soaking in the extra-large deep bathtub surrounded by fragrant bubbles. Her hair was pulled up on to top of her head.

I felt my cock stiffen at the sight of her sexy body surrounded by bubbles. "May I join you?"

She gave me a sexy look. "I would be disappointed if you didn't." She watched as I slowly removed my t-shirt and jeans and dropped them on the floor, revealing my black boxer briefs. I finally removed them, exposing my aroused shaft.

She licked her lips, then scooted forward as I slid in behind her, pulling her between my legs. She leaned back on my chest and I wrapped my legs around her.

She slid her hands up my inner thighs. "You feel good."

I kissed her on the neck and moved one palm down to her sex. She parted her legs. I put my fingers inside her and began to move. She clenched around my fingers and soon let out a loud moan.

She turned around to face me, kissing me on the lips.

"May I wash you?" she whispered.

I smiled.

She picked up the fragrant soap, rubbed it between her hands, slowly lathered my chest, then squeezed water from her sponge to rinse me. When she glided her soapy fingers down one arm to my hand, I locked my fingers with hers and pulled her to straddle me. Our lips met. My hard cock met her entrance. I grabbed the back of her ass, pulled her towards me, and entered her.

I leaned my head on the back edge of the tub and closed my eyes. I thanked fate, the universe, or whoever that higher power was who blessed me with this woman.

CHAPTER 23

Charlotte

We were in Dmitri's kitchen at the breakfast bar. I talked him into allowing me to cook breakfast—a vegetable omelet with a side of cut fruit. He made us cappuccinos. I was barefoot and wearing one of his button-down shirts. He wore pajama bottoms and a t-shirt. I'd been at his place now for three weeks.

"This is really good," he said. "I didn't know you could cook."

It pleased me he'd said that. "Well, now you know."

There was silence as we ate.

"I should really go to my place. I want to learn what Jax is up to."

"I can take you. I need to check in at my office. I can stop by afterwards and pick you up. Bring you back here."

"Or you can stay with me at my place." I grinned. "I can cook for you in my own kitchen. I'd like to show you that tiara if you want."

"I can stay at your place for a few days. I don't want you to be alone; not until this situation is resolved."

"I wouldn't be alone, you know? My brother is there." When he'd said 'not until this situation is resolved,' my heart fell into my stomach. I couldn't imagine not being with him. He made my world feel brighter. Of course, I knew we couldn't be tied at the hip. That wouldn't work for either of us.

"Why do you think Adeline wants your tiara?"

"The only thing I can think of is that she views it as a crown. She was born a princess and I wasn't. I know she's estranged from her family, so there is that."

"It's possible she's just crazy," he said.

"I'm positive she's crazy, but how she got that way is the real story. I do know she looked up to her brother in a worshipful way, and when he married me and moved to the US, she didn't handle it well," I offered by way of explanation.

"That doesn't warrant being estranged from her family," he said.

"True. There are things I don't know about her, and that is one of them. I would love to know how she hooked up with your uncle."

"I'd like to know that too," he said. "I phoned my father yesterday and asked about my uncle. My father said he didn't know anything about Sergei and your former sister-in-law. My father claimed Sergei had merely bragged about having a young Danish princess as his girlfriend but no other details."

There was a brief silence, then I stood and began clearing off the breakfast bar.

"You cooked so I'll clean up." He kissed me on the cheek, then took the plates from my hands and went to the sink. His touch always sent tingles through my entire body. I wondered if this would last forever.

* * *

Dmitri left and it felt strange to be away from him. The whole thing between us just felt too good to be true. I wanted to hold on for dear life. My track record with men wasn't great. Actually, none of them stayed, whether through death or boredom. But none of them were as perfect for me as Dmitri—not even Lars, which hurt me to admit.

I didn't want to hold onto Dmitri too tight; he might feel smothered. That's the reason I wanted him to come to my place. He could leave whenever he wanted. I would hate it, but I didn't want him to view me as needy.

I was in my bedroom, unpacking my bag from staying at Dmitri's. An unsettling feeling overcame me and I instantly wondered where my brother was. He had been acting strange ever since the death of Mick and the discovery of everything on that flash drive. Was *he* hiding something?

I walked out of my bedroom and down the stairs in search of my brother.

"Jax. Hey, dude."

No response.

I walked into the kitchen and noticed there was a paper on the kitchen counter. I walked over and picked it up. It was from Jax.

Charley,

By the time you read this I will have been long gone. There is so much I haven't told you, and I'm not as innocent as I've led on. I pushed Mick to steal that money, but in those last days before he was murdered, he shut me out. I wanted to figure out what had happened, but I couldn't. I thought you could.

Sorry. You are better off without me. The whole world is better off without me. Please know that none of this is your fault. I'm leaving this planet my way. See you on the Other Side.

Jax

My first instinct was to run upstairs. My heart was pounding as I made my way to his room, down the hallway from mine. Once there, I opened the door and peered inside. All of his things were still there, even his laptop.

I pounded down the stairs and towards the kitchen door that led to the garage. When I opened the door, I instantly saw Jax hunched over his steering wheel, blood all over the inside.

My heart was pounding so hard when I opened the car door. What I saw was shocking and heartbreaking. He was clearly gone.

I fell to my knees, sobbing so deeply I didn't think I could breathe.

"Jax!" I screamed.

CHAPTER 24

Dmitri

When I drove into an empty spot in front of Charlotte's house, it was buzzing with police and an ambulance. I quickly got out of my car and rushed to her open front door.

"Who are you?" asked an NYPD officer holding a clipboard.

"Charlotte is my girlfriend. I need to get to her."

The officer nodded and I went inside. I saw her sitting on the couch in the living room. Her eyes were red and tears were running down her face. I rushed to her and sat beside her. An NYPD detective was sitting on the sofa across from her.

I threw my arms around her; she put her head on my chest and wept bitterly. I wanted to ask what had happened but now didn't seem like the time. I would find out soon enough. I just wanted to be there for Charlotte.

"Ms. Bjorn," the detective said. "Is there anything you can tell me?"

"No," she whimpered.

"Thank you," the detective said.

It was clear to me someone was dead and in her house. The kitchen door that led to the garage was open. The conversation was loud from the medical examiner and police.

"Surely Charlotte doesn't need to hear all this, officer. May I please walk her outside?"

"Sure. You might want to go to the back. The ambulance is in the front. We will come to get you both when it leaves."

With my arm around her waist, we walked to her back patio. We were alone.

"What happened?" I handed her my handkerchief.

She took it and wiped her eyes and blew her nose. "Jax shot himself in his car in my garage. He left a note. I folded it up and have in my pants pocket. I don't want to give it to the police. He said there was a lot I didn't know about him and he had a part in the theft of that money. I'll show you the note when the police leave," she said.

Her last statement confirmed my earlier suspicion. "I'm sorry."

We remained standing. I kept my arm around her and she rested her head inside my shoulder. I knew there wasn't anything I could say to make her feel better. My job was to only be present for her. Twenty minutes passed in silence except for her crying, which came in waves. I was worried about her; Jax was her only family besides her aunt.

"Ms. Bjorn," said the detective, who had stepped into the patio. "Your brother is now in transport. I don't believe we have any further questions for now. Your brother's Mustang will be towed shortly. It needs to be taken by the NYPD."

She nodded and looked up at me.

"Do you have any idea of other details?" the detective asked.

"No," she said.

The detective nodded and walked back into the house.

"Let's go back inside and pack up some of your stuff. Then we'll go back to my place, okay?"

"Okay," she said.

The detective had left his business card on the coffee table right before he and the last two officers left, closing the door behind them. I walked to the door and locked it then climbed the stairs to Charlotte.

There was a light on in a room down the hallway. I walked in that direction and found her there. I knocked twice.

"Hi."

"Please come in," she said.

It was her bedroom—very feminine with crisp white linens and a canopy hanging over the bed. There was a beautiful crystal chandelier in the center of the ceiling.

"How are you holding up?"

She was sitting on an upholstered chair in a sitting area, her eyes bloodshot and puffy. "I don't know. It doesn't seem real."

"I'm sure." I sat down in the chair across from her.

"I need to go into my brother's bedroom, but I didn't want to go in there alone. I want to take his laptop with us back to your place. I have a feeling there might be some clues about what all he was into." She pulled out the suicide note and handed it to me.

I read it. "Okay. Let's go."

I knew it was better to just get this over with rather than her thinking about it too long and breaking down again. We stood and she led the way further down the hallway to a bedroom on the far right. She flipped on the overhead light.

The bedroom was in perfect order—bed made and no clutter. There was a small desk with the laptop on top.

"I suspect most everything on this computer is password protected, but something a good hacker could get into—unless you have that skill," she said.

"Let's take it to my place and I'll give it a try. Sometimes people keep small password books; perhaps he's got something like that in this room."

"Yeah, let's look around. I can check the dresser drawers if you don't mind going through that desk."

I nodded.

We began rooting through all of the drawers. I was about to call it quits when I found a small black day planner. I opened it up and flipped through it. When I got to the very back, there were passwords written down.

"I found something." I showed her the calendar book. "There are some passwords written in the back. That doesn't mean all of them are current, but at least there is something to start with." There were also quite a few phone numbers, but I decided she might want to go through those herself.

"Any sign of his cell phone?" she asked.

"I see a charging cable, but not the phone. Maybe we should look around more. Hopefully, it wasn't in the car the tow truck hauled away."

"He used to leave it in my library a lot. Maybe it's in there. I hope so. I bet there's a ton of information in it," she said.

"Let's finish up in here, then go to your library."

The library was a grand scale place; collector's books filled virtually every shelf. The oversized desk was intricately carved mahogany. Even the chairs facing the fireplace were high quality leather. But most impressive was an original Vincent Van Gogh painting behind the desk. I knew it was authentic. I found it difficult to understand she hadn't had any home security system until recently.

"Here it is," she said, picking up a phone from a round wooden table between the two leather chairs.

"Is it password protected?"

"Yeah, it is."

"Let's put that with the laptop and we can work on them at my place. It's possible we can figure out what that password is."

"Sure."

"Do you need some time to pack up?" I asked.

"I have my bag ready in my closet. I just need to get it."

"Let me."

"Okay. My closet is on my third floor. Just go through my bedroom closet and you'll see a set of stairs. It's up there. I'll try to find something to put that computer and phone into. My brother is sure to have that in his room."

I was shocked when I entered her closet. It was the size of a bedroom, with built-in shelving, hanging rods, and even another crystal chandelier. Her packed bag was sitting on the floor next to a long upholstered pink velvet bench. I couldn't help but smile—it was so her.

I flipped off the light and walked back down the stairs. I found her in Jax's room. There was a backpack where she put the laptop and the cell phone. I slipped the suicide note inside the bag.

"I've got the laptop and cell phone. And if you have my bag, there is only one thing left," she said.

"What's that?"

"I want to open my safe and show you that tiara my former sister-in-law is hounding me for."

I nodded and we made our way to the first floor, stopping to put the suitcase and backpack on the floor in front of the door. I followed her to the library. She went to that priceless painting behind her desk and opened it up like a small door. Inside was the safe. She put her thumb onto a reader and then punched in a series of numbers. When the safe opened, she reached in the far back for a cherry wooden box with a brass front latch and placed it onto the desk. When she opened it, I was stunned. The diamond and emerald white gold tiara definitely looked regal; something you would expect to see on a royal.

"Wow" was all I could say.

"It was custom made for my wedding. I know it's worth a lot of money, and I don't know when I would ever wear it again. It's sentimental—and the reason I won't let Adeline have it. Truthfully, I would place it with Christie's or Sotheby's to sell it before I would let her have it," she said.

"I understand."

She put it back into the box, locked it in the safe, and swung the painting over it. I now understood why her former sister-in-law wanted it.

"Ready to go?"

"Yeah," she said and gazed up into my eyes.

She seemed so vulnerable. I wanted to pull her into my arms and hold her. But I knew the sooner we left her house, the better. There was a dark energy permeating the whole place—it was palpable—and I couldn't wait to get out of here.

CHAPTER 25

Charlotte

It was seven-thirty. We had just finished dinner—we had Chinese delivered. Dmitri and I were sitting outside on his patio; he had a whiskey and I had a glass of white wine.

I leaned back on the headrest of the chair and gazed at the night sky. Dark thoughts filled my mind. Everyone I love dies. My parents, Lars, my baby, and now my brother. Would Dmitri be next? I just couldn't bear the thought, and another wave of tears came. Only this time was deeper and I couldn't stop the wailing and the shaking. I put my hands over my face.

I felt Dmitri's hands underneath me as he lifted me up. He carried me to his chair and placed me on his lap, my cheek resting on his chest. I felt kisses on my head as he held me tight.

"It's good to get it out," he whispered.

After about half an hour, I decided to get it together. A shower might help clear my head. I kissed him and made my way to the bathroom.

I was numb as I undressed and stepped into Dmitri's shower. I allowed the warm water to completely wash over me, like that would cleanse off all the darkness. Grief threatened to bury me in the abyss. More tears came.

Somehow the tears stopped; my head seemed clearer. I got out of the shower and toweled off. I grabbed Dmitri's white terry robe from the wall hook and put it on, my wet hair falling to my shoulders. I padded my way to the living room and found Dmitri still outside, but now he was holding a guitar. A classical melody filled the air. I walked out into the patio and sat in the chair beside him. He smiled at me and then the melody on his guitar changed, and he began to sing: "Charlotte, my love, the sun comes with you…"

I couldn't believe what I was hearing. His deep baritone was beautiful and filled my soul. Where tears had been, there was now joy instead. I felt all the passion in his words and it made me love him even more. How could I have been so lucky to have met him? I'm no one special. Actually, I'm a complication I wouldn't wish on any man.

"That's so beautiful. I didn't know you could sing and play guitar. Did you write that?"

He grinned wide. "Yeah, while you were in the shower."

He'd actually written a song just for me. No one had ever done that before. It warmed my heart. "You're a man of many talents." I leaned over and kissed him on the lips.

He leaned his guitar against the wall and pulled me onto his lap.

"I've never loved a man the way I love you—not even Lars, and it hurts me to say that."

He pulled me tighter and kissed me again.

"Everyone I have loved dies and I'm scared of losing you too." I finally said it and wondered if it was too much.

"I don't want to lose you either," he said. "I've been smitten with you from the very first time I laid eyes on you, and that would be from your modeling days."

"Why didn't you pursue me, then?"

"Bad timing. I was stuck in two business deals with my father, and knew I would have to leave for Moscow. When I v returned and went to the party you attended, things went south."

"I'm sorry. Raven was a shameless, egocentric person. I spent the bulk of my time in lock up hating who I was. You deserve someone so much better than me." I was ashamed. Even though I wasn't guilty of the crime, I was in a back room in a hotel having mindless sex with some guy I barely knew. Garth was the first and only man I'd been with since Lars died and it was only a single time.

"Charlotte, I'm not so perfect. There are things about me I'm not proud of," he said. "My father is a Russian oligarch who has close ties to Putin. For years I had to walk a tight line where that's concerned. I don't want to be involved in any of my father's business dealings any longer, and the last business was that hair salon. It was merely a place for money laundering. Right now, all my business dealings are honest and free and clearly mine. You have nothing to worry about where I'm concerned."

"The rumor in the models' circle was that you were in the Russian mafia. That's why I asked you the question when we had our first date."

"Actually, it's called Bratva and I've done all I can to distance myself. My Uncle Sergei, on the other hand, is in knee-deep, and he's with your former sister-in-law now."

"That's frightening." I wondered how far Adeline would go to get my tiara.

"Yes, it's frightening and I don't want you to live alone."

I didn't want to be a burden "I have security on my house now, so I should be safe." to him. Who knows what Adeline might do to get my tiara? I wondered if she was also involved in all the rest of this. Trouble always seemed to follow her.

His brow furrowed deeply. "You would be a prisoner in your house, because anytime you might leave to go shopping or anything else, you would be a target. You would need a bodyguard."

"What about you? All that video footage implies you are also being watched."

"I'm not altogether sure what that's about," he said.

"I can't help but wonder if my brother was involved in some way with your uncle."

"I've thought about that too. Since neither of us want to be involved with any of that, I'm considering telling my father about the flash drive. But I don't want it to look like you know anything about any of it. I can't tell from the files on that drive if any of that cryptocurrency had been cashed out. My father is friends with Igor Smirnoff; I'm sure he would appreciate any information about this."

"Then that pulls you right into the whole thing."

"And the reason I've been reluctant until this point to divulge anything to my father. I've also wondered where Sergei was getting all of his recent money. He's the black sheep of the family, and what he'd inherited from my late grandfather is sure to have been all used up at this point."

"All this looks very bad, and it's not something we can go to the police with—US or Russian."

"True."

"Another idea. It would seem that when Mick was killed, the police should have gone into his apartment and done a search. A computer is generally scrutinized. That would leave either of us out of it."

"I'm not so sure about that. Unless they suspected he was involved in something nefarious, I don't think the search would have happened," he said.

"What if we just anonymously send the flash drive to the police?"

"Bad idea. They wouldn't want to get involved since it would turn political. Relations between Russia and the US are tenuous enough," he said.

"Sounds like your father is the best call, then."

CHAPTER 26

I was in the bedroom at Sergei's New York City apartment. We arrived back after several weeks in Germany. It was close to eleven and Sergei still wasn't back from his business meeting. He was supposed to be back by eight. I paced the floor in sky-high heels and red bustier with matching G-string—Sergei's favorite lingerie and one he'd purchased for me. Impatience took over and I went to the nightstand. I grabbed my cell phone and began typing. I planned to set the stage for him to help me get that tiara.

I'm so hungry for you. I need to taste you. Yummy...

I was sure that would get him.

Sure enough, in less than twenty seconds, my phone pinged: *You want it don't you?*

He always needed his ego stroked. *I sure do. You please me so completely. You are the very best lover.*

My phone pinged: *Ten minutes.*

I replied with a heart emoji. I went to my lingerie drawer and pulled out a small packet of white powder. Cocaine. I poured a tiny amount on the top of my hand and snorted it. I wasn't in the mood to have sex with Sergei, but knew I better get in the mood. He was my meal ticket, a way to get what I wanted.

I heard the front door of the apartment open, and sauntered out to him in the living room, very aware he noticed my sexy outfit by his crooked grin.

"Hello, handsome," I welcomed in my most sultry voice. I went to him and kissed his lips. There was a strong stench of alcohol.

"Hey, baby." His words were slurred. "Ya missed me, huh?"

"I sure did. I am hungry for you." I was actually wondering where he'd been. I wanted to hit him up for help with my plan to get that tiara. Now he was drunk; that might be a problem.

I wrapped my arms around him and slid my hands down to his butt, pulling him towards me. I felt his manhood and knew he wanted me.

"You seem tense, my love. I think you need me to give you a massage."

He grabbed my crotch and stuck his finger inside me. "The only massage I want is your lips on my dick," he said.

"Your wish is my command." I licked my lips and took one of his hands. I led him to the bedroom.

"Candles. Nice touch," he said.

"Only the best for you." I guided him to sit on the edge of the king-sized bed. I unbuttoned his shirt, making sure to explore his hairy chest, as I knew he liked that. "Sexy man." I slid off his shirt completely.

"You know it," he said.

I slid onto my knees and slid off his shoes, and took the toe of each sock into my front teeth, pulling each off. Sliding up to him, I guided him to lay on his back; I undid his pants and pulled them off at the bottom hem.

My hand went gently onto the front of his underwear, teasing him.

He growled.

I pulled his underwear down and slid them to the floor. My hands slid down the top of his thighs, then went upwards on his inner thighs. I ended at his erection with both hands, with the tip of my tongue gently on the top, making circles.

He groaned and arched up.

I finally gave him what he wanted, the way he wanted it. Experience had taught me how he liked his sex, and I made sure to give it to him. Each time I'd up the ante, keeping him hungry for me. I wanted him to be putty in my hands.

Sergei was now snoring. I worked him with all I had and no doubt he was down for the count. I got out of bed and padded to the bathroom to shower. I was careful to put scented lotion on my entire body afterwards. I walked back to bed and slid in nude beside him. My plan was to sex him up again in the morning.

* * *

My plan worked exactly as I wanted. I teased him until he couldn't help himself and then when the time was right, I went for it.

"Do you like fucking a princess?"

He grinned. "I sure do."

"I want to make you feel like a king."

He smacked me on the butt. "That you do."

"I need my princess crown, so I can wear it for you."

"A crown, huh? I didn't know you had one," he said.

"I sure do, but your nephew's girlfriend stole it from me. Can you help me get it back? You are so powerful and strong."

"Where is it?" he growled. "I'll get it for you."

"Will you?" He was sitting on the edge of the bed as I straddled him. I ran my fingers through his sparse hair, then bent down and lightly sucked on his earlobe.

"You bet I will. Where is she?" he asked gruffly.

"She is with your nephew. I bet she wears my crown for him, and that's not right. It's supposed to be for you to see on me. You are my king."

"Yeah, I want that," he said.

"Oh Sergei." I ran my tongue down the side of his neck.

CHAPTER 27

Dmitri

The medical examiner had called this morning and asked Charlotte what to do with her brother's body. It was painful watching her tell them to cremate him. She was struggling and barely got the words out. We talked about it last night. Besides one aunt, there weren't any other living relatives. She also didn't know of him having any close friends, so a big funeral wouldn't happen. She wanted to spread his ashes in the ocean.

I decided to phone my father today and I really dreaded it. I put it off for as long as I could. The information on that flash drive was lethal. I wanted it out of Charlotte's and my life. How could I get it to my father in a safe way? Emailing it without encryption was dangerous. I wasn't completely sure who to trust.

I grabbed my cell and walked to the outside patio and sat. I dialed my father.

"Hello, my son. It's nice of you to call."

"I hope you are doing well?"

"I am. So, what do I owe the pleasure?"

"I have some disturbing information and I don't know what to do with it. I thought you might know."

"Okay, please tell me about this."

I told the whole story from beginning to end. He listened intently. "I need that flash drive and computer. I do know about that missing money," my father said.

"Given the political situation, I don't feel safe just putting these into the mail and sending to you that way. What do you suggest?" I asked.

"I'll get back with you on how to transport these."

"There's more." I went on to describe the details of Charlotte's and my relationship, as well as concerns over Sergei and Adeline.

"I understand now why you'd previously told me about Sergei's new girl."

"Yes."

"I need to think about this and get back with you. Sergei is a scoundrel and there's no telling what he would do if he thinks we're onto him."

"I understand."

"What's this Charlotte to you?" my father asked.

"Papa, she's the one," I declared honestly.

"Are you sure?"

"Positive. I want to marry and have children with her. She means everything to me." I'd never shared my intimate feelings with my father before.

"Okay. That's all I need to know. I'll get back with you."

I sat back in the chair and tried to get my thoughts together. I wanted to go through everything on Jax's laptop. There might be other clues. He claimed he wasn't innocent. Whatever it was, he couldn't live with it. Perhaps I should copy the entire computer on to an external drive before I gave it to my father. I hated doing anything without Charlotte's permission. Would she give it?

"Is everything okay?" Charlotte asked as she sat beside me.

"I think so. I just spoke with my father and he's going to get back with me. I told him the whole story. He's anxious to get the flash drive."

"I don't want either of us to be affiliated with anything on that drive. There's also the issue of my brother's laptop."

"I wanted to ask you about that. Are you okay with me going through the whole thing, then giving my father the laptop? There might be clues," I said, unsure of how she'd react.

"Of course you can go through it first and then give it to your father. I'm scared what you might find, but maybe there will be answers for me too. I wished we could have gotten into my brother's cell. I'm positive there is a ton of information in there."

Jax's cell phone had fingerprint ID rather than just a passcode.

I reached over and held her hand. I couldn't get enough of her. She was the woman I waited my whole life for. She taught me how to love. I knew I wanted to marry her, but was it too soon? Would she say yes?

"I wonder if that tiara of mine is the cause of all the troubles with Adeline. She actually threatened you and I don't understand why she would have done that," Charlotte said.

"It does seem strange; the timing coincides with the stolen money."

"Yes, it does."

"I'm positive my father can handle this," I said, trying to reassure her.

"I've decided to give the tiara to my former mother-in-law. I'm not in the royal family anymore," she said.

"Unless your former in-laws asked for it back, then you aren't under any obligation to return it."

Charlotte wore a far-away expression. "I've thought long and hard about this, and I believe it's the best thing to do. I plan to contact my former mother-in-law and talk to her about it. It will feel awkward, but I want to do this."

I squeezed her hand. I knew why she wanted to do this. It was because of me and I didn't like it. "Is there more that you want to tell me?"

She nodded. "That tiara is left from my marriage to Lars, and it doesn't have anything to do with us. It's like a wedding band. It represented him and me. He's been gone for a very long time and I want to release it. It's time." Her eyes filled with tears.

"I'll support whatever you want to do."

She wiped her tears with her hand. "This feels right. If my former mother-in-law decides to give it to Adeline, then so be it. But I don't think she will. It should be with the other family jewels."

"I want to help you, but I don't know how."

"You can't. This is a journey I have to take alone."

She stood and bent down to kiss me, then walked back inside. I saw her grab her cell phone from the kitchen counter, and walk down the hallway towards the bedroom. What she just said hit me hard. She was going to give up a thirty-million-dollar tiara to protect me. Part of me didn't want her to do it, yet another part of me wanted her to.

* * *

My cell rang. The caller ID showed it was my father. I answered it.

"Hello, son."

"Hello, father."

"I have spoken to Igor, who is one of the owners of that stolen money. Of course, he definitely wants any information he can get that will provide clues towards getting that money back."

"I understand."

"Do you know where the lockers are at the airport near you?" he asked.

"Yes."

"Go to locker number 5023. Put the flash drive and the computer into this locker. The PIN is 978156. Text me when you have done this."

"I will." We disconnected.

I already purchased an external drive to copy everything on that computer. I hated to do this without first going through the computer himself, but I hadn't been able to break through that password— nothing in Jax's day planner had worked. Regardless, I was going to try one more time. Maybe Charlotte knew of something her brother might use.

I walked to the bedroom and found her laying on the bed, sobbing. I sat on the side of the bed and rubbed her back. She didn't even acknowledge I was there. It killed me to see her this way. I felt helpless, and I didn't do helpless well.

I moved to the other side of the bed, got in beside her, and pulled her into my arms. Her head rested on my chest; her crying eventually stopped.

"Thank you," she said.

"I'm here for you. You've got to know that."

"I do. I feel these complications are my fault. I want to do something to make it right."

"I know." I held her in silence for thirty minutes before I heard her take a deep breath.

"I love you so much," she said.

I kissed her on the top of her head. "My father called and came up with a plan on how to get the flash drive and laptop," I told her.

"That's good."

"I think the hard drive should be copied onto an external drive before I get it to him."

"If you think that's best."

"I do. Unfortunately, I haven't been able to get into the computer without the password. Do you happen to know something that your brother would have used?"

"I can offer suggestions." She pulled away from me, and sat up. "We can try now, if you want."

"Sure, if you're okay."

"I am." She grabbed a tissue from the nightstand and blew her nose. "I want to go to the bathroom and wash my face, then I'll meet you in your office."

I nodded and watched her walk to the master bathroom. I made my way to my home office. I just put the computer on my desk and powered it up when she walked in.

"I might know a few important dates he could have used," she said.

"Okay."

"Try 1121997."

"I'm in. What does that date mean, by the way?"

"It's the date our parents were killed in the car accident."

"That's an important date for sure." I wrote down the numbers on a small notepad. It would make it easier for my father to get into the laptop. "I'm going to copy the whole computer onto this external drive, then I need to take both items to where my father told me."

"Where is that?" she asked.

"To a locker at the airport. He gave me the locker number and the PIN to get inside. I'm to leave these and it will be taken to Moscow from there."

"That's smart. If we are still under someone's surveillance, then it's better not to have any courier here," she said.

"My thoughts exactly. I shouldn't be gone longer than forty-five minutes. It's probably better that I go alone."

She nodded.

CHAPTER 28

Charlotte

My conversation with Astrid Bjorn, my former mother-in-law, had gone much better than expected. The woman was charming as always, and seemed delighted I had called. It was easy to tell Astrid about the troubles I was having with Adeline over the tiara. Astrid insisted I didn't need to return it to her. We went back and forth about it until Astrid finally agreed it should be placed with the rest of the royal jewels.

She insisted I travel on the royal private jet to bring her the tiara. Her personal assistant, who I remembered from Lars' and my wedding, would accompany me.

I was grateful my passport was still valid. The plan was for me to give Astrid twenty-four hours' notice so she could arrange the flight. I would stay at the palace once there.

Images from the day Lars had given me the tiara flooded my mind. He'd been so proud and had quite ceremoniously put it on me. While I never had any official title from the queen, Lars had called me a princess ever since he crowned me that day. A part of me was dying inside at the decision to take it to his family home. How would he feel about me doing this? Would he approve?

If things had gone differently, our son would have been next in line after Lars for the throne. We might have had a little girl, and I could have given her the crown one day on her own wedding day.

I began to feel guilty for loving Dmitri—for wanting him more than life itself—for hoping we could have what Lars and I hadn't.

Would Dmitri understand my need to make this trip? I knew I needed to do this alone, and worried if he might be hurt. Should I tell him, or just leave a letter behind? This was the only decision left. The others had been made.

I heard the elevator door open and knew Dmitri had returned. I turned from my seat outside; I left the sliding glass door open. He'd been gone almost two hours.

He gave me a kiss, then sat on the chair beside me. "Hi, beautiful."

"Did everything go okay with getting both those items inside the locker?"

"Yes and I'm glad it's done. Hopefully, that's the end of it."

"I hope so too." I sensed there was something else going on with him, but didn't want to ask. I had my own dilemma. "My conversation with Astrid, my former mother-in-law, went better than I'd expected."

"I'm glad to hear that. I didn't want to pry."

"I want to take my tiara to Copenhagen and give it to her. She's going to send the royal jet to pick me up. I'm to stay at the palace." My heart was racing.

"I can take you," Dmitri said.

"I know and I love you for that. The thing is, I have to do this alone. I have unfinished business there."

"I want to keep you safe," he said, his tone matching the concern on his face.

"I will be safe. The royal jet and my escort are as safe as it gets. You're going to have to trust me with this. I love you, Dmitri, and I don't want anything to come between us."

He ran his hand through his hair and took a deep breath. "I do trust you. I just don't trust anyone else."

"I know. This will be hard for both of us."

"When do you want to go?" he asked.

"Soon. I'm to give Astrid twenty-four hours' notice and she will have the plane at the airport here for me."

"When you're ready to come back, I'll fly to Copenhagen and travel back with you," he said.

"Thank you."

I wasn't sure how long I wanted to stay in Copenhagen. I was torn. Queen Astrid was my only link to Lars. This trip would be difficult on many levels; I also knew this visit would be the last. Part of me was sad while the other was very ready to move forward with Dmitri.

I wanted to change the direction of our conversation. "I'd like to see if there is anything interesting about my brother on his computer. I know the external drive could show me that."

"I can set up my computer with the external drive and you can search away. I haven't had time to go through it myself, so I can't say what might be interesting or not."

"There might not be anything at all."

"Or there might be a lot," he said.

I knew Jax kept secrets and the reason he'd ended his life might be on that computer. His few belongings in my house hadn't uncovered anything. I told the police to just keep the Mustang—I didn't want it back. What for?

"I can make another copy of the external drive if you want. It would be easy to do and allow you to more comfortably read on your own laptop. I feel like I need to keep a copy so I can look through it thoroughly. That stolen money and video surveillance worries me. I need to get to the bottom of it."

I stood. "I'm okay with a copy."

He grabbed me at the waist and pulled me to his lap. "Did I tell you how luscious you are today?"

I couldn't help but giggle, and then our lips met. I felt his rigid shaft against my ass and desire ignited for him.

"I can't ever get enough of you," he whispered and his kiss deepened.

Tingling sensations filled me—like electricity and a magnet all in one. I wanted him with a ferocity, needed him to take me away to a different time and place. To a place without rules, personal histories, or fear.

"Take me to bed. Make love to me—I want all of you—don't hold back."

I knew he knew what I meant. All our prior lovemaking had been gentle, passionate, and he'd focused almost entirely on pleasuring me. I knew there was more caveman inside of him, and that's the man I needed.

He was quiet while he carried me to the bedroom and when he got to the doorway, he looked at me with questioning eyes.

"Yes."

He carried me to the edge of the bed and sat me there. But I stood and went to him, unbuttoning his pale blue Oxford shirt and opening it up. I ran my hands over his hard abs and pec muscles and traced my tongue over one of his nipples. When I lightly ran my teeth over it, I saw him grin.

We kept our eyes fixed on each other, as I slid his shirt off and it fell to the floor. My hands traveled to his belt and I unbuckled it, then unzipped his dark washed jeans.

He was quick to take the cue. He slid out of his shoes and jeans, leaving them on the floor. He untied my silk kimono and it glided to the floor. I stood nude in front of him. My hands pushed his boxers to the floor. Our eyes remained fixed on each other the whole time.

He guided me to the edge of the bed, picking me up and placing me in the center. I felt his hands part my knees before his fingers went inside of my wetness.

He pulled out of me and put his fingers in his mouth. "Sweet as honey."

He crawled to me and traced his tongue across my lips, passionately kissing me as his tongue entered my mouth. It was wickedly erotic to taste myself on his mouth.

I wrapped my legs around his waist and arched myself towards his hard shaft as he entered me and began thrusting.

"More!" I yelled. "I want all of you."

His thrusting became faster and faster, then harder and deeper.

I clenched around him and felt the orgasm build. I let out a primal sound that I didn't even recognize came from me.

He turned us over so I was on top of him and he lifted me up by my hips. I straddled him and began pumping him, harder and harder like I'd never done before. Then a climax came again and I screamed out his name.

He pushed me back and turned me onto all fours, lightly smacking me on the ass. Just enough to sting.

I moaned in pleasure, so he smacked again and reached around and lightly pinched one of my nipples.

"God, yes," I moaned. The combination of pain and pleasure intensified the whole experience.

His tongue traveled downward, tracing my back and down to my wetness.

He entered me from behind and began pumping—gently at first but he quickly picked up speed, going deeper, and thrusting more violently.

"Yes, yes," I cried. "Come with me!"

He kept thrusting— speed increasing like I'd never felt from him before. His beast was loose and so was mine.

His hands were on my butt cheeks and he squeezed. I could feel him getting bigger inside of me and knew he was close—then it happened.

He gave out the loudest moan I'd ever heard and I rode the wave of ecstasy, more satisfied than I'd ever been. We had claimed each other.

CHAPTER 29

Dmitri

I was in the kitchen and coffee was brewing. It was nine-thirty in the morning and Charlotte was still asleep in bed. I reflected on the evening before. The primal pounding sex was unexpected, but I knew she needed it. Maybe I did too. I was shocked at my own raw performance with her. I'd not been this animal in a very long time. I wondered how she would feel about it this morning.

"Good morning," Charlotte said. She was wearing the silk kimono from last night. She came to me and put her arms around my waist.

"Good morning to you too." I kissed her on the top of her head.

"I'm calling Astrid today."

Now I understood why she wanted me the way she did last night. I dreaded her leaving and had a dark feeling about her trip to Denmark.

"I need to go to my house and retrieve that tiara," she said.

"I'll take you today."

"Would you spend tonight with me at my house?" she asked. "I want to feel your body beside me in my bed. I want to cook for you. I want to take your picture so I can see your face when I'm gone."

"Oh Charlotte." I put my arms around her and held her tight. "We can do all that."

She was tugging at my heart strings. I planned to ask her to marry me and give her the diamond engagement ring I bought yesterday while out. Was now the time? I wasn't sure it was.

I poured each of us a cup of coffee.

"I'm going to call now. There's a six-hour time difference. It's three-thirty in the afternoon there," she said.

"Sure."

She picked up her cup of coffee and went to the bedroom.

I took my coffee cup and walked to the patio outside. My thoughts turned to the external drive I promised to have ready for her. It would take several hours to copy the whole thing. She might want to take her laptop with the external drive on the flight.

I got the process started and returned to the kitchen. Charlotte was already there and had pulled out a frying pan. There were eggs and bacon from the refrigerator on the counter. She wore a sweet smile. "Hungry?"

"I am. What are you making?"

"How about scrambled eggs and bacon?"

"Sounds good to me. What can I do to help?"

"How about setting the table outside on the patio? It won't take me long to cook our food. It would be nice to eat outside."

"I'll set us up."

The weather was unseasonably warm with a slight breeze. A perfect morning for eating outside. The round wrought iron table and chairs sat on the farthest back wall. There were flowering plants in three planters along the side wall. It was a pleasant space to be in and have breakfast.

I took the white tablecloth and placed it on top the table, then returned to the kitchen. She was busy cooking when I got two glasses from the cabinet, filled them with water, and took them outside.

When I returned inside, I took a seat at the breakfast bar and watched her cook. I imagined what it would be like to have her with me all the time. Just the thought of it warmed my heart. But there was an inner voice telling me that her visit to Denmark wouldn't be for a mere couple of days. She said there was unfinished business but hadn't volunteered what it was. I seriously wanted to know. Perhaps she would volunteer something before she left.

* * *

Our bags were now packed and ready for the drive to Charlotte's place. We got into the elevator and rode down to the garage. I put both bags into the trunk of my Aston Martin.

I pulled out of the garage and proceeded to the road. We were silent. I put a hand on her knee and gave her a wink. She blushed and smiled.

I pulled onto her street.

"You can drive around to the back and pull into the garage. There is plenty of room for your car," she said.

"Sure."

When we got to the back of the house, she hopped out of the car and punched in numbers on the side of the garage door. The door opened and I pulled next to her red Mercedes with the black convertible top. The license plate said RAVEN. It felt strange seeing that.

"I haven't had time to get my license plate changed," she said, clearly noticing I'd seen it. "I haven't driven this car either, and won't until that license plate is different."

"I can help you do that, if you want."

"We can talk about it when I return. Maybe I'll get rid of the car and purchase a new one. It holds bad memories," she said.

I went to the trunk of my car and retrieved our bags. She led to a door in the far back of the garage and opened it and went inside. We entered the kitchen. I followed her as she flipped on the lights along the way.

"Shall I take these bags upstairs?"

"That would be great," she said.

I glanced at her on my way upstairs. She opened the refrigerator and the side freezer door. Then she walked inside her pantry.

Once upstairs, I flipped on the light in her bedroom and placed both bags on the floor beside the small closet door with the stairs inside. I walked to the double window and glanced outside. The view was of the front of her building. When I turned around to leave, I couldn't help but notice a small florist card on her nightstand, propped up against the lamp. Curious, I lifted it up. It read: *Enjoyed last night, Deuce*. I smiled, remembering when I sent her those roses, and was touched she saved the card.

I was back downstairs and watched as she was searching through a cookbook.

"Do you like Thai?" she asked.

"Love it."

"Great."

I took a seat at her round oak kitchen table.

"I know you like shrimp because that is what you'd ordered on our first date," she said.

"Yeah," I gave a light laugh, "I'm surprised you remembered."

"Everything from that day is fixed in my mind."

"Is that right?" I laughed again.

"It is." She turned to look at me and gave a wide smile. "Would you like some wine?"

"Sure. I see you have it racked underneath your prep island. Shall I uncork it?"

"Yes, please." She reached into a drawer and pulled out a cork screw, then handed it to me.

I noticed there were quite a few dark wines and very high-quality ones at that. I spotted a 1998 Ravenswood

Winery Merlot and wondered what the story was. Beside it was a 1980 Lakespring Merlot and I pulled out that one. I knew she enjoyed merlot.

I uncorked the bottle and grabbed two wine glasses from the cabinet she pointed to. I poured her a glass and set it on the counter where she was preparing food, and returned to sit at the table. I watched her expertly cook. The smell was delectable—curry, ginger, lime, and a lot of other items I was clueless of.

It wasn't long before she put a lid on the skillet and set the timer for twenty minutes. She brought her glass of wine over to where I was, set it on the tabletop, and walked over and put her arms around me.

"Thank you for everything," she said. "I don't know how I could have made it through it all without you."

"I will always be here for you, if you want me?"

"I will always want you." She kissed me on the lips.

"I want to marry you, Charlotte. Will you marry me?"

"Yes, yes, yes!"

I pulled out the ring from my jeans pocket, opened the case, and put the fifteen-carat Lorraine Schwartz emerald-cut diamond ring on her finger. It was a perfect fit.

CHAPTER 30

Dmitri

The dreaded time of Charlotte's departure had arrived. I loaded her bags in the trunk of my car and went back inside. I sat on her living room couch waiting for her to come downstairs.

I reflected on the previous evening and was grateful I'd gone ahead and proposed to her. Even more so that she had accepted. Our lovemaking had been sweet, our bodies finding pleasure in each other, then satiated and exhausted, finally slept.

"Picture time," she announced, wearing navy slacks with navy pumps and a pale pink silk blouse. Her long, wavy hair fell to her shoulders. She had her iPhone in her hand.

I hadn't noticed she'd come downstairs.

"Where do you want me?" I said, deliberately cheerful.

"The first picture I want you exactly where you are sitting now." She began clicking the camera on her phone. "Now, I want both of us together. Will you hold the camera? Your arms are longer than mine."

"Sure." I held her phone and took selfies of us sitting beside each other on her couch.

She turned and gave me a kiss on the lips. "There's one more thing: I'd like you to have the security code for my house and a key. Just in case," she said. She pulled out a key from her pocket and handed it to me. "The security code is the same as the one used on my brother's computer. I've written it down in case you don't remember." She handed me a piece of paper with the numbers on it.

"Okay, if that's what you want."

She nodded. I put the key on my key ring and tucked the small piece of folded paper in my wallet.

"I'm ready now," she said.

The drive to the Teterboro private airport took half an hour. I drove through the gate and directly to where the plane was parked. It was easy to spot as it was clearly labeled with the Danish royal insignia. I got out of the car and went to her side and opened the door, then went to the trunk and pulled out her suitcase.

A tall, lanky middle-aged man in a black pilot's uniform approached us. "Charlotte Bjorn?" he asked with a strong Danish accent.

"Yes," she said.

"I'm Captain Helmit Jorgensen, the pilot for the royal family of Denmark."

She offered her hand. "It's nice to meet you. Please allow me to introduce my fiancé, Dmitri Zhukov."

He and I shook hands. "Are you ready to leave?" the pilot asked.

"I am."

The pilot motioned to a stocky man in his mid-thirties, who approached and carried her suitcase to the plane.

Charlotte turned to me and put her arms around me, then planted a kiss on my lips. "I'll call you once I'm settled," she whispered. "I love you."

"I love you too."

Then she let go of me and walked with the pilot to the plane.

I went back to my car and leaned against it; I stayed that way until the plane took off. It felt like a piece of my heart just flew away.

CHAPTER 31

Charlotte

I entered the luxuriously designed interior of the plane holding my navy leather tote, which held the tiara. The inside of the plane looked like a fully modern living room, with two tan leather sofas and matching recliners and dark red carpet.

"Ana." I spotted my old friend. I went to Ana and gave her a hug, then took a seat across from her. Ana was Astrid's personal assistant. She and I were the same age. Ana had been a wonderful friend when Lars and I had briefly lived at the palace. She was still a strikingly beautiful blonde—tall and stylishly slim. She was attired in a black pantsuit and her hair in a neat chignon.

"It's so nice to see you," Ana said. "The queen wanted to travel with us, but it was too much of a security risk."

"I understand. I have butterflies in my stomach. It has been such a long time. Not since Lars' funeral."

Ana reached over and squeezed my hand. "I know."

"Ana, I feel so much shame. I wasn't even sure Astrid would want to see me. I didn't commit that crime, but I couldn't prove it."

"That is history. Whatever happened is over and done with and we should move on." Ana was loving and kind. I always felt I could tell her anything.

"Thank you for saying that. You look well. How is your family?" I asked.

"My father's health isn't good, but my mother is well," Ana said.

We spent the time in flight reminiscing and drinking a little wine. I learned that not much had changed. Royal decorum was what it was. Ana had never married. Neither had Astrid remarried. Her husband, the king consort, Lars' father, had passed away before Lars and I married.

Eight hours later, the plane landed on the runway of the royal airport. A black limo was waiting for us when we descended the stairs out of the plane. The weather was quite crisp and there was a light drizzle of rain. A light-skinned man with blond hair dressed in a black suit met us at the bottom of the stairs with a large umbrella.

"Ms. Bjorn," he greeted.

"Yes."

"Allow me to escort you to the car."

I nodded and walked with him underneath the umbrella, then got inside the back of the limo. Ana got in after me.

My suitcase was carried to the trunk of the limo and placed inside. The limo began moving and the windows darkened. I was just barely able to see the picturesque Nyhavn waterfront canal. It was familiar. I'd traveled this road numerous times.

"I wish the weather was better, so we could sightsee," Ana said, breaking the silence.

"I know. This was never the best time of year to visit Copenhagen. But it is still great to be back." The knot in my stomach further tightened. We were close to the palace.

The lovely tree-lined entry to the road leading to the palace was visible, as the driver had lowered the dimness of the back windows. I was grateful for that; the view was spectacular.

The driver drove around the back of the palace and to the family entry, a massive stone walkway. The limo stopped and a chauffeur I'd not seen before opened the back door.

"Madam," he said.

Ana and I climbed out of the car, and a butler was at the back entry to greet us. "Welcome back, Ms. Bjorn," he said. I recognized him: an elderly gentleman with a crop of close-cut white hair. He wore the same style black suit, white shirt, and tie uniform that I remembered.

"Hello, Mr. Henriksen. It's most pleasant to see you again." I was always careful to address all the royal staff by the surnames out of respect. Ana had been a close confidant.

I knew I'd never see this palace again after this visit. It wouldn't be fair to Dmitri.

"Your luggage will be delivered to the Trygve apartment," he said.

I remembered that apartment well, as it was where Lars and I had lived when in Copenhagen.

Ana and I followed behind the butler down the Great Hall. Ornate antique tapestries lined the left side of the wall with a massive stone fireplace in the center of the wall that was original to the castle in the fifteenth century. The right side of the wall was glass, displaying the lovely outside gardens. Numerous sitting areas were arranged in this room with ornate Louis XV salon suite furniture with gilded legs and arm rests. All the upholstered fabric matched in red sculptured velvet. The fifty-foot ceiling had black wrought iron drop chandeliers were evenly spaced above the opulent floor. At the end of the corridor was a Gothic-style arched opening.

"I will leave you here," Ana said. "Oliver will escort you to Queen Astrid's Sofia parlor."

I had forgotten about the strict formality here. "Thank you, Ana." I silently followed the butler.

I entered the salon and curtsied. "Your Majesty."

"Charlotte," she said and rose from her seat. She walked to me and embraced me in a motherly hug. "Please call me Astrid, like before."

Astrid was a beautiful woman with short dark hair with streaks of gray, reminding of the passing of years since I'd last seen her. Although only five-feet four-inches tall, she appeared more powerful than her height. Her pale complexion had turned somewhat sallow and her pale blue eyes were sad.

"It is so wonderful to see you." I really meant it too. I loved her dearly.

"It is likewise. Please have a seat beside me," Astrid said.

Queen Astrid's parlor was a most regal, but intimate sitting room. The walls were covered with ivory silk panels. In the center of each panel was an elaborate gilded motif. Virtually all the wood in the room was gilded. A crystal and gold chandelier hung overhead the seating area of two Louis XVI upholstered settees in shiny golden silk fabric that sat facing each other. There were matching chairs on each of the ends. The ceiling had a hand-painted Renaissance-style mural. Priceless oversized oil portraits of six family ancestors hung on the walls. An antique Persian rug was on the floor.

"How have you been, love?" Astrid asked.

"I'm doing well, and I'm grateful you agreed to see me."

"I haven't heard from you in many years, and none of my letters to you were ever answered."

"I never received any letters," I replied, confused. I wondered why. "I thought you didn't want to have anything to do with me."

"Why would that be the case?"

"Because I was in prison, even though I wasn't guilty."

"It seemed suspicious to me, as I knew you well and didn't believe you capable of such a crime," she reassured me.

"Thank you for saying that. I'm trying to find a way to clear my name."

"If there is anything at all I do to help you with this, please let me know."

"I appreciate that." I reached down to the floor where my leather tote was and pulled out the cherry wooden box. I opened it so the tiara was visible. I pulled it out of the box and held it. "I have brought the tiara Lars gave me for our wedding. He crowned me that day and said I was his princess. He always made me feel that way too. Lars and I loved each other so very much. This tiara represents our love. It is one of my most prized possessions for that reason. And because of that love I believe it should be with the royal family jewels. I'm hoping you agree."

"You really don't need to give that up. Lars had that specially made for you. It was a gift of love," Astrid said.

"There's something else." I reached back into my leather bag and pulled out a small velvet case. "This diamond and emerald engagement ring was your mother's. I believe you should also have this back." My eyes filled with tears.

"If this is truly what you want, then yes, I will accept your tiara and the engagement ring. Please tell me why, after all these years, you have decided to do this," she asked.

"I never thought I could love again after Lars died, and he will always have a place in my heart. That will never change. But I have found love again." I lifted my hand to show Astrid my diamond engagement ring from Dmitri.

"I see."

"It would be wrong of me to have this tiara and your mother's engagement ring when I remarry. I believe these should be with the Bjorn family jewels. Lars was the crown prince."

"I understand. But I will hold the tiara for you for as long as you want me to. If you change your mind, I will return it to you. I do want my mother's engagement ring back and I thank you for bringing it to me," Astrid said.

I handed Astrid the wooden box and the ring, and began to sob.

Astrid wrapped her arms around me until I regained composure and I took the tissue she offered. "What can I do for you?"

"Please allow me to visit the crypt where Lars and Erik are entombed. I need to spend some time there."

"Of course. I can get the bishop to go with you if you like."

I blew my nose. "Thank you, but I would like to go inside alone." I paused briefly and stared across the room.

"It seems there is something else you want to talk about," Astrid said.

"You've always read me well." I gave a weak smile. "I want to talk to you about Adeline."

Astrid straightened. "Go on."

I told Astrid everything. I even told her about Adeline's relationship with Sergei Zhukov. She took a deep breath and wore a somber expression. "Adeline has gone off the rails. She stormed out of this room our last conversation and said she was done with the family," Astrid said.

"I knew she never approved of me marrying Lars, but I'd thought in time we could have a healthy relationship. Unfortunately, it just never happened. Things progressively got worse when Lars passed away."

Astrid patted my knee. "I know. I hoped she would change her mind about the family once she was on her own and realized things out in the world were much more difficult than she'd had at home. Hers was a very sheltered life and I coddled her too much. I deeply regret it. Her father had warned me about that, but I was stubborn. She was my only baby girl. I should have listened to my husband."

"You didn't know. She's such a beautiful woman and I can see how men would be attracted to her. I worry about her. The man she is with isn't an honorable man. I know this because he is my fiancé's uncle and the very blackest of sheep in the family."

Astrid's eyes filled with tears.

I put my hand on top of Astrid's. "It pains me to tell you all of this. I wish I could help her, but I know she won't let me."

"I will take care of this. Her life seems to be in danger," Astrid said. "Perhaps her brother Harald can get through to her."

"I do hope so. Harald is a good man." Harald was now the crown prince since Lars passed away. Adeline was the youngest of the three children.

"Shall we have tea?" Astrid asked.

"Yes, that would be lovely."

* * *

I retired for the evening in the Trygve apartment. It was the same opulent space I remembered. Astrid and I had talked for hours following dinner. It was now eleven.

I picked up my phone and walked to a seating area in the small receiving room in front of the bedroom. I checked the time. With the six-hour time difference, it would be five in New York. I dialed Dmitri's number. He picked up right away.

"Good evening, beautiful," he said before I could even say anything.

"Good evening to you too."

"How are things going?"

"Everything is good. I returned the tiara to Astrid as well as the diamond and emerald engagement ring Lars had given me. It's a family heirloom. It had belonged to Astrid's mother and it should be with her now."

"I understand," Dmitri replied.

"Astrid and I had a very nice visit. She's a lovely person."

"I'm sure she is. What are your plans?"

"There is something I need to do tomorrow." I paused. "I miss you so much."

"I feel the same," he said. "I want to book a flight to Copenhagen and bring you back here."

"Yes, I want that."

"I will arrange and call you back in the morning," he said.

"I can't wait to put my arms around you."

"Soon, my love," he said.

CHAPTER 32

Adeline

"Galem, what do you mean Charlotte is visiting my mother?" I was in Sergei's New York City apartment alone. Galem was my informant at the palace in Copenhagen where he was a staff member. We used to smoke pot together and frequently I invited him to my bedroom for a late-night romp. We shared the same kinks and both of us knew there weren't any strings attached.

"She arrived this afternoon and has been visiting with your mother," Galem said.

"What about?" I was now pacing the living room. More like stomping my feet.

"I could only hear bits and pieces of the conversation. From what I was able to hear, Charlotte brought her tiara and the royal engagement ring Lars had given her, and gave them to your mother."

I threw my shoe across the room. "Fuck!"

"I just thought you would want to know."

"Follow her if she leaves the palace and let me know where she is. I'm hopping the next plane to Copenhagen. That bitch is going to pay."

"What are you going to do?" Galem asked.

"Don't worry about it. Nothing will come back to you and I will compensate you generously." I hung up. I was still stomping the floor when Sergei came through the front door.

"What is going on, my sweet?" he said.

"My crown is now at my mother's. Your nephew's girlfriend took it there today. How am I supposed to have it now?"

"We can go there and ask your mother for it."

"It's not that simple. I'm not welcome there anymore," I lied.

"Oooooh," he said and came to me then put his arms around me. "We can have another crown made for you. It won't be the real jewels, but we can copy it. You can wear your crown for me then."

"No!" I broke away from his embrace. I stomped my foot on the floor and folded my arms in front of me. "I want *my* crown!"

"Well, well. Having a temper tantrum, are you?" he said, laughing.

I was quick to refocus. Without Sergei, I didn't have any money. I needed to get a plane ticket to Copenhagen right away.

"I want to go to Copenhagen and figure a way to get it."

"Okay. Tell me how you want to do that."

"I will figure it out when I get there. Would you arrange a plane ticket for me so I can leave right away?" I gave him my best pouty face and managed to will a few tears for added effect.

"I won't be able to travel with you this soon," he said. "Would you like for me to arrange a security detail to accompany you?"

"Actually, I know of two guys at the palace who will help me. I've known them since I was a teenager, but they are greedy. I just need to be able to pay them." I needed money to compensate Galem and the rest of the money would go in my pocket.

"All right, I can do that. Would five thousand be enough?" he asked.

"That would be enough for one of them."

"Okay, ten thousand," he said. "I'll arrange the flight now."

* * *

I was seated in the first-class section of a Delta Airline international flight to Copenhagen. I sent a quick text to Galem letting him know my arrival time. He replied with a thumbs-up emoji.

I fastened my seat belt and sat back. The pilot announced takeoff.

The first hour of flight I already drank two vodka gimlets and had requested a third. The flight attendant served me lunch instead: chicken broccoli divan and a cup of coffee. I cursed at her but the flight attendant just ignored the comment.

The in-flight movie was boring so I turned it off and opened my iPad. I decided to search the web and see if there was anything interesting. This flight was going to be eight hours in the air, and I'd take a taxi to a hotel. I would phone Galem from there.

I considered what my next move was going to be. Since I wasn't going to ask my mother for the crown right away, the idea of causing harm to Charlotte sounded fun. Actually, I had toyed with the idea of disfiguring Charlotte's face—give her a few scars to see in the mirror. She'd know what it was like to be rejected by any modeling agency. There wouldn't ever be a "Raven" again. Or maybe I could just shave her head and smack her around a bit. Hmmm. The trick would be to catch her. Galem was my inside guy and I could rely on him, or at least I used to.

Sergei gave me the money. I sweettalked him and gave him the mind-blowing sex he liked last night and again this morning. That seemed to appease him.

It had now been an hour since my last vodka gimlet. I motioned for the flight attendant to bring me another drink. She was quick to bring it.

CHAPTER 33

Charlotte

I was grateful for the hospitality the queen had shown and now I was ready to go to the crypt. It would be my very last time. It would hurt but I was compelled to go. Whether Lars' spirit would hear me, I didn't know, but I had to try; there were things I needed to say. I also wanted to send love to my baby. Both deaths had all but destroyed me, and I had taken a destructive path in my grief. Things were different now. I had a chance at love and a good life. I hoped Lars would be happy for me.

I was dressed warm in leather pants and a fleece-lined London Fog hooded raincoat as the weather was still cold and rainy. The chapel and family crypt were at the farthest end of the estate and required vehicle transport to get there. Astrid had offered the help of a staff member to drive me.

Armed with an umbrella, I made my way to the waiting limo. A tall and lanky blond-haired man opened the back door. I got inside, the driver closed the door, and soon I felt the car moving. In less than ten minutes, we arrived. The driver got out of the car and opened my door, then escorted me to the chapel while holding up an umbrella for me.

"Do you know how to get to the lower lever where the crypt is?" he asked.

"Yes, I do. Thank you for asking."

"I will wait outside for your return," he said. There was a nice portico with a cement bench.

"Thank you, Galem."

CHAPTER 34

Dmitri

I was in my office at home trying to get some work done, but I couldn't concentrate. I had this gut feeling something was off and couldn't shake it. When I'd spoken with Charlotte last night, she sounded fine. So what was it then? Maybe it was that call from Adeline. Clearly that woman was a real whack job. When I last talked to Charlotte, I decided not to tell her Adeline had made another threatening phone call. This time it was specific. She demanded the crown and claimed that if Charlotte didn't give it to her, there were going to be dire consequences. I didn't tell Adeline the crown was now with her mother.

I decided to go ahead and travel there, and searched for the first direct flight to Copenhagen. There was one early the next morning, so I booked it. I would phone Charlotte when I arrived.

I Googled the location of the Bjorn family estate to see where it was from the airport, then arranged a car rental and a hotel room. I wasn't going to assume I could stay at the palace. Actually, I didn't want to stay there. It was Charlotte's late husband's family, and staying there didn't settle well with me.

The next morning, I just barely made it on time to the gate for the Delta international flight to Copenhagen. I'd been lucky to get the very last first-class ticket.

I put my two carry-on bags into the overhead storage bin and settled into my seat when the pilot announced they were ready for takeoff.

Half an hour after takeoff, the fasten seat belt light went off. I reached into the storage bin, pulled out my laptop and the external drive of Jax's computer, and placed them on the pulldown tray.

I began by looking through all the items on the desktop. There was one folder that stood out. It was labeled MISC PERSONAL. I opened the folder and found a document labeled JOURNAL. I opened it right up; it wasn't password protected.

The journal was quite long, almost two hundred single-spaced pages. I decided to read the whole thing since I had the time on the long flight.

Much of the information in the first part of the journal detailed hookups from various gay clubs in New York City. It wasn't until I got to page fifty that things really got interesting. There were details of several sexual rendezvous with Igor Smirnoff. Jax had even taken him to Charlotte's house while she was in prison. There were graphic details of how Igor would put on Charlotte's makeup and dress up in Charlotte's clothes, even her underwear, and prance around the bedroom before he and Jax had sex.

Jax had another journal entry where he secretly recorded one of their sexual sessions and there had been a phone call Igor had received prior to their intimacy. Igor spoke in Russian and Jax later had it translated. That was when he learned of the cryptocurrency. Also, I saw my father's name as one of the crypto owners.

Jax decided that he should be a paramour of Igor's and thought he could get more information about all that money by spending more time with Igor. Once, when Igor was out making a liquor run, Jax nosed around on Igor's computer. When he found information about the crypto, he copied the file onto a flash drive and slipped it into his jacket pocket.

Mick had been privy to the whole thing. Jax, Mick, and Igor had numerous threeways together and both Jax and Mick schemed on ways to get the cryptocurrency and launder it. They planned to take the entire but never got it done—or so Jax thought. Turned out Mick double-crossed Jax; Mick enlisted Sergei to handle the crypto transfer. Jax didn't know until he snooped on Mick's computer and saw the activity. That was the information he copied onto the flash drive and gave to Charlotte.

My stomach burned knowing my father's name was also down as part owner of that cryptocurrency. I knew my father was now in possession of all this information from the journal, and I worried what would come of it. I closed the laptop when the flight attendant stopped by. Then, I heard a woman's voice in the background screaming profanities—something about not getting another vodka gimlet.

"May I serve you lunch? It is chicken broccoli divan," the flight attendant asked.

"Yes, that would be nice. Thank you."

The food was mediocre but at least I wasn't hungry any longer. I ordered a whiskey and drank it slowly. Nagging thoughts of Charlotte in Copenhagen flooded my mind. I tried to dismiss it as missing her, but my gut said otherwise.

I picked up the laptop again and kept reading. There was a full page about Jax trying to figure out where Charlotte's tiara was; he was certain it was in her house and not in a safety deposit box. He finally discovered the safe behind the painting in her library office. He tried everything he could think of to get it open. The combination wasn't a problem, but getting her thumbprint was; the safe wouldn't open without it.

There were details of Jax's cocaine use and how his bank account wasn't keeping up with his habit. It detailed how Charlotte had an administrator at the bank who deposited fifteen thousand dollars a month into Jax's checking account.

Seems she had continued to financially support him even once she returned home. I found this surprising.

Jax had been the one to tip off Sergei about where Mick would be on the night of the murder. Jax didn't know it would lead Mick being murdered, and he felt guilty about it, like he'd done it himself. Mick had wanted out of the cryptocurrency swindle but Jax didn't. He told Sergei about it after the conversion about the crypto. Jax thought the crypto was now in gold bars and he and Sergei were going to split it. The plan had been that the gold bars would be hidden in Switzerland under a fake company name owned by another fake company from yet another company. All those company names were in this journal. My father would be sure to spot this information as well.

The details about Igor's trysts with Jax and Mick were sure to raise an eyebrow with my father. Igor was married and had adult children.

Jax told of how Sergei insisted Adeline be present during several of their meetings about what to do with the stolen money. He had complained about it, but it didn't get any further than that.

I now knew Sergei was the sole person who had possession of the stolen money. This looked bad. As much as I wasn't fond of Sergei, I still feared for what might become of him.

As the journal neared the end, there was mention of Jax was darkly depressed and how life wasn't worth it anymore. He'd written how he'd not done anything much with his life and didn't want to live it any longer.

I closed the document and shut down the laptop. I sat back in my seat and took a final swallow of whiskey. There was still five hours to go. I picked up my cell, made sure I was connected to the plane's Wi-Fi and began composing a text to Charlotte.

Hi Beautiful

I decided to go ahead and get a flight to Copenhagen. I arrive in five hours. I have a hotel suite reserved. I'll phone you from the hotel. I hope all is well on your end.

Love you babe

My phone pinged quickly.

I'm so happy to hear from you, and also that you will be arriving soon. I miss you so much and I'm anxious for us to return home together.

I love you so much—with my heart, my soul, and my body.

See you soon, my love.

I replied: *I love you too. Soon I can show you.*

I put down my phone and leaned back in the seat. My mind played out the scene of seeing Charlotte get into that royal jet and then the plane taking off. In no small way, I felt humbled. Charlotte was going to the royal palace of Denmark and meeting with the queen. She was even giving her tiara back for me. I vowed to spend the rest of my life living up to her—making her feel she was *my* princess.

My thoughts were interrupted by the same loud-mouthed woman as before, who was again demanding another vodka gimlet.

"Ms. Bjorn, I must insist we wait a bit. I can serve you coffee or a non-alcoholic beverage."

CHAPTER 35

Charlotte

The family chapel was a Gothic red brick building and could seat seven hundred people. It was quite ancient—built in the same year as the palace and still in use for services on Sundays. The interior of the nave was in pristine condition and there were two rows of pews on either side of a wide aisle. The room was four times longer than it was wide. The amazingly tall ceiling was domed with gilded wooden beams. A single pulpit was on a raised gilded stage. A gilded wooden triptych—three panels that illustrated the sufferings of Christ—was on the wall behind the pulpit.

I walked through a wide hallway on the left side of the vestibule and at the very end, an archway led to stairs going down. I took these stairs to the crypt. The alcove with Lars and Erik's sarcophagi was the last on the right. I walked through the arched doorway to both sarcophagi.

I went to Erik's sarcophagus first and put my hands on top. "My sweet son, I loved you even before you were born and I love you still." I closed my eyes and said a prayer.

I next went to Lars' sarcophagus and putting both hands on the top, bent down, and kissed it.

"Lars, the life we shared was beautiful, and when you left this world, I was shattered. I hope you are enjoying heaven and have been able to see our little son. I thought I couldn't ever love again after you died, and I was alone for many years. But I have found love again. His name is Dmitri and he is a very good man. I know you would like him. He's kind and loving and fun. I feel like I have a chance to live a good life with him. I'd been dying inside for way too long without you. Now I am finally alive. You will always be in my heart, sweet man." I kissed the top of his sarcophagus again.

"Yeah, yeah, yeah," a voice behind me mocked, followed by three slow claps.

I was startled and turned around to face Adeline. "Why are you here, Adeline?"

"Why shouldn't I be here? Lars was my brother, who is dead because of you," Adeline said.

"I don't know why you continue to believe that. Lars' plane crashed. It had nothing to do with me."

"He was flying to pick you up in New York and if he'd not done that, then he would still be alive today!" she snapped.

"Do you even hear what you're saying? It's crazy talk."

"When you married my brother, you decided to make my mother yours. You poisoned my mother's mind against me, so she would love you more than me."

"I did no such thing. Couldn't you accept that Lars wanted to marry? If it wasn't me, then it would have been someone else. I know you looked up to him, and he loved you very much."

"No, no, no." Adeline wagged her finger side to side. "You don't get to do that. Try to talk yourself out of this one."

I walked toward Adeline but stopped when she pulled out a gun. "What are you doing?"

Adeline was waved the gun around. "Don't you even get close to me, bitch."

"Why are you calling me that? What have I done to you that you hate me so much?"

"You have got to be kidding! More like what haven't you done? You're a mere peasant whom my brother, the crown prince, married. You were, and still are, way beneath him. Way beneath me too." She gave a smirk full of disdain.

"Your brother and I fell in love and it was way before I even knew he was a royal."

"Right! And you expect me to believe that? Then there's the issue of you weaseling in on my mother—spending so much time with her that she didn't even have time for me. You made it so that she loved you more than me!" Adeline screeched.

"That's ridiculous! She and I were just getting to know each other. I do love her dearly, like a mother. But she loves you very much; nothing will ever change that."

"Well, she's not your mother, she's mine. Then there's that tiara."

"Yes, I would like to know what your issues are with the tiara Lars had *made for me*."

She was now pointing the gun and making tiny circles at my head. "You aren't a royal. *I am*. I should have that tiara."

"I gave that tiara to your mother. So I do not have it any longer. You should be happy about that since you didn't want me to have it."

"Right! Then there's the modeling agency and how you poisoned the owner against me. She wouldn't hire me."

I knew I should tread lightly on this one so I tried to stroke Adeline's ego. "No, I didn't. You screwed that up all by yourself. If that agency didn't want to sign you, then why didn't you try another agency? You were and still are a beautiful woman and will still make a great model."

"Liar!" Adeline screamed. "But I got even with you, didn't I?"

"What do you mean?"

"How do you think you were sent to prison? Marilee and Zahara hated you almost as much as I did. All I had to do was give them the idea and the means to frame you.

How were we to know the guy had already done coke? You getting blamed for his 'murder' was just a bonus."

"I'm not surprised."

Adeline's smirk darkened. "How did you like Grace?"

I flashed on all the abuse Grace had inflicted on me in prison. "What about her?"

"I paid her royally to harass you. Sergei got someone to videotape you so I would see you getting out. Grace was supposed to take you and smack you around for me. She said your brother got there to pick you up too soon. Too bad." Adeline gave a boisterous laugh.

"Grace harassed me all right. I was raped by her and her cohorts repeatedly. I feared for my life the whole time I was there. I ended up at the infirmary for two weeks after one of the rapes. I sincerely hope I can have children after what they did to me."

Adeline laughed some more. "I got into your house when your brother wasn't living there. I drove that Raven car a few times. I thought about trashing it, but decided it was too much trouble. I didn't want anything to do with you any longer, or my family for that matter. I have myself a sugar daddy now who will do anything I want."

"That must be Dmitri's uncle, Sergei."

"Damn right! And he's filthy rich too. I got lucky with him. Those parties I attended with Zahara and Marilee had some powerful men there. That is how I met Sergei."

"I don't think he's as rich and powerful as you think."

"Wrong! I overhead him talking about all this cryptocurrency he had with some other guys," Adeline said.

I now understood who one of the thieves was. "You know he's married, don't you? His wife is in Russia."

"Big deal. He doesn't love her, he loves me."

I was tired of playing this game and knew I had to somehow stifle it. I didn't believe Adeline would really use that gun. "He isn't good for you. You deserve someone worthy of you. I know you aren't a killer, Adeline. This isn't who you are. Please put down the gun and let's talk this through."

I studied Adeline and believed I'd finally gotten through to her. So I stepped forward to attempt to get her to put the gun down. Then I heard a *pop* and was overcome with excruciating pain as I fell to the ground.

Everything turned black.

CHAPTER 36

Charlotte

I found myself suspended on the ceiling of the crypt and looking down at the floor. I was curious where I was and who was on the floor. I studied the woman and noticed the diamond engagement ring.

How is that possible? Am I dead?

A pulling sensation and a sense of traveling moved me like a vacuum through a tunnel. There was faint music playing and it became more vibrant as I approached a golden light. The light was bright but it didn't hurt my eyes. I felt immense love like I'd never felt before and I wasn't afraid or alone. A beautiful luminescent lady traveled beside me, but remained silent.

The lady finally spoke, not with her mouth but with her mind, "Do you know where you are?"

"I think I must be in heaven. Is that right?"

"Yes, you are." She smiled wide. "There is someone who wants to see you."

"Okay."

"Hold my hand," the lady said.

I did as she instructed and we were quickly in a beautiful meadow where the color of the flowers was more vibrant than I'd ever seen before. I walked on the soft grass and bent down to touch one of the flowers. The feeling of love radiated from the flower to me.

I saw someone walking towards me. It appeared to be a man—a very tall man. It was Lars and I began running towards him and jumped into his arms.

"My lovely princess," he said and kissed me on the lips.

I took my fingers and traced the side of his face. "I've missed you so much."

"I've missed you too, my love," he said. "Erik is here. Would you like to see him?"

I could hardly contain my excitement. "Yes, yes, yes!"

"Let's go," he said. We floated above the ground, traveling quickly. I was still in his arms.

Soon we were in a small schoolyard where children were playing. Lars set me on the ground. One little boy approached when he saw us. He had light blond hair like Lars.

"Erik?"

"Yes, Mommy?" he said.

I went to him and bent down to embrace him. I picked him up into my arms. Joy filled my soul. I glanced up at Lars, who was smiling. I kissed Erik's cheek and felt the warmth of his body.

"I am so happy now with my family."

"You cannot stay," Lars said. "It's not your time."

I hugged Erik tightly but knew I had to let him go. His big violet eyes looked like mine. "Just a little longer."

"Mommy, I love you. I have to go now."

I kissed him on the cheek one last time, then watched as he ran back to the other children.

Lars took my hand and soon we were floating very fast towards a building that looked like the Bjorn palace. The front doors opened wide as we stopped in front of them. I glanced down and noticed I was now wearing my dress from the wedding reception. Lars had on his tux from our wedding.

"Shall we?" he said with a smile and a wink.

I put my hand on his arm and we walked inside to the royal ballroom. An orchestra was playing our favorite song. Lars led me to the center of the dance floor.

"Shall we dance?" he asked.

"Yes, please." My soul was bright and joyful.

Lars led me in a Venetian waltz. The energy was electric as we spun around the dance floor. The feel of his body against mine was thrilling. We played out the memory of our wedding dance.

As the dance concluded, he spun me one last time, then the tiara appeared in his hand.

"I crown you Princess Charlotte Bjorn." He placed the tiara on my head. "My princess, my lady, my love." Then he took my hand and kissed the top of it. He pulled me into his arms and kissed me again, while I held on for dear life, not wanting to let go of him.

The energy changed and we were floating again. Lars held my hand and we approached a massive crystal cathedral. It was so breathtakingly beautiful; I was in awe. A being appeared in the front of the cathedral wearing a long hooded white robe with a golden cord around the waist. I knew the being was there for me.

"I must leave you now, but I will return," Lars said and kissed my hand.

I climbed the steps to the being. Whether male or female, I couldn't tell. They escorted me down a long hallway to an open double door, then stopped and turned to me.

"Your council is waiting to see you," the being said, not with any audible voice but straight to my mind. "I will leave you here."

I walked inside and to the front of a long bench-type desk where seven hooded beings were seated. The hoods were pulled over their heads so I couldn't make out who they were. The one in the center spoke.

"Do you know why you are here?"

"Yes, I remember from before."

"You have a choice to make, but first, you must review the life you have lived until this point."

Suddenly I was surrounded by a panoramic viewing screen as my entire life played out. I wasn't only watching but was experiencing it. When I got to the part when my baby died, an awareness filled me; I understood Erik wasn't supposed to live. Then, the plane crash. The awareness came again how that was supposed to happen. Both Erik's and Lars' lives cut short, blueprinted before they were even born.

The life I led following Lars' death played out and I was filled with shame, disgust, and hatred for myself. The life review stopped and I was left facing the council.

"Before you make a decision to stay or go back, you need to see what your future will be if you return," said the being in the center.

I was again surrounded by a panoramic viewing screen but it was scenes of me and Dmitri—the beginning of our relationship played out first. Then, scenes filled the screen of how happy we were and enjoying a family. Life was good. At that moment, I was filled with hope and deep, penetrating love for Dmitri. At this thought, the panoramic viewing screen disappeared.

"We see you have made your decision. It is a good one." The center being stood and motioned to my earlier escort who came forward, and I knew to follow.

I walked out of the cathedral and Lars was waiting for me. "Shall we walk?" he asked.

I took his hand. "Yes."

"I heard you speaking to me at the crypt," Lars said. "Erik did too."

"I've done some things I'm very ashamed of and worry how you might think of me."

"No one is perfect, Charlotte," he said. "Go back and live the rest of your life. Dmitri is a good man. I'm grateful you found love again."

There was so much love in his eyes and when he kissed me, I knew this meant goodbye.

I didn't know how, but I found myself hovering above my body in a hospital room. There was a breathing tube down my throat, connected to a ventilator, wires on my chest, and an IV in my arm. I saw Dmitri in a chair beside the bed, holding my hand.

Without any thought at all, I felt myself being sucked back into my body with a jolt.

I gasped and opened my eyes.

Dmitri suddenly stood. He put his hand on my head, then reached down and kissed my forehead.

"You've come back," he said and I saw tears in his eyes.

I couldn't speak but I blinked my eyes twice. He brought up my hand and kissed the top of it. I squeezed it.

Dmitri used the call button by my bed and a nurse came quickly. "I see she's awake," the nurse said with a strong Danish accent. "I will get the doctor."

Again, I squeezed Dmitri's hand tightly.

The doctor appeared with two nurses trailing behind him. He bent down to speak to me. "Ms. Bjorn, can you hear me? If you can, please blink three times," he said, also with a very strong Danish accent. I did as he instructed. "You are in the hospital and I am Queen Astrid's personal physician, Dr. Aksel Nielson. You have been shot. The bullet went into your spleen and I have removed the bullet. You were unconscious for two days. We almost lost you." He straightened his posture. "I would like to examine you now." He pulled out his stethoscope and placed it onto my heart, my lungs, then my neck. He removed the sheet and placed his hands on my legs. "Can you feel my hands?"

I blinked three times and then squeezed Dmitri's hand.

"All is good," the doctor said and patted my arm. "I will test your breathing shortly and if all is well, that breathing tube can be removed."

I blinked three times.

CHAPTER 37

Dmitri

Two weeks passed. Charlotte had gone through many medical tests, including two MRIs. One was for her torso and the other for her head. Apparently when she fell to the ground after being shot, she hit her head. Fortunately, there wasn't any brain bleed or concussion, and her body was healing nicely.

The bedroom lights were dimmed in the hotel suite in Copenhagen. Queen Astrid wanted us to stay at the palace, but Charlotte and I insisted otherwise. She was laying down with her eyes closed.

"Why the tears?" I asked when I entered the bedroom. I knelt beside her and took hold of her hand.

"I just love you so much," she said.

I kissed the top of her hand. "I almost lost you. Your heart stopped and you had to be defibrillated."

"I know. I went to the Other Side," she said.

My eyes filled with tears. "Can you remember anything?"

"Only vague images, and no matter how hard I've tried to recall it all, it's futile." Her eyes met mine. "One thing is certain, and I know this to be a fact. Our love for each other brought me back."

"My God."

"Dmitri, hold me." The tears ran down her cheeks. "I want and need to feel you against me. I want to know you are really here and this isn't just a dream."

I gently lifted her up and into my arms. I was careful of her wound. She put her arms around my neck and kissed me on the lips more passionately than she had the strength for taking things further.

I carried her to the living room and sat on the couch.

"What do you remember about being shot?" This was the first time I broached the subject. The police who came to the hospital to question her hadn't been able to get her to talk. Charlotte had instead deferred to Queen Astrid, who somehow managed to call them off.

The Queen put two of her Royal Life Guards, who were the royal police, in charge of Charlotte's security detail. These two men were posted outside her hospital room and even followed me whenever I went outside.

"It was Adeline who shot me," she said.

"There was security footage in the crypt—audio and video."

"Were you able to see it?" she asked.

"Yes, I did."

"What happened next? Did the Royal Life Guards get her?"

"Unfortunately, no. Somehow, she managed to get away. There is still a search going on to find her. All the airports and train stations, both in Denmark and the US, have been notified to keep on high alert for her. But my suspicion is that she's long gone, and I can't help but think Sergei got her," I informed her.

"I'm afraid Adeline is rotten to the core. I know Astrid is devastated. She and I talked about Adeline before I ever went to the crypt. Astrid was going to find Adeline and force her to come home. She was worried about her," Charlotte said.

"The queen and I spoke briefly. She mentioned something about that, but my concerns were for you, so I really didn't engage with her all that much."

"I do understand and I'm sure she did as well. She really is a lovely person," Charlotte said.

"I did gather that much."

"What are we going to do now?"

"That's all up to you."

"Let's go home," she suggested.

"The queen offered her royal jet to take us home when we're ready. Shall I contact her?" I asked.

She hugged me tighter. "Yes, yes, yes!"

CHAPTER 38

Adeline

I managed to get on the train from Copenhagen to Hamburg, Germany, without being caught. Once there, Sergei sent a guy to pick me up in a car and we drove to Berlin, where a chartered plane flew us to Munich. Sergei was already in Munich taking care of some business.

"What have you done, my sweet?" Sergei was sitting on the main deck of his yacht smoking a joint. We were in the North Atlantic Ocean on the way to Accra, Ghana, to purchase gold bullion. He had cashed out the cryptocurrency in Germany and deposited the money into the Bank of Ghana.

"I took care of a family matter about my crown." I sauntered to Sergei in a skimpy pink thong bikini. I sat on his lap and took a hit off his joint.

"Okay." He grinned, taking another hit off his joint, and put his free hand inside one of my bra cups and squeezed a nipple.

"Ooooo. You know what I like." I knew I had to be accommodating since he was asking about what had happened Copenhagen. I hoped to distract him.

"How did you take care of that matter?" he asked.

"Well, that bitch stole my crown and gave it to my mother when she should have given it to me. So, I made that bitch pay."

"Really? Now, how did you do that?" he asked.

I wondered if he already knew exactly what happened, but he wanted to hear it from me. "I shot her, but I didn't kill her. She deserved it."

"Well, well, well. I didn't know you had that in you." He gave a wide grin. "Maybe I should have used your skills in my business." He took off my top and pinched the other nipple.

I gave him a sexy moan. "Oh, Sergei, I am so wet for you." I took my hand and guided a finger inside my thong, then pulled it out and inserted it into his mouth. He sucked my juices from my finger.

"Take off your swimsuit bottom and pleasure yourself for me." His grin was disgustingly crude.

I did exactly what I knew he wanted—sexing him up till he was thoroughly exhausted, which didn't take long. It never did. I'd always been careful to stroke his ego, make him believe he was a real stud muffin.

He was now laying back on the lounger on the deck, snoring loudly. I got up from the lounger and grabbed my swimsuit, then sauntered nude to the swimming pool on the upper deck. I didn't care how many of the staff members saw me naked. After all, I was Sergei's and this was his boat so I was the queen of this ship. I could do whatever I wanted and it would be fine.

Once I had my fill of swimming in the pool, I grabbed a plush towel from a side table and wrapped it around myself. I made my way to our suite. I grabbed a pair of white short shorts and a bright red halter top. My sexuality was my greatest power with Sergei and I intended to keep it going.

I pulled out my cell phone and checked the world news. I wanted to see if there was anything in there about shooting Charlotte. Turned out there was. Actually, it was a breaking news item. "Princess Adeline of the Bjorn Royal Family of Denmark is wanted for attempted murder of her former sister-in-law, Charlotte Bjorn, widow of the late Crown

Prince Lars Bjorn..." It went on to tell how all the airports, train stations, and ports of entry had been notified to contact the police in Copenhagen. There was even a reward offered for my capture of 6,979,950.63 Danish kroner, which was the equivalent of one million dollars.

I shuddered! How could I keep from being captured? How far would Sergei go to keep me from prison? For the time being, we were out to sea and once we arrived in West Africa, I would probably still be safe. I believed it was doubtful the Ghanian Border Patrol would be a problem, but getting back into the US would certainly be a problem. For the first time in my twenty-five years of existence, I was scared. For all my prior brazen behavior, I never worried about repercussions. Now I certainly did. I believed if anyone could get me out of this situation, it would be Sergei. I would focus on that. I put my phone back on the nightstand and padded back to the main deck where I'd last seen Sergei.

Only Sergei wasn't where I'd left him. I searched him out and found him at the bar, pouring vodka into a glass over ice.

"Hello, my sweet," he said. I walked to him and gave him a kiss on the cheek. "A vodka gimlet?"

"Yes, that would be perfect."

He motioned to the bartender, who dutifully obliged. "Let's take our drinks to the sitting room," he said. "We need to talk."

"Of course." My heart was almost beating out of my chest as I followed him to our suite.

He closed the door and sat on the white leather couch. He patted the cushion for me to sit beside him. "I need to figure out what to do with you," he said. "I can't afford any trouble."

I took a large swallow of my drink. "Tell me what you mean?"

Just then two burly men appeared. Sergei nodded. They both came to where I was and one guided me to stand.

"These men will escort you back to Copenhagen. Your mother is expecting you," Sergei said.

"What?!"

"I'm sorry, Adeline, but this is the way it has to be. Your mother will make sure you don't have to go to jail for what you have done, and I won't be harboring a fugitive." Sergei wore a stern expression. "Dax will escort you to the ship that is approaching. Both he and Radimir will take you on the boat and get you back to your home. Please go to the bedroom and pack all your things." He kissed me on the cheek.

I threw my glass across the room. It shattered against the wall. "This is horse shit!"

Sergei nodded at Radimir, who took my arm and forced me to walk to the bedroom.

* * *

I was now on board a mere fishing boat. It was me and the two men Sergei had assigned to escort me. The captain was speeding across the ocean back to Hamburg, Germany. We were to then travel by car to Berlin.

I sat in my seat on the main deck, frozen. I was shocked at what Sergei had done to me. While I knew it wasn't ever true love between us, I really believed he was addicted to me. Also, I knew he was turned on by the fact I was an authentic princess. My mind was racing, trying to figure out what had changed in him. I knew his crimes were way beyond anything I'd done. Actually, I knew enough about his dealings to land him in prison. I thought this knowledge alone was enough to keep me secure with him. What was I going to do now?

Traveling on this boat was a far contrast to Sergei's yacht. It was a bumpy ride and not at all comfortable. Also,

I was hungry, but no one offered me anything to eat or drink. Both escorts kept their eyes on me the whole trip till we arrived at the port in Hamburg.

The small port was somewhat isolated from the main one. Dax and Radimir guided me off the boat to a waiting taxi. We all got into the backseat and the taxi was quick to begin moving.

The taxi eventually pulled into a private airport. The short drive brought us straight to the plane with the familiar Danish royal insignia. The ladder was down and Radimir forced me out of the taxi and onto the plane. Two Royal Life Guards met me at the bottom of the stairs.

One of the guards motioned to someone to get my bags.

"We will take care of the princess from here," one of the royal guards said and handed Radimir an envelope.

I knew this must have been the reward money. My stomach burned. Sergei didn't even have the decency to not take the damn money.

* * *

The two Royal Life Guards who had accompanied me on the plane escorted me out of the limo's backseat and into the palace. They led me to Queen Astrid's Sofia parlor. I found my mother seated on the settee and I walked to stand before her.

"Hello, Adeline," my mother said. "Please have a seat." She pointed to a matching side chair.

I did.

"I'm seriously concerned about your behavior with Charlotte. She almost died because you shot her," Mother said. "What do you have to say about this incident?"

"I have nothing to say." I sat stoically with a blank expression.

"Nothing?"

"I have nothing to say," I repeated.

"Very well." Mother motioned to one of the Royal Life Guards. "Please escort Princess Adeline to the tower and sequester her there."

The two Royal Life Guards came forward. One secured my arm with his hand and forced me to go with them.

I heard my mother sobbing once I was just outside the door. I didn't have it in me to care.

CHAPTER 39

Charlotte

It had been two and a half months since the shooting and I was feeling well. Dmitri had waited on me constantly, making sure I didn't do anything to exert myself.

The morning sun was just rising when I got out of bed in Dmitri's bedroom. I was careful not to wake him. I'd worn a silk chemise, so grabbed my robe from the chair beside the bed and wrapped myself up in it, then headed out of the room.

I padded barefoot into the kitchen, flipped on the light, and pulled out a mug out of the cabinet. Grabbing a coffee pod, I put it into the coffeemaker. As the coffee was brewing, my mind reflected on the past two and a half months. It had all been a blur—doctor's appointments, police reports, and reporters who hounded me for my "side of the story." I'd taken it all in stride. The doctor said my healing was going well and gave the okay to return to normal activities as I could tolerate. The one thing missing was intimacy with Dmitri; he hadn't touched me since the incident and I wanted him so bad that it hurt.

With my coffee mug in hand, I went to the sliding glass door to the outside patio and opened it. I went to my favorite chair and sat.

The orange glow of the rising sun was lovely above the city skyline. There was a chill in the air but I didn't care.

The coffee helped warm me. Memories of my brother filled my mind, and the pain of his loss ached in my heart. I knew there was so much about Jax I'd not known. I knew I should look at the contents on the external drive from his computer, but I just didn't have it in me to do it. I was afraid of what I might find. Dmitri had already gone through it, and when I asked him about it, he said I needed to read it for myself. I knew that wasn't a good sign.

My thoughts turned to Adeline. I struggled to understand why she hated me so much. All the things she said before the shooting were absurd. She'd clearly lost her mind and now Astrid would have to deal with it. I sincerely hoped Adeline wouldn't have to go to jail, that Astrid would be able to use her royal power as queen to handle Adeline. She clearly needed psychological help and Astrid would ensure Adeline got that.

Reflecting on the humiliation of being incarcerated and the hell I'd gone through filtered through my mind. Because of what was said on the security video from the crypt, I was closer than ever to clearing my name. I wondered how it would all go down with Marilee and Zahara once I had my day in court. I wanted to feel good about this, but somehow, I didn't. You can take the hammered nail out of a piece of wood, but the hole is still there.

I felt like crying, but was sick and tired of crying. It was time to get back to life. It felt like it had been forever.

I stood, bringing my empty coffee mug back inside, went straight to the kitchen, and opened the refrigerator. I decided to cook breakfast. It would be the first time since I'd been back. Dmitri had insisted on doing everything. I wanted to show him I was fine.

I pulled out the frying pan from the cabinet and the bacon from the refrigerator. Then turned on the burner and went to work.

"Good morning, beautiful," Dmitri said as he entered the kitchen. His tousled hair and slight beard shadow were sexy on his handsome face. And those light gray eyes always made me swoon. He was dressed in navy and red pajama pants and a dark t-shirt.

I smiled wide. "Good morning to you too."

He walked to me and put his arms around my waist from the back, and planted a kiss on the side of my neck. "That bacon sure smells good."

The scent of his body sent shivers through me. When I felt his hard shaft against my back, it took everything inside of me not to turn around and touch him.

"I love your cooking," he whispered in my ear.

"That's a good thing because I enjoy doing it for you."

He gave me one last kiss on the cheek before he pulled away. "What can I do to help?" he asked.

"Set the breakfast bar and some orange juice would be good," I answered.

"I'm on it."

I worked my magic—poaching eggs, toasting English muffins, and making a simple hollandaise sauce. Dmitri watched from where he was seated at the breakfast bar as I assembled—the English muffin, the bacon, poached egg, and finally hollandaise sauce on top. I plated our food and handed Dmitri his plate first and placed mine on the breakfast bar beside him.

"Eggs Benedict, wow. You made it look so simple too. You certainly know what you are doing." He winked, grinning.

I decided this was the day I was going to seduce him. I was more than ready and he needed to know it.

"My God, this is good!" he said right before he put another fork full into his mouth. "How did you learn to cook like this?"

"My mother. She was a great cook and I found I actually like doing it."

I got up from the barstool and started gathering the plates.

"No, no, no," he said. "Sit. You cooked; I clean up."

I laughed. "I won't turn that down." I moved to where he was standing and stood in front of him. I put both arms around his neck and planted a kiss on his lips.

He responded by deepening the kiss.

"I need you—need your bare skin next to mine. Please don't push me away."

"I don't want to hurt you."

"You won't."

Our eyes met.

Dmitri bent down and lifted me up into his arms. He kissed me and began walking to the bedroom.

CHAPTER 40

Dmitri

I carried her to the foot of the bed and sat her there. But she stood back up and placed her hands on my chest and reached underneath my t-shirt to bare skin. I pulled my shirt over my head and tossed it onto the floor. Her hands explored my chest with hungry, lustful eyes.

I took the front of her silk robe, pushing it off her shoulders, and removed it, letting it fall to the floor, and lifted the hem of her chemise over her head. She stood before me nude.

She reached for the top of my pajama pants and slid them down. I helped her by kicking them off. I stood before her nude.

She licked her lips at the sight of my rigid shaft as I shortened the distance between us and guided her to sit on the edge of the bed.

She reached behind me, placed her hands on my ass, and pulled me towards her lips. We kept our eyes on each other as she wrapped her hand around my cock and moved it downwards.

She slid her tongue on the top of my cock and made tiny circles with my pre-cum, teasing me. She licked down the length of me and back upward, then took me deeper into her mouth before she began sucking and moving at a voracious pace.

"Oh God, Charlotte!" I moaned. I knew I was close to coming.

I placed my hands on her shoulders, pulling her up and guiding her to lay back on the bed I crawled after her so I was kneeling over her.

My lips met hers and my tongue entered her mouth as I deepened the kiss, hungry for her.

I raised both her arms over her head, then traced my tongue down her neck to her collarbone. My tongue traveled further to her breast, to her nipple, and put it into my mouth and sucked.

She called out my name and arched her back.

I did the same to her other breast, tracing my tongue down to her scar, and lightly kissed around it.

My hands gently parted her legs before my tongue traced her inner thighs up to her clit. I sucked it gently and inserted a finger inside her. She was dripping wet.

"I need you, Dmitri. I need you inside of me!" she called out.

I entered her gently, making sure she was ready for me.

She arched her back, deepening me inside her.

I began moving—slowly at first and then more, going all the way inside her—pounding and pounding. She met me thrust to thrust, our bodies in perfect harmony. I took her like never before. Sweat dripping off my brow, I could feel her clenching around me, both of us climbing and arriving at the same place together. We both cried out as we went over the edge into bliss.

Her head was now resting on my chest. We laid silently for a while.

"I should get into the shower," she said.

I tightened my arms around her and kissed her on the top of her head before releasing her. "Sure, shall I join you in a few minutes?"

"Please do," she said and smiled wide.

I watched as she padded her way to the bathroom, admiring her beautiful, shapely ass. As soon as I heard the shower running, I got out of bed and turned on the lamp on top the bedside table. I glanced over to the center of the bed sheet and noticed a copper T-shaped item, about the size of a quarter. It had what appeared to be a string on the end. It was Charlotte's IUD.

Emotions filled me of what the ramifications of this discovery could mean. I was ready for a child with her; I wanted a child with her. But would she be ready for that? Would she want that too?

I picked up the IUD and took it with me into the bathroom. I placed it on top of the counter before getting inside the shower with her.

When she saw me, a huge smile appeared and she met me with soapy hands that she rubbed across my chest, around to my back, and down to my ass. I pulled her close and planted a passionate kiss onto her lips.

Once again, our hands were all over each other. At one point she tried to get me to penetrate her, but I pulled away and instead pleasured her with my hand. With what I now knew, a conversation needed to take place before I could be inside her again.

Charlotte was the first to step out the shower. She grabbed a white fluffy towel from a wall hook beside the shower. As she was toweling off her hair, I watched as she stared at the sink counter and walked there. I stood behind her and wrapped my arms around her waist.

She turned to face me with questioning eyes.

I pulled her close, and bent down and kissed her. "I found this on the sheet of the bed."

"What should I do?" There was anxiety in her voice.

"Do you want to have my child?" I asked, nervous about what her answer might be.

She was quiet for what seemed a very long time. She seemed to be studying my eyes. "I do, but only if that's what you want," she replied. "It's not only my decision to make. You would be the father."

My smile brightened. "Let's have a baby."

She went onto her tiptoes and planted a kiss on my lips.

Our fire for each other once again ignited and it was but a brief moment before we were once again in bed.

* * *

Three Weeks Later

I was in my office at home in front of the computer, scanning locations for a get-away spot for us to get married. I planned to bring this up to Charlotte after finding a place. After much searching, I came across an exclusive resort in Barbados, and decided that might be the place. I hoped she would agree.

My heart was full as I pondered possibly becoming a father. Thoughts of my childhood ran through my mind, and I wanted my own child's life to be different. I fantasized of a life and family with Charlotte, even when the mere notion of it was preposterous—when she was a model, even while she was in prison. I felt an instant attraction to her from the very beginning, and had all but given up until fate shined on me and she appeared through my doorway and in my barber chair. From that moment on, my hunger for her reignited.

My thoughts shifted to when Charlotte had been shot and I'd completely lost it—more afraid than I'd ever been of possibly losing her. I knew we had a chance to carve out a family life together, and I wanted that with her more than anything. I thought of what I heard on that security video from the royal crypt. Charlotte had voiced her concerns about being able to even get pregnant due to the rapes while in prison. I decided to get that thought out of my head.

CHAPTER 41

Andrei

A palatial limestone structure in a French Renaissance style was nestled in a lush forest surrounded by a velvety lawn. The fifty-thousand-square-foot mansion had thirty-five bedrooms, forty-three bathrooms, and sixty-five fireplaces. This was my Belyaev Mansion, located outside of Moscow.

I was sitting in my favorite leather chair in front of the fireplace in the smoking room—a quite masculine space with cedar walls and a massive stone fireplace that went all the way up the twenty-five-foot-tall ceiling. I had a scotch in one hand and a cigarette in the other. The log in the fireplace crackled and my mind wandered to thoughts of my son.

I remembered all the years Dmitri assisted me. I knew my son grew to resent the illegal dealings and I'm sure he believed I wasn't an honorable man; though Dmitri never once said anything, I could see it in my son's eyes.

Dmitri had taken the ethical route once back in New York City, forgoing the backroom politics of my lifestyle and had cultivated his own. He distanced himself from Moscow. I was proud of my son. Dmitri had managed quite well with his own business endeavors.

I reflected on the conversation Dmitri and I had last. He came to me with the incriminating information on that laptop. Didn't have to, but did. That spoke volumes—how he still had affection for me.

I knew my divorce from Marissa, Dmitri's mother, had been rough on him. At first, Marissa prevented me from seeing or speaking to him. Eventually, it was he who reached out when he was eleven and our relationship grew from there, and Dmitri moved to Moscow.

Dmitri was a smart kid and even more so as a young adult. When he wanted to go to Yale University to pursue business, I enthusiastically supported him. Dmitri had excelled and went on to get his MBA.

I took full advantage of Dmitri's expertise and because of that, my businesses soared. My dynasty in Russia wasn't shabby by any means to begin with, but I'd wanted to infiltrate the US. I'd done exactly that.

Dmitri was sure to know what was on that computer. He was much too smart not to look it over thoroughly before relinquishing it. The information was ugly, and involved my brother Sergei, as well as embarrassing details of my friend Igor's sex life. Igor and I would have to come up with a plan to deal with this. While the absence of the cryptocurrency and its fifty-fifty ownership between me and Igor wouldn't compromise either of our holdings, it was more a matter of principle. Between Igor and me, the world wasn't too big for us to find Sergei and deal with him.

I found the surveillance videos to be most concerning. Why were Dmitri and Charlotte being watched? Was Sergei planning to kidnap them? While that didn't make any sense, I knew that Sergei wasn't too bright. Also, what was it with the videos of the meetings in that restaurant?

Then there was the murder attempt from Sergei's Danish princess on Charlotte. I wasn't surprised Sergei gave the girl up; he probably even took the reward money.

But I was hurt Dmitri hadn't phoned when Charlotte was shot and in the hospital. I knew Dmitri was smitten and planned to marry her. Did he think Sergei and I were tied together with the thievery of the crypto? I needed to know.

Dmitri was my only child—sole heir to everything I had. More than that, I loved him deeply.

I glanced at my watch. It would be one o'clock in New York City. I picked up my phone and called Dmitri.

"Hello, Papa," Dmitri answered on the second ring.

"Hello, my son. How is your lovely lady doing? I heard about her misfortune on the news."

"She's healing nicely. The shot went in her shoulder and just barely missed her subclavian artery. She lost a lot of blood. I almost lost her. The doctor had to use a defibrillator," Dmitri said.

"Is there anything I can do to help?" I asked.

"I don't think so, but I do plan to marry her as soon as she is able. I have to talk to her about the details, of course. If it's possible, I would like you to be at the wedding."

I felt a smile on my face and a warmth in my heart. I knew my son loved me. "Of course I will be there. Just let me know when."

"On another matter," Dmitri said. I knew Dmitri was choosing his words carefully. "What do you think about the information on that computer? Particularly, the document labeled Journal?"

"Do not worry about any of this, my son. Igor and I will get our money back. Sergei has gone rogue. We will handle this. You just enjoy your fiancé and let me know about the wedding."

"I certainly will." Dmitri momentarily paused and cleared his throat. "Jax was Charlotte's brother, but that's where it ends. She is the one who discovered his body and the suicide note. It pretty much spelled out his guilt. The details in that Journal document tell the rest of the story. She—no, *we*—need this behind us," Dmitri said.

"That you do. Do not worry. This will be taken care of."

CHAPTER 42

Sergei

I sat on a deck chair as the captain eased the yacht into a slip at the port of Tema in Accra, Ghana. I was to pick up the gold bullion here.

Amadou Osei was Paramount Chief of the Ashanti Tribe and lived in the village of Kumasi. Mr. Osei was a graduate of Harvard and a successful businessman. I believed Osei was the perfect one to get the gold from. Fifteen billion dollars, to be exact. The transaction would take place on my yacht. I had arranged for a New York City banker to be present during the transaction. I would next get the bullion to a Swiss national bank for vault storage via a private plane. I would personally take the bullion with two security guards who were already on my yacht. I could cash out whenever I wanted. At the moment, I was more than fine with my money.

I had already spent one billon and had the rest of a second billion in a German bank. My yacht wasn't cheap and neither were the staff's salaries. I'd also spent quite a bit on Adeline—buying her gifts and lots of cocaine. But I didn't care about what I'd already spent. There was plenty more where that came from. I was living the high life and planned to find another girl to take care of my needs. A business acquaintance would take care of that for me. I could take my pick of ladies off my computer from the comfort of my chair. She wouldn't even cost more than one million dollars.

CHAPTER 42

Adeline

I paced the floor in the apartment in the tower of the palace. My two-thousand-square-foot space had been recently updated with all new modern plumbing, heating, and air conditioning. The decor was consistent with the rest of the castle—palatial but ancient. Rumor had it the ghost of King Triston III, my great-great-great grandfather, roamed the halls. I'd yet to see him, but was on high alert. This was my prison cell. Royal Guards stood watch outside the only door. There wasn't any possibility of escape.

The more I paced, the angrier I got. Sergei was a slimy jerk and it disgusted me how I'd allowed him to use me. I wanted to get back at him, but hadn't come up with any plan yet. I knew about his most recent thievery of cryptocurrency, but not the important details that could really do any damage to him. But I would figure this one out—maybe even use it as a bargaining chip to gain my freedom.

My mind moved to the incident with Charlotte in the crypt. I knew I shouldn't have pulled the trigger of the gun. Actually, I only planned to use it as a prop—scare the crap out of Charlotte, get her on her knees begging for mercy. Things had escalated and I lost it, screaming details of how I'd framed Charlotte for murder. Since I hadn't actually done the deed myself, I wasn't worried. But stupid Charlotte moved toward me and on reflex I just shot. I had forgotten about the security cameras inside the crypt. I now realized I was doomed, but I wasn't going down alone. Hell no! Marilee and Zahara were going down with me for that murder. There's no way I was going to prison and they would be free.

I went to my allowed computer, which had only limited access to the internet. I searched for information about the shooting. There wasn't anything more than what I'd already read. Then I searched out Marilee and Zahara. There wasn't any information about either of them. Next, I pulled up Facebook and put in Marilee's name. She was there all right, but I didn't have the capability to message her or make any comments—nothing that would show Marilee I was trying to get in touch with her.

On a whim, I tried to contact Sergei. Why not? Maybe I would get lucky.

Nope! Didn't work.

I got up from the computer and began pacing, cursing, and screaming. Anything at all to release the pent-up emotions. I was so enraged that I didn't hear the knocking at my door. When I turned around, I was face to face with my brother Harald.

"Hello, sister of mine," he said. "Just wanted to pay you a visit. May I sit?"

"Sure." I walked to the pale green upholstered couch and he took the matching chair across.

He jumped right in. "You know you're in some deep shit, right?"

"Yeah," I said, defeated. I loved my brother very much and felt shame for the first time. I knew I'd disappointed him.

"There's so much evidence against you and the Danish Ministry of Justice has it. When Charlotte was taken to the hospital, they came to the crypt and found the cameras. We had to relinquish the tapes to them. I don't think you can get out of this," Harald said.

I began to cry. This was the first time in years my emotions broke. I'd never allowed myself to be vulnerable enough to shed tears. There was always a plan and an ulterior motive for everything I did; it was just my mode of operation.

Harald stood and sat beside me, putting his arm around me. I leaned into him and wept bitterly. He pulled me tight and tried to comfort me.

CHAPTER 43

Harald

I had watched the videotape. The chief of police had contacted me. I was struck with anger that Charlotte spent six years in prison all for a lie. Maybe my sister hadn't done the actual framing, but it was her idea and she didn't come forward during Charlotte's trial. That spoke volumes about her character. Then to add insult to injury, she paid an inmate to harass Charlotte. What Charlotte had endured was horrendous.

I realized how Charlotte's name had been seriously tarnished, and therefore the Bjorn family name as well. Most of all my late brother. I knew no one could have loved Lars more than Charlotte—and he her. She was a good person who everyone in the family adored, with the exception of my sister Adeline.

Adeline's sobbing stopped. I reached over to the side table and grabbed a tissue for her. "I want to help you, Adeline, but I don't know what I can do."

"Maybe I can get a plea deal," Adeline said.

"Perhaps, but you must remember; it's not only that you shot Charlotte, but you caused her to spend six miserable years in prison. I don't know of any judge or jury that would give you leniency for these crimes. While Charlotte has recovered from the gunshot, the fact remains that she lost six years of her life because of your scheme. And worse, she has lived with undeserved shame. Adeline, for what? Please tell me. I want to understand."

"Mother loved her more than me," Adeline said. "She wasn't even a true royal, but she was treated like a princess. She even had a crown. I am the princess—not her."

"Your title might be stripped because of your crimes. It's up to Mother now. You should talk to her."

Adeline's expression was stoic. "I don't know if I can," she said.

"You must try," I urged, trying to get through to her.

"I miss our father. He loved me and treated me like the princess I am."

"You're a grown woman now and everything you do has consequences—good or bad. When we were young, our parents could take care of our mistakes, but as adults that isn't possible."

Adeline just stared across the room. She was silent—a dark, faraway look in her eyes.

"Talk to me, Adeline."

She just continued staring across the room. No words— not even tears.

"I want to help you, but I can't if you don't talk to me."

She turned to face me but didn't say a word.

* * *

"Mother, I believe Adeline is mentally ill."

We were in her parlor. I had a glass of bourbon, Mother a glass of white wine. I told my mother everything I discussed with Adeline.

"I don't understand how she can think I don't love her," Mother said.

"It sounds to me more a matter of jealousy of Charlotte. And I've yet to hear any real reason from Adeline of why."

"I keep seeing that video in my mind, and it scares me what Adeline is capable of. I don't think she should be out in society and it grieves me seriously to know this."

"What do you plan to do?" I asked.

"I must seek counsel."

"Perhaps a psychiatrist should evaluate Adeline. She might be granted leniency if she went to a mental health institution until she is well," I suggested.

She took a final swallow of her wine. "I am sure that will be considered."

CHAPTER 44

Charlotte

"Hi, Aunt Lydia! I'm so happy you called." I was sitting outside on Dmitri's patio. It was ten on Sunday morning. I had a steaming cup of coffee in my other hand.

"Pearl and I just returned from Machu Picchu. We were at a monastery retreat and only returned home late last night. I was shocked to learn about Jax and also what happened to you. Pearl and I didn't have any electronics the whole time we were at the monastery," Aunt Lydia said. "Do you know why Jax killed himself?"

"I had no clue he was depressed enough to do himself harm. His partner was murdered and Jax had moved back in with me. I spent some time at my fiancé's house, and when I returned, I discovered his suicide note. I found his body inside his car in my garage."

"My God," Aunt Lydia said. "Then how are you doing? It was all over the news about your former sister-in-law shooting you. Is there anything I can do? You and your fiancé are welcome to come and stay at our place if you want to just get away. We'd love to see you and meet your guy."

"Thank you for the invitation. Right now, I'm not sure what our plans are. There's been so much drama and I'm ready for all that to just fade away."

"Do you have any plans for Jax's ashes?" Aunt Lydia asked.

"I'm not sure what to do. He loved the ocean, so I was thinking about spreading them there. But he also loved your place, so spreading them out into the desert might be an option too. I just don't know." I felt a little guilty I'd not taken any action at all about Jax's ashes. They were in a carved wooden box with gold etching on top, sitting on a shelf in my home office library.

"Either way I'm sure it's fine. You could even have the ashes buried next to both your parents. There's space there," Aunt Lydia said.

"Thank you for the suggestion. I hadn't thought of that, and that might be the better choice. I'll think it over," I answered gratefully.

CHAPTER 45

Dmitri

I held her tight, her head resting on my chest. Our lovemaking had been tender. Gratitude filled me for the love I'd found in her. I longed for Charlotte to be pregnant with my child. Our child.

I would do everything humanly possible to keep her safe from the evil clutches of Sergei. The man didn't deserve to even walk the ground Charlotte stepped on.

Then, there was the issue of clearing Charlotte's name. She made me promise not to do anything till she felt better. It was now time. All the evidence on the video should do it. I would phone a lawyer tomorrow morning and get the process started. Also, that private investigator might be able to find evidence. He'd not been able to locate Zahara, but she could have gone back to her home country of Somalia. The other woman, Marilee, had been in a drug rehab facility but was released. Her current whereabouts were unclear. The PI was still working on it. Marilee's father was a prominent attorney in New York City, and it would be an embarrassment to him when his daughter was incriminated. The man would do everything in his power to keep his daughter out of prison.

I would make sure when Charlotte was exonerated, it made it to the television news as well as the front page of the newspaper. She deserved at least that.

* * *

"Abernathy, Collins, and Seales," answered a high-pitched voice on the phone.

"This is Dmitri Zhukov. I would like to speak with Grant Collins." I met the man at a cocktail party I attended several years ago with a date. Grant Collins wasn't cheap, but he was one of the best around.

"Hi, Dmitri. What can I do for you?" Grant Collins said.

"I'd like to bring my fiancé in to see you. Her name is Charlotte Bjorn."

"Yes, I remember that case well."

"We have enough evidence to exonerate her. I was hoping you would consider representing her."

"I would love to meet with you and Charlotte. I'll send you back to my secretary and ask her to find you the soonest time to come in," he said.

"Thank you. We really appreciate this. While Charlotte cannot get back those six years in prison, she can at least have her name cleared."

"I understand completely."

Satisfied with initiating things with the attorney, I needed to get Charlotte out of the house. It wasn't fair for her to feel caged. Dancing and dinner out seemed perfect. The Upstairs Jazz Club might be nice. They had Mediterranean food and generally had a live band for dancing.

I began to ponder security. Actually, I should phone my father and see what progress there was in locating Sergei. Sergei was the one keeping us enjoying freedom.

"Hello, my son," my father answered.

"Hello, Papa. I hope you are well."

"Yes, very good. Now what do I owe the pleasure of this call?"

"Any news about Sergei? I'm worried about Charlotte's safety. It would be easy for Sergei to grab her and try to use her as leverage."

"I understand. The news isn't good, I'm afraid. Word has it he's hooked up with Oleg Popovvicht," my father informed me.

"Isn't he the sex trafficker of young women?" I asked.

"The same. Seems Sergei purchased one of his girls after he sent the Danish princess back to her mother. This one is young and from Poland. Both Igor and I want to get our money back first, then hand him over to the Polish police with evidence of human trafficking. Sergei is such a coward, he would probably give up Popovvicht to stay out of jail himself," Father said.

I was shocked. "How in the world are you going to do that?"

"Do not worry, my son. I have my ways."

"I know you do. I just want to keep Charlotte safe."

"I understand. For now, hire security detail, then try to live a normal life. I will keep you posted."

"Yeah, I'll hire bodyguards. She isn't going to like it, but it is what it is."

I decided to get personal bodyguards, but dinner and dancing for tonight was out. Better to arrange so we could get out of the house.

* * *

I found Charlotte in the kitchen making cinnamon scones. She kept busy most of the time cooking and baking. I knew it was to keep from being bored, but was grateful for all the scrumptious food. Groceries were delivered almost daily, since going to the grocery store was out.

"Beef Wellington is for dinner, with steamed green beans and carrots," Charlotte said with a grin. "I hope you'll be hungry."

I gave her a smile. "I don't think kings eat better than I do every day."

She was now beaming. "Your Royal Highness, would you like to sample my sourdough bread? It's fresh out of the oven."

I walked to her, grabbed her at the waist, and kissed her on the neck. "Royal Highness, huh?" I gave her a light pinch on her butt. "I would love some of your bread."

She gave out a giggle, then dusted my nose with some flour on her hand from the scones.

"Be careful, my love, or I will take you to the bedroom. You look so sexy in the kitchen."

She pushed the wooden bread board my way and pointed to the butter.

"Eat your sourdough bread, my lord. Tell me what you think. I found the recipe on the internet. My cookbooks are in my kitchen at home," she said.

I felt a pang of sadness at her saying 'my kitchen at home.' I felt her home was here with me.

She must have noticed my expression after she said that, as she wiped the flour off her hands and walked to me, stood on her toes, and put her hands around my neck. Her eyes met mine. "Wherever you are is home for me," she said. "Always know this."

"Thank you."

She gave me a kiss. "Now, eat some of my bread." She smiled wide.

I did just that—sliced a large piece and buttered it heavily. I sat on the bar stool in front of her and took a bite. I closed my eyes, savoring the tangy flavor, chewy texture, and crisp, crackly crust. "Damn, this is good."

"Success then. I was thinking about making crème brulée for dessert," she said.

I grinned. "I'm going to be your dessert."

She giggled. "Okay, no crème brulée, then. *You* are yummier!"

I sliced a second slice of bread, buttered it, then went back to my barstool. It was three o'clock. We hadn't had lunch as breakfast was late and huge—Eggs Benedict, sliced fruit, and homemade cinnamon rolls.

"I made an appointment with an attorney for tomorrow to handle your case," I informed her, hoping to brighten her mood.

"Thank you. I'm anxious to clear my name and not feel like dirt whenever I go anywhere in the city. Although we haven't gone anywhere in a while," she said.

"That brings up my crappy news. I spoke with my father again and Sergei is still on the loose. Seems he purchased a girl from a human trafficker." I took the final bite of sourdough bread.

"That's terrible," she said.

"Yes, it is." I told her all the details from the phone call with my father.

She grimaced since we previously dismissed the notion of bodyguards. "Bodyguards, huh?"

"Yeah, I get it. I wanted to take you out to dinner and dancing. But that's out."

"I would love us to go out to dinner and dancing. We haven't danced together since our first date," she said.

"I know; I remember that evening well."

"Me too." She popped the Beef Wellington into the oven and set the timer. "When you took my hand and led me to the dance floor, I was surprised. But when you pulled me close to dance, I knew there was something. I felt it right away."

I couldn't help but grin. "Is that right?"

"Then when you walked me home, it took every bit of self-control I could muster not to ask you to come inside."

I laughed. "If you only knew how bad I wanted you that night, it would have scared you away."

"We happened so fast. When I look back, it seems unreal," she said.

"It was definitely fast. I've never felt the way I feel about you with anyone else."

She smiled wide. "And here we are."

CHAPTER 46

Charlotte

I stepped out of the large luxurious shower with gray basketweave tile walls in a bold graphic design. It had two rainfall showerheads above and two handhelds, one on each side. Dmitri definitely had good taste.

I grabbed a fluffy white towel off a hook outside the shower. With a towel wrapped around me, I made my way to his walk-in closet. It was another impressive space with cedar drawers, shelves, and hanging rods. The farthest wall was a full-walled mirror. Dmitri had made space for me.

I pulled out a drawer where my underwear was; there were only three pairs left. Dmitri's washer and dryer were off the kitchen in a laundry room, but there weren't any lingerie drying racks. My La Perla bras and panties couldn't go in the dryer.

Up until this point, I didn't want to go to my place. Not since Jax died. I was ready to go there now. Dmitri's was definitely a man's space—no makeup mirror, no special shelf for my perfumes, no accessory shelves, or everything else I loved about getting dressed.

I wanted to scream! I kept busy cooking and reading books on my iPad. Enough! Tomorrow, we were going to see the attorney and our two new bodyguards were going to accompany us. Now was the time to talk to Dmitri. I grabbed my long silk multicolored Arabesque print kimono and put it on.

It was eight-thirty when I walked towards the media room where he was watching a football game. I went inside. The theater-size TV had the game on and Dmitri was at the bar on the far side of the room mixing a drink. He smiled wide when he saw me.

"Can I fix you a drink?" he said.

I walked to the bar, deciding not to talk over the television. "Club soda would be nice. We're trying to get pregnant, right?"

He grinned. "Maybe you already are."

"Maybe." I took a deep breath. "I want to talk to you about tomorrow."

"Sure. Let me stop the TV." He paused the game.

"We have that appointment at ten with the attorney."

He took another swallow of his drink. "Right."

"I'd like to stop at my house afterwards to get some things, then go to Bloomingdales."

"Sure. You know those two bodyguards have to be with us." He gave a sour look, showing he wasn't excited about it either.

"I know you probably have to go to your business office at some point. How are you able to handle things now?"

"My administrative assistant has been emailing me the things I can handle that way. But you're right. I do need to stop in." He took another swallow of his drink.

"What kind of business do you have? I feel kinda stupid that I don't know."

"I'm an investor in stocks and properties. I own three restaurants and a nightclub. I also own a small winery in Napa Valley. I actually own this building we're living in."

I smiled wide. "Guess that's why you have the penthouse all the way at the top."

He laughed. "You would be right."

"You know, I've never seen that video from the security footage in the crypt."

"Let's have a seat." He walked to the seating area. I followed and sat beside him. He turned the TV off, then took my hand. "I don't think it would be a good idea for you to see that and I'll tell you why." He brought my hand to his lips and kissed the top of it.

"I do want to know why."

"You've already lived through that once, so why should you again? It's quite disturbing."

"I get what you're saying but maybe I don't remember it all."

"I suspect the lawyer is going to play it tomorrow while we're there. You will, of course, have the option to leave the room if it's too much," he said.

"I understand."

He pulled me close. My kimono slipped open and my thigh was exposed. He drew me to him and our lips met. He slid his hand up my thigh, then kept going upward to the gusset of my red silk panties, moving them aside as he slipped a finger inside me.

I moaned into his mouth; he deepened the kiss, then inserted another finger and hooked it. I quickly rose to an apex of pleasure and screamed out his name.

He lifted me up into his arms and carried me to the bedroom.

* * *

Dmitri took as well as he gave and we both were thoroughly spent. He held me close as we drifted into blissful sleep.

CHAPTER 47

Charlotte

Dmitri and I entered the offices of Abernathy, Collins, and Seales on the second floor of a high-rise building in Manhattan. Dmitri looked handsome in a black Armani suit with a white shirt and striped tie. I wore a navy double-breasted blazer dress that hit right at the knee. I had on nude high-heeled pumps, my hair in a stylish low chignon, and large gold hoop earrings. My tan Stella McCartney handbag was looped around my arm.

Dmitri opened the glass office door and I walked inside the waiting room, which was tastefully furnished in modern style with several large oil paintings hanging on two walls. Dmitri followed and the two bodyguards trailed behind. They were both over six feet tall and muscular. One was brown skinned with a shaved head and the other had short red hair.

"Charlotte."

I glanced at where the voice came from. A woman entered the waiting room and I recognized her instantly—another colleague from those modeling days.

"Dahlia." I went to her and gave her a friendly hug. I noted how changed the woman was from our modeling days. Her dark brown hair was pulled back into a tight, severe bun. She wore heavy dark-framed glasses and no makeup. Her black pantsuit was boxy and ill-fitting. One would never know Dahlia had once been a top-paid runway model.

"Actually, it's Sarah. Dahlia was my runway name."

"I hear ya. No more Raven either."

Both of us laughed.

"My God, what are you doing here?" she asked.

"We have an appointment with Grant Collins," Dmitri piped in.

"Sarah, I'd like you to meet my fiancé, Dmitri Zhukov," I introduced her. "Dmitri, Sarah. We modeled together."

"It's nice to meet you, Dmitri," Sarah said.

I held out my engagement ring for her to see.

"Nice," Sarah said and gave me a wink. "I'll take you to Mr. Collins, but let's talk afterwards. Okay?"

"Sure." I was anxious to learn about Sarah. There was sure to be a story there.

Sarah glanced at the two bodyguards and then at Dmitri.

Dmitri turned to the bodyguards. "You should both stay in this lobby until we return."

The two men nodded.

Sarah led to a corner office where the door was open. She knocked on the side of the door. "Mr. Zhukov and Ms. Bjorn," she announced.

"Please, come in." He stood and walked to greet us and offered handshakes. "Charlotte, Dmitri—I'm Grant Collins." He gave us a wide Hollywood smile. "Please have a seat." He motioned to the two burgundy leather chairs in front of his desk. Dmitri and I sat. Grant Collins went to the door and closed it, then went back to his place behind his desk. "What can I do for you?"

"As you know, Charlotte was sentenced to six years for manslaughter. We have evidence that proves she's innocent," Dmitri said.

"Please go on," Grant said.

"I have video footage you should see, then you can draw your own conclusions. I also witnessed something the night of the crime that could potentially help," Dmitri said.

Grant gave his attention to me. "I see."

"I spent those years in hell for something I never did. I can't ever get those years back, but I can get my dignity returned. I want my name cleared."

"I completely understand. Dmitri, please tell me what you witnessed that night," Grant said.

Dmitri went on to describe what he witnessed. The lawyer nodded and wrote notes on a yellow legal pad. "You said you have a video for me to see," Grant said.

Dmitri pulled out a flash drive from his jacket pocket and handed it to Grant.

"Let me get the conference room set up for us to view this video," Grant said.

Dmitri and I watched as Grant left his office briefly, then returned. "Please follow me," he said and led the way down a hallway to a medium-sized conference room with a long table. A large video monitor on the wall was already powered on and there was a remote control on the table.

Dmitri took a seat across from Grant. I sat next to Dmitri.

"Before we get started, is there anything you can tell me, Charlotte, that preceded this?" Grant asked.

I told all about my trip to Copenhagen and the full history I had with the royal family. I detailed the issues of Adeline's jealousy and her wanting my tiara. Then I told him why I was in the crypt. Grant took notes the whole time.

"Thank you."

"Grant," Dmitri said. "That video is pretty graphic, and I've told Charlotte that at any point she is free to leave the room. She's already lived it, so why do it again?"

"I agree," Grant said and looked at me.

"I prefer to step out. I do know what happened, of course. Dmitri watched this security video and I trust him with this." Dmitri took my hand and squeezed.

"Very well." Grant stood and left the room, coming back with Sarah.

"Let's get a cup of coffee," Sarah said with a smile.

"Sounds good." I followed her to a break room a few doors down. There was an espresso machine, three round tables with chairs, and two couches.

"Cappuccino?" she asked.

"That would be nice." We were seated at a table across from each other. "I'm surprised to see you working here. What happened?"

"I got into a bit of trouble myself. Hilda sent me on a shoot on a yacht. I was the only model. I immediately sensed the photographer was sleezy and I should have walked out right then, but I didn't."

"I thought you were like me and only did runway?"

"Not all of us were lucky like you. I didn't get asked for as frequently and had to take on other shoots."

I felt bad for her. "Sorry."

"Anyway, the guy was trying to get me to take off my clothes."

"What?"

"At first it was just outfit changes where there wasn't much privacy. On the last change, the guy came at me and demanded to take pictures. I was naked except for a thong. I told him no, but he got aggressive. I knew he was going to overpower me, so I grabbed the first thing I could find—a pair of five-inch Gucci stilettos, and took the heel and jammed it in his shoulder when he tried to pull me down. The heel of the shoe went deep into his lower shoulder, but he still tried to come at me. So then I kicked him in the balls and ran out—first grabbing a dress from the shoot. I threw it on once I was off that ship. There were others on the yacht, but no one tried to help me," Sarah told.

"What happened next? None of this was your fault— you were a victim."

"I was reported to the police by the photographer before I even got a chance to get to the police station. The guy said I assaulted him for no reason, and some of the crew members on the ship confirmed his story," Sarah said.

"Unbelievable. I've heard of these things happening, but never knew anyone who actually lived through it."

"Long story short, Hilda fired me. I spent some time in jail and had to go back to school to learn a skill. So I am now a paralegal," she said.

"Wow! Guess we both went through hell because of that job."

"I can't help but believe Hilda knew about that photoshoot. There were some other things that didn't add up with her. Also, some younger models disappeared and we never heard about them again. One even recently. I knew her—Jenna."

"I know her too. She was with Hilda when I had dinner with my brother at an Italian restaurant on my first day out," I told her.

"Hilda wouldn't ever say anything when asked about any of them. I don't think she cared. She just wanted to make money and quickly replaced them with new models."

"It's not an easy life. I remember doing coke just to be able to get on that runway wearing that skimpy underwear with those wings."

"I get it. But look at you now. Engaged to a sexy hunk and you look *incredible*!" Sarah said.

"Thanks."

Our conversation was cut short when Grant came into the room. "Shall we go back to my office?" he asked.

I nodded and rose from my seat. "It was nice talking to you and catching up," I said my goodbyes, then followed Grant.

CHAPTER 48

Charlotte

Dmitri and I were at my place. The meeting with the attorney had gone well. Grant was certain he could clear my name with all the evidence we provided.

I went upstairs to gather more clothes to take back to Dmitri's. He was in the living room talking to the bodyguards.

I walked upstairs to my dressing room and sat on the pink velvet bench. I glanced around, trying to take it all in. I missed this space. I must have been sitting there for a while because Dmitri appeared.

"Is everything okay?" he asked.

"Everything is fine. I just like being in here. It reminds me of how much I enjoy being a girl." I gave an embarrassed laugh and stood.

"I will build you an even bigger girl-room than this," he said with a serious expression.

"Actually, my biggest thing right now is not having a lingerie drying rack in your laundry room. I don't have a place to dry my panties. That is why I'm running out and need to buy new ones."

He gave a roaring laugh. "Why didn't you tell me?" he asked.

"Well… I'm not entirely sure."

His expression was tender. "Don't lie to me."

"Your place is so masculine and you designed it to be exactly the way you want. I can't just come in and demand changes."

"Yes, you can," he said.

"Oh Dmitri." I put my arms around him. "All I ask for is a place to dry my undies."

"I'll make that happen right away," he said. "We need a place that isn't mine and isn't yours, but *ours*. It probably needs to be somewhere else," he said.

"I know, you're right. This house was Lars' and mine, and those memories will always be here. I know that isn't healthy for us. Then there's the fact my brother died by suicide here."

"Once Sergei is caught, we'll be free to live the way we want. We can look for properties online, but at some point, we'll have to physically go there. I'd like to be as close as possible to my office. Right now, it takes me only twenty minutes to get there. Anything outside of the city would make my commute much longer."

"I know the location of your place is ideal. Maybe we can think of something."

"We will," he promised.

"I wanted to mention something to you that I learned from Sarah yesterday."

"Sure."

"She made a strange comment about the old modeling agency I used to work for. She said there were models who seemed to disappear. Young models. She said that Hilda, the owner, never would talk about it and nothing seemed to get done about locating them. I know you mentioned Sergei buying a girl from a human trafficker. I can't help but wonder if these missing models are related to that guy Sergei got his girl from."

"It could be related, but I'm not sure what either of us could do about it," he said sadly.

"I get it. It just bothered me. Sarah told me who the most recent missing model is, and I saw her the evening of my release from Bedford. She was at a restaurant and Hilda was with her. Her name is Jenna; she's from Poland. She can't be older than seventeen. Sarah told me about her own bad experience. Seems Hilda sent her to a photoshoot on some yacht. Sarah said the photographer seemed sleezy, but she went ahead with the job anyway. Then, the guy jumped her like he wanted to rape her. She defended herself, hurting the guy in the process, then fled. Turned out the guy called the police on her before she was able to report him. The police questioned everyone on the yacht and they sided with the photographer. Hilda then fired Sarah."

"Did she give the name of the photographer?"

"No."

"Hmm," he said and took a deep breath.

"I just need a minute to grab some things and we can leave."

CHAPTER 49

Dmitri

Charlotte and I were back at my place. She decided to skip Bloomingdales. I dismissed the bodyguards and was grateful to be alone with Charlotte. Having bodyguards wasn't my style. I could defend myself, but I was overprotective of her.

I pulled out the lower left drawer of my desk in my home office. I found my unloaded gun in the back of the drawer and a box of bullets in front. I'd not used that gun since my father had returned to Moscow, but I certainly knew how to handle it.

I closed the drawer and stood. I'd allowed myself to get soft—not working out or training. I picked up my phone and dialed the trainer I had previously worked with.

"Dmitri!" he answered after the first ring.

"Hi, Pete. Hope all is well with you."

"Great. What can I do for you?"

"I need to train. Can you help me out?"

"How soon?" Pete asked.

"Right away."

"You're in luck; I don't have any clients until tomorrow morning. Eight o'clock?"

"Yep."

"Good. See you then," Pete said and we ended the call.

I found Charlotte in the bedroom reading a book. "I need to talk to you."

She straightened in her chair, and put the iPad down on a side table. "Of course," she said.

"I don't like the idea of bodyguards. Staying holed up in this penthouse isn't really living."

"I don't like it any more than you do," she said.

"I'm pretty good at defending us myself. There are things you don't know about me."

"I suspected as much," she said. "I knew you would tell me when you were ready."

"I haven't trained in a while and must return to it. My private gym is in the basement of this building. No one else has access to it but you and me. I've phoned a trainer I've used before and he will be here at eight so I can get started. There's also a pool if you feel like swimming."

"I would love to swim in the pool, but I didn't bring a swimsuit," she said.

I smiled and gave her a wink. "We can both go tonight if you want. No swimsuits needed."

"Please tell me more," she said.

"We can talk later. Training will take a while."

CHAPTER 50

Charlotte

I remained seated on the chair in the bedroom, reflecting on what Dmitri had just shared and how his demeanor had changed. I'd never seen this side of him before. His eyes were steel and his jaw tight when he left for the gym. It was frightening and sexy at the same time. There's something tantalizing about a strong alpha man.

I sat further back in the chair and laid my head on the cushy backrest. My mind shifted. It had been three weeks since the IUD fell out, and I couldn't remember when I had my period before that. I wondered if the thing hadn't worked for a while before it fell out. I thought I might be pregnant. I was catching myself feeling moody, occasionally nauseous. and lightheaded. Should I tell Dmitri? Or go to the drug store and get a pregnancy test myself? Although how could I do that? Maybe I could phone a pharmacy and have one delivered?

I did exactly that and hoped it would arrive while Dmitri was at the gym.

My cell pinged thirty minutes later, saying the delivery person was waiting in the lobby. Fortunately, the pharmacy was only a block away. I made my way to the lobby, secure in seeing the two familiar building security guards there.

I rode the elevator back up to Dmitri's and went into the bathroom to do the test.

It was positive.

I was frozen. I wanted to be absolutely sure it wasn't a false reading. I opened another kit and did it again.

Positive.

I left the two test sticks on the bathroom counter with the results showing. I wanted him to see for himself.

I returned to the chair in the bedroom feeling anxious. I just wanted to tell someone—almost anyone—about the news. Then, my thoughts turned to baby Erik. Sadness came over me and overshadowed my excitement.

I brushed the dark thoughts aside and decided to get busy in the kitchen; it was calming. I decided to make an apple pie.

When Dmitri appeared, I was in the kitchen and rolling out pastry. He'd been gone for several hours.

"How was your workout?"

"Good. I hadn't realized how out of shape I'd gotten. He'll be training me every day. It will be early mornings so the rest of the day won't be screwed," he said, walking over to me and kissing me on the cheek.

I couldn't help but grin. "You already look chiseled to me."

He laughed, clearly less tense than before he left for the gym. "What are you making?" he asked.

"An apple pie."

"Yum. Sounds good." He kissed me again. "I'm getting in the shower."

I all but held my breath as I watched him make his way to the master bathroom, wondering if he would know what those pregnancy sticks were.

I put my rolling pin down, wiped my hands, and walked to the bedroom. I stood just inside the bathroom door and pointed to the tests on the counter.

"What?" he asked and turned to me.

I walked further inside.

His eyes were wide. "You're pregnant?"

"I am. I suspected, so I called the pharmacy down the corner and had these kits delivered to the lobby."

He picked me up into his arms and kissed me. "Are you happy?" he asked.

I felt tears running down my face. "I'm scared."

He carried me to the bedroom and sat me on the edge of the bed gently. He got on his knees in front of me and held both of my hands. "We will do this together. I'll be with you every step of the way. What happened to you before won't happen this time."

He guessed what I'd been thinking.

"I do want our baby."

"Me too. Very, very much," he assured me. He raised my hands to his mouth and kissed the tops of them.

"I thought it wasn't possible to love you more, but now I love you even more than that."

His hand stroked the side of my face. "I want us to get married soon."

"Me too."

* * *

True to his word, Dmitri had phoned an interior designer and sent pictures of the laundry room. She said she knew exactly what was needed for lingerie hanging space, a laundry folding space, a rod for hanging, and arranged for a carpenter to do the work. Also, a plumber would come create a tub sink for handwashing delicates. The project turned out much nicer than I had asked for.

The penthouse had four bedrooms. I walked down the hallway to one of the three guest rooms. This bedroom was the closest to the master bedroom. I went inside and walked around, trying to decide if it might work for a nursery. It did have a convenient ensuite with a bathtub that wasn't too deep.

I walked to the window and gazed out. The view of Central Park was nice and I imagined being in this room, rocking our baby. It was something I'd longed to do with Erik but it never happened. Maybe this time things would be different.

I decided I wanted to get married at Aunt Lydia's. Dmitri was okay with it and all I needed was for Aunt Lydia to agree. I was hoping for a wedding in two months; I knew I wouldn't be showing by then, though my pregnancy didn't need to be a secret. I wanted as many positive vibes as I could get—Aunt Lydia and Pearl were as positive as it came. I thought the situation with Sergei would be resolved before then. From what Dmitri had described of his father, the man had powerful ways to get things taken care of. I hoped this was the case.

I picked up my cell from the nightstand in the bedroom, walked to the living room, and sat. It was too chilly to sit outside, which was my favorite place for a phone call.

"Hello, Charlotte."

"Aunt Lydia, how are you and Pearl?"

"We are very good. We're talking about taking another vacation. Don't know where yet, just someplace fun."

"Sounds good."

"How are *you* doing?"

"I'm pregnant." I just blurted it out. It felt good to tell someone other than Dmitri.

"Congratulations! Let me tell Pearl." I heard her calling for Pearl to come to the phone. "I'm putting you on speaker phone," Aunt Lydia said.

"Girl, you have got to be over the moon," Pearl said. "I'm not surprised though. Lydia and I had a feeling."

"Was it a vision?"

"Yes, and a very good one," Pearl said.

"Good. I know I can't go through what I did before with Erik."

"Do not worry. All will be well. Do you want to know the gender?" Pearl asked.

"You know that?"

"Sure do. Do you want me to tell you?"

I suddenly got quiet. "I'm not sure. I just want to know if my baby will be born healthy."

"Yes, very healthy," Pearl said.

"We will do a blessing for your baby and your pregnancy tonight. It's the new moon," Aunt Lydia said.

"I appreciate that. You know, when I stayed with you two, it was the most peaceful and wonderful experience." Both Aunt Lydia and Pearl made a knowing sound. "I wanted to ask you both a question. Would you consider allowing Dmitri and I to get married at your place?"

"That would be delightful," Pearl said.

"We would like that," Aunt Lydia said.

"Thank you. I was hoping, but I didn't want to just assume. I'm not sure of the timeline yet." I went on to tell a whitewashed version of how Dmitri needed to take care of some business prior to us getting married.

"Whenever you are ready, just say the word. We will make it happen," Pearl said.

"Love you two."

CHAPTER 51

Adeline

"I have a food tray for the princess." Galem lifted the silver dome to show the food.

"You may enter," said the Royal Life Guard. He was stationed outside the door of my sequestered apartment.

Galem nodded; the guard opened the door and Galem walked inside.

"What the fuck?"

He took his pointed first finger over his mouth as he was facing me with his back to the guard. "Dinner is served," Galem said and lifted the silver dome to show pork tenderloin with a cream sauce. He discretely pointed to the inside top of the silver dome. Galem waved goodbye and left. The door was closed and locked afterwards.

I reached inside the dome and grabbed the cell phone and passport taped to the top. I took the items to my bed and put them underneath the mattress. I planned to further inspect the items once I finished my meal.

Some time had now passed and it was eleven o'clock. I knew there was little chance of anyone coming to see me at this time of night so I went to where the two items were hidden and retrieved them.

The passport was of a woman with red hair and dark-framed glasses by the name of Ingrid Beirn—the cleaning lady. The cell was a burner phone and I was able to easily link to the full internet with it. Marilee was easy to message on Facebook. Hopefully, she would reply to my message.

My brain was racing. *What was Galem suggesting? Would he actually help me escape?*

I walked to my window of my prison apartment and gazed outside. The window faced the back of the property, but how could I escape so high up? There was only one door to the apartment and no attic access.

The cell phone rang.

"Hello?"

"Adeline, it's me," Galem said.

I walked to the bathroom and closed the door so the guards outside couldn't hear. "Hi and thank you for the cell and passport, but what can I do with them besides talk with you?"

"I believe I have a way to get you out of there," he said.

"How?" I asked skeptically.

"How good of an actress are you?"

"Depends. What do you have in mind?"

Galem went on to explain his plan. I listened eagerly and knew I could pull it off. "I appreciate this but what do you want in return?"

"I want that emerald ring your late father gave you," he said.

I always wore this ring. It was priceless and a part of the royal jewels. "That's worth a hell of a lot of money. Plus, what can you do with it? Pictures of it were in the news when my father had given it to me for my sixteenth birthday. Anyone in Denmark will recognize it."

"Not your problem. That is my price," he said.

"Okay. If that is the only way I can get out of here, then fine. What good would it do me in prison anyway?"

* * *

Each subsequent day, Galem brought me various items taped underneath that silver food dome: a short curly redhead wig folded inside out and stuffed inside a baggie, black heavy-framed glasses, hand-binding cords, masking tape, and a vial of ether.

Yeah. I can do this. Ingrid was about the same size as me.

I had put each of these items inside the closet in pockets of my clothes. Tomorrow was the day to execute the plan. Once I was safely outside of the palace grounds, I would meet with Galem and give him the ring. I still had cash from Sergei and there was enough to get a plane ticket to New York City. I'd drain my trust fund while in Denmark, and purchase prepaid credit cards in ten thousand dollar increments once in the US. I'd be set. In theory anyway.

Marilee replied and said she would pick me up at the airport. We would figure out the rest then.

CHAPTER 52

Marilee

"Hello, Daddy."

"I need to talk with you right away," he said.

My heart was racing. By the tone of his voice, I knew something wasn't quite right. "What's wrong?"

"Can you come to the house tonight? Your mother is visiting her sister in Georgia. We will have privacy to talk."

"Okay. What time?"

"Seven," he said. "I'll be home from the office then."

"I'll be there."

I suspected what the call was about. I'd been carrying the guilt of what happened to Charlotte and it had been eating me up for over six years. I knew Zahara and I shouldn't have done what we did.

I tried to numb my guilty feelings with drugs but it seemed to make things worse once the drugs wore off. The subsequent depression was enough to make me end it all, to be completely free of the guilt and fear of getting caught and ending up in prison just like Charlotte.

I knew there was enough heroin in my top drawer to get high three more times. I went to the drawer and pulled out my kit, then filled the syringe with the entire amount.

I walked to my bed and laid down, waiting for the inevitable.

I was ready.

CHAPTER 53

Charlotte

"Charlotte, this is Sarah from Grant Collins' office."

"Hi, Sarah. It's great to hear from you."

"I have good news and bad news," Sarah said. "The good news: the judge who looked over your case evidence has agreed you are not guilty."

"My God! I have waited so long for this."

"Yes, you have. Mr. Collins wants to see you in his office to go over things," Sarah said. "There is time available for three tomorrow."

"I'll check with Dmitri but I suspect it will be fine. And the bad news?"

"Marilee killed herself."

I was stunned. "What?"

"Yeah. She was found with a needle in her arm. There was also a suicide note," Sarah said. "She told the whole story of how she was the one who'd framed you and Zahara was just standing beside her. There was also mention of how Adeline had planned the whole thing."

"Wow!"

"Shocking, I know! I just wanted you to hear it from me before it hit the news. Call me back if you need to reschedule for tomorrow."

I sat in the living room, momentarily stunned. Finally! It really happened!

I made my way to Dmitri's office and knocked. He was at his computer.

"Hello, love," he said.

"I just received a call from Sarah at the lawyer's office. The judge declared me not guilty."

"Finally. It's about time," he said. He pulled me to him and sat me on his lap, then kissed me on the lips.

"I've wanted this for so long. It's hard to believe it finally happened. Now I don't have to feel the humiliation and shame anymore. I want the whole world to know I'm innocent."

"You deserve *at least* that," he said. "Perhaps the lawyer can arrange for it to be in the newspaper and on the news."

"Sarah said we need to go to the lawyer's office and go over a few things. She said three tomorrow is open. Can you make it?"

"Yes," he said and held me tight.

We sat quietly for a while. He stroked my hair and kissed me on the top of my head, then placed his hand on my belly. "We need to get an appointment with an obstetrician," he said.

"We really don't know how far along I am. That IUD came out pretty easily, and it shouldn't have. It's possible it never actually worked."

"The doctor can tell us," he said.

"The first trimester scares me. That's when miscarriages seem to happen most frequently."

"Do not worry." His hand remained on my belly. "Our baby is fine."

"I just thought of something."

"What's that?"

I gave him a naughty look. "We've not gone downstairs and swam in that pool."

"Want to go now?"

"I do."

He gave me a kiss. "Let's grab some towels and go."

I felt a playful smack on my ass when I stood. I giggled and threw him an air kiss.

* * *

The farthest wall of the gym was clear glass and the pool could be seen through it. The door was on the far right. Inside the pool room, the remaining three walls were painted a light tan and the sconces' brightness could be adjusted. There was stone tile halfway down the walls and on the floor around the pool. The pool itself was longer than it was wide—fifty feet long, twenty feet wide—and the water was seven feet deep at the farthest end. There was a cutaway in the back that resembled an alcove but was actually a whirlpool for two people.

"This is very nice."

"I think so." He was quick to strip off his clothes and dive in.

The sight of his chiseled, muscular body always took my breath away. I feasted my eyes as he swam the length of the pool using strong strokes.

I quickly stripped off my t-shirt, yoga pants, and panties. I hadn't worn a bra—Dmitri liked that.

I dove into the warm water and swam underneath, and didn't resurface until in front of him. He tried to grab me at my waist, but I swam away playfully and dove deep into the water. I came up through his legs from behind and he grabbed at me as I came up for air.

"Race you down the pool, but you have to do the breast stroke."

"Game on," he said.

I gave a wide smile. "I get to say go."

We got into position at the first end of the pool.

"Go!"

I kicked off and flew down the pool, doing my favorite stroke from my days on the high school swim team. I knew

I was a bit rusty but it was instinctive. I was fast but I heard Dmitri behind me.

"I win!"

"Shit! How in the hell did you do that?" he asked.

"High school swim team." I beamed. "If we'd tried the backstroke, things would have probably turned out differently. That wasn't my best event."

"Then next time it will be the backstroke, for sure. I need to reclaim my male pride." He gave a boisterous laugh, then made his way to me and picked me up at the waist. I wrapped my legs around him and my hands went behind his neck.

"You are full of surprises. I would never have guessed you were a strong swimmer, let alone on a high school swim team."

I giggled. "I keep you guessing so you won't ever be bored with me."

"Never bored," he said and slid his hands to my butt and squeezed.

"Let's try out that whirlpool."

He winked. "Race you there with the backstroke."

"You play dirty."

He grinned. "You have no idea."

This time he said *go*. We both jumped off and raced down the pool.

I flew, getting to the end ten seconds before he did.

"Damn! You're like a little fish."

"I prefer to think mermaid." I raised my brow and gave him a naughty look. I pulled up and out of the pool, wiggled my butt, then plunged into the whirlpool.

He got into the whirlpool and pulled me to him. "And you're all mine."

I straddled him, ran my hands down his chest, and stopped at one of his nipples. I gently squeezed it before putting it into my mouth and sucking. His eyes went dark with lust and remained fixed on mine.

"Only yours," I told him.

I felt his rigid shaft against me. Tingling sensations fired through me as I ground myself against him, giving just the right amount of friction to ignite me. His hands squeezed my ass and I took his shaft into one hand and stroked him. I heard him moan and his shaft grew even harder as I rubbed the tip on my clit.

I felt his fingers on my forbidden zone and he inserted a finger. A new wave of arousal coursed through me and when he moved his finger to my g-spot, I couldn't hold out any longer. I screamed out his name while I rode the wave.

He picked me up and floated to the other end of the spa and turned me facing the wall. He wrapped his hands around my waist and planted himself inside me from the back. He began pumping, faster and faster, harder and harder. With each thrust, I met his.

My inner muscles gripped him and I knew I was close.

"Come with me," he said.

I gave out a loud primal moan with him as he filled me with his seed.

CHAPTER 53

Andrei

I was in my study smoking a cigar. I was the *Pakhan*—don of the Zhukov Bratva. Dmitri was my sole heir and I had expected him to take over once I retired. Unfortunately, Dmitri had chosen to distance himself. I dreaded the call to my son with the news Dmitri needed to hear I knew this was the best way to get Sergei. I had trained Dmitri well when he moved to Moscow at eleven. He was *Pakhan* material.

"Good morning, Son."

"Good morning, Papa," Dmitri said.

"Sergei is on the loose in New York City."

"Go on," Dmitri said.

"Igor and I got most of our money back, but Sergei got away. He has his men with him. You and your fiancé are in danger."

"What is the plan?" Dmitri asked.

"I'm sending ten of my best men, plus Gustav and Polvalaski, who are already in NYC. You will be in charge, and Gustav will be your second," I laid out.

"Do you want Sergei alive?" Dmitri asked.

"Yes, if possible, and sent back to Moscow. I will send a private plane once you have him. Sergei has five men and I'm not sure how loyal they are to him."

"Sergei had a girl with him. What about her?" Dmitri asked.

"My source said Sergei killed her and threw her body into the ocean off the coast of Portugal."

"Any leads where Sergei might be?"

"Not yet."

"When can I expect contact from Gustav?" Dmitri asked.

"Tonight."

CHAPTER 54

Dmitri

I sat back in my desk chair and realized I needed to talk with Charlotte about this latest. The appointment with the lawyer in the judge's chambers was quick and simple. A news announcement had been written up by the paralegal and approved by the judge. The lawyer took care of sending it in to the news. There wasn't any fanfare. I knew Charlotte wanted it that way and I would have phoned the television news channel myself if I'd not just received this call from my father.

I was torn. I didn't want to be involved with the Bratva; I didn't want to be a sitting duck either. The Zhukov Bratva was a powerful force in Russia and their arm spread to New York City when needed. It hadn't been necessary in many years until now.

How much should I tell Charlotte? To tell the full truth would scare her. To not tell her anything was wrong.

I made my way to the kitchen where I knew Charlotte was making a cake.

"Hi, beautiful." I walked to her and kissed her on the lips, then took a seat at the breakfast bar across from her.

"I hope you feel like chocolate lava cake for dessert tonight. I've been craving chocolate lately." Charlotte put on oven mitts and pulled the cake pan out of the oven. She sat it on top of a wire cooling rack.

"Sounds decadent."

"You seem like you have something you want to tell me," she noted.

"I do."

A furrow formed on her brow. "You look serious."

"Let's go to the living room and have a seat."

She removed her apron and followed me. I sat on the couch.

"Sit beside me." She did as I asked. I placed my hand on top of hers. "I just received a phone call from my father. There have been some new developments regarding Sergei."

"Okay…"

I squeezed her hand before I told her, "My father was able to recover most of the money Sergei stole, but wasn't able to actually get Sergei. According to my father's source, my uncle is now here in the city."

"What does that mean for us?" she asked.

"It means we're sitting ducks if nothing is done about it."

"Why is that? We don't have anything to do with that situation," she said.

"The thing is, Sergei knows my father and Igor are on to him and have recovered the bulk of the money he stole. He is a desperate man and will do whatever it takes to keep himself from being captured and returned to Moscow. The most obvious would be to use you as leverage."

"I don't understand."

"Think about it this way. Would anyone grab the man if he had you captive and threatened you?" I asked.

She was trembling. "I don't like where this is going."

"Have you ever heard of the Bratva?"

"No…"

"As I've mentioned before, my father is a powerful oligarch in Russia. He has close political ties there. As most oligarchs do, my father has his own army to protect his interests. His is called the Zhukov Bratva. I have been asked to head the search and capture of Sergei and return him to Moscow."

Tears were streaming down her face. "Oh God, no!"

I put my arm around her and held her tight. "I won't be doing this alone. My father has arranged for twelve of his best men to work with me. I can handle this."

"When?" she whispered.

"Not sure. I'm expecting a call from the second in command tonight. I will know more then."

"I'm afraid. If anything happened to you, I know I couldn't go on. You are everything to me." Her eyes met mine and I saw her fear.

"I've been out of the Bratva for quite a few years but I haven't forgotten what to do. Nothing will happen to me. Sergei will be outnumbered. I can handle this, Charlotte."

She began to cry again. "This Bratva is the Russian mafia, isn't it?"

I tightened my hold on her. "You have nothing to worry about, my love. I will always protect you. This one thing with Sergei will destroy us if not properly handled. The New York City police won't do anything. We have to take care of it ourselves."

She put my hand on her belly. "Our child won't be harmed in any way. I am taking care of this for our family," I assured her.

She lifted her eyes and met mine. "You are a good man. I don't want this to harm *you*."

"Believe me when I tell you this: I do not want to have to take care of this. I just have to."

"I believe you."

Just then, her cell began to buzz. She glanced over to the end table where it was sitting. It was her home security alert. "Oh no!"

She handed her phone to me.

I took her cell and stared at the screen. Adeline was clearly visible roaming around inside Charlotte's house. She wore a short, curly red-haired wig and heavy black-framed glasses. Even with this disguise, it was clearly Adeline. We watched in horror as she went to the oil portrait over the fireplace and sprayed bright red paint over the face of "Raven" while mumbling gross obscenities. She next went to the library office and ripped the priceless Vincent Van Gogh painting off the wall, fully exposing Charlotte's safe. Adeline sprayed a huge X on the front.

Next, Adeline ran up the stairs, then back down, holding one of Charlotte's suitcases. She grabbed the oil painting and made her way out to the garage. We watched as Adeline put the items into the trunk of Charlotte's car, started up the engine, and left with a screech of the tires. It was a mere seven minutes afterwards that a police siren was audible and an officer was outside of Charlotte's front door.

Adeline was long gone. She hadn't been inside the house long, but it was still enough time to wreak havoc. She ransacked Charlotte's closet, grabbing everything from underwear, shoes, tops, and jeans. She even grabbed one of Charlotte's designer silk evening gowns and matching shoes, and clutch purse.

Charlotte stared in disbelief as she and I went room to room, checking to see what had been ransacked.

The police did their due diligence—wrote up a report, took Charlotte's and my statements, took pictures. Also, the security system footage was forwarded to the department.

"It's a good thing you weren't here," I said to Charlotte once the police left.

"Yeah." She walked around her living room and stared at the Raven portrait. "Why?"

"Jealously makes people do terrible things."

"I can't believe she was able to get out of Copenhagen, let alone end up back in New York." I could see by her expression her mind was racing. "What do you think I should do? Should I phone Astrid and report what just happened?" she asked.

"Not sure. It's possible we shouldn't do anything but sit and wait. I suspect she might lead straight to my Uncle Sergei."

"Why do you think that?" she asked, skeptical but curious.

"She's alone and desperate. I suspect she still has Sergei's contact information."

"You're probably right. Can't someone track my car? That license plate is a dead giveaway."

"I feel certain at this point she's in some borough, like the projects in Queensbridge. She could steal a random license plate, throw yours away, then drive to a neighborhood where the car won't stand out so much."

"So now what?" Charlotte asked.

"Don't worry about this. I will take care of it." I put my arm around her waist. "Let's get anything you want from here and return to my place."

CHAPTER 55

Charlotte

I went to the kitchen and pulled out two favorite cookbooks, then went upstairs to my closet, packed up random items, and put them into a suitcase Adeline hadn't snatched.

I was back in the living room. "Do you mind carrying my suitcase downstairs?" I was protective of my pregnancy, not wanting to lift anything heavy.

"Of course," Dmitri said. His cell rang. He pulled out his phone and spoke in Russian. He hung up and walked upstairs.

Damn! That was the call he'd been waiting for. I guess it's game on. I felt like throwing up.

* * *

Eight o'clock. I knew I had to remain calm. Dmitri assured me he knew what he was doing and I didn't have anything to worry about. I knew absolutely nothing about his world—a world where a family had their own army and police. Should I feel safer? Truthfully, a part of me did. Then, there's another part of me that worried for his safety.

I had absolutely no confidence in conventional law enforcement and knew there wasn't any way in hell they would capture Adeline or Sergei. Both deserved to be held accountable for their deeds and the NYPD wouldn't do a damn thing. Maybe they couldn't.

Dmitri left an hour ago and I was alone in this penthouse. It would be smarter to get busy doing something rather than pacing the floor like a cat.

It was after midnight when he returned from his meeting. When he left, he was in his black Aston Martin. But when he returned, he pulled into the garage in a black SUV with tinted windows and bulletproof glass. I know this because he told me. Seemed he kept it at his office garage.

The change in him was astonishing—eyes of steel, tightened jaw, his chest even seemed to have grown broader. He was a certified alpha man. My confidence in him rose to a level I hadn't known possible. He was so sexy that I wanted to jump his bones. I didn't get the chance though, as he'd gone straight to his office, talking in Russian on a new phone I'd never seen before.

He did kiss me when he'd gotten home last night, but it wasn't the sensual kiss I'd grown accustomed to. It was the same when he left this morning, while I was still in bed.

I needed to work off some of the tension burning inside me. I might as well go to Dmitri's gym and swim in the pool. Anxiety wasn't good for the baby, and right now, my anxiety had climbed to the roof. Swimming used to be the balm for my soul. I knew it would help me now.

Dmitri gave me the passcode and programmed my handprint into the scanner. It felt strange getting on the elevator to go to the pool alone.

Fortunately, I remembered to get a swimsuit from my closet yesterday. Even though I knew this area was private, it felt strange to skinny dip without Dmitri.

The water was warm when I dove in. It felt liberating to swim the full length of the pool and back again. I kept swimming laps—changing from the different strokes I loved. When my energy was spent, I turned on to my back and allowed my body to float. I closed my eyes and allowed my thoughts to drift.

Dark images from that day in the crypt flooded my mind. Anger filled me for how I'd been a victim that day. I used all the power of persuasion I knew on Adeline. I remember trying to feel sisterly love for her, realizing she was deeply hurting. Now that was all gone. Adeline needed to be on the receiving end of the same crap she had been aiming at me.

I felt this darkness raging inside of me, and I didn't like it. This wasn't who I was. Even after the hell I went through in prison, I held on to what degree of light I could. But there was a shift in me. If Dmitri were here, I would talk it out with him. He calmed me, bringing reason and truth when my racing mind couldn't see it.

CHAPTER 56

Dmitri

I stepped off the elevator and into the living room fully expecting to see Charlotte. I walked to the bedroom and not finding her there, went from room to room of the entire penthouse. I went outside to the patio and not finding her there either, began to panic. The only place I'd not checked was the gym. I got back into the elevator and rode it down. When I stepped out, I was relieved to see through the glass wall she was floating on her back in the pool. I noted her eyes were closed.

"How's my mermaid?"

She opened her eyes and smiled. "Care to join me?"

I gave a wide grin, then quickly removed my clothes and dove into the pool, swimming underwater until I got to her. She met me with open arms and wrapped her legs around my waist. She kissed me and I deepened it.

My fingers traveled to her top and untied it, then threw it to the outside of the pool. I did the same with her swimsuit bottom—untying the sides and freeing her from it.

"I like you better naked." Her belly was starting to swell and her breasts were fuller—a reminder of our growing baby. I found her even more sexy.

She gave a sweet smile, but I saw lust in her eyes. "Is that right?"

She broke loose from me and swam under the water but I wasn't going to have any of that. I needed her underneath me.

I swam to her and grabbed her waist, then pulled her into my arms. I carried her to the other end of the pool and up the steps. Grabbing a towel from a side table, I wrapped it around her. "To the bedroom?"

She gave a lustful smile, then kissed me on the neck. "Yes."

I carried her to the bedroom and placed her in the center of the bed. I crawled over to her and kissed her lips. My kiss was tender at first but my hunger for her took hold and the kiss quickly became ravaging. She met me in like manner and I felt her hands around my back as her fingernails dragged down to my ass.

One hand traveled to her sex. She was soaking wet with desire when I put two fingers inside her and she clenched around me.

"Take me," she whispered.

I did just that—entering her gently but when she arched her back for more, I found myself pounding into her. I pumped and pumped, wanting to take everything I could from her. She squeezed my ass with her hands as she continued to climb that mountain with me. The more I took from her, the higher she coaxed me.

I felt her clamp tighter and I could hold back no more. I released with a loud growl that thundered about the room and I heard her call out my name.

I held her tight with her head was now resting inside my shoulder. The beast in me had been let loose and I was astounded she met me there. I kissed her on the top of her head. "God, I love you."

She kissed my chest, then lifted her chin to look into my eyes. "I love you too."

I reflected on my day. The meeting with my father's men had gone well. We orchestrated a plan to start our search for Sergei. All twelve were familiar with New York City's geography and would go straight to work. I expected a report the next morning.

I knew Charlotte wanted to know what was going on. But I didn't intend to tell her all that much. There wasn't any point in getting her anxiety any higher than it already was.

"Tomorrow afternoon is the appointment with the obstetrician. Are you going to be able to make that?" she asked. Her head remained tucked inside my shoulder.

"Yes, of course." I'd actually forgotten about it, too lost in the issues of Sergei and Adeline.

"I'm sure I can reschedule if it would be better for you," she said.

"Absolutely not. This takes priority." I held her even tighter, realizing too late I pounded her like a beast and she was carrying my child. A question for the doctor, maybe?

"I admit I'm anxious about this appointment. I'm hoping to learn a due date," she said.

"I'm sure we'll get that," I told her, hoping to set her at ease.

"I've been thinking about where our baby can have his room."

"*His* room?"

"I know, I know. A little boy keeps popping into my head. He has brown hair the same as you, and his eyes are the same color as yours."

"Maybe."

"The guest bedroom closest to ours would work well. What do you think?" she asked.

"That might work. Let's think about it." What I was really thinking about was more along the lines of how devastating it would be if she didn't carry our baby to term. Both of us would be shattered and dismantling a nursery would only add to the grief.

"Yeah." She kissed me on the chest. "I shouldn't get so excited so quickly. I've walked this path before."

"I've got to get you out of this penthouse. You've been cooped up here much too long. I think we would be safe to have dinner out at one of my restaurants if we use precautions."

"Yes, let's do it. I don't even care where we go."

I chuckled lightly, trying to lighten the mood. "It's three now and I can get reservations for six. Is that good?"

"Yes, yes, yes." She giggled, then hopped out of bed, and headed for the shower.

* * *

When Charlotte stepped into the living room wearing a dark royal blue form-fitting dress with tall strappy heels, she took my breath away. Her long, wavy hair was down, touching her shoulders just the way I liked it, and she wore her makeup light. Her natural beauty was perfect.

"Wow! You are absolutely stunning!" I walked to her and kissed her. I put my fingers in her hair, remembering the first time I did that while she sat in my barber chair. Her perfume was the same too and still intoxicated my senses.

"You look incredibly handsome yourself. I always swoon when you wear that suit and tie," she said and smiled sweetly. "It reminds me of the time you surprised me at that restaurant on our first date."

I laughed at that memory. I'd wanted to impress her—to shed that hippie look that was in character for the hair salon but not who I really was. "We better get out the door if we are going to make our dinner reservation."

She nodded and grabbed a jacket that matched her dress. I helped her put it on. She picked up her small clutch purse and we got into the elevator.

"This car is about as safe as a vehicle can get," I told her once were inside. "We should use this car exclusively until the Adeline and Sergei business is over with."

She glanced at me and smiled—her luscious lips giving me a hard-on. I knew I should get us on our way quickly before I grabbed her and we didn't leave at all.

CHAPTER 57

Dmitri

Haut De Gamme was an upscale restaurant I owned in the heart of Manhattan. I pulled the SUV into a covered entry and two valets greeted us. One opened Charlotte's door and the other took my car keys.

"Madam, shall we?"

Charlotte slipped her hand through my arm, and we made our way down the red-carpet runner to a wide entry door.

A young Latino man greeted us and opened the door. "Good evening, Mr. Zhukov. Madam."

The inside reception area was elegant but small. A middle-aged man greeted us from behind a wooden podium. "Mr. Zhukov, madam, please follow me."

The man led us through a crowded, dimly lit, long, narrow dining room. The white-clothed tables were arranged in intimate seating against the two side walls. We continued towards a back area, where a door led to a tiny private dining room with space only for a single table and it was already set for two.

"How nice," Charlotte said. The waiter had already taken our drink orders and she and I were alone.

"I like the privacy of it. The front desk won't let anyone in without a reservation, so we should be fine." I studied her.

She smiled wide. "I'm impressed. You own this, right?"

"It's been mine for the past two years."

"It feels great to be out. I'm not going to lie," she said.

I put my hand on top of hers on the table. "I bet. I appreciate how you've been so patient with needing to stay inside the penthouse. Just know it isn't forever."

"I know it's for security reasons, but that doesn't make it any easier," she said. "I love you for it, though. I just wish I felt more confident in *your* safety."

I wasn't certain our dining space was free of any listening devices. "We can talk more about this when we get home."

"I understand."

The waiter returned with our drinks—scotch for me and club soda with lime for her. The waiter took our meal orders and then left.

"My father wants to be present when we get married. But the thing is, I don't want to wait. How would you feel about a justice of the peace wedding?"

"I'm fine with that. But what's the rush? I was hoping to have our wedding at my Aunt Lydia's."

"Are you having second thoughts?" I asked, worried.

"No second thoughts. I'm ready to be your wife," she said.

"We can stop at a jewelry store after the obstetrician appointment tomorrow and buy wedding bands. Then, we could get married the next day."

She nodded.

The waiter returned with our food—filet basquaise for me, bar noir grillé for Charlotte. Fancy names for cod filet and grilled black sea bass, respectively.

"Is there something you aren't telling me?" she asked.

"I want to claim you as mine—that you aren't the widow of the late Crown Prince Lars Bjorn but you are Mrs. Dmitri Zhukov. I don't want the mother of my unborn child to have another man's last name."

"It bothers me too. Something we've not talked about, though, are our individual financial situations. Neither of us is poor," she said.

"What do you want to do?" I asked.

"I don't want any secrets. I'll lay all mine out and I'm hoping you will do the same."

"Agreed. Is there anything else?"

"Nothing we have to do before we marry, like you introducing me to your parents. I want to meet them, even if we have to travel to where they are."

"Do you want a pre-nup?"

"Not unless you do."

"No. To me, a pre-nup means someone is already putting together an exit plan, even before they get married."

She smiled. "I feel better now. This is something that's been on my mind."

"Do you already have a financial manager?"

"For some of my money in the US, I do. His name is Oscar Benet and he is a vice president at Vanguard Westend Bank. It doesn't have to stay that way. I just needed someone while I was in Bedford Hills. I have off-shore accounts I've managed myself. Basically, that money has just been sitting there for over six years. There's actually one million in cash in my home safe. I have stocks and CDs too. I'm sure I can use advice on all that. You're the one with the MBA."

"We'll sit down together and work out all the details. Is there anything else?"

"I don't think so. How about you?" she asked.

I felt myself smiling wide. "No. I'm ready for us to be married."

"Me too."

We had just finished eating when a three-piece band began to play.

"Would you like to dance?"

A wide smile appeared on her face. "Yes."

A piano player, drummer, and a bass player were on a stage riser. A small dance floor was right in front. The male piano player began to sing "Sway," a Michael Bublé song.

I stood and offered my hand, and led her through the doorway to the very back of the main dining room. I led her to the dance floor. We were the only ones there. I took her hand into mine and put my other around her waist; she put her free hand around my neck. Soon we were gliding on the dance floor. She followed my lead easily. It wasn't long before I felt all worries fading away. Her in my arms and dancing was magic. It was exactly like the very first time we danced and she melted into my arms.

CHAPTER 58

Charlotte

We were back in the penthouse living room. "Thank you for a lovely evening."

He winked, then removed his suit jacket and draped it over a kitchen chair. "The night is still young."

"It is." I gave him a naughty look, removed my jacket, and put it on top of his. I reached behind my back and unzipped, letting the dress fall to the floor and stepped out of it. Now only in strappy heels and a sheer navy bra and matching panties, I stepped back while maintaining eye contact.

"My lovely minx," he said with a raspy voice and lusty eyes.

I grinned. "You have no idea."

He stepped forward to undo my bra, but I stepped back again. Turning so my back was facing him, I unfastened my bra. I bent forward, showing him my ass, and I dropped the bra to the floor.

"Nice," he crooned.

I raised up and turned to face him with my hands across my breasts. I massaged them seductively and pinched my nipples lightly, throwing my head back with a soft moan. I took my hand and pushed aside the gusset of my panties. I began to finger myself, before putting my finger into my mouth and sucking it clean.

"Oh yeah," he encouraged me.

I stepped towards him and guided him towards the sofa and he sat. I got on my knees in front of him and slowly unbuttoned his shirt. I put my hands on the top of his thighs and moved closer between his legs. When my lips met his, his tongue went into my mouth in a hungry and savage way, further igniting the raging fire inside me.

My hand traveled to the large bulge in his pants and I ran my palm over him.

His hands reached up to me, but I wiggled out of them and traveled my tongue down the side of his neck, down his chest, pausing only to suck one of his nipples and trace my teeth against the other.

He gave a low growl. "My God, woman."

My eyes met his and I grinned wickedly. My tongue traveled further downward. When I got to his belt, I unfastened it and undid his pants. He raised his ass up so I could pull his pants and boxers off at the same time.

My hands now on the base of his cock, I traced the head with my tongue and moaned as I took him in my mouth and swirled my tongue through his pre-cum. I took him into my mouth as far as I could and I began bobbing up and down, finding a solid rhythm.

I felt him getting more rigid as I gently pulled back and traced my tongue over his balls while my hands remained at the base of his cock.

"Woman, you're killing me," he growled.

"Patience, my love."

I rose from my knees and straddled him, rubbing my wetness against his rigid cock before I put him inside of me. I began going up and down on him deeper, faster and faster.

"My God," he called out, then he grabbed behind my knees, and stood up off the couch—still inside of me—and walked us to the bedroom.

He stopped at the end of the bed, lifted me up, and crawled us to the center. He began thrusting and pounding, allowing his beast to take hold as he held both my hands over my head.

"Come for me," he growled.

I clenched my inner muscles around him and arched my back.

"DMITRI!"

He let me ride the wave till I finally came down, then he rolled us over so I was on top of him. I began going up and down on him, faster and faster.

"Come with me, love."

I felt him swell larger and harder and my inner muscles clenched around him again. I knew he was close and so was I.

He let out a thunderous growl. I screamed out. We reached the same place together.

CHAPTER 59

Dmitri

It was seven and I had just finished my workout with my trainer. Charlotte was busy in the kitchen preparing breakfast when my phone rang. I glanced at the number before I answered it. "*Da?*" I walked to my office and sat. We spoke in Russian.

"Hi, boss. We have a lead," Gustav said.

"Okay. Tell me more."

"We found the girl outside an apartment in Queens. She knocked on a door, no one answered, and she got back into the stolen red Mercedes. She switched license plates."

"Any sign of Sergei?" I asked.

"Not yet, but we will keep a tail on the girl. She might lead us right to him," Gustav said.

"When you locate Sergei, call me first. I must deal with him myself. Just keep him till I get there. Same for the girl."

"Will do," Gustav said.

We ended the call, and I walked to the kitchen. "That was the call I'd been waiting for. Adeline has been located."

"What now?" she asked.

"They will keep a tail on her. I'm convinced she'll run to Sergei."

"That's good," she said.

"Do I have time for a shower before breakfast?" I asked.

"You do. I'm making Belgin waffles with sausage on the side. I want to cut up fruit too. So take your time."

I stepped into the shower and my thoughts traveled to my father. I wanted to phone him today to share the latest. This needed to be done before we left for the obstetrician as there was a seven-hour time difference.

* * *

Breakfast was complete and Charlotte was now in the shower. I took the opportunity to place the call to my father.

"Hello, my son," Father answered on the second ring.

"Papa. I hope you and Marta are well." I wanted to get the small talk over with first. My father expected that.

"We are well. Do you have news for me?" Father asked.

"Yes. The Danish princess is definitely back in New York and I'm certain she will lead us straight to Sergei. Gustav called and said they are tailing her."

"That's interesting for sure," Father said.

"On another matter. Charlotte and I will marry tomorrow at the courthouse. I don't want to wait."

"Why the rush?"

"She is pregnant," I offered as explanation.

"An heir. Congratulations."

"I wanted you to be here for the wedding, but it was before I knew Charlotte was pregnant. We can plan a time for us to get together at a later date. She's anxious to meet you."

"And I her," my father said. "How far along is she?"

"We will find out today at the doctor's office."

"Keep me posted, Son."

"I will."

I pulled open the lower left-hand drawer of my desk, pulled out my gun, and loaded it. I took out the concealed-carry holster and sat it on my desk. I hadn't carried a gun since my father had gone back to Moscow. A familiar knowing filled me—an invisible steel armor I'd been trained to wear.

I picked up my cell phone and sent Gustav a text: *Any updates?*

The reply was quick: *Still tailing her. She'd stopped into a parking lot for a while and got on her phone, then got back on the road and is still driving.*

My reply: *I'll check in afterwards.*

Gustav replied: *Okay, Boss.*

* * *

At nine-fifteen, we pulled into the parking lot of Dr. Marian Levitz, obstetrics and gynecology. I got out, walked to Charlotte's side, and opened her door. I touched the holster inside my jacket, secure it was where it needed to be. After a perusal of the parking lot to ensure things were safe, I helped Charlotte out of the car.

We entered the modern building and immediately saw the receptionist, a middle-aged woman with short brown hair dressed in medical scrubs. "May I help you?" she asked.

"I'm Charlotte Bjorn and I'm here to see Dr. Levitz."

The woman checked Charlotte in and told us to have a seat in the waiting room, a comfortable and modern space with several sofas, cushy chairs, and tall live plants in two corners and on several side tables. There were two tasteful framed prints on the walls. One was of a beach scene and the other a mountain scene.

Charlotte took my hand and held it as we sat beside each other on the upholstered sofa. There was only one other woman in the waiting room and she was very pregnant and alone.

"Ms. Charlotte Bjorn?" said a woman at an open door. She wore the same scrubs as the receptionist and had a clipboard in her hand.

"Yes," I said. I stood up with Charlotte.

"Who are you, sir?"

"I am Dmitri Zhukov, Charlotte's fiancé and father of our baby."

The woman nodded and smiled. "Please follow me."

Charlotte was soon in a hospital gown and sitting on the exam table. I was in a chair alongside the wall of the small exam room.

There was a quick knocking at the door, then a woman in her early fifties walked in. She was just over five feet tall, medium build, with short graying hair and with dark-framed glasses. She wore a white lab coat with her name embroidered on the upper lefthand pocket.

"Hello, Ms. Bjorn. I'm Dr. Marian Levitz." She glanced at me.

"Nice to meet you. My fiancé Dmitri Zhukov is here with me," Charlotte said.

She took a seat near a computer. "Great to meet you both."

The doctor talked to us about what to expect from the appointment and the subsequent ones. Next, she did her examination. "You are over four months along. I would like to go ahead and do an ultrasound today, if you are both okay with this?"

We both agreed and were soon ushered to a room down the hall. A technician came in and began the ultrasound. "Yes, there's your little one," she said and pointed to the monitor. "He looks perfect."

"A boy!" Charlotte glanced at me and I felt myself smiling wide as I held Charlotte's hand.

"Yes, definitely a boy."

CHAPTER 60

Adeline

I drove through the Taco Bell in Queens, bought a burrito, then pulled into a parking spot. I started to take a bite of my burrito when my phone rang. The caller ID showed it was Sergei. "Hello, handsome, have you missed me?"

"My sweet, of course I have missed you. It was most unfortunate how things ended with us. How are you doing?" he asked.

"I'm fine and now in NYC."

"Is that right? How is that?" Sergei asked.

"I have my ways. I miss you so much," I said, hoping to get his interest.

"It is most fortunate. I am also in the city. We should get together."

"I was hoping you would want to see me."

"Where are you staying?" he asked.

"I haven't checked into a hotel yet."

"In that case, you should stay with me. Would you like that?" he asked.

"Yes, but only if I can sleep in the bed with you." I wanted to be sure to hook him. I knew his preferences and sincerely doubted he'd been able to get that from anyone else.

His voice was husky. "Oh, is that what you want?"

I knew I had his full attention. I gave my sexy voice. "I do. You are a sexy man. Only you can satisfy me."

"You want it, don't you?"

"You know I do."

"Go to the episcopal church parking lot in Queens. Stay there. Two of my men will get you. They will be in a black SUV. You will recognize them," he said.

"I can't wait to see you."

"Yes, my princess."

I quickly removed the wig and ran my fingers through my long black hair. It fell in soft waves down my back. I removed the thick-framed glasses, checked my makeup in the mirror, and applied some lip gloss I found in my purse. Last of all, I gave a single spray of perfume.

Less than twenty minutes later, I pulled into the church parking lot. The black SUV was already there. I turned off the engine and watched as two men got out of the SUV. I recognized them—the same men who escorted me to that wretched fishing boat.

"Ms. Bjorn," Dax said. "We are here to transport you to Mr. Zhukov."

"Hi, Dax. I need you to get my suitcase from the trunk."

He nodded, followed me to the open trunk, then took the suitcase and carried it to the SUV. I got in the backseat and Dax sat beside me.

"Hello, Radimir." He was the driver. He nodded.

"What do you want to do with the car?" Dax asked.

"Nothing. Just leave it. I don't want it."

He smirked. "Very well."

CHAPTER 61

Dmitri

Charlotte and I were just exiting the city clerk's office with our completed marriage license. We already purchased matching wedding bands. My cell beeped with a text message. I waited till we were in the SUV before reading the message.

GUSTAV: *The girl was picked up in a black SUV. Following them now. She left the car in a church parking lot in Queens*

ME: *Let the other men know to be on high alert, but don't send them in yet. Keep me posted*

GUSTAV: *Will do, Boss*

I took my gun out of the glove compartment and placed onto the center console.

"Is everything okay?" Charlotte asked.

"Yes."

We drove silently till we got to my building and entered the garage. I walked to her side of the car and opened the door. We rode the elevator to the penthouse.

We stepped into the living room, and I immediately walked to my home office. I sat at my desk and placed my gun inside the drawer and closed it. Then, I picked up my cell phone and dialed my father. The phone only rang once.

"*Da?*" We spoke in Russian.

"Adeline was picked up by two of Sergei's men. Gustov and Uri are tailing them. How do you plan to get him to Moscow once I have him?"

"I'll send one of my jets for Sergei and my men," my father said.

"What about Sergei's men?" I asked.

"Shoot them," he said bluntly.

"And the girl?"

"Send her back to her mother. She should deal with her. Not our problem."

I sat back in my desk chair. Darkness filled me. The life I worked so hard to be free from was back. I heard a light knocking on my office door. It was Charlotte. "Please come in and have a seat."

"Talk to me," she said.

I took a deep breath and stiffened. "Adeline was picked up by two of Sergei's men in a black SUV. She left your car in a church parking lot in Queens. I'll wait a day, then get one of my men to bring it back to your house. It's best we don't get the police involved."

"I understand," she said.

"I have some things I don't want to do but it is the only way. Do you trust me?" I asked.

"With my life," she said and walked over and gave me a kiss. "You are from a world I don't understand. But I know *you*. I trust *you*."

"Thank you." I pulled her to my lap. "When I have Adeline, would you like to talk to her before we send her back to Astrid?"

"Yes," she said. "I'm tired of being her victim. She needs a taste of her own medicine. I learned a thing or two during my six years in lockup. I had to in order to survive."

"You have the right to do that." I placed my hand on her belly. "Just don't forget, our baby is growing inside you. You can't allow yourself to get overly stressed."

"I know," she said.

"Are you ready for tomorrow at eleven?"

"Yes, I really am."

"Two of my men will escort us to the city clerk's office for our wedding. It's a safety thing."

"I understand."

* * *

Charlotte was in the walk-in closet preparing to dress for our wedding ceremony at the courthouse. I was on my side of the closet about to put on a pair of pants when my cell beeped from on top of the leather bench in the center of the closet. I reached over and picked it up.

GUSTAV: *Sergei is definitely with the girl at a house in Soho*

ME: *I need to know how many men he has with him. Check on their security*

GUSTAV: *I only see two men outside. Not sure of inside*

ME: *Keep me posted. And be careful*

GUSTAV: *Will do, Boss*

"Is everything okay?" Charlotte asked.

"Yes."

"Is there anything you can tell me?"

"Not yet." We just finished dressing when my phone rang. I took the call in Russian. "Our ride is here. We should go to the lobby and the car will be out front."

"Sounds good," she said and we got into the elevator.

CHAPTER 62

Charlotte

Our wedding ceremony was a stark contrast from the gala Lars and I had. But I felt it was right for Dmitri and me. The love we shared didn't need to be a pomp-and-pageantry event. When we put on our wedding bands, I felt so much love for him. I knew I always would.

A secretary at the city clerk's office offered to take our picture. I was grateful I wore a solid white knee-length lace dress. The secretary even had a fake bouquet for me to hold. Dmitri had worn his black suit and we did make a lovely pair. I planned to have a bridal portrait painted at a later time with a proper gown. I wanted this. It would replace that Raven portrait Adeline had ruined. Fitting, as I hated that portrait.

Dmitri arranged for us to go to dinner and out dancing later that evening. It was nice, but two hours into our evening, his cell buzzed. We needed to leave; his men had captured Sergei and he needed to be there.

"After all of this is over, I'll take you on a proper honeymoon," he promised.

So, once again, I was alone in the penthouse. My anxiety was through the roof and it was pointless. I knew Dmitri didn't want to be involved with the Bratva, but he was involved now. There wasn't any other way to define it. How was that going to affect us in the future?

CHAPTER 63

Dmitri

I arrived at the location in Soho. Five of my men were outside.

"Hi, boss."

"Boris." I nodded. "Who's inside?"

"Gustav and the rest of our men. Sergei only had five men. We shot them dead before they shot us."

"You did good." I walked to the back sliding glass door and went inside. Gustav met me. "Where's the girl?"

"Alexei and Vlad have her in a bedroom in the back," Gustav said.

"How much did the girl see?"

"Not much. When we found her, she was in a back bedroom sleeping. We kept her there," Gustav said.

"Good," I said, walking to the living room. Sergei was tied to a chair. "Uncle." I pulled out a chair from the adjoining dining room. I flipped the chair around so my hands rested on top of the back of the chair as I straddled it, facing Sergei. "You're in some deep shit."

"It appears so," Sergei said.

"What do you have to say for yourself?"

"There seems to be some misunderstanding."

"About what? That you stole seventeen billion dollars from my father and Igor?" I asked incredulously.

"Hmm, let me see. I don't know anything about that," Sergei denied.

"I didn't expect you to admit to it. The thing is, what's left of the funds has been recovered by my father and it has your fingerprints all over it."

"Is that right? So, now what are you going to do, Nephew?"

"Looks like you get a one-way trip to Moscow, compliments of your brother."

"That's not necessary, Nephew. We should strike a deal," he said, attempting to bargain.

I gave a roaring laugh. "You're in no position to make any deal." I stood and walked to the kitchen down the hall. I phoned my father; it only rang once.

"Yes?" my father answered.

"We've got him."

"Good. Get him to the Teterboro airport in an hour. I already have my jet there. Gustav and Uri will handle things from then on. Good work, Son."

"Of the other men, who stays here and who goes back to you?"

"You keep four men and send the rest back with Sergei."

"Which four? I'm not Bratva—only your son. You are the *Pakhan*."

"Yes, I am *Pakhan*. But as my son, you are expected to take my place when I'm gone," my father said.

I wanted to wait until Sergei was gone before I brought Charlotte to see Adeline. There needed to be some cleanup done here first. I walked back into the living room.

"Looks like you get the express to Moscow," I told my uncle. "Aklm and Polvalaski, stay here." Both nodded. "Gustav and Uri, come with me."

I led both men to the kitchen. "*Pakhan* wants you two in charge of getting Sergei back to Moscow. Gustav, you will be first in command, and Uri, you will be second. The Bratva jet is at the Teterboro airport and will leave in an hour. Four men are staying here with me and all the others will travel back with you on the jet."

"Yeah, boss, got it," Gustav said.

Uri nodded.

"Are you sure Sergei only had five men?"

"That's all we found here. We've been watching this place for several days and no one else has been around," Gustav said.

"Which means there could still be more. I don't want to take chances. We need to get this place cleaned up quickly and leave. I'll take the girl with me."

"What should we do with the bodies?" Uri asked.

"Dump them off the Brooklyn Bridge."

CHAPTER 64

Charlotte

It was now seven and I had only slept a few hours. I was struggling—why hadn't he called? I couldn't live like this forever. The world of the Bratva was a terrifying mystery.

I decided to get out of bed and walked to the kitchen for some coffee. I put a pod into our Keurig and a piece of bread into the toaster. I was just finishing my coffee when my phone rang. It was Dmitri.

"Good morning, beautiful."

"Good morning, love. Please tell me all is well and you will be home soon."

"Yes and yes. Do you still want to see Adeline?"

"Absolutely! Do you have her?" I asked, eager.

"Sure do. Can I take her to your house?"

"Yes. I don't want her here."

"I agree. My guys will stay with her there and I'll come home and get you," he said.

"Sounds good."

When Dmitri came home, he found me inside our closet. "How's my girl?" he asked.

I turned and went to him, still in my bra and panties. I stood on my tiptoes and kissed him. "I won't be long. Just trying to find a pair of pants I can still zip."

"My little guy is growing," he said as he put his hand on my belly. "I'll take you shopping once this thing is settled."

I kissed him again and he walked to the living room.

I ended up with charcoal grey leggings, an oversized lavender sweater, and black shortie boots. I grabbed my hobo purse and went to the living room.

"Are we ready?" he asked.

"Yes."

The drive to my house was somber. I pondered how I wanted to confront Adeline. Should I beat her up? Or make Adeline listen to what I wanted to say?

Dmitri put his hand on my thigh and I put my hand on top of his. He pulled around the back of my house, opened the garage, and drove inside.

I was the first to go inside. Once in the kitchen, I found Adeline tied to a kitchen chair, facing me. All the blinds on the windows were closed. Two of Dmitri's men were sitting at the table.

"Well, well, well, look what the cat dragged in."

"You bitch!" Adeline spat at me.

I pulled my hand back and slapped Adeline hard across the face. I wondered if I broke one of her teeth.

"Just try spitting at me again, you idiot." I paced in front of her slowly. "Now, let me see. You framed me for murder and I went to prison for six years." I threw back my fist and nailed Adeline's shoulder. She wailed. "You trashed my house, stole my car, my painting, and clothes. Oh yes, you also shot me. Hmm, what should I do with you?"

Adeline smirked. "You can't do anything to me. My mother is queen."

"That's interesting. You know, I could kill you and dump your body off the bridge in Brooklyn. Your mother would never know who did it. Actually, maybe I will. You definitely deserve it," I said. "What do you think, Adeline?"

"Just shoot me. I don't care," Adeline said.

"Oh no. Just shooting you is too merciful. You don't deserve that at all. Maybe I will take one of my kitchen knives and start carving you up. Nice and slow. I will cut out your tongue first, then tape your mouth shut so you can't even scream. How would you like that?"

Adeline's face was a deep red and there was terror in her eyes.

I went to my kitchen drawer. I pulled out a large butcher knife and walked back to Adeline. "This is a nice carving instrument," I said, waving it in front of Adeline's face. I grabbed a large handful of her hair and whacked it off with the knife. "Oops!" I threw the hair at her.

"*Stop*! I'm sorry, Charlotte," she cried.

"What? I don't think I heard you." I was still waving the knife.

"I said I'm sorry. I shouldn't have done all that shit to you."

"Why did you do it?"

"Because I hate you! That's why!"

"Not a good reason, Adeline," I said sarcastically before grabbing another handful of hair and whacking it off. "Oops." I threw the hair in Adeline's face.

"*Stop*!" Adeline screamed. "If you let me go, I promise to never bother you again."

"Just like that, huh?" I grabbed the last handful of long hair and whacked it off, leaving Adeline with a full head of choppy, uneven, short hair.

"What else can I do?" Adeline asked.

"If I *ever* see you, hear from you, or learn you did anything at all to defame me, I will come after you and carve you up into tiny little pieces and put them into a black garbage bag for the trash collectors to pick up. Do you understand?"

Adeline nodded.

"I didn't hear you."

"Okay! You won't ever hear from me again."

"That also includes you being a tattle to your mother about our little encounter right now. If I find out *anything*, I will come for you and you won't walk away," I vowed.

"Okay… I'll keep quiet," Adeline said.

I pulled my fist back and punched Adeline's jaw hard; she screamed.

"That's so you know I mean business." I glanced at Dmitri and nodded.

Dmitri stepped forward and faced Adeline. "You can be sure I'll come after you if you don't comply with what Charlotte said."

Adeline nodded.

"You're lucky we're sending you back to your mother. The police here would love to get ahold of you. Attempted murder, breaking and entering, stealing a car, framing Charlotte. These crimes would surely buy you room and board at Bedford Hills. You might even be able to team up with Charlotte's old roomies there."

Adeline was trembling.

Dmitri glanced at me and I nodded. He stood and motioned. "I'm impressed how you handled Adeline. She deserved all that and more."

"Yeah, she did, and I would have gone further if I wasn't pregnant."

"Do you want to call Astrid or should I?" Dmitri asked.

"I should be the one. I'll do it now."

* * *

I dialed Astrid's private number. She answered on the third ring. "Hello, dear."

"I hope you are doing well."

"Yes, I am."

"I wanted to let you know that Dmitri and I have Adeline. We were wondering if you wanted her to come back to you?"

"Yes, I absolutely do," Astrid said. "Please tell me how you got her."

"Actually, she broke into my house, spray painted red everywhere, took a priceless painting, and stole my car. I have her on my security video doing it. She was with Dmitri's Uncle Sergei, who is wanted in Moscow. Dmitri was able to capture Sergei and arrange for him to be returned to Russia. Adeline was there with him."

"I'll send my jet to get her and Royal Guards to secure her. It will arrive tomorrow afternoon. I will have the pilot text you with the time," Astrid said. "I am so sorry she has caused you so much grief."

"Thank you for saying that, but it's not your fault. Adeline needs psychological help."

"Yes, she does."

"I tried to talk to her, but she only spat at me and mocked me. I ended up slapping her in the face. Her spitting was the last straw. So when you see her bruised up face, you know it was from me."

"I understand and won't hold that against you," Astrid said.

CHAPTER 65

Dmitri

It had been four weeks since Sergei was returned to Moscow and Adeline to Copenhagen. Life had calmed for us. We were sitting in the media room and at the bar; we had just finished eating dinner. I was pouring myself a whiskey. Charlotte was seated on a barstool, drinking mineral water.

"Would you like to go shopping tomorrow?"

"That would be nice. Where were you thinking?" she asked.

"There's a maternity wear shop on the Upper East Side that might be nice."

"I would love that. My clothes are only getting tighter."

"As they should." I grinned and walked to her and placed my hand on her belly. "You are sexy as hell—even more so pregnant."

"I hope you still think that when it's time to have our baby," she said.

I kissed her on the lips. "You can be sure I will."

"Have you heard anything more from your father about Sergei?"

"No, and I need to call him. I've been dragging my feet on that because I don't want any further involvement."

"I get it," she said. "I haven't phoned Astrid either. I'm not sure that I will. The whole thing was terrible. Now I have to figure out what to do about my house."

"Did you want to keep it?" I asked gently.

"No. It needs to be sold but it can't be in its current condition," she said.

"It would be easy enough to hire people to handle things. We just need to make sure all the items you want to keep are removed first."

"You know what my closet looks like, so that might be a problem."

"I promised you a girl-room and I will deliver. I know just the person to call who can make that happen. This penthouse is over ten thousand square feet. There is definitely space. Anything else?"

"My cookbooks, kitchen knives, and wines," she said. The priceless painting was never recovered.

"Done. Anything else?"

"I don't think so. The things inside that house represent the past. I only want to focus on our future."

"What about your car?" It was back in her garage.

"That should be sold too."

"You've got things inside your safe. What about those?" I asked.

"The cash can be deposited into the bank. The rest is what I wanted you to look over," she said.

I was grateful she fully trusted me. She didn't have as much money as I did, but still had a substantial amount. I motioned for us to walk over to the couch to sit. "We can look over the financials within the next day or so. The other items I can arrange to be handled for you. I don't want you doing any heavy lifting. I'll call the architect and designer tomorrow to get your girl-room started. I'll also include the nursery."

"That sounds wonderful." She began to chew the inside of her lip.

I noticed she always did that when there was something she wanted to say but was hesitating. "What are you thinking about?"

Her eyes met mine. "I want to hold off on furnishing the nursery until my eighth month."

"You heard what the doctor said. Everything looks perfect," I said, confused.

"And I truly hope nothing changes," she said.

I pulled her onto my lap from where she was sitting beside me. "We can do whatever you want but I still want to plan."

She kissed me on the neck. "What would you like to name him?"

"What would you like?"

"I want you to choose. You are the father and he is your son. It should be you," she said.

"Are you absolutely sure of that?"

"Yes, I am sure," she replied.

"Are you opposed to a Russian name?"

"Of course not," she assured.

"I want to name him Nikolai."

"I like that. What about his middle name?"

"In Russia, the child's middle name is the first name of the father with *-yovych* at the end, which means 'son of.' So, it would be Nikolai Dmitriovych Zhukov."

"Very nice. So that would mean your middle name is Andreiyovych," she said.

"Yep." Just then my cell rang. I glanced down. "That's my father."

She nodded and jumped up from my lap.

We spoke in Russian. "Hello, Papa."

"Good evening, my son."

"I hope you are well."

"Yes, very well," Father said.

"How is Uncle?" I asked.

"I gave him to Igor to deal with, and it appears Sergei is now dead," Father said.

"He was a traitor. But he was your brother, so it can't be easy for you."

"No, it's not easy. But that is not why I called. How is your lovely wife doing?"

"She's doing well. The doctor said Charlotte is into her fifth month of pregnancy and we will have a son."

"Wonderful!"

"His name will be Nikolai Dmitriovych Zhukov."

"A nice strong name. I'm glad you chose a Russian name," Father said.

"Charlotte asked me to name our son and she likes the name I chose."

"You have a smart woman," Father said.

"I know. I still can't believe she's my wife," I said, shaking my head a little in disbelief.

"Talking about wives, I ran into Tatiana a few days ago. She was asking about you," Father said.

"Is that right?" I asked.

"She still hasn't gotten over you."

"That was an arranged marriage for you to form an alliance with the Solvaviche Bratva. It was hell for me. I tried, it was a mistake, I moved on. She should as well."

"I agree. Unfortunately, her father is still pissed. Apparently, she has gone to him recently and has asked him to get you back."

"Hell no!"

"I'm just the messenger."

"I don't get it. That was over fifteen years ago. Why now?"

"She claims she had your son," Father said.

"No way! She's bluffing. We only had sex twice the whole time we were married and I wore a condom both times. It was in the first month we were married, and clearly she wasn't pregnant those last months. She's stupid if she thinks I would fall for that," I raged. "A paternity test would easily confirm it."

"Seems she wants her son to be deemed your heir."

"What do you suggest?"

"Let it play out. See if she does anything. Since she never remarried, it's possible she just wants her son to believe you're his father. Perhaps she is ashamed of who the real father is," Father said.

"The whole thing is ludicrous. If she pushes, I will demand a paternity test and I want it done in the States. That way I can be sure her father doesn't try to taint the results in his daughter's direction."

"That's a good plan. But make no mistake: she intends to make trouble, though I cannot understand what she believes she will gain."

"With her, it's hard telling. Thank you for letting me know."

"I'm hoping you and Charlotte will plan a visit here soon," Father said.

"I'll discuss it with her. She mentioned her desire to meet you and also my mother. Charlotte doesn't have any family members still living with the exception of an aunt in California."

"I will send my private jet for your travel," Father said

"I appreciate your offer."

I contemplated what my father had shared. I knew it wasn't biologically possible I was the father of Tatiana's son. But why would she be stupid enough to try this? I knew I could easily call her bluff, but perhaps an interaction with me was all she really wanted. I had no desire for that either.

"I see you're off the phone," Charlotte said. "Is everything okay? Your expression tells me it isn't."

I'd not heard her return. "Everything is fine," I lied.

CHAPTER 66

Charlotte

The morning was quite lovely as we stepped out of Dmitri's SUV in the parking lot of In The Mommy Way maternity shop. The air was slightly chilly and I wrapped my blazer as tight as I could around my belly. It definitely wouldn't button.

I think Dmitri was more excited than I was when we began shopping. He insisted on picking out items and me trying them on for him. I was surprised by a few things he'd chosen, and of course, I agreed to everything. I wouldn't deny him this pleasure. By the time we finished, there were so many items, Dmitri had to make three different trips to the car. I sincerely hoped it all would fit on my side of Dmitri's closet.

I found myself touching my belly frequently. It must be an instinctive pregnancy thing since I didn't even realize I was doing it. Dmitri did it too when he was close to me. I'd never seen a man want a child the way he did. I found myself comparing the experience to that which Lars and I shared. Lars wasn't ever as involved. He was more accepting and considerate, but never seemed as attracted to me as he was before I became pregnant. Dmitri's affections for me were the polar opposite and I so loved him for it. Also, the sexual aspect was different—more intense, exciting—and I craved him almost constantly. Lars stayed away, like being pregnant was a disease. I did love Lars, but it was more of a worshipful love. I saw it clearly, so different from Dmitri and me.

I never thought of these things before. I just assumed all expectant fathers were this way. How wrong I was!

We just got back on the street to begin our ride home when Dmitri's cell rang. He picked it up and took the call in Russian; I could tell by his expression and tone of his voice he was angry. I thought something was wrong last night when he spoke with his father. Dmitri had brushed it off but now I was certain something was amiss. Again, he wouldn't tell me anything when I asked him. I was positive it was Bratva related.

I began to worry more and more. How did this Bratva affect us? Or, more importantly, how would it affect our son? I was really a simple girl—from a simple background—and naïve in so many ways.

Back at the penthouse, dinner was over and we were sitting in the media room. He poured a glass of whiskey and I had a glass of ginger ale, sitting side by side as we always did.

"I know something is wrong and you're not telling me."

He took another swallow of his drink, a large one. "Yeah, you're right."

"That last phone call was from Petr, one of my men. He said my ex-wife is in town and wants to see me. She asked for my address and phone number. I told him not to give it to her," he said.

I was surprised at his concern over his ex. "Why not?"

Dmitri stood and walked to the bar and refilled his empty glass. His jaw tightened as he stared across the room. I knew this was bad and he didn't want to tell me. He was back at the couch next to me. "Before I tell you this latest, I need to tell you the whole story first."

"Please do. I want to know it all."

"I told you previously my marriage to Tatiana was made in hell, but that's not the half of it. It was actually an arranged marriage—a way to form an alliance between two rival Bratva families. Not my idea but I did agree to it to please my father. From day one, it was hell. There was zero chemistry; actually, we only had sex twice in that first month and never again. Both times I wore a condom. I'm telling you this because she's trying to claim her fifteen-year-old son is mine. It's not possible," he said.

"Wow! That's huge."

"There's more. By her claiming her son is mine and a Zhukov heir, it allows her family dominance over mine. Seems her father is pushing for this. He's been angry all these years because the marriage didn't work out."

My stomach was now in knots. "Now what?"

"My father said he ran into her a few days ago, and he suggested I just wait for her to make a move. Looks like she has. Now I have to deal with her. Since a paternity test would prove I'm not the father and she knows it, I seriously doubt she will agree to any test. Even if she does agree, unless the lab here in the US handles it, her father can make false claims. And it would start an all-out war between my family and hers," Dmitri said.

"What are you going to do?" I asked.

"I have to talk to her, but not here. I also need reinforcements because I can't imagine she's alone."

"That can only mean one thing. If she murders you and a DNA test isn't done, her claim might stand."

"Exactly."

"How can you safely meet up with her?"

"At my office in the city, with my four men at my side. What I learn will determine what future steps I take," he said.

"How strong of a presence does her family have here in the city?"

"I'm not sure. I haven't kept up with that since I disassociated with the Zhukov Bratva. Now, I'm back in it and it really, really sucks!"

I knew my world could be shattered but said, "I want you to teach me how to use a gun."

He pulled me onto his lap, held me tight, and kissed the top of my head. "I can handle all of this. I've been groomed since the age of eleven to be the next *Pakhan*. We may need to go to Moscow," he said.

I sat quietly on his lap for a while. "I will go anywhere with you."

"Tell me what you're thinking about?" he asked.

"I want to know about your childhood in Russia. You've never told me anything about it. I sense you went through a lot."

"That's a story for another day, my love. It isn't anything I would want anyone else to go through. I promise you, I am a changed man. I'm not that younger man anymore," he said.

CHAPTER 67

Dmitri

It was ten on Sunday morning. I was in my office with Viktor and Petr, two of my men. Boris and Maksim, my other two men, were in the reception area of the lobby. All my professional staff were off for the weekend. Tatiana was due to arrive at any moment.

There was a knock on my office door.

"Yes?" I called out.

The door opened and Boris stepped inside and closed the door. "Tatiana's here and she is alone," he said.

"Petr, get Maksim, and you and he nose around the building. I'm not convinced she truly came here alone."

"Yes, boss. I'm on it," Petr said and walked out.

"Boris, keep vigil in the lobby."

Boris nodded and asked, "Should I bring her in here?"

"Yes."

Viktor took a seat on the sofa on the right wall.

Tatiana stepped into my office wearing a pink blazer and matching trousers. I barely recognized her. There was a hardness in her face.

"Tatiana," I stood and greeted her, then motioned for her to have a seat in front of my desk. I was careful not to be warm towards her.

"Dmitri. It's nice to see you," she said in Russian and glanced around my office. Her eyes fell on a picture of Charlotte on a shelf.

"What brings you to my neck of the woods?"

"I just happened to be in New York City and thought I would look you up," she said.

My right brow rose. "Is that right?"

"I just wanted to see you," she said and her eyes went to Viktor.

"Why?"

"I've come to tell you that we have a son."

I gave a roaring laugh. "Bullshit!"

"Why do you say that? We were married once," she said.

"Unfortunately, that is true. But we both know you are lying."

"Pavel is fifteen years old and we were married when he was conceived," she insisted.

"You do understand biology, right?"

"What are you saying?" she asked.

"We only had sex two times and that was the first month of our marriage. Both times I wore a condom. If I'd gotten you pregnant then, I certainly would have noticed in the remaining eleven months we were married."

"There were other times," she said but couldn't look me in the face.

"Maybe in your dreams."

"He looks very much like you."

"Whatever! He's *not* mine!"

"I can't believe you would deny your own son," she said. "Pavel believes you are his father and that's what is on his birth certificate. After all, we were married at the time. So, in essence, you are the father."

"You're obviously delusional. What game are you trying to play, Tatiana?"

She fidgeted and chewed her lip. "No games, Dmitri."

"I'll tell you what. You get a paternity test done, here in the States, then we can talk. Actually, I want two paternity tests. One done here in New York and another done in London. The samples need to be collected by a doctor here."

"We can get a paternity test done in Moscow," she countered.

"Hell no! I need something I can rely on to not be tainted by your father."

"That's just not convenient for Pavel. He is in school and I don't want his studies to be interrupted."

"Too fucking bad!"

"We can have lunch together and talk this over. Maybe we can get to know each other again," she said, trying to persuade me.

"Another hell no! I'm not interested in you. I am a married man and my wife is carrying my child."

"I see," she said. In a flash, her hand had slipped into her purse. She pulled out a gun and pointed it at me.

"*What are you doing now?*"

"What does it look like, you asshole?"

Viktor was quick to kick Tatiana's hand and the gun fell to the floor. I was swift to retrieve it, then placed it on my desk. I grabbed Tatiana by the front of her collar and threw her against the wall, holding her there.

"*What in the hell is wrong with you?*" I yelled right in her face. "Who is the real baby daddy?"

"Dmitri, stop!" she cried out.

I grabbed her by the throat with one hand and held her tight against the wall. "Tell me now, Tatiana, or you are through." I tightened my grip on her neck.

"Pavel is a Zhukov."

"*Who?*"

She was trembling and her face was dark red.

"*Last chance!*" I yelled and further tightened my grip on her neck.

"S-s-sergei," she stuttered. "Sergei is the father."

I let go of her and she fell to the floor. "I should kill you now."

"Pavel needs his mother!" she cried out.

I glanced at Viktor. "Stay here with her."

Viktor nodded.

I took Tatiana's gun from the top of my desk and put in a drawer. I grabbed my cell and walked out of my office to a conference room down a hallway. I shut the door and dialed my father's number. My father picked up on the second ring.

"Hello, my son."

"Hello, Papa. I have a situation here with Tatiana and I need your advice."

"Yes?" Father said.

I told him the entire story.

"The boy lives with his grandfather and Tatiana doesn't live there. If she wasn't Fyodor Solvaviche's daughter, I would say shoot her. But I don't want a Bratva war. I will contact Fyodor and get back with you. Meanwhile, put her somewhere and hold her there," he said.

"Okay. Does the Solvaviche Bratva have a presence here in New York City?"

"Yes, but it is small. I'm sending you more men. Hold off on doing anything until you hear back from me."

"Will do."

With her hands bound around her back, Tatiana was led to the building elevator by Viktor and Boris. They followed me. We got into the elevator and rode to the basement level, directly to the parking garage. Tatiana was put into the backseat of my SUV. Viktor got in beside her. Boris got into the front passenger seat and I got behind the wheel. Maksim and Petr followed in their black SUV.

We traveled for an hour till we were outside the city, and finally stopped at an isolated and abandoned warehouse. We all got out; Viktor held Tatiana's arm tightly. I led the way to a paint-chipped brown door, took out a key, and opened it. I walked inside and flipped on a light. I was surprised it still turned on after all this time. The stench of mildew and stagnant dust hit me in the face. The cement floor was heavily stained— a reminder of the many incidents that created those stains.

"Take her to that chair." I motioned to an old and dusty floral print upholstered chair. The chair was one of two that sat near a far wall.

Viktor nodded and guided her there.

"Boris, you sit with her." Boris nodded and took the other upholstered chair beside her.

"Maksim and Petr, keep watch outside."

"Yeah, boss," Petr said and both men walked outside.

I motioned to Viktor who then followed me to a far end of the warehouse where she couldn't hear us talking.

"*Pakhan* will call me and let me know what to do with her. We only assume she had some of her father's men watching her, though I have no evidence of that."

"Better to be safe," Viktor said.

"And to stave off a Bratva war. I have no desire for that."

Two hours later, my cell rang. The screen showed it was my father. We spoke in Russian. "*Da?*"

"Fyodor says Tatiana has gone rogue. She teamed up with some of Sergei's men after his death," Father said.

"I thought my men killed them all. Who's left?"

"Not sure but one of them was her boyfriend. Fyodor does want her back. I have agreed to send my jet and men to retrieve her as a show of goodwill," Father said.

"She claims Sergei is the real father of her son, which does make him a Zhukov."

"I find that difficult to believe. More of a convenience for her to claim. Since Sergei is dead, I will need to ask Igor to exhume his body and get the necessary DNA. At any rate, she cannot claim you as the father. Therefore, your legitimate heir will be from Charlotte."

"I don't care what happens to Tatiana. I just want her out of my life," I insisted.

"I agree," my father said. "I want you and Charlotte to also be on my jet. We need to spend time together. She is a Zhukov now."

"Very well. It will have to be a brief visit as I'm preparing Charlotte's house to be put on the market. It was trashed inside by Adeline and a lot has to be done."

I was filled with dread for this journey to my homeland. I knew I had to face my demons, that darkness I tried to be rid of for the past ten years.

CHAPTER 68

Charlotte

The June weather was clear, mild and sunny. I wore one of my new outfits Dmitri bought me: a pale blue cotton knit dress that prominently displayed my baby bump. The matching blue leather cross-strap pumps with chunky three-inch heels completed the look.

Dmitri was quite handsome in all black—designer jeans, t-shirt, and jacket. His black boots made him even taller than his six-foot four-inch height.

We were at the private airport in New York City and waiting in the SUV. I watched as two burly men stepped down the stairs of the Zhukov jet and met Viktor, one of Dmitri's men, who held the arm of a tall and slender woman with long black hair. She wore a pink pantsuit and high-heeled pumps. She held her head high and wore a stoic expression. Viktor handed off the woman to the two burly men, who then guided her up the stairs into the plane. Viktor waited a few minutes before he took the stairs up and inside. He then returned outside and nodded at Dmitri.

"We should go ahead and board now," Dmitri said. "Petr and Boris will bring our luggage on to the plane."

Dmitri opened my door and helped me out of the SUV. I put my hand into his arm and we made our way to the plane.

When we entered, Dmitri greeted the pilot and copilot in Russian. An attractive blonde in a royal blue pantsuit met us. "Welcome Mr. and Mrs. Zhukov. My name is Ingrid and I will be your flight attendant for this trip," she spoke in English with only a slight Russian accent. "Please follow me." She led us to a stairway and pointed. "Up these stairs is your bedroom and bathroom." She continued walking towards the middle of the plane into a living room, where there was ample space for the four men and Tatiana in one of the two seating areas. Tatiana was seated between two of the men. Her eyes darted up and down, checking me out, and she gave a sour expression. I could tell Dmitri noticed.

In the back of the living room was a table and chairs for eating.

The flight attendant continued walking and led the way to a conference room with a door that closed for privacy.

This jumbo jet was even more luxurious than Astrid's royal jet.

Dmitri walked to where Tatiana was sitting and addressed the man to the right of her. "Take her to the back of the plane and secure her in the conference room. I don't want her looking at my wife," he said. He spoke in English and I knew it was because he wanted me to know what he said.

The man nodded and escorted Tatiana to the back. Once she was out of view, Dmitri introduced me to the three remaining men. All three spoke English and gave a respectful smile and a nod. The pilot soon spoke over the intercom that it was time to take off, so everyone sat and buckled their seatbelt. Dmitri and I sat beside each other on a white leather sofa against the right wall. He took my right hand into his and we awaited takeoff.

The travel time was ten hours to the Zhukov private airport. I spent much of the time in the bedroom resting. The conversations in Russian between Dmitri and his men were exhausting. What I really wanted to do was go to the conference room and talk to Tatiana. I didn't know if she spoke English but I had to try.

I decided to go downstairs from the bedroom and through the sitting area to the conference room. Dmitri's back was to me while he was busy talking to his men. I was able to quietly get to where Tatiana was being held. When I entered the room, Boris stood when he saw me.

"I want to talk with Tatiana," I told him.

"Go ahead," Boris said and moved to stand against the wall.

I sat in a chair across the table from her. "Do you speak English?"

"Yes, I do," Tatiana said.

"Good." I took a deep breath, trying to collect my thoughts before I spoke. "I understand you made a visit to see my husband."

"That is correct."

"Why?" I asked.

"That is between Dmitri and me. It isn't any of your concern," she said.

"Actually, it is. I know you pulled a gun on him."

"Yes," she replied.

"Why did you do that?" I demanded.

"He was my husband before he was yours. There was unresolved business. He ruined my life and after fifteen years, I decided to get my revenge."

"For what? Another man's son you are trying to trick my husband into believing is his? Dmitri told me the whole thing. Aren't you embarrassed? That claim is too easy to disprove. My son will be the rightful heir and you need to accept that. It is unfortunate you have led your son to believe a lie. I suggest you remedy that and leave my husband in peace."

Tatiana began roaring with laughter. "You really are stupid," she said.

"Tell me about that. What am I stupid about? You seem to know the answers. Tell me."

"You're stupid enough to come back here and think I would even talk to you. You think you're so high and mighty. Bet you didn't know Dmitri is a coldblooded killer."

I froze and my breath hitched. I couldn't believe what she just said. The conversation Dmitri and I had about his childhood flashed in my thoughts.

"Thought so," Tatiana said and gave a mocking laugh.

I stood. "I came here to offer you grace but I can see it was a waste of my time. Burn in hell, you bitch!" I turned to leave.

"Wait!"

I turned around. "I'm listening."

"Andrei is the real father of my son," she confessed.

"I'm listening."

"If I tell Andrei this, he will have me killed to save face."

"Why is that?"

"Because our affair was during the time Dmitri and I were married," she said.

"Wow!" I sat back down. "Does Dmitri know this?"

"No. After he tortured me, I yelled out it was Sergei," she said.

"One lie after another. Don't you know the saying *the truth will set you free*?" I questioned.

"It won't in this case," she countered.

I glanced over at Boris, who was still standing against the wall. His eyes looked like saucers, then he shook his head.

"The only thing that will save you is a paternity test. It might be embarrassing but you have already initiated a paternity claim. First on to Dmitri, then Sergei, and now Andrei. Whose is it really? Liars can't *ever* be trusted. Especially in situations like this."

"A paternity test that shows Andrei is the father could start a Bratva war. Is that what you want?"

"You started this. What did you hope to gain by digging up this history? You let it go on for fifteen years," I countered.

"My father has been questioning me lately quite firmly. He is demanding to know who Pavel's father is."

"What did you tell him?"

"That Pavel is Dmitri's son," Tatiana said.

"When, actually, Pavel is Dmitri's half-brother." I rose from my seat and pulled away from the conference table. "Dmitri must know the truth. I am going to ask him to come in here and you will tell him yourself. Boris has been witness to our conversation." I glanced over to Boris, who nodded.

Tatiana became silent, her expression grim. "I thought you came in here to offer me grace" she said.

"This isn't grace worthy, Tatiana. This is the stuff that breaks up families, causes Bratva wars, and a whole lot of anguish for everyone involved. Most of all you."

As I made my way out towards Dmitri, it was clear how the Zhukov Bratva was all about family—protection and support of—whatever that looked like. On one hand, that felt secure and comforting. On the other, terrifying. I couldn't even fathom Dmitri as a coldblooded killer. There had to be more to this story. Or not. Tatiana was a liar.

Dmitri spotted me instantly. I motioned for him. He stood and came to me. "What's going on?"

"Tatiana has something important she needs to tell you. Boris was a witness to the conversation I had with her." I reached up and kissed him on his cheek, then left him to go inside the conference room without me.

CHAPTER 69

Dmitri

I went inside the conference room and spotted Tatiana. I pulled out a chair and sat across from her at the conference room table.

"Hello again." I put my arms on the table and folded my hands. "What have you got for me? Charlotte seems to think there is something you need to tell me. Go ahead and spit it out."

Without any hesitation or preamble, she said, "Pavel's father is Andrei."

"*Fuck!*"

"Andrei doesn't know it either. My father was pushing me to name who Pavel's biological father is and I knew if I said it was Andrei, it would cause serious problems."

"So, you were cheating on me with my father! *Real* classy! What made you think it was okay to name your son's paternity on to me?"

"Because he was conceived during our marriage," she admitted.

"So, you were willing to pass off my half-brother as my son?"

She didn't answer.

"You know you're going to pay like hell for this. You should never have lied."

"It takes two to tango, as they say," she threw back.

"This only proves you are a worthless whore. I can't look at you any longer." I stood, glanced at Boris, and left the room.

It was clear to me I needed to have a conversation with my father. The betrayal made me feel sick inside. There had to be more to this story than Tatiana was telling. I found it difficult to believe my father would sleep with his own son's wife.

I walked to the back and up the stairs to where Charlotte was. She was sitting in a chair reading a book on her iPad. When she saw me, she put down her device. "Do you need a drink?" she asked.

I took a seat across from her. "Yeah."

She stood, walked to the minibar, poured some whiskey, then handed it to me.

I swallowed half of the glass.

"Are you okay?" she asked.

I glanced at her but didn't say anything. I downed another large swallow of whiskey. My thoughts traveled to the time period when I was married to Tatiana. I searched my brain for any clues Tatiana was fooling around with my father. I recollected her going to my father for advice on her ballet career numerous times. Other than that, there wasn't anything suspicious.

I finally spoke, "Looks like I have a half-brother." I finished my glass of whiskey.

Charlotte got out of her chair, walked to me, and sat on my lap. She put her arms around me. No words were said. She only held me tight.

* * *

We arrived at the Zhukov Estate in regal fashion. We were met at the family airport with two limousines. Charlotte and I rode in one, Tatiana and the men in the other.

The ride was somber. Charlotte sat close to me, her hand remaining on my thigh.

It was only a ten-minute drive before the car came to a stop in front of the mansion. Two butlers appeared. One approached our limo and opened the door. "Welcome, Mr. and Mrs. Zhukov," the butler said in Russian.

"Thank you, Aklm. Please speak in English. My wife doesn't know Russian."

The butler nodded. "Very well, sir. It's a pleasure to meet you, Mrs. Zhukov, and welcome to the Zhukov Estate."

"Thank you," Charlotte said.

"Sir, your father is waiting for you in his office. Mrs. Marta is waiting to meet your wife in the salon."

I turned to Charlotte. "Are you okay with this?"

She glanced up at me and gave a sweet smile. "Yes."

I bent down and kissed her on the lips.

The butler at the door opened it wide and we entered. The four men with Tatiana trailed behind.

A lady's maid was inside the foyer and greeted Charlotte in English. The woman led her through the massive foyer to a wide hallway.

"Sir, please follow me," Aklm said.

"Tatiana and Boris need to also come."

Aklm wore a questioning expression, then nodded.

"Boris, please bring Tatiana. We are going to see my father."

Aklm led them down a long corridor to a set of heavy wooden doors. He knocked, opened the doors wide, and I was first to enter.

"Hello, Papa." I stood in front of my father's large ornate wooden desk.

"Son." Father stood and walked over to embrace me. "It is so nice to finally see you. Please, let us sit more comfortably." We moved to a seating area in front of the fireplace. Tatiana and Boris stood by the wall beside the door.

"I trust your travel here went well?" Father asked.

"Yes. We were most comfortable and the pilot and flight staff were quite hospitable and professional. Thank you for arranging this." I gave a guarded smile. "Your new jet is quite nice and luxurious."

"I see we have Tatiana and Boris with us," Father said and glanced at them. "Tatiana, please come over here and have a seat."

She did as he instructed and sat in an upholstered chair across from him to the right of me.

"Seems you've got yourself into a bit of trouble," Father said. "What do you have to say about all this?"

She was visibly shaking and her hands gripped the sides of the chair. Her face was dark red.

"Yes, I am waiting," Father said.

Tatiana just spit it out. "Pavel is your son."

Father straightened in his chair and wore a rigid expression. "What?"

"Pavel is your son. A paternity test will confirm this," she said.

"And you waited fifteen years to tell me this?"

"I didn't want to tell you at all but my father was pushing for me to name the biological father. Since I was married to Dmitri at the time Pavel was conceived, I just said he was Dmitri's son," Tatiana blathered.

"Fuck!" Father screamed.

"That's what I said." I kept my eyes on my father, who didn't acknowledge what I'd said but focused on Tatiana.

"I need a paternity test done and it will be collected by my personal physician," Father said. He turned to Boris. "Take her to the East Wing of the mansion and lock her up in one of the suites."

Boris came forward and escorted Tatiana out of Father's office.

"We need to talk," Father said once he and I were alone and the door closed.

"Yes, we do. Please explain how this happened. You have to know I'm not taking this revelation well."

"I'm sure." Father paused, staring into the distance. He wore a deep furrow on his brow. I remained silent, not wanting to say something in anger I might later regret. "Son, there is no delicate way to say this. So, I'm just going to spit it out and tell you exactly what happened. There was only a single incident. No other times. This was two months before you divorced. Tatiana came to me in this study while I was working. I'd been drinking pretty heavy. It was late at night. She sauntered in, closed the door, then took off her clothes. She came in and began seducing me. I regretted the incident immediately afterwards. My behavior was wrong and I knew it. I felt shame and should have told you, but I didn't. I was a different man then. I can only hope you will someday forgive me," Father said.

"Tatiana shared this with Charlotte while we were on your plane traveling here. It's a lot for me to take in. What are you planning to do now?" I asked, trying to process everything.

"I must go to her father and admit the whole thing. I'm sure it won't go well. I also have to tell my wife. She and I weren't married then, but it still shows a lack of character on my part. She needs to hear this from me."

"Pavel is your son and my half-brother. If it wasn't for Charlotte getting Tatiana to talk, she would have continued the charade. She actually told me Pavel was Sergei's. How convenient, considering he is now dead."

"A paternity test is the first step. I'm sure Fydor Solvaviche will want this. If the test is positive, Fydor and I will have to come up with some agreement. It isn't necessary for you to be involved," Father said.

"I should probably be there when you initially meet with him. He may have questions."

"As you wish."

CHAPTER 70

Charlotte

The decadence of the Zhukov Estate was mind blowing. It was even more opulent than the Bjorn palace in Copenhagen. All the furnishings and artwork were museum quality. There was a lot of gilded wood and the gold wasn't just spray paint but actual gold.

I found Marta to be a delightful woman of fifty-five years old. She was twenty-five years younger than Andrei. She was attractive, tall and slim. She was stylishly dressed in a LaFayette148 metallic-leafed jacquard black pantsuit and wore three-inch black pumps. Her blonde hair touched her shoulders in loose waves. She wore full makeup; her bright red lipstick matched her long fingernails. For all her formality, she was quite warm and friendly. I liked her instantly.

She arranged for a formal tea to be served for the two of us and I enjoyed our conversation. She openly shared her disappointment at never having any children of her own. She wanted to know all about my pregnancy and even hinted at Dmitri and I staying at the mansion until our baby was born. This surprised me but I made no commitments. Given the latest debacle with Tatiana, it was doubtful Dmitri would want to stay long at his father's place.

Marta was quite chatty and we visited for several hours. I was surprised Dmitri hadn't returned and grew concerned.

Marta couldn't have known about the latest regarding Pavel and I wasn't one to tell.

* * *

I heard the door of our suite open and was pleased to see Dmitri. I was sitting on an upholstered chair with my shoes off and my feet elevated on an ottoman.

"Hi, beautiful," he said and walked to me and bent down for a kiss. There was a solemn expression on his face.

"Hi. How did things go?"

He took a seat beside me. "It went better than I expected, actually. It's still a mess but I have confidence what my father told me is correct." Dmitri then told all he and his father discussed.

"It's good to have it all out and in the open. This revelation is sure to surprise your half-brother. Perhaps in the end, the alliance hoped for with your marriage to Tatiana will actually come about through your half-brother."

"It's so like you to see a bright side," he said and gave a weak smile.

"We are all only human and mistakes come with the package. At the most, all we can do is pick ourselves up from the rubble, dust ourselves off, and move forward in a better direction. That's it. Forgiveness is hard. I know this one well."

Dmitri stood and walked to me. He bent down and lifted me up into his arms and carried me to the bed.

"I need you, Charlotte," he said.

Tingling sensations shot to my core. I wanted him too—badly. I stood and turned around for him to unzip my dress and let it fall to the floor. When I turned to face him, I put my hands onto his shirt, unbuttoned it, and let it join my dress on the floor.

My hands explored his smooth, sculpted chest. I kissed my way down his chest and rang my tongue down to his belly. I unbuckled his belt.

Dmitri was quick to take charge; I knew that was what he wanted. He unbuttoned and unzipped his pants, letting them fall to the floor with his boxer briefs. His cock was fully erect and I licked my lips as our eyes met. My arousal rose and I scooted to the center of the bed. He came to me.

I felt his heat on top of me as his lips met mine, and the scent of him further fueled my own fiery need for him.

His hands traveled down my breasts and removed my bra. Then his fingers slid to the sides of my panties and he pulled them off.

I felt his palm against my sex, then one finger went inside me. My knees parted and I heard the sound of my wetness as he pumped inside of me with his fingers. With his thumb circling my clit, I experienced electric pleasure course through my body as I rode the waves.

He pulled his fingers out and put them in my mouth. The taste of myself felt wicked and sensual.

His lips met mine and his tongue darted in and out of my mouth hungrily. My hands wrapped around his ass as I arched against his hard shaft.

His thick and large cock then entered me and began pounding into me with a primal intensity. My pleasure climbed with each thrust and I clenched around him.

"Oh God, Charlotte," he moaned.

His pumping and thrusting became even more intense. I felt him get bigger and the crest of orgasm erupted.

I screamed out his name.

His moans soon turned into a growl—we reached the same place together.

My head rested on his chest and his arm was around me. I could hear his heart beating and it matched my own. He kissed me on the top of my head.

"I love you, Charlotte. I love you so much." He pulled me tighter against him.

"You are the air I breathe and my thoughts are of you almost constantly. Sometimes I fear all of this—us—is only a wonderful, incredible dream, and I will wake up and it will all be gone."

I felt his hand upon my belly and just as our baby kicked inside of me.

"Nikolai," he said.

"He loves you too," I whispered.

* * *

Dmitri and his father had met with Fyodor, Tatiana's father. I was grateful to learn things had gone well. The paternity test did confirm Andrei was the father of Pavel. Dmitri told me how both men planned to meet again to discuss future plans that would affect Pavel. Dmitri said we should leave for home and return at a later date once the situation calmed down. He felt it wasn't his place to be involved. He was certain he'd done his part and it was for Fyodor and Andrei to work out.

Our two days in Russia hadn't left time to explore the large city of Moscow. I really wanted to but didn't push. Dmitri had been tense the whole time we were at the estate. I knew it would be best for us to leave.

Once again, we were inside the Zhukov jet. There were also ten of Andrei's men with us. It had been decided they would reside in New York City and Dmitri was to be their leader. But for what activities, I didn't know. I knew Dmitri would further explain things to me once we were home. At least I hoped he would.

There was a change in him, like he was now carrying a heavy burden. His jaw would tighten more and more, and there was a distant look in his eyes. I wished he would share what he was thinking. I wanted to share his burden and lighten his load, but I knew that wasn't possible. No doubt the Zhukov business he tried so hard to be independent from was now back in his life. I worried about him but felt helpless to do anything about it. The claim Tatiana made when we were in the jet haunted me. I wanted to ask Dmitri about it but wondered if I should. I'd never seen any sign whatsoever that he was a killer. If he'd ever killed anyone, I was positive it had been warranted. The world of the Bratva was foreign to me and it seemed like they had their own laws and ways of enforcing them. Perhaps I was being naïve. Or, maybe, I didn't want my world shattered.

CHAPTER 71

Charlotte

The next four months flew by. I was well into my ninth month of pregnancy. The renovations to add a massive closet for me took almost a month to complete. But now all my precious belongings from my old closet were inside this new one. It was much larger and more luxurious than my old closet. Dmitri was true to his word.

My wanted items from my old house were now at our penthouse and Dmitri had arranged for the house to be emptied out and prepared for the market. There were interested buyers and it was just a matter of time till it sold.

My car sold and I was grateful to be rid of it. No trace of Raven existed now and I was happy about that.

Nikolai's nursey was complete and all that was left was for him to be born. Dr. Levitz assured me he was quite healthy and would be a big baby. I wasn't looking forward to the pain of labor and delivery, but was anxious to hold Nikolai in my arms. It would happen soon, as I already reached my due date. Dmitri was ecstatic and my soul was delighted to know this.

He hired a nurse assistant to stay with me during the days or evenings when he was out of the penthouse working. Lisa was an athletic twenty-five-year-old with short blonde curly hair and she wore red-framed glasses. I enjoyed her company.

The early October weather was warm and sunny with a slight breeze. Outside on our roof patio, I sat on a lounger with my feet up. Lisa was inside preparing lunch when I felt my first strong contraction. I decided to stand up and walk to the kitchen when another contraction began, stronger than the first.

"Lisa!" I called out.

She was quick to appear. "Yes?"

"I'm having contractions. Please call Dmitri."

She nodded and grabbed her cell.

Dmitri was at our penthouse in twenty minutes and my contractions were steady at five minutes apart. He scooped me up into his arms and we got into the elevator. Lisa held my packed bag and got inside the elevator with us.

He gently put me into the front passenger seat of the SUV, now our regular vehicle. Lisa put my bag into the back seat, wished us well, and left for home.

"Ten minutes, my love," Dmitri said as he maneuvered the traffic towards the hospital.

I nodded just before another contraction came, then closed my eyes, and breathed through it.

By the time we were inside the maternity ward, my contractions were steady at every one and a half minutes. I was rushed into a labor and delivery room and was prepared to give birth.

Dmitri stayed by my side the entire three hours. Such a contrast from my first baby, which took two days. Nikolai was ten pounds, seven ounces, and twenty-three inches long, born October 3. He had curly light brown hair and light grey eyes, just like his father. When he let out his first cry, joy filled me. He was alive, well, and perfect.

Dmitri was the first to hold him as I was still being attended to. His smile beamed pure love as he held our son. I watched as he kissed him on the forehead and held him close. He whispered something to Nikolai. My heart overflowed.

* * *

I sat in a rocking chair in Nikolai's nursery. I had him in my arms as I nursed him. He was such a sweet and perfect baby. I felt blessed.

Dmitri walked through the door, bent down, and kissed me. "How's my little guy?" He bent down and kissed Nikolai on the top of his head.

"He's nursing really well. We're almost done, so if you want to hold him you can."

"Yeah. I'd like that very much." Dmitri went to the changing table and pulled out a burping cloth. He knew the drill well. I was so proud of him.

I stood and handed Nikolai to Dmitri. "I think you're the perfect dad."

He sat on the rocker. "I want to be," he said as his expression turned serious. "Thank you for giving me a son."

"Thank *you*. It was a joint effort, after all." I winked.

He gave a pure smile. "It sure was."

* * *

It had been six weeks since Nikolai was born. Everything had gone well. We kept Lisa around for an extra set of hands for a few hours each day. Today I arranged for her to spend the afternoon. The doctor had finally given me the okay for sex and I was more than ready.

I sent Dmitri a text: *Any interest in a naughty interlude? Lisa is staying with Nikolai for a few hours*

Dmitri: *Oh yeah! What do you have in mind?*

Me: *Meet me downstairs at the pool*

Dmitri: *Sans the swimsuit*

Me: *I want to watch you remove your clothes. You are a beautiful and sexy man*

Dmitri: *20 minutes*

Excitement fueled me as I made my way downstairs to the pool. I was more than ready to be with my husband again. I wanted to feel his bare skin against mine and finally act on my desires.

I stripped and dove into the pool. The water was the perfect temperature as I swam some laps. It wasn't long before I spotted Dmitri walking through the doorway. He was still in his work clothes: black slacks, black shirt, and matching jacket.

"I see my mermaid."

"Yes, you do, my handsome husband," I replied while treading water.

I watched with hungry eyes as he removed his jacket and draped it over a chair, then took off his shoes. He removed his shirt. His smooth, chiseled chest sent thrilling sensations straight to my center. He gave a lustful grin as he removed his pants and boxer briefs, showing his erect cock. I licked my lips. He dove into the water and swam to me.

I wrapped my legs around him and our lips met. I felt his hands grip my ass cheeks and he pulled me tighter to him. I felt his cock slide over my clit and I deepened my kiss, so hungry for him.

He lifted me and carried me to the stairs at the end of the pool. I stood as he grabbed two long cushions from two lounger chairs and put them on the floor side by side on the outside of the pool. He guided me to lay on the center of my back. He knelt in front of me and parted my knees.

I felt his hands slide over my sex and entered two of his fingers inside me. I felt myself clench around his fingers as his thumb glided over my clit. The ecstasy came quickly and his tongue darted in, out, and over my wetness.

"Oh God, Dmitri," I moaned as another crest of pleasure rose and I rode the wave.

"You taste like honey." He rose and kissed me on the lips. I tasted myself on his tongue and my arousal rose again. I wanted him inside of me and I couldn't wait a second longer.

As if he'd read my mind, I felt him enter me. Gently at first but when I arched my back to him, he went inside me further.

"All of you!" I demanded. "I want all of you."

I felt him oblige me, going all the way inside me, and the tingles of electricity began to rise. He began pumping and pumping and I felt the wave begin anew. I clenched around him as he thrust in and out of me more quickly.

"Come with me, my love," he said as his thrusting became even harder. Pounding and pounding into me. I felt a mounting pleasure building up. I clenched even tighter still around him. My brain was halted and my body alone was in control in a primal intensity I'd never felt before. Dmitri picked up his pace, pounding harder and harder as I fell over the edge, exploding in ecstasy. Bliss fired through every part of my body. I screamed out his name in a loud voice that echoed through the pool room.

He let out a loud primal growl and I felt him release his seed inside of me. I knew we were once again one.

We laid there quietly. My head was on his chest. I felt his heart beating and I kissed him there.

"I've missed us," I said.

"Me too." He kissed me on top of my head. "You know, we may have just made another baby."

"Maybe we'll have a girl this time," I replied and our eyes met. I couldn't help but smile.

He gave a roaring laugh and pulled me tighter to him. "I'm okay with that."

For More News About D K McLaughlin and Other Great Books, Signup For Our Newsletter:

http://wbp.bz/newsletter

Word-of-mouth is critical to an author's long-term success. If you appreciated this book please leave a review on the Amazon sales page:

https://wbp.bz/raven

Romantic Mystery from WildBlue Press

WildBlue Press, 2016   WildBlue Press, 2017   Lost Canyon Press, 2018

Janice Boekhoff's Earth Hunters Series embarks on captivating journeyes where ancient secrets reveal timless truths and pave the way to love and faith. These suspenseful blend heart-stirring adventure, romance, and wholesome themes.

In **CREVICE**, Elery Hearst delves into the depths of Arizona's Lost Dutchman's Mine. The quest for her family's legacy transforms into a soul-searching adventure, intertwining her fate with Lucan Milner. Together, they navigate a labyrinth of old wounds and emerging threats, their faith and emotions intensifying amidst the rugged terrain.

CREATED takes us to the lush, mysterious jungles of Costa Rica with Paleontology Professor Travis Perego. His pursuit of a revolutionary discovery challenges the boundaries between science and faith. Teaming up with Lenaia, a woman harboring her secrets, they face the wilderness, their ethical convictions, and their unresolved histories. In their journey, the struggle to safeguard their discoveries is as daunting as their quest for personal redemption.

In **CASCADE**, we meet Geologist Lenaia Talavera, who gets more than she bargained for when she's called to Mt. Rainier to investigate an act of sabotage. Not only is she forced to confront her left-over feelings for her ex-boyfriend—feelings her current boyfriend wouldn't appreciate—but women from the nearby town are disappearing… only to be found dead.

Unraveling these mysteries might not be easy, but it could be the key to a profound renewal of their lives and beliefs.